Dwight Kemper

# Who Framed Boris Karloff?

Midnight Marquee Press, Inc.
Baltimore, Maryland, USA

Acknowledgements

The following were very instrumental in getting this book to press: Sara Jane Karloff Pratt, Catherine Kemper (for proofreading the first galleys, which she hates doing but did it anyway), Frank Dietz (for a great cover), The Barnes and Noble Mystery Readers Club (and specifically Mary Ann Lynch), Gene Cothran, Joe Kane (each for their input and criticism), Paul and Denise Ruben, Southern Pacific Railroad Yahoo Group (Louis Adler, Ken Harrison, Ken Kellogg, Larry Mullaly and Tim Zukas) and Scott Essman. And of course, Gary and Susan Svehla for knowing who Boris Karloff, Basil Rathbone and Bela Lugosi were and believing a fictional mystery about them might just be worth publishing.
–Dwight Kemper
May 2007

This novel is a work of fiction and all events described are from the imagination of the author. While many of the characters are based upon real people and the actual filming of *Son of Frankenstein*, *Who Framed Boris Karloff?* is a work of fiction and in no way should be considered historical fact.

ISBN 13: 978-1-887664-74-5
ISBN 10: 1-887664-74-2
Library of Congress Catalog Card Number 2007927358
Manufactured in the United States of America
Printed by Odyssey Press
First Printing by Marquee Mysteries, an imprint of Midnight Marquee Press, Inc.,
    May 2007
www.midmar.com

This book is dedicated to:

Boris Karloff, Basil Rathbone and
Bela Lugosi, who gave me inspiration...

Sara Jane Karloff Pratt,
who gave me her support and encouragement...

And to my ex-wife, Cathy Kemper,
who says she never gets the credit!

# INTRODUCTION

When an author asks you to write the foreword for his book, it's a pretty terrifying task, especially if the book is titled *Who Framed Boris Karloff?* and Boris Karloff just happens to have been your Father!

The above aside, I had the best time reading *Who Framed Boris Karloff?* I was "hooked" early on, and couldn't wait to be led down yet another wrong road. I followed wrong lead, after wrong lead; wrong suspect after wrong suspect, knowing full well my Father could never have "done it!"

I learned more Hollywood "truths," more Hollywood "history," and more Hollywood "secrets" and looked behind more Hollywood "doors" than I ever did growing up in Hollywood.

Watching Tinseltown's bogeymen trying to solve a murder in this cleverly written story was a pure joy for this reader who was led page after page towards a totally unexpected conclusion.

—Sara Karloff

# CAST OF CHARACTERS

BORIS KARLOFF – Frankenstein's Monster in *Son of Frankenstein*. A gentleman who would never kill anyone and yet he was found standing over the body.

BASIL RATHBONE – Actor, master swordsman, formerly with British Intelligence in the Great War, Rathbone played Baron Wolf von Frankenstein in *Son of Frankenstein*. Having just finished making *Hound of the Baskervilles* for 20th Century Fox, could Rathbone use Sherlock Holmes' methods to find who framed Boris Karloff?

BELA LUGOSI – Hungarian actor forever typecast as Count Dracula. Lugosi played "Old Ygor" the crooked-necked, grave-robbing blacksmith in *Son of Frankenstein*. Known for being temperamental, Lugosi had a grudge against Martin F. Murphy and was overheard wishing him dead.

ROWLAND V. LEE – Producer/director of *Son of Frankenstein*. His methods had put production behind schedule and Martin F. Murphy had plans to replace him. Was that reason enough to kill?

JAMES WHALE – Openly gay director of the first two *Frankenstein* films, he was brought in by Martin F. Murphy to replace Rowland V. Lee as director of *Son of Frankenstein*. Surely he had no motive....

MARTIN F. MURPHY – Studio Production Manager. He had a chip on his shoulder regarding directors who wasted company money. He was the perfect victim of the perfect crime.

CLIFF WORK – Vice president in charge of Production at Universal Studios. Work would do anything to finish the much-anticipated *Frankenstein* sequel—but did that include covering up a murder?

EDDIE "THE BULLDOG" MANNIX – Hollywood "fixer" and tough guy. If you had an actor who may have killed someone and you wanted to cover it up, you called Eddie Mannix.

TONI "LEGS" LANIER – Eddie's dame, described by mobster Mickey Cohen as "the only one in LA with balls." She was hard drinking, fast living and quick tempered.

JACK P. PIERCE – Makeup wizard responsible for the entire pantheon of Universal Studios' Monsters. He worked without a contract and his methods were slow and meticulous. Did he direct his attention to detail to committing murder?

LIONEL "PINKY" ATWILL – Typecast as the oily villain. He drove around town in a bullet-riddled Rolls Royce and attended sensational murder trials. Is he a murderer or just a red herring?

JOSEPHINE HUTCHINSON – Baroness Elsa von Frankenstein in *Son of Frankenstein*. Was she an innocent British actress, or a scheming murderess?

JOHN P. FULTON – Special Effects man. Was murder his finest effects work?

WILLIAM HEDGCOCK – A technician thoroughly familiar with the high-voltage monster-making apparatus used on the set of *Son of Frankenstein*.

PETER MITCHELL – A photographer for the publicity department who had been working at the studio for only two weeks. Wide-eyed, star-struck innocent or crafty killer?

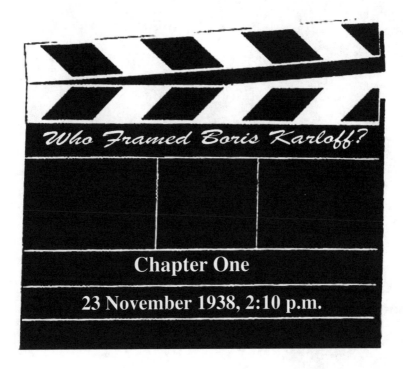

**Chapter One**

**23 November 1938, 2:10 p.m.**

"*Son of Frankenstein*," assistant director Fred Frank shouted as he held up the clapperboard, "production 931, Wolf von Frankenstein meets Monster, take one."

The clapperboard clacked.

"Action," said producer/director Rowland V. Lee.

Basil Rathbone as Baron Wolf von Frankenstein stood in the foreground of the laboratory set built on Universal Studios Stage 7, his body deliberately placed in front of the worktable before him to keep a surprise hidden from his co-star. In the background, a curtain of backlit steam representing boiling sulfur rose up from a 30-foot well sunk into the floor of the soundstage. Hiding just inside the well was the unsuspecting Boris Karloff in full Frankenstein Monster makeup.

"Okay, Basil," instructed the director, "grab the knife from the table there and slip it in your pocket."

Rathbone did as he was told, slipping a long surgical knife into the inner pocket of his two-tone tweed hunting jacket.

Lee shouted, "Okay, Boris. Come out of the pit and lurch toward Basil."

There was a heavy clump, clump, clump as Karloff lumbered ever nearer, making Basil wonder why his character didn't hear the Monster "sneaking" up behind him. Karloff's huge green hand gripped Rathbone's shoulder. The heavy gray-green greasepaint gave the Monster a corpse-like pallor when photographed through special filters on monochromatic film. It also tended to get on everything

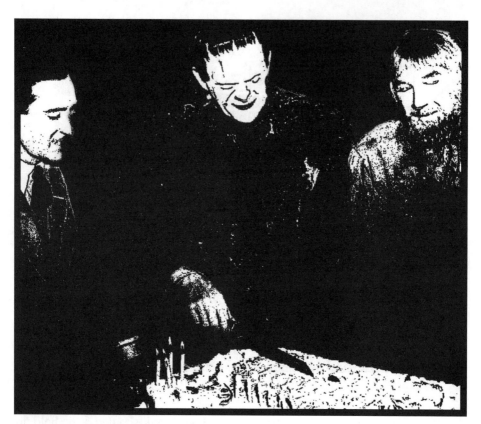

**"Well, what are you waiting for, Boris?" asked Rathbone. "Make a wish and blow out the candles."**

Karloff touched. In contrast, Rathbone's aquiline features were painted red so the special filters didn't wash out his features.

Instead of flinching in terror, Basil smiled up at the Monster. A pencil thin mustache pasted to his upper lip emphasized Rathbone's dashing good looks. He stood aside so Boris could see his surprise. It was a huge cake with a spray of icing flowers framing the inscription, "HAPPY BIRTHDAY, BORIS." The horrific features of Frankenstein's Monster broke into a wide grin as Basil led the cast and crew in song. A Universal Studios photographer popped off a series of flashbulbs to capture the moment as Rowland V. Lee and Bela Lugosi, in full Ygor makeup, joined Karloff and Rathbone around the worktable to sing "Happy Birthday" to the hulking giant.

Rathbone picked up a specimen jar from the worktable and handed it to Boris. "We all thought you might want this so you could enjoy your cake." Floating in the specimen jar was Boris' dental bridge that he had removed to create an indentation in the Monster's right cheek.

"Yeah, that," added Lee, "and because without it we can't understand a word you're saying."

The actor smiled gratefully, turned around and discreetly slipped the bridge in place. Turning back, he said, "Thank you."

"I like Karloff better without the bridge," joked Lugosi in his trademark Hungarian accent. "Then it is not just Bela no one can understand." Behind the fake yak -hair beard, rubber-crooked neck and shaggy wig Bela Lugosi flashed Ygor's snaggletoothed grin.

"Well, what are you waiting for, Boris?" asked Rathbone. "Make a wish and blow out the candles."

There were 51 brightly burning candles on the cake. Karloff surveyed the mini inferno and chuckled. "It's a good thing I don't have the Monster's fear of fire."

After pausing to make a wish, Frankenstein's Monster blew out the candles with one great exhalation that was met by cheers and applause.

"What did you wish for?" asked Bela, passing Karloff a knife to cut the cake.

Boris tugged at the neckline of the Monster's brown fur jersey and quipped, "A cooler costume." He took the knife and began divvying up pieces to the cast and crew.

"Boris," Lee said, holding a small package, "not only is this your birthday, but you're also a first time father," referring to the birth of Boris' daughter earlier that morning. "That being the case," Lee continued, "the special effects department made these for you. Actually, they're for little Sara Jane Karloff."

The Monster graciously took the package and tore away the wrapping. Inside was a special pair of bronzed baby shoes. They were miniature versions of Boris' Frankenstein boots.

Karloff smiled. "The perfect thing for my little monster."

"Ah, there he is!" effused an unexpected visitor who sauntered onto the set swinging a bamboo cane and walking a bit unsteadily. He was tall, wispy and wore a fetching Panama hat and a white suit. A folded paper with "Western Union" quite visible on it was tucked carelessly in the breast pocket. Director James Whale smiled as he made a sweeping gesture that nearly knocked him off balance. "There's my Monster, who appears to have not only become civilized," he noted the bronzed Monster shoes, "but has procreated. Whatever would dear Henry Frankenstein have said about that?" He put his hand to his lips like a little boy who had just said a naughty word. "Oops. Now it's *Heinrich von* Frankenstein, isn't it? I see the studio is still catering to the whims of the German market."

Boris smiled broadly and took Whale's hand. "James! What brings you to Universal Studios!"

"Thought I'd see how my Monster was faring in the hands of a new director." As Boris released his grip, Whale became aware of the green makeup now smeared on his hand. He held it gingerly away from his white suit with a look of drunken annoyance.

"Oh, I am sorry, James," Boris said, noting Whale's distress. Gesturing at his costume he said with a helpless shrug, "You're welcome to wipe your hand off on the back of my shirt. It won't show on camera."

"Nonsense," Whale smiled weakly as he tucked his cane under his arm to free up his clean hand. He reached for the handkerchief in his breast pocket and unfurled it with a practiced snap of the wrist. "A gentleman always comes prepared."

"I was so terribly sorry to hear about poor Colin passing away last year," Karloff said, referring to his *Frankenstein* co-star Colin Clive.

"Ah, yes, dear Colin." Whale sighed as he looked in the direction of Stage 28, otherwise known as the Phantom Stage, on which the Castle Frankenstein interiors had been erected. "Very decent of you to honor Colin's memory with that lovely painting, Rowland," he said, referring to the portrait hanging over the fireplace mantel on the Castle Library set. "Might I trouble you for it when shooting wraps?"

"I'll see what I can do," Rowland said, avoiding Whale's gaze by picking at his cake with his fork.

"So kind of you. The artist captured dear Colin's angelic features perfectly." He smiled wryly as he wiped his palm clean. "Ah, Colin. Much like Dante's Mephistopheles, he was a beautiful angel, but ultimately condemned by the fates and his own shortcomings."

"What were you doing on the Phantom Stage?" Rowland asked, eyeing Whale suspiciously.

"Just poking about a bit," was Whale's impish reply. He stuck the green-stained hanky in the breast pocket of Rowland's double-breasted gray suit as he turned his attention to Basil. "But where once we had the father, I see we now have the titular son." He gazed at Rathbone with mock sympathy. "How are you bearing up under this '*Frankenstein* curse' I've heard tell about?"

"So sorry about that, Jimmy," Rathbone said. "The publicity mill at Universal came up with that ridiculous notion."

"As I recall, the ballyhoo went on to crassly give the deaths of Colin and dear 'Old Baron Frankenstein' Frederick Kerr as proof of the curse's existence. It also maintained that you said—"

"'There's nothing in it,'" Rathbone quoted with a shake of his head as he gazed down at the floor. "Publicity made up my alleged quote. The whole thing is in very poor taste."

"Think nothing of it. I'm sure wherever Colin is, he's laughing about it." Whale staggered closer to Basil and leaned in on his cane. "I've heard good things about your performance as Sherlock Holmes. *Hound of the Baskervilles*, wasn't it?"

"Indeed," Rathbone said, noting the alcohol on Whale's breath. "For 20th Century Fox. It won't be released until next year but preview audiences have been most kind."

Whale stepped back a bit and displayed himself as if he were a runway model. "So, dear detective, what might you deduce about me?"

"If I were to use the methods of the Great Detective," Rathbone said, as he straightened up and eyed Whale with a Sherlockian demeanor, "you've been drinking in the early afternoon. Obviously, you've been trying to forget some unpleasantness. I would assume having something or other to do with Colin Clive and bitter, yet fond, memories of him that some recent incident has stirred up."

Whale smiled with genuine admiration. "Bravo," he said. "Indeed, I have been raising a glass or two to the dear boy."

"You are very finely dressed," Rathbone said with clipped Holmesian speech, "so you obviously have important business on the lot. I would say you have a late afternoon appointment with Martin F. Murphy, the Studio Production Manager."

Whale was visibly taken aback, exactly like any visitor to 221-B Baker Street who suffered the intense scrutiny of the Consulting Detective.

"How on earth did you know that?" Whale asked.

"Elementary, my dear Whale. From the telegram, there on the floor." Rathbone noted the paper with a wry gesture. "It fell from your breast pocket when you reached for the handkerchief. See there? Murphy's name and the time of your appointment, both plainly visible."

Whale gave Rathbone a Puckish grin as Rathbone picked up the telegram and handed it back. Sticking the telegram back in his pocket, Whale said, "My God, you're good. I imagine all that fencing you do has sharpened your wits. Very good, my dear Mr. Rathbone. I doff my cap to you, sir."

Rathbone smiled. "My time in British Intelligence still serves me well."

Whale stood at attention and saluted. "Ah, yes. The Great War. Doughboys in the trenches, and all that."

"I was Patrol Officer for the Second Battalion, Liverpool Scottish," Rathbone said, proudly. "I remember one mission in No Man's Land. I was camouflaged as a tree to spy on the enemy's position when—"

Lugosi sighed heavily and grumbled, "Again with the war stories! All the time, the war stories! I have war stories, too. Do you see Bela boring people with *his* war stories?"

Rathbone smiled and gave Bela a genial pat on his humped back. "So sorry, old man." To Whale he said, "I hear you distinguished yourself admirably in the Great War, as well."

Whale made a deliberately camp gesture. "He also serves who only stands and minces." In a more somber tone, he added, "But, yes, I did indeed see to my duty to the best of my ability."

"Why does Murphy want to see you?" Rowland abruptly interrupted, no doubt recalling a memo leaked to the *Son of Frankenstein* set 11 days earlier:

UNIVERSAL PICTURES CORPORATION
Inter-Office Communications
FROM: M. F. Murphy, Studio Production Manager
TO: Cliff Work, Vice President of Universal Studios Production
SUBJECT: *Son of Frankenstein*

Due to necessity of meeting release date and in order to get value of cast already on salary, this picture started production Wednesday, November 9. Operating under conditions like we are, without a script, is extremely difficult for all departments concerned in physical production and, more importantly, most expensive. We have no way of determining just how long this picture will take in production and nothing concrete upon which to substantiate any detailed figures we might attempt to compile as an estimated budget...

The memo was dated Saturday, November 12, 1938. No doubt Murphy leaked the memo himself to give Rowland some incentive to stay on schedule.

"What *does* Murphy want to see you about, Jimmy?" Rowland asked more pointedly.

"Why, my boy, I am here because—"

"Because *I* asked him here," a gruff voice said. This, and a slamming stage door, announced the arrival of Stage 7's second unexpected visitor, none other than Martin F. Murphy himself. The short, stocky executive took one look at Frankenstein's Monster scooping up another bite of birthday cake and said, "What the hell is this? Why aren't you shooting?"

"Keep your shirt on," Lee said. "It's just a little celebration for Boris. It's his birthday and he's a new papa."

Murphy glared at the cake and the bronzed Monster shoes. "Oh yeah. Congratulations there, Boris."

"Thank you," Karloff said, always a proper British gentleman, even to someone who brought a decided chill to an otherwise cheerful afternoon.

Rowland added, "We'll get back to work just as soon as we clear this cake away and," he indicated the studio photographer, "we get a few more shots for the papers."

Murphy reached into his jacket and produced a solid-gold cigarette case from the breast pocket of his silk shirt. He unsnapped the case, selected a Camel, then snapped the case shut. After tapping the end of the cigarette against the case, he stuck the cigarette in his mouth, returned the case to his pocket, and waited.

Seeing his chance, the photographer fumbled in his pockets for a lighter and lit Murphy's cigarette. "There you go, Mr. Murphy, sir."

Murphy took a puff and eyed the photographer. "Who the hell are you?"

"Uh, Mitchell, sir. Peter Mitchell from Publicity. I started working on the lot two weeks ago."

"Yeah, well, keep up the good work." Murphy pushed past the photographer and confronted Lee. "We're behind schedule, Lee! The head office is on my case about this production. They keep asking me, how far along are we in the script? I tell them, why, Mr. Rowland V. Lee doesn't believe in scripts. The head office says to me, how the hell can somebody shoot a movie without a goddamn script? So I says, Mr. Rowland V. Lee, the producer and the director of this fine production, has everything under control. He's got it all in his head. So I come on the set and what do I see? Frankenstein with cake all over his puss and a crew, a *paid* crew, standing around *not* shooting a movie! I tell you, it's enough to drive a man crazy!"

Murphy began to pace back and forth, puffing angrily on his cigarette. "This party is bad enough," he said. "Did Karloff have to delay shooting this morning by rushing off to the hospital just because his wife had a baby?" He stopped and looked reproachfully at Karloff. "And what was this business about you going to the hospital wearing the Monster makeup?"

"Honestly, Martin," Boris said, remembering his morning at Hollywood Presbyterian Hospital, "what would you have done if you were me?" Trying to keep a straight face, he added, "Now, mind you, because I didn't stop to take the makeup off, I had a bit of difficulty convincing the nurses and attendants at the hospital that I wasn't an invader from Mars."

Murphy grew pale. "Oh God, tell me you're kidding! If you scared any of the other expectant mothers—! I can see the lawsuits!"

Boris began to chuckle. "Take it easy, Martin. I'm only joshing. Seriously, I went over to visit Dorothy before Jack even had time to put the makeup on me. That story was a fairytale concocted by the *Los Angeles Examiner* to sell papers."

Murphy let out a sigh of relief. "Thank God!" He took another drag on his cigarette.

"As for my leaving when I did, what else was a man who just learned he'd become a father to do?"

"Still—" Murphy grumbled.

"Tell you what," Boris said, ever the diplomat. "What if I agree to work gratis on the last day of shooting in lieu of my absence this morning?"

"That would help," Murphy relented. He shot Lee an angry scowl and said, "But that doesn't get *you* off the hook! We wanted to make this monster show a $250,000 production. But that wasn't good enough for the great Rowland V.

Lee! This is an epic production, you said. It should have a bigger budget and be in Technicolor, you said. So, after convincing the head office to make this movie the first Technicolor picture Universal ever produced, after changing the Monster's costume for Technicolor, after building sets for Technicolor, after shooting a lot of footage in Technicolor, what do you do? You scrap the idea of Technicolor!"

Lee stood his ground. "I explained to Cliff Work about that."

"All those tests! All those very *expensive* Technicolor tests! Not to mention the Technicolor cameras and the equally expensive and downright pain in the ass Technicolor consultant, all of it thrown out on a whim from you! Why, Lee? Just tell me why?"

"Jack Pierce couldn't get Boris' makeup to look right in Technicolor."

"So you fire the makeup man, not scrap the Technicolor! I would think a 47-year-old producer with your experience would be a hell of a lot more cost conscious! Pierce isn't under contract. We can fire him any time we want."

"Boris would never agree to that," Lee said, looking to Karloff for support.

"No," Boris said with a shake of his squared head, "I never would. Jack is the best makeup man in the business. I owe him a lot."

"He's 10 years out of date! There are younger makeup guys coming up with newer and more economical kinds of monster makeup. Why, Boris, there's this one guy who could make you up in half the time it takes Jack Pierce."

"In half the time, perhaps, but not as well," Boris insisted.

"Well, never mind that," Murphy said with a dismissive wave. "I want to know what the hell this guy is still doing here," indicating Bela Lugosi. "What's the story, Lee? You were supposed to shoot all his scenes in one week!"

Lee got right in Murphy's face and yelled, "You goddamn sons of bitches wanted Bela for $500 a week. That's a goddamn insult! Well, I'm going to keep Bela on set from the first day of shooting to the last day of shooting and there's not a goddamn thing you can do about it!"

"Like hell there isn't," Murphy said. "I'm replacing you with Jimmy Whale!"

A hush fell over the soundstage. Rowland V. Lee and Martin F. Murphy stood locked in each other's withering stare, each waiting for the other to flinch. It was Whale who broke the silence, standing off to the side, looking from one man to the other like a spectator at a tennis match. "What I wouldn't give for a bag of popcorn," he said.

"SHUT UP!" the two shouted at Whale.

"Listen up, Lee," Murphy said, his index finger giving emphasis to every word with staccato pokes to the director's chest. "I'm here to get this production back on schedule."

"Is that so?" Lee snarled.

"Whale here knows how to bring in a movie on budget and on time. Hell, he brought in *Wives Under Suspicion* under budget and five days ahead of schedule!" He waved his hand in Lee's face. "FIVE DAYS! And Whale brought the movie in $30,000 under budget!" He threw an arm around Whale's shoulder and hugged him gruffly. "Now this is a director! Sure, he's light in the loafers, but damn it, he knows how to make a picture that makes a profit!"

Whale appeared amused by this display. He patted Murphy's cheek with mock affection and said, "You flatter me, Martin." With an elfin twinkle in his eye, he added, "Give us a kiss," and pursed his lips.

Murphy quickly let go of Whale and kept a safe distance. Clearing his throat, the production manager took a long drag on his cigarette and threw it to the floor. He snuffed the butt out with the toe of his shoe. Finally he said, "So that's it, Lee. You can either bring this production back on schedule or collect your pink slip." He stabbed a thumb in Whale's direction. "Meanwhile, Mr. Whale and I have some details about his next picture to discuss. Like whether it's going to be this one."

Murphy snapped his fingers and pointed at the photographer. "Hey, you, what's your name?"

"Uh, Mitchell, sir. Peter Mitchell. I've been working in Publicity for—"

"Yeah, whatever. You're with me and Whale."

"You know, Martin," Whale smiled wickedly, "in the circles in which I travel this is considered an invitation to a *ménage à trois*."

Murphy grabbed Whale roughly by the arm and steered the tipsy director toward the exit while Mitchell followed. "Whale, just shut your trap, will you!"

The stage door slammed shut.

The cast and crew stood transfixed. After a long pause, Rowland turned and addressed the set. "Well, you heard the man! Put this cake away, take the damn bridge out of your mouth, and let's make a goddamn horror movie!"

Rathbone gave Boris and Bela a half smile. "Well, gentlemen, I guess the party's over."

**Chapter Two**

**23 November 1938, 9:35 p.m.**

"More steam!" Lee shouted into the sulfur pit. Halfway down the 30-foot well, a grip was sitting in a chair at the entrance to an access passageway. "More steam," the director repeated. "And make it look HOTTER!"

"Yes, sir, Mr. Lee, sir," the grip's meek voice echoed up from the well.

Down in the pit, the grip was frantically changing colored gels on the back light and twisting valves on strategically placed steam pipes. After repositioning the fan, he leaned over the edge of the passageway and shouted, "How's that, Mr. Lee, sir?"

"I want to see a sulfur pit and all you're giving me is a Turkish bath! Make it look like there's boiling sulfur in there, goddamnit!"

"I'm sorry, Mr. Lee, I'm doing the best I—"

An ear-piercing scream echoed up from the well, followed by a muffled thud.

"What the hell happened?" Rowland shouted down.

"I leaned over too far, I guess," the chagrined grip called up. "But I'm okay. The stuntman's pad broke my fall."

Lee motioned to some stagehands. "Go down there and get that idiot back into position."

Shaking his head, Lee stormed back to his director's chair with the Frankenstein Monster following after him. "Wowan, uh ow oor upseh, buh—" Boris began.

Glowering irascibly, Lee barked, "Stop mumbling, Karloff!"

Boris paused to compose himself, then deliberately enunciated, "Row-land, I know you are up-set, but, ta-king it out on the crew will not sol-ve a-ny-thing and," he gestured at the pit, "you could cause an-o-ther ac-ci-dent."

"Another accident, huh?" Lee's outstretched hands clutched at the air as he bellowed, "If I had Murphy's neck right now, what I'd do to him wouldn't be an accident!"

A stagehand signaled that the grip was back at his post in the sulfur pit. Lee shouted, "PLACES!"

Rathbone and Lugosi joined Boris on their marks.

"Take heart, gentlemen," Rathbone whispered to his co-stars, "this is the last shot of the night."

"Is the camera ready?" Lee called.

Supervising the camera operator and checking the scene composition, director of photography George Robinson said, "Camera ready."

"That film better not jam this time, Robinson!" Lee cautioned. "Sound ready?"

Wearing headphones, sound supervisor Bernard B. Brown looked up from his control board. "Sound ready."

The assistant director held up the clapperboard. "*Son of Frankenstein*, production 931, Ygor pets Monster, take five." Clap went the clapperboard.

Lee shouted, "ACTION!"

As the camera rolled, a gravelly cackle gurgled up from Bela's throat as Ygor petted the Monster's sheepskin jersey. Very slowly, Boris let a crooked half-grin twist around one corner of the Monster's mouth. Rathbone expressed Wolf's growing apprehension as he observed the gruesome pair. They played out the scene, then held their poses until Lee shouted the all-important, "Cut. Print it. That's a wrap! Let's call it a night!"

A very audible sigh of relief issued from the cast and crew.

Boris went over to his "Monster chair," a slant board that allowed him to rest between takes in a nearly upright posture in full costume. Next to the slant board was the small table where he kept his ashtray and the water glass for his dental bridge. Boris slipped the bridge into place and lurched toward Robinson, who had turned his attention to a stagehand who was arranging a wooden dummy on the operating table. It was a replica of the Monster used to set up shots and lighting effects.

"Do you have the time?" Boris asked.

"A little after 9:30," Robinson said, checking his watch. "I guess that gives you, what? Six, maybe seven hours sleep before your 5:30 makeup call?"

Karloff sighed. "You're not taking into account the three hours it takes to get out of this makeup."

"That's the glamour of show biz."

After the dummy was put into position, Robinson checked the tableau in the viewfinder he kept around his neck. He had technician William Hedgcock roll over a piece of Kenneth Strickfaden's monster-making apparatus and had it placed beside the operating table. The control box was a complicated amalgam of glass radio tubes and toggle switches. Hedgcock took a cable with a strap on one end and wrapped the strap around his wrist.

"Clear for test," he shouted.

Hedgcock walked over to a giant rheostat and knife switch mounted on the laboratory set's main wooden support column. He threw the knife switch and dialed up the rheostat, then returned to the control box and threw a toggle switch. The control box was an impressive sight to behold as the glass radio tubes pulsated and the Jacob's ladder on top of the arrangement flickered with electricity crawling between two antennae.

"Clear Tesla coil!" Hedgcock warned.

Robinson moved Boris well back before signaling to Hedgcock that it was okay. Hedgcock threw another toggle switch. The laboratory came to life as seven-foot arcs of electricity shot across the stage from a giant Tesla transformer straight into electrodes built into the operating table and other strategically placed electrodes around the set. Shouting over the noise, Hedgcock said, "Mighty impressive, huh? Kenny Strickfaden dubbed that transformer 'Megavolt Senior' or 'Meg Senior' for short. And boy, howdy, she puts out a lot of juice! That's three quarters of a million volts right there!"

With his fingers in his ears blocking out the noise, Karloff smiled politely at Hedgcock, then leaned closer to Robinson and said, "I don't mind telling you that I get rather nervous around all this high-voltage stuff."

"You don't have to worry about a thing," Robinson shouted. "You ever see those 'electric man' acts at the circus?"

"Yes, I have."

"They use the same stuff. Those daredevils can shoot lightning from metal thimbles on their fingertips. As long as you're properly grounded like Bill over there, the voltage goes harmlessly over your body."

"And if you're not properly grounded?"

Robinson hesitated a moment, then admitted, "Well, you could get cooked from the inside out."

"I see," Boris said with concern.

"Don't worry, Boris. The head office would kill us if anything ever happened to you."

"That isn't very reassuring. By the way, where is Kenny? He's the one usually running the light show."

"Universal's just renting the equipment, so Bill over there is in charge of the effects. Next to Strickfaden himself, Hedgcock's the best there is."

"Hey, Robinson," shouted the director over the din. "Turn that thing off!"

"Do you want this scene set up for tomorrow or not?" Robinson growled back.

Hedgcock looked up from his work and appeared to be straining to hear as Lee said, "Yeah, later, but I want to make an announcement before you guys have a chance to rush off!"

Robinson got Hedgcock's attention and made a cutthroat gesture. The technician switched off the control box, dialed down the rheostat and disengaged the generator knife switch. "End test!" he shouted.

Now that the set was quiet, Lee cupped his hands and called, "Hey! Gather around a minute, you guys! I have an announcement!"

Hedgcock went over to Boris and Robinson and said, "Say, did I hear you right? Did you say there's a shoot tomorrow?"

"You heard right," said Robinson.

"But tomorrow's Thanksgiving. The old man doesn't expect us to work on Thanksgiving, does he?"

As the crew gathered in a circle, Lee said, "Look, I know today's been rough and I've been pretty rough on all of you."

"You can say that again," a stagehand muttered. The crew grumbled in agreement.

Lee did his best to ignore the murmur of dissent. "I know tomorrow's Thanksgiving and naturally you wanna spend Thanksgiving with your families, but we've got to save this picture. We're behind schedule and we gotta catch up."

Hedgcock grimaced. "We got Union rules about this, Lee. Thanksgiving is a national holiday."

Over the general murmur of agreement, Basil whispered to Boris, "The natives are getting restless."

"Yeah," a carpenter said, "are we saving this picture or your job?"

The murmuring grew louder as Boris whispered to Basil, "All they need now are torches and pitchforks."

Lee stared them all down. "Now listen, fellas. Sure, I'm trying to save my skin. But we've put a lot of work into this picture. If the studio takes it over now, you guys may be out on your asses, too. James Whale may want to bring in his own crew and start from scratch."

The crowd fell silent.

Sensing he was gaining ground, the director added, "Look, suppose I have the commissary cater a big Thanksgiving spread right here on the set. You can all bring your families and we'll make it a publicity thing so the head office won't squawk. But if we don't make Thanksgiving a working day, this picture could be sunk."

The silence in the ranks was palpable. The crew turned away to talk amongst themselves. After conferring with each other, Hedgcock stepped forward as spokesman. "If they're willing to work tomorrow," he said, indicating Boris, Basil and Bela, "we'll work tomorrow, too."

Everyone looked to the actors expectantly.

"Well, Boris," Rowland asked, "what do you say?"

After a pregnant pause, Karloff said, "For the good of the picture, I'll be here."

"As will I," said Basil.

Lugosi said, "Save me a drumstick and I will come."

Bela's remark broke the tension. The crew laughed.

Lee smiled for the first time that evening. "Okay, now that that's settled, the front office wants a script, so I'll give them a script. I'm going to have Willis Cooper on the set and have him write pages of dialogue just before we shoot."

"*Just* before we shoot?" Lugosi exclaimed.

"That's right," Lee nodded. "Lines fresh out of the typewriter. I believe this will make your dialogue sound more natural, you know, if you read the lines just before the cameras start rolling."

Lugosi was visibly upset. "Please, it is bad enough trying to make up the words as we go, but you cannot just put a script in front of me and expect me to remember the words. I need time to memorize them."

"Don't give me that bull," Lee shot back angrily. "You're all the time saying what a great actor you are! Well, goddamnit, ACT!" Lee gathered his notes and was about to storm off when he noticed Bela's hurt expression. The director sighed and said, more gently, "I'm sorry, Bela. You know I've been in your corner fighting with the studio about your wages. Honest, I've been on your side from the start. It's just I don't have time for you to act like the temperamental Hungarian prima donna. Not now."

Bela nodded. "I understand, Rowland. Forget it."

Lee gave the crew a last look. "Be on the set bright and early. Have the wives and kiddies here at one o'clock. We'll get this goddamn picture done SIX DAYS ahead of time, if I have anything to say about it!"

Lee left the set in a hurry before anyone else could argue with him. The crew grumbled resignedly amongst themselves as they headed out, leaving Boris, Bela, and Basil to ponder the situation.

Boris smiled at Bela and said encouragingly, "Lee is just tense. You understand. Don't take it personally."

"This is all that Murphy's fault," Lugosi glowered as he removed his crooked teeth and spat at the floor. "That is for you, Martin Murphy!"

"Boris is right, old boy," said Rathbone. "Tonight Lee was simply full of 'sound and fury, signifying nothing,' with apologies to the Bard for twisting his words to make my point. After Lee's had a good night's sleep, tomorrow will go much better for all of us. And we'll all have a feast into the bargain."

"Tomorrow," Bela said venomously, "tomorrow Bela will have no appetite. Tomorrow will only be better if Murphy is dead! Only then will things be all right again!"

"Watch yourself, Bela," cautioned Rathbone with a mischievous smile. "Incriminating lines like those are usually uttered in badly written mystery plays, usually before the deadly deed is done by the end of the first act. Besides, I have a plan that doesn't involve anything so extreme as murder."

"What is it then that you suggest we do?" asked Bela, sitting down in his canvas chair.

"Simple," said Rathbone, pulling his chair up next to Bela's. "We'll inform Mr. Murphy that if he replaces Rowland, we'll walk off the picture, all three of us."

Bela smiled. "Yes, that is a good plan!" He turned to Boris. "What do you say, Boris? We stand together, yes?"

Boris stood silent for a moment before uttering a hesitant, "Well—."

"Boris," said Rathbone, "it will only work if the three of us stand together." He held out his hand like a character from a Musketeer swashbuckler. "What do you say? All for one and one for all?"

Bela put his hand on top of Rathbone's. "Yes, all for one!"

The two looked expectantly at an uneasy Boris Karloff. With a sigh he said at last, "I'm sorry. I can't."

Bela was shocked. "What! You would let that Murphy fire our director?" He shook his head and grimaced. "You disappoint me, Boris. I never took you for a coward."

Karloff bristled. "Now that's just uncalled for! I've never backed down from a fight when the cause was a just one."

"So, why do you hesitate now?" Bela demanded. "Isn't saving our director just cause enough for you?"

"Yes, but you fail to appreciate the position this puts me in."

"Ah, Bela, I see his point," said Rathbone. "It's because the other man is James Whale." He looked up at Boris. "That's it, isn't it?"

Boris nodded. "Everything I am today I owe to Jimmy Whale."

"Bah!" Lugosi bellowed. "Don't remind me."

Basil gave the Hungarian a shocked look. "Now where did *that* outburst come from?"

Lugosi shifted uneasily in his chair. "I was offered *Frankenstein*, to play the Monster. I turned it down. I said to Carl Laemmle, Jr., 'You don't need an actor for that part. Anybody can moan and grunt! I need a challenging part—a part where I can ACT!'"

"I see," said Basil.

Behind the yak hair and makeup Lugosi's features were twisted into a bitter scowl. "And yet, it was Karloff's moaning and grunting that made him a star. A star greater than Bela." After a long silence, he added, "Not that I hold a grudge or anything."

"Uh, yes, well," ventured Boris, hoping to return to the original subject. "About Jimmy Whale—he would never admit it, but he's hit something of a rough patch since last year's disaster *The Road Back*, and I don't want to interfere with his chances for a comeback."

"What is that, this *Road Back*?" Bela asked.

"Oh, I heard about that," Rathbone said. He turned to Bela and explained, "It was Whale's sequel to *All Quiet on the Western Front*. The Nazi Party wouldn't release the film in Germany until all the antiwar sentiments were cut from the picture. Isn't that right, Boris?"

"Yes," said Boris. "Charles Rogers, who was vice president of production at the time, took the film away from James and butchered it. But James bore the brunt of the critical backlash, and now he's directing B-movie fodder like *Wives Under Suspicion*." Imploringly, he added, "Before we take any action, let me talk to James. I owe him that much."

Rathbone nodded in agreement. "Yes, that's really the only fair thing."

"Bah!" scoffed Bela. "You English, all you do is talk. We Hungarians do, we don't talk."

He pulled off his wig, got up, and left the soundstage in disgust.

Karloff sighed. "That could have gone better."

**"That could have gone better."**

Dwight Kemper

"Oh, he'll get over it." Rathbone reached into his pocket for a cigarette, offering the pack to Boris.

"I wish I could believe that, Basil." The Monster took a cigarette and Rathbone gave him a light. Taking a drag and exhaling smoke, Boris said, "As you may have already gathered, Bela has been known to hold a grudge."

## Chapter Three

### 23 November 1938, 10:37 p.m.

The pungent smell of chemicals that filled the Jack Pierce makeup studio mingled with freshly brewing coffee. Boris Karloff stripped off his sweat-soaked Monster costume and got into a terrycloth robe just as Basil Rathbone was getting ready to head home.

"In and out in under an hour," Boris said, enviously.

"What can I say," Basil said, stopping to check his reflection in a mirror. "It doesn't take long to remove that red Indian makeup I have to wear."

Taking the glass coffeepot from the hot plate, Boris poured himself a half-cup. "You really ought to consider growing a mustache, Basil," he said. "It suits you."

"Tried to once," Basil said, feeling his naked upper lip. "Ouida complained that it tickled."

"Well, there is that," Boris said with a smile.

"Only half a cup?" Basil asked, indicating the coffee. "Afraid it will keep you awake?"

"No, this is just the chaser," Boris said. Next to the hot plate was a bottle of whiskey. Boris mixed a generous amount of whiskey with the coffee and then sat down in the makeup chair.

"I didn't know you were an Irish coffee man."

"It helps me brace up against the pain of getting this makeup off. I used to take a full tumbler of plain whiskey back in the *Bride of Frankenstein* days. Remember, Jack?"

In a corner of the bungalow, the diminutive Jack Pierce in his white doctor's smock was the quintessential mad scientist preparing to operate. His black slicked-back hair, his thin, trim mustache and piercing gaze added to this impression. "I remember, Boris," he said in a gravelly Greek accent tinged with a touch of Brooklyn.

"Now I add two parts whiskey to one part coffee and mix with a generous amount of harsh language." Taking a sip, he asked, "By the way, how are those adoption proceedings coming, Basil?"

"As quickly as one can expect with these things. The young lady carrying our future child is expected to deliver in April. Honestly, you'd think dear Ouida was the expectant mother, the way she's been insisting we need larger living quarters."

"What are you hoping for?" the Monster asked.

Basil smiled. "Well, if it *is* a boy, I can teach him to fence and jump ramparts." Basil gave Boris a hearty salute. "I'd better leave you to suffer in peace."

"Good night, Basil."

"Good night, Boris. Good night, Jack."

"Yeah, yeah," said the irascible makeup man. "See you tomorrow." Jack was busy gathering the necessary solvents for the procedure.

After Rathbone's departure, Boris asked, "Where's Bela," noting the empty makeup chair next to him.

Pierce grimaced as he soaked a sponge with isopropyl alcohol. "Bela's in one of his moods again. He strip off his costume and went home still wearing the yak hair. He's going to have a hell of a time getting off that spirit gum at home. It'll serve the bastard right. He's always been a pain. Even way back with *Dracula*. Did you know he insisted on doing his own makeup?"

"Really?" said Karloff, being polite, well aware of the long-standing feud that existed between Pierce and Lugosi.

"'I did my own makeup on the Broadway stage,' he says to me," Pierce groused doing a poor impression of Bela's accent. "I wanted to make Dracula look like a monster. All Lugosi did was slick back his hair and put on eyeliner. He looked like a goddamn waiter!"

Realizing that nothing he could say in Bela's defense would smooth Pierce's ruffled feathers, Boris sat quietly and studied his reflection. He contemplated the heavy eyelids, the gray-green pallor, the rubber overhanging forehead and squared skull piece that the slightest movement of his head made slosh with trapped perspiration. His neck still showed scars where Pierce had first attached the electrodes back in that long hot summer of 1931 for the first *Frankenstein*. It was during his initial outing as the Monster that Boris had sustained a chronic back injury. Shaking his head, listening to the slosh, slosh, slosh, Boris wondered why he had let himself get talked into revisiting a role that involved 30-pounds of makeup and padding that exacerbated the pain in his back. The $3,750 per-week salary Universal offered certainly made a third go 'round as the Monster seem very appealing. But it was Rowland V. Lee's willingness to compromise that clinched the deal. After all, it was Lee who came up with the idea of the Monster being in a coma for the first half of the movie! That way, Karloff could lie down on a nice hard operating table. The special effects department proposed sparing Boris' back even further by flying Bela Lugosi on wires so the Peter Pan rig bore the actor's full weight in a scene where the Monster carried Ygor's dead body down into the Frankenstein crypt. But no amount of money, special effects or Irish coffee could hide the creeping realization that Boris may have made a big mistake accepting the role again. The sight of Jack rolling his instrument table near Boris' makeup chair intensified this feeling.

"Ready, Boris?" Jack asked, poised to operate.

Karloff sighed, finished his Irish coffee and resigned himself to the ordeal yet to come. "Very well, Jack. Do your worst."

It was at that opportune moment that Jimmy Whale, who must have been psychic about when to make an entrance, knocked on the open door of the makeup studio.

"Jack," Whale smiled. "How have you been, you old monster maker?"

Had anyone else dared to interrupt the curmudgeonly Pierce while he was working, there would have been fireworks for sure. But when Jack Pierce saw the intruder was James Whale, he smiled broadly and took the director's hand, shaking it vigorously. "Jimmy! So good to see you again!"

"God," Whale said, surveying the makeup studio, "this place hasn't changed a bit. Still have your rogue's gallery, I see."

Whale was referring to a display of plaster life masks hanging on one wall. Casts of everyone Jack Pierce had ever had in his makeup chair were lined up row upon row, including recent casts of Boris Karloff and co-star Basil Rathbone. They all hung there in mute witness to the goings on in Jack Pierce's *sanctum sanctorum* of greasepaint and spirit gum.

"Yes, they all my children," Pierce said, smiling broadly.

"I see that one of your children is missing." Whale pointed to a blank space in a row of recent casts. "What happened? Did one of your actors get you riled and you gave their bust a bust?"

"Nah, the nose just got chipped. I gotta cast new one."

The director chucked Pierce under the chin. "Temper, temper. Always throwing things when your children get naughty." He turned his attention to Boris. "Ah, but this child," Whale said, spreading his arms out dramatically as he approached. "This child I had a hand in creating." He stood behind the makeup chair so their reflections shared the mirror. "I must have made dozens of sketches of that wonderfully angular face." He posed as if for a daguerreotype family portrait, his white suit rumpled and hair out of place,

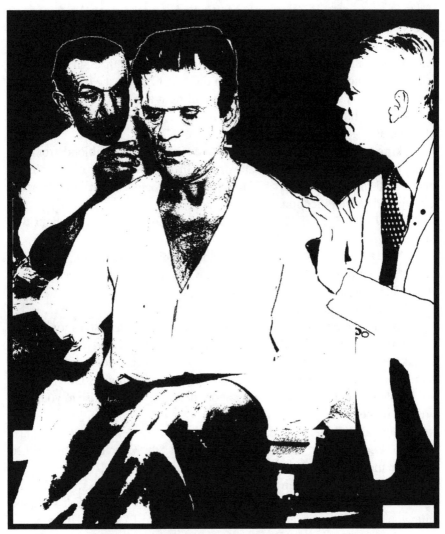

"Jack, how have you been, you old monster maker?"

and said, "We make quite a gruesome pair, don't we, Boris? God, I still re-member the words you uttered when you saw yourself in Pierce's makeup for the first time!" Effecting a lisp, Whale said in a rather good impression of Karloff, "I think that thith will be the motht thenthathanal thing to be theen on the thilver thcreen."

Boris smiled at the memory, then said, "You and Mr. Murphy must have had quite a long meeting. It's after 10 o'clock."

"Is it?" Whale said, checking his watch. "Egad! So it is! I thought it was rather late. Dear Martin was wining and dining me all day, trying to convince me to take on your little film. He even had that delightful young man from the publicity department—you know, the beautiful boy who was taking pictures of you at the party this afternoon—Martin had him take a couple of snaps as we conferred in his office over brandy and cigars." He checked his reflection in the mirror. "Obviously a bit too much conferring. I look like an unmade bed." Grabbing a comb from the makeup table, he ran it through his tousled hair. "I woke up alone, stretched out on the couch. At least Martin was kind enough to pull a blanket over me before calling it a night."

"Are you bleeding?" Boris asked, noting a few drops of red on James' white lapel.

Taking a monogrammed hanky stained with traces of blood from his breast pocket, Whale dabbed his nostrils. "Just a nose bleed. It's nothing. I took a spill on Martin's carpet." He returned the hanky to his breast pocket and winked at his reflection.

"Um, Jimmy," Karloff said, fumbling for the right words, "about this business with Rowland and Murphy—."

Whale turned to give Boris a disarming smile as he held up a staying hand. "Think nothing of it, old boy. Don't worry your flat head about it. I told Martin I'm not interested."

This was a great relief. "Really?"

"Do you honestly think I want any part of another monster movie? I'm done with them. Hell, I've done *Showboat*, my pride and joy! My new agent is soaking Universal for a bloody fortune and cut of the profits for *The Man in the Iron Mask*. Monsters are the last thing I want on my résumé."

Whale gave Jack a consolatory pat on the back. "No offense to you, dear monster maker."

"None taken," Pierce said.

"No, Lee can keep his position as director. Oh, Murphy did his best to convince me otherwise. But I dug my heels in and said no."

Just then the phone rang. Pierce answered. He looked perplexed as he listened to whoever was on the line, then said, "Really? Now? It's a good thing you called. I was just about to take the makeup off." He held the receiver against his chest and asked Boris, "Are you up to a couple more shots?"

"What?" Boris said, confused. "But Rowland said we were wrapped for the day."

Pierce shrugged. "He says he needs you for a couple of pick-up shots with Pinky," he said, referring to Lionel Atwill, who was playing the role of the one-armed Inspector Krogh. "Pinky" was his very unlikely nickname.

"Pick-up shots?" Karloff protested. "My scenes with Lionel aren't for days yet."

"I guess Rowland got another one his brainstorms and called Pinky and Pinky said okay."

"But who made Lionel up? You obviously didn't do it."

Pierce shrugged. "All I know is what Rowland tells me. He says he wants you back on the set in costume, so if you gonna do it, we gotta put you back in costume."

Karloff sighed. He didn't relish donning that padded outfit again. But he was a professional and if spending another hour in makeup on some improvisational scene would help wrap production quicker, so be it.

"Tell Rowland I'll be right there," he said, resignedly.

"Boris said he'll be right over," Pierce said to the other party on the phone.

"I say, Boris," said Whale as Pierce cradled the receiver and Boris slipped out of his robe and pulled on a fresh pair of underwear and a fresh black undershirt, "why don't you take my studio cart? It's just out front. Actually, it's Murphy's cart."

"What are you doing with Murphy's studio cart?" Boris asked, leaning on Whale for support as Jack Pierce buckled Boris into the steel leg struts that gave the Monster his characteristic lurch.

Whale gave a slight shrug under the burden of Karloff's weight. He grunted and puffed, "Since he—left me for dead—in his office—I didn't think he'd—mind my commandeering it." Looking down at Pierce, he asked, "How are you—coming, Jack, old man?"

"Almost ready," Pierce said, holding open the first pair of the two pairs of pants Karloff wore. Boris stepped into them and Jack tugged the pants up the actor's stiffened legs. Karloff could feel poor Jimmy buckle under the strain. The actor shifted his weight to ease up on the willowy director. After the two pairs of pants came the spare double quilted padded suit that had been airing out since late that afternoon. Then Karloff donned the brown tunic, the shaggy coat, and the boots. It took a bit of doing, but in a little under 20 minutes with Jack's and James' help, the Frankenstein Monster was ready to menace the Universal Studios lot again.

Whale was done in. He leaned against the makeup table, dabbing his perspiring face with the monogrammed handkerchief. "I'll be glad to walk you out," Whale offered. "Just give me a moment."

"Are you sure you don't want the cart for yourself?" Boris asked as Pierce did a quick touchup of Karloff's hands, paying particular attention to the blacked ends of his fingertips.

It was then that Boris remembered that Whale had earlier used his hanky to wipe off the green makeup left on his hand, and that Whale had stuck the soiled handkerchief in Rowland's pocket. Looking over at James as he mopped his forehead, Boris could just make out the monogram "B. S." Boris figured James must have borrowed the hanky. It would be just like James to brazenly snatch a hanky from somebody just because he needed one. Shrugging it off,

Boris said, "You could drive me over to Stage 7 and then use the cart to get back to where your car is parked."

"No, wouldn't hear of it," Whale said as he stuck the hanky back in his pocket and poured himself a cup of coffee. "It's a lovely night and I could do with a bit of a walk. Clear out the cobwebs and all that."

After a few quick sips of coffee and after checking his hair and clothing in the mirror, he said, "Besides, Boris, I'm sure dear Martin would insist on lending his cart to Universal's leading horror star."

"Don't let Bela hear you say that," Boris chided, but only half-joking.

A final dusting of fuller's earth on the now resurrected Monster's clothing and Boris was ready to follow James Whale out the front door. Effecting his talking Monster voice, Karloff grunted in full character, "You—lead—way. I—follow."

Whale giggled delightedly. "I just love how you do that!"

"Wait, Boris." Pierce pointed to his cheek.

"Oh, yes." Boris took out his dental bridge and put it in a glass of water. He sucked in his cheek so Pierce could give the hollow a quick dab of black makeup.

Pierce nodded his approval. "Now you're ready."

Murphy's studio cart was just as Whale had left it, with one wheel up on the curb. Boris got in. It was a bit of a tight fit and the strut-stiffened legs didn't help matters any. But he somehow managed it with a little effort and a lot of grunting.

"Comfy, are we?" Whale asked, obviously amused at seeing the Frankenstein Monster behind the wheel of a studio cart.

Karloff smiled and nodded.

"Well, I'm off then," Whale said, about to gallantly doff his hat, then realizing he wasn't wearing it. He smoothed his hand over his hair instead.

Boris made an inviting gesture at the empty passenger seat.

"I'm parked on the other side of the lot, up by the Phantom Stage. Besides, the sooner you get to the set, the sooner you can get out of that costume and go home." He waved and said, "Ta."

Boris waved then placed his huge foot on the accelerator.

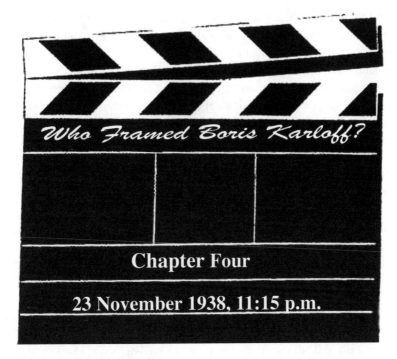

**Who Framed Boris Karloff?**

## Chapter Four

## 23 November 1938, 11:15 p.m.

Boris arrived on the set and found Stage 7 deserted. There was no film crew present. The overhead studio lights were dark. The Strickfaden machines were on. Huge Tesla transformers crackled. The control box radio tubes pulsated, the Jacob's ladder crawled and fizzled.

In the pulsing lights and "Meg Senior's" jagged arcs of lightning Boris saw what he thought was the camera set up dummy burning to a crisp on the operating table. But the closer Boris got, the more he began to realize that the dummy wasn't a dummy at all. Karloff's eyes widened with horror. It was the still, lifeless, and smoking body of Martin F. Murphy!

Remembering what he saw Bill Hedgcock do during the equipment test, Boris ran to the main control panel and yanked open the huge knife switch. The room was plunged into darkness and deathly silence, disturbed only by the sound of hissing, charred flesh and the pungent cookout stink of barbecued pork.

Having been blinded by flashing lights and sudden darkness, all Boris could see were blobs of color against black. He felt his way in the dark, hunting for the operating table, all the while being mindful of the open sulfur pit at the back of the laboratory set.

He found the operating table and reached out for the body, feeling down the right arm until he came to the wrist.

"Oh, my dear God," Karloff said as he felt for a pulse, but found none.

Just then a stark beam of light and an exclamation of "Jiminy Crickets!" startled Boris. The actor looked up and squinted. He held up a hand to protect his eyes from the glaring flashlight beam.

A studio security guard stared open-mouthed at the improbable scene of Frankenstein's Monster bent over the body of his hapless victim.

"Jiminy Crickets!" the guard repeated as he fumbled for his gun. "Uh, d-don't you move. I got you c-covered!"

Boris stood transfixed for a moment, then realized how all this must look. He raised his hands and said, "I'm Boris Karloff." Unfortunately, without his dental bridge, this came out sounding like, "U'm Borwith Kahwoff." The rest was equally unintelligible as he endeavored to explain, "Rowland Lee, the director of *Son of Frankenstein*, called me to the set. I found Martin Murphy lying here dead. He's been electrocuted. You must call for an ambulance at once."

"I can't understand a word you're saying and I don't care," the guard said, obviously half scared out of his wits. The muzzle of his revolver was shaking so wildly that Boris was afraid it might go off.

"I'll stay right here," Boris said in as soothing a voice as he could muster, trying to enunciate without his dental bridge. "But Mar-tin Mur-phy is dead. E-lec-tro-cu-ted. Call the po-lice and an am-bu-lance."

The guard maneuvered himself to the studio phone, keeping the flashlight beam and the gun aimed at Karloff the whole time. "You—you just stay right there while I call the police."

All Boris could do was roll his eyes and sigh, but at least now his vision was coming back into focus and he could see.

From the burn in Murphy's jacket it would seem all the arcs of high voltage current were attracted to something in the breast pocket of his shirt. Boris reached in and pulled out the executive's gold cigarette case. Boris felt a shudder as he remembered what Robinson told him about being cooked from the inside out by the Tesla coil if you're not properly grounded. As he returned the cigarette case to Murphy's pocket, Boris spotted what looked like crumpled notepaper clutched in Murphy's right hand. The fingers were curled in a death grip and a residue of cooked flesh had stuck to the paper. Boris wanted to alert the security guard, but saw the guard was too preoccupied to listen.

It was a strange balancing act to behold as the nervous guard wrestled with the task of dialing the phone while holding the flashlight and keeping Boris covered with the revolver. Somehow he managed it, with a clever use of one armpit for the flashlight, his chin for the receiver while he dialed the phone with his free hand, and held the gun on Boris with the other hand. It was obvious to Mr. Karloff that the security guard had definitely missed his calling not turning his talent into a Vaudeville act.

Dwight Kemper

Once the guard finished dialing, he grabbed the receiver from under his chin, waiting to be connected with his party and finally said, "Hello, studio police department? This is Jenkins, studio security. I just caught Frankenstein red-handed murdering a guy!" There was a brief pause. "No, I ain't drunk! He's standing right here big as life! Seven feet tall and all green! There's a dead guy on the operating table and everything! He says the dead guy's name is Marvin Murray."

"No," said Boris, feeling very frustrated. "Mar-TIN Mur-PHY."

"Oh, he says it's a guy named Mar-TIN Mur-PHY." There was another pause, followed by, "What do you mean, 'he who?' Frankenstein! He says it's a guy named Martin Murphy—I dunno, maybe it is *that* Martin Murphy! How should I know?"

Boris sighed as the security guard nervously hung up the phone. "N-now you just stay right where you are until the police g-get here."

As the guard kept Boris covered, he absently rubbed under his chin, then looked at the palm of his hand. He grimaced in disgust, exclaimed, "What in the world—!" and wiped his hand on his pants.

Now all Boris could do was wait patiently for the Universal Studios police to arrive. He felt supremely confident that the authorities would simply take his statement and then get down to the business of finding out what had really happened here tonight.

As it turned out, things weren't going to be quite that simple.

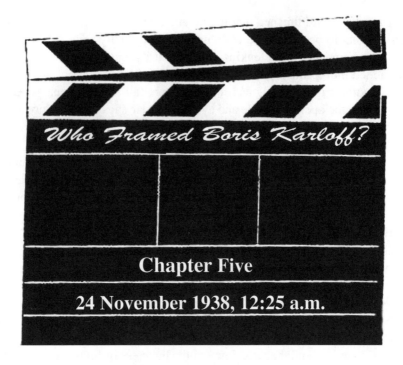

**Who Framed Boris Karloff?**

**Chapter Five**

**24 November 1938, 12:25 a.m.**

Loud curses and growls filled the master bedroom at 516 Linden Drive in Beverly Hills. Although the two wiggling forms under bedcovers seemed to be wrestling, these two were most definitely not enemies—on top, Eddie "The Bulldog" Mannix, so named because he was short and squat, his face was round and flat and, like a bulldog, he could rip a guy's throat out; his willing opponent—Toni "Legs" Lanier, a 20-something brunette, ballsy, hard-drinking, hard-loving, an Irish broad who got her gorgeous gams and her nickname dancing with the Ziegfeld Follies.

The telephone on the nightstand began to ring.

The one time New Jersey Palisades pug peered out from under the sheets. "Who the HELL's calling me at THIS goddamn hour?"

"Oh, Eddie, don't answer. Who gives a damn who's calling?"

Not one to deny Toni anything, Eddie ignored the phone and pulled the bedclothes back over the both of them.

But try as he might, Eddie couldn't keep his mind on Toni.

"Oh, Christ," Eddie grumbled, throwing back the sheets and glaring at the still ringing telephone. "Maybe it's Mayer or Strickling. It could be important." The 40-plus tough guy was Louis B. Mayer's second-in-command and absolutely essential to Howard Strickling, head of M-G-M's publicity department.

"Screw Mayer and screw Strickling," Toni said.

Toni pulled Eddie closer to her, but it was no use—Mannix could still hear that goddamn ringing telephone. He jerked the sheets back again and looked over at the bedside table with a frown of concern.

"Jesus," Mannix said, "maybe Gable got drunk and hit another pedestrian or somethin'."

Toni grabbed Eddie's face in a violent twisting grip that would have given a lesser man whiplash. She glared into his eyes and said with venom, "Edgar J. Mannix, if you ignore me one more time for work, I'll make you sing falsetto with my knee, you sonofabitch!"

Eddie loved it when Toni talked to him like that. The tumultuous noise of Toni, Eddie, the creaking bedsprings and the ringing telephone all blended together into a clashing, discordant crescendo of passion.

They came up for air as Eddie flopped down between Toni and the damn telephone. It had now been ringing for a full 10 minutes. He reached over for the handset and hesitated, asking Toni, "Is it okay if I get it now, baby?"

Toni managed to croak, "Yeah, sure."

Eddie's demeanor switched to "The Bulldog" as he picked up the handset. "Whoever the hell this is, you better make it DAMN important!"

"Eddie, I need to call in that favor."

Mannix instantly recognized the voice. It was Cliff Work, vice president in charge of production over at Universal Studios.

"You gotta come right over," Work pleaded.

"Now?" Eddie looked over at Toni.

Like a satisfied Venus waiting for Mars to come back for seconds, Toni's arms were draped seductively over her head, her long dark hair spilled out over the silk pillow like a chestnut waterfall. Her full breasts were heaving.

Eddie sure had no desire to abandon Toni. "I'm in the middle of somethin' here. Try me in the morning."

Eddie was about to hang up when he heard Work say desperately, "It can't wait till morning! You're the best fixer in Hollywood and I need you to fix something right away!"

"Fine. Sure. In the morning." He brushed his hand over Toni's thigh. "Mmmm," she purred.

"I told you it can't wait! You said I could call in the favor anytime! Well, this is anytime!" As Eddie moved the handset to its cradle, he heard Work say, "Or do I have to remind you about what happened at Pinky's weekend sex party?" Eddie immediately put the handset to his ear and listened. "Remember, Eddie? Those naked pictures of you and that underage starlet? I smoothed things over with the mother without you having to resorting to—well, to doing to the mother like you did to your ex-wife."

"Hey, leave Bernice out of this," Eddie growled.

The former Mrs. Bernice Mannix had been killed in a car accident on the 18th of November 1937. The "accident" happened in Palm Springs where Bernice had been living in quiet and well-paid exile since 1934 when Eddie first became involved with Toni. Strangely, Bernice's death came soon after she had threatened to publicly sue Eddie for divorce on the grounds of "cruelty and infidelity."

Hearing Bernice's name mentioned made Toni's lips tighten and not in a good way. "What about Bernice?" she hissed. "Who the hell is that?"

Eddie winced. "It's just business, baby." Eddie kissed her. "A guy needs a favor." He turned on the nightstand light and fumbled for his glasses. As he did, he said to Work, "Okay, you made your point." He searched the bedside table drawer for a pad and a pencil. "Gimme the lowdown and make it good."

As Eddie jotted down the details, Toni heard, "Yeah—okay, then what? Yeah—So what did you do?—Uh huh—An' what did he do?—Okay—So, how many guys are in on this?" He scribbled on the pad, then said, "Okay, that's not a problem. So what did they do with the you-know-what?—Good. Tell those guys to stay put till I get there." Eddie put down the pad and pencil and was about to hang up when something the other party said made him pause. As Eddie listened to Work ramble on, he looked over at Toni and made a "yak, yak" gesture, then said into the mouthpiece, "Relax, will ya. Just leave it to me. Oh, and I wanna see you and Kar—" he stopped himself from naming names as he glanced back over at Toni, who was watching him intently, he said, "—you and the *other guy* in your office." He listened to Work and grumbled, "What the hell do I care if he's still in makeup? Just keep the guy there till I can talk to him!" He hung up and tore the page out of the pad.

"Who was that, baby?" asked Toni as Eddie got up to get dressed. Her voice was filled with concern.

"Like I said, a friend calling in a favor," he said, stepping into a pair of boxer shorts.

"What kind of favor?" Toni asked, although she had a pretty good idea.

"I can't say," Eddie said. "If it was another dame, I'd tell you, you know that." It was understood between them that they both had appetites that no one person alone could satisfy. Mannix and Howard Strickling had opened a high-end private brothel in the Hollywood Hills where stars and executives could party and not worry about scandal rags catching wise. It was an open secret Eddie kept a private suite there and frequently used it to sample the stable of talent.

Eddie stepped into his walk-in closet and pulled on a pair of pants and grabbed a shirt and a tie. He stuffed the torn out page in his pants pocket.

"How long will you be gone?" she asked suggestively.

She kicked away the bed sheets, displaying herself provocatively as Eddie checked his reflection in the dressing mirror. Damn, Toni looked good!

Dwight Kemper

"I ain't sure, doll," Eddie said, fumbling with his tie as he bent down to kiss her, "but keep your motor runnin' for me, anyways." He sat on the edge of the bed and pulled on a pair of socks and tied his shoes. "This could take a while."

Toni hugged Eddie from behind and held a black ring box in front of him. "Don't forget the ring I bought you."

Mannix smiled and took the box. "Hey, baby, I said I'd never go nowheres without it, didn't I?"

He slipped the gold ring with the tiger-eye stone on his stubby digit. Toni had presented it to him on the day they set up housekeeping on Linden Drive. Because he couldn't legally marry her at the time, the ring became the closest thing to a wedding band.

She took his hand now and kissed the ring. "There, you big lug. Sealed with a kiss. Now you can't take it off."

Eddie kissed her again. Her warm body felt good. It was going to take a powerful force of will on his part to make Eddie get out of that bed. He held her and said, "Believe me, baby, if this wasn't so damn serious, I'd say to hell with 'em. But I gotta go."

"I know, darling," she said, exaggerating the word with a long, breathy "ah." "I'll wait up for you."

He kissed her again. "You better, doll."

The Bulldog got up, grabbed a jacket hanging on a nearby valet and headed out on what he thought was going to be another routine "fix it" job.

It wasn't.

# Who Framed Boris Karloff?

## Chapter Six

## 24 November 1938, 2:07 a.m.

Cliff Work sat behind his desk. He wore a pair of pants under his bathrobe, shoes without socks, and a worried expression. Work was a beefy no-nonsense industry veteran, but like all industry veterans, he was constantly on the verge of a nervous breakdown. "You know how I got where I am today?" Work asked as he set out a row of medicine bottles of various shapes, sizes, and colors for various stress-related ailments. "Because Charlie Rogers broke the first commandment of the studio system: 'Thou Shalt Not Lose Money.'"

Flanking Cliff Work was Eddie Mannix. Sitting on Work's couch in Monster makeup and stocking feet, listening to Work but keeping a sharp eye on Mannix, was the prime suspect in the murder of Martin F. Murphy, Boris Karloff. While Mannix stared Boris down, he fidgeted with his ornate gold tiger-eye ring, a ring that Karloff surmised had left its impression in many a man's jaw.

"Rogers cost the studio over $3,000,000," Work said, grabbing the first pill bottle. "The head office is banking on the success of a *Frankenstein* movie, so guess who has to deliver the goods? Me, that's who." He shook a pill into the palm of his hand, then gulped the pill down with a glass of water. As Work read Boris the riot act, he repeated this procedure with each bottle along the line. "Your green greasepaint fingerprints were on the lever running the electrical machinery," shake, shake, rattle, rattle, pop, swallow, gulp, "and on the steering wheel of Murphy's personal studio cart," shake, shake, rattle, rattle, pop, swallow, gulp, "and on Murphy's gold cigarette case!"

"I told you how that happened," Boris interrupted.

Shake, shake, pause, "Did you know about the bloodstains found in the back of the cart?" Resume shake, shake, rattle, rattle, then pop, swallow, and gulp.

Karloff was taken aback. "No."

Over Work's medicinal maraca accompaniment Mannix chimed in, "There was also a bloodstain on the rug in Murphy's office."

Boris fell silent for a moment. A bloodstain in Murphy's office and another in his personal studio cart? Could Jimmy Whale—?

Work paused between pill popping and added grimly, "There was a note found in Murphy's hand, a note signed by *you* asking him to meet you on Stage 7." Clutching his stomach, Work reached for another bottle and poured out a tablespoon full of chalky white liquid and swallowed it. "This is playing HELL with my ulcer! I hope you're happy." Grimacing at the taste of the medicine, Work said, "You were seen by the security guard standing over the body. The film crew saw you arguing with Murphy."

"I wasn't arguing with him," Boris corrected. "We had a disagreement about Jack Pierce. That's hardly a motive for murdering a man."

"What about the note?" asked Mannix, holding up the very note in question between his immaculately manicured fingers. The nails shown with clear polish. He handed the note to Boris and said, "That's your signature, ain't it?"

Boris recognized his signature. It was unmistakable. But the note itself had been typed. The paper struck Boris as strange, too. It wasn't your typical notepaper. The short top edge felt frayed as if it had been a page torn out of a book. The sides of the remaining three corners felt unusually stiff. The size and smooth texture of the paper reminded Boris of something, but he was too upset to collect his thoughts. He said, "Why would I type a note and then sign it? Wouldn't I write the whole note? Obviously anybody could have typewritten the note and traced my signature."

"It don't look traced to me," Mannix insisted, taking the note back. He cleared his throat and read the contents aloud. "'Need to discuss your outrageous behavior this afternoon. Meet me on Stage 7 or I won't finish the picture. Signed, Boris Karloff.'"

Boris stared intently at Work. "What possible sense does it make my luring Murphy onto Stage 7 if other evidence hints that he was attacked in his office and the body transported to Stage 7 in his studio cart?"

"It doesn't make sense," Work said, popping another palm full of pills. "That's why we're going to help you out of this jam." He looked down at the label on the bottle for the pills he had just swallowed. "Oh, crap, this is Rogers' prescription."

"You should have the police check all the typewriters at the studio. There's a 'd' on that note with a break in it."

"That would raise too many questions, Boris," Work said.

Mannix leaned in close. Boris detected a heavy perfume that couldn't have been aftershave. Mannix had stubble on his face. "The ambulance boys had to pry this note out of Murphy's cold, dead hand. That means he was holding the letter signed by you when he croaked. You know what will happen to your career if the press catches wind of this, Mr. Monster? They just love juicy details like that."

Work interrupted with a loud clearing of his throat and gestured for Mannix to back off. "Well, that's not going to happen. Boris, you're too valuable to Universal Studios to let something like this get into the papers. Now, we know someone was obviously setting you up. I mean, you just don't look the type to kill anybody."

Mannix smiled. "What are you talking about, Cliff? Boris here looks exactly the type. His bread and butter depend on it. At least that's what Mr. and Mrs. Average American will think. And they sure the hell won't give a damn about bloodstains on a rug."

"Now see here—" Boris began, but was cut short by Cliff Work.

"Just sit and listen, Boris. Like I said, you're too valuable to have this reach the press, or the courts. So we asked Eddie Mannix—"

"Yes," Boris said pointedly, "I know Mr. Mannix's reputation as a 'fixer.' We've met before." He looked intently at Mannix. "Remember, Eddie?"

Work looked up at Mannix. "You two know each other?"

Mannix shrugged. "Sure. Karloff did some work over at M-G-M. *The Mask of Fu Manchu*. That Myrna Loy was a real doll."

Boris smiled sardonically. "That was our first meeting, the cordial one where Eddie played the role of welcoming representative for Mayer and Strickling. Things were less cordial a year later. Remember THAT encounter, Eddie?"

"Sure, I remember. What's your point?"

"It was 1933 and Eddie was working on behalf of the Studios, trying to 'fix' the threat of the emerging Screen Actor's Guild—by any means necessary. I and the other 12 founding members had to meet secretly, going to extremes like making telephone calls from payphones and parking our cars blocks away from where we were meeting. After one such covert rendezvous I returned to my car. Back then, I drove an English Auburn, and I was shocked to find the headlights had been smashed and the tires slashed. And speaking of incriminating notes, there was a note left under the windshield wiper. It read simply: 'Stop the Union, or else.' And it was signed, 'Eddie Mannix.'"

Eddie shrugged. "Those were different times."

Boris stared Eddie down, but kept smiling. "Indeed they were, Mr. Mannix. Indeed they were. The Screen Actor's Guild beat the odds and became a thriving union despite your best efforts." Boris' expression became hard. "I'm

Union member number nine, and damned proud of it. And I greatly resent your being brought here tonight."

"Now look here, Karloff," Eddie began angrily.

"KNOCK IT OFF, EDDIE," Work shouted.

Mannix reluctantly backed off, but kept a sharp eye on Karloff as Work popped another pill and said, "Okay, so like I started to say, we asked Eddie here to loan himself out from M-G-M to help us clear up this little matter."

"Cover up, you mean," said Boris, the green makeup hiding how flushed with anger his face was getting.

"You say 'cover up,'" Mannix said as he took Work's ashtray and set it in front of him. "I say there ain't nothing to cover up. See?" He folded up the incriminating note and lit a match. Setting one edge of the note alight, he said, "Now you see it, now you don't."

Boris shot up from the couch and tried to stop him. "You can't do that! There's a real murderer out there and if you destroy the evidence—"

Mannix grabbed Boris' wrist and held it in a powerful grip. The Bulldog's gold ring caught the glint of the flames dancing in the ashtray. Boris noted that the tiger-eye stone was carved into the relief profile of a conquistador. "Temper, temper, Franky. See, we don't care about some other killer that may or may not be out there. We just care about you. This is for your own good. Take Fatty Arbuckle. He was acquitted and the jury even apologized to him and everything. Y'know what happened to Arbuckle? He died a broken man, is what. See, the public don't care about the truth. They believe what the papers tell 'em to believe. The papers said Arbuckle was a killer, so no matter who said what after that, Arbuckle was a killer."

"Be reasonable, Boris," Work said, practically begging. "We just want to save your career—and mine, too, if you want to know the truth."

"At the sacrifice of a man's life?" asked Boris as he watched the note turn to ashes.

Mannix let go of Boris' wrist and patted him on the back. Karloff felt a chill creep down his spine. "Hey, Murphy's dead already. Nothing we do can change that. So we take care of the living. We take care of you."

"Boris," Cliff Work said, "we're closing down production for a few days to give Eddie here a chance to, well, to do what he does best. In the meantime, we'll put you on paid vacation for a week. Go home, do some gardening, play some cricket, or whatever you enjoy doing. Forget this ever happened."

"Because believe me," added Mannix, "by the time I'm through, this whole thing *will* never have happened."

Boris Karloff sighed and sat down. Outwardly resigned, but inwardly seething.

## Chapter Seven
### 27 November 1938, 9:53 a.m.

Boris was puttering around in his garden at his Coldwater Canyon home, although "puttering" was hardly the word to describe his mood. "Brooding" was more like it. Usually the three-plus acres with its lawns, hedges, and fruit trees, a place he referred to simply as "The Farm," was a great comfort to Boris. He regularly took pleasure in working with the soil and tending to his 400-pound pet pig Violet. But this morning found the tall, gaunt figure, whose sun-darkened complexion betrayed his British/East Indian heritage, taking little pleasure in his digging.

Karloff was quite a sight while gardening under the best of circumstances. He always did his gardening in what he called "me wickies," which consisted of a pair of swimming trunks and a top hat.

This was the sight that met Basil Rathbone as he strolled up the walk to the rear of the Spanish style split-level home. Boris had phoned last night and asked Rathbone to drop by this morning. Rathbone stood there a moment, dressed in funerary black, his hands in his trouser pockets, watching Boris toil away with a garden hoe. When, after a while, Boris had failed to acknowledge his presence, Rathbone said good-naturedly, "Burying another body, Boris?"

Boris looked up from his digging. By his demeanor, Rathbone expected him to utter one of his guttural Frankenstein's Monster growls. Instead, he

Dwight Kemper

simply said, "Oh, hello there, Basil. Sorry. I didn't see you." Noting Rathbone's attire, Boris added, "I see you're going to Murphy's funeral today." He resumed his digging.

"Judging from your attire, it appears you will not be attending."

"It was suggested I keep a low profile," Boris said darkly.

"By whom?"

"It's a long story, Basil."

"You seem quite—distracted. Frustrated that the picture's been delayed, are you?"

Karloff stopped his digging, removed his top hat and wiped the sweat from his brow. "No, Basil. It's something far more serious than that." He was about to resume his gardening, but tossed the hoe aside instead. "This is pointless."

"Not if it makes you feel better."

"That's the problem. It doesn't."

Rathbone gave Boris a look of concern. "It's not about Dorothy or the baby, is it? Complications with the C-section?" In preparation for his role as Wolf von Frankenstein, Basil had been boning up on his medical jargon.

"Dorothy is doing all right under the circumstances, an infection of some sort. But the doctor assures me she'll be fine after a week or two in hospital. The baby is doing just fine and will be home soon with a nurse to look after her." Boris fell silent for a moment, then added, "But that's not why I've asked you to meet me here."

"Then why all the mystery?"

Instead of answering, Boris acted the role of the perfect gentleman host and gestured for Basil to join him on the slate patio.

"Thirsty?" he asked. "I made a pitcher of lemonade."

Basil sat down and smiled. "Mind putting something a bit stronger in it, old boy?"

Boris smiled back. This was the first time he'd smiled in days outside of recent visits to the hospital to see Dorothy and the baby. "Gin?"

"Or vodka, whatever you have on hand."

Boris returned momentarily, sans top hat, wearing a bathrobe. He brought out a pitcher of lemonade and two glasses filled with ice on a silver service, along with Thursday's neatly folded newspaper.

Basil looked up and chuckled. "Seeing you this way, Boris, I'm reminded of the butler you played in *The Old Dark House*. That is, if the butler had been wearing a bathrobe and a pair of swimming trunks."

Setting the tray down on the glass topped patio table, Boris said, "If Jimmy Whale could have rationalized such a costume, I very likely would have been." Filling the first glass, he handed it to Basil. "Your 70-proof lemonade, Mr. Rathbone."

Boris poured himself a glass and sat down. His mood shifted back to brooding as he nursed his lemonade. He watched his two dogs, a black Scotty, named Whiskey, and a white west highland terrier, named Soda, playing together around the pool and barking at the ducks in the water. Such a homey scene usually soothed him, but Karloff felt tense.

"Are you going to tell me what this is all about?" Basil said, breaking the silence. "Your phone call was intriguingly cryptic."

"Basil," Boris said at last, "someone is using me. I don't like being used. For some reason someone has gone to great lengths to make me look like a murderer."

"Oh? A murderer?" Rathbone said, eyebrows raised. He chuckled, thinking Boris was joking and asked, "And whom have you supposedly killed?"

Boris hesitated a moment and then said, "Martin F. Murphy."

Rathbone was taken aback. "What? Really, Boris, you shouldn't joke about a thing like that."

"Do I look like I'm joking? Martin F. Murphy was murdered."

"Murphy died of a heart attack. He was found in his office, or so I've heard. In fact, the front office said the production was going to be shut down out of respect to Murphy's memory and shooting would resume Monday."

Boris' face became a grim mask as he looked off into the distance. "I see Mr. Mannix has done his job well."

"Mannix? Eddie Mannix? What does he have to do with—" Rathbone stopped abruptly as Boris took the newspaper from the tray and thrust it at him. It was folded to the obituaries.

"The newspapers published the cover story Mannix invented. Read it for yourself."

"I've already read it," Basil said, glancing at the newspaper. Along with Murphy's obit was a recent photo. The caption read, "In happier times, M.F. Murphy smiling over brandy and cigars with director James Whale." Jimmy and Murphy looked very chummy. They were seated on Murphy's leather sofa, grinning from ear to ear, mirroring each other with a snifter of brandy in one hand and a large stogie in the other. The imagery had Whale's direction all over it. The article went on to read, "Funeral services will be held Sunday afternoon at 2 o'clock, November 27th at the Edwards Brothers Colonial Mansion, 1000 Venice Boulevard. After the services, the body will be taken to Angelus-Rosedale Cemetery for cremation at the Rosedale Crematory."

Looking up from the paper, Basil said, "So all this is a cover story?" Realization was slowly setting in. "It all makes perfect sense now. The one-week production delay after all the fuss about being behind schedule. The set closed off to the cast and crew." He studied Boris' face and said, "Perhaps you'd better start from the beginning."

"It all began soon after you left Jack's studio," Boris said. He told Rathbone everything that had happened, going into great detail: Jimmy Whale's visit to Jack Pierce's makeup studio, Whale's rumpled clothes, the bloodstains on his lapel, the monogrammed hanky, the phone call, the way Murphy was found, the meeting with Work and Mannix. Everything.

"I see," Rathbone said, after Boris went silent again. "So, someone appears to have gone to a great deal of trouble framing you for Murphy's death." His aquiline features became thoughtful. "Quite clever, really."

Now it was Boris' turn to be taken aback. "I beg your pardon?"

"Think of it, dear fellow. Whoever conceived of this murder plot has committed the perfect crime. By making one of Universal Studio's most valuable properties the prime suspect, he or she will almost certainly get away with it. The studio will see to that."

Boris fidgeted with his lemonade. The ice cubes tinkled against the crystal walls of the glass. "And there's not a thing I can do about it." He paused dramatically. Boris had been rehearsing what he was about to say over and over in his mind since that night in Cliff Work's office. After the deliberate pregnant pause, he added, "Unless—" and let the word hang there in the warm morning air.

Karloff gave Basil the sideways and suggestive glance of someone about to propose committing an act of mutiny.

Basil, consummate actor that he was, took his cue.

"You don't mean—" Rathbone said, letting his sentence hang there unfinished along with Boris' "unless."

"You were a member of British Intelligence in the Great War," Karloff said. "And you demonstrated a very keen deductive skill on the set the other day."

Rathbone's finely sculpted nostrils twitched with excitement. "Ah, so you think we should take the case on ourselves!" He mulled this over a moment. "Of course, you realize, it's one thing to play a detective and quite another thing to investigate a real murder, particularly one where clues have no doubt been destroyed."

"Eddie Mannix is very thorough, indeed. But I think between the two of us, we might just be able to pull it off."

Rathbone felt galvanized at the suggestion. But he hesitated. "The question remains, my dear Mr. Karloff, why?"

Boris knitted his brows. "Why what?"

"Why bother? After all, you're in the clear. The studio has seen to that. As far as the outside world is concerned, there never was a murder. Murphy died of natural causes. They're even cremating Murphy's body, making an autopsy impossible. Why not simply pretend the whole thing never happened?"

Boris studied Rathbone carefully. He realized that Basil wanted his assurance that Boris was fully committed to the endeavor.

"Basil," Karloff said at last, "I can't let a murderer escape unpunished. Whoever committed this crime thought they could use me for their own sinister purposes. To let Martin Murphy die like this, at the hands of such a cold-blooded assassin, goes against everything I believe in. I realize that one false step and I could find myself facing a murder charge, or worse—the killer might come after the both of us. But I'm willing to take that risk. There's just one problem."

"Dorothy's still laid up in hospital," Rathbone said, leaning forward. "Our investigation might place her and the baby in jeopardy. Yes, that does complicate things."

Boris took a sip of lemonade. After a moment, he said, "I could keep the baby out of harm's way by sending Sara Jane and her nurse on holiday at some resort. But Dorothy is another matter."

"We could wait until she's fully recovered. Only—"

"Only, the longer we wait, the less chance we have of catching the murderer."

"So what would you propose?"

"I've been giving the matter a great deal of thought," Boris said. "We might hire a bodyguard to stay with Dorothy while she's in hospital."

Rathbone nodded. "Yes, you could do that. But a bodyguard would raise questions. Dorothy's really in no condition to be unduly alarmed."

"We could avoid that if the bodyguard were disguised as a private nurse."

"That would do the trick. That is, if you know of any lady bodyguards."

"I wasn't thinking of a woman," Boris said. "I was thinking more about a man who's very good at not looking like a man, but can protect my wife, if things should come to that."

Basil was more than a bit skeptical. "Had you anyone in mind?"

Boris took another sip of lemonade and said, "I think I know just the man for the job. He is, shall we say, an acquaintance of Jimmy Whale's."

Rathbone smiled. "Looks good in a wig and a dress, does he?"

"Amazingly good, in fact," Boris smiled back. "Works as a bouncer at a Los Angeles gentlemen's club called Mae's where he also doubles as a female impersonator. His real name is Julian Walker, but he calls his lady persona Julie."

"What sort of fellow is this Julian/Julie?"

"He was twice decorated in the War for heroism. No one suspected he was a transvestite, although he once told me that he wore a bra and panties under his uniform."

"I see," Basil said, looking uneasy. "Good thing the man wasn't in my regiment."

"After the War he came to America with a traveling British vaudevillian troupe, touring first the Bijou and then the Orpheum circuits before settling in Los Angeles."

"How on earth did you come to meet him?"

"He was a guest of James' on the set of *Frankenstein*, and in full drag. No one suspected the fellow was, well, a fellow. I still remember John Boles chatting up this stunning looking young lady, trying to get her phone number. That is, until Jimmy asked the fellow to remove his wig."

Rathbone exploded with laughter. "That sounds like typical Jimmy Whale, all right!"

Boris smiled. "Poor John. He looked greener than the Monster did. He very nearly clobbered James right there and then."

Recovering his composure, Rathbone considered the variables of the problem and said, "You do realize, of course, that Whale may have committed the murder. His happening upon you at the makeup studio was a bit too coincidental. Those bloodstains on his suit and handkerchief might have belonged to Murphy. He may have deliberately set you up by putting you in the very studio cart used to transport the dead body. Any acquaintance of his might compromise Dorothy's safety, even unintentionally."

Karloff shook his head. "James doesn't have the physical strength to drag a body around. I believe things happened just as he said. James was passed out on Murphy's couch when the killer came upon Murphy and killed him. Later James woke up, found himself alone in a darkened office, which explains why he didn't see the blood on the rug, and then he unwittingly took Murphy's cart before the killer had a chance to wash out the bloodstains. As for the phone call, unless James is a ventriloquist I doubt he had anything to do with it. He was right there beside me while the killer phoned Jack."

"He may have had an accomplice make the call," Rathbone posited.

Karloff gave this some thought, but rejected it. "James has no motive. You were there. Murphy couldn't say enough good things about him."

"Maybe Whale resented being used as a pawn to bring Rowland back in line."

"No," Boris shook his head. "James didn't seem the least bit resentful. In fact, he told me his agent was getting him plenty of money for an upcoming picture, *The Man in the Iron Mask*."

"That could be the very motive right there," Rathbone said excitedly. "Perhaps Murphy insisted Whale either take on *Son of Frankenstein* or Murphy would cancel any of Whale's future projects. Whale was drunk. He might have struck out with some weapon of opportunity, a letter opener or a desk lamp. You have to admit, dear fellow, that the crime scene does rather take on the characteristics of James' morbid sense of humor."

"That still doesn't change the fact that James lacks the necessary strength to move the body."

Rathbone gave Boris a wry smile. "To quote a line from *Hound of the Baskervilles*, 'That's why so many murders go unsolved, Watson. People *will* stick to facts.'"

Boris didn't have a comeback for that. He just sat there silently.

"Still, you know Whale better than I," said Basil as he put down his lemonade and steepled his fingers. He arched one eyebrow in thought. "Just to be on the safe side, though, why don't we use this cover story when we hire this friend of James' as a bodyguard. Tell him that you've been getting some threatening fan letters and you're worried about Dorothy's safety. She doesn't know about the threats and you don't want her to worry, so he's to play his role around her at all times."

"Yes, I like it. I think that will work nicely."

"So it's settled, then?"

"Yes," Boris said. "Yes, it's settled. Well, as soon as we hire Mr. Walker. We'll stop by the club tonight and make him a proposition."

"I wish you wouldn't put it quite that way, Boris," Rathbone said, shifting uneasily in his chair. After a moment, he stroked his chin in thought. "All that remains now is for me to arrange for my own wife's protection. Ouida has been hinting that she'd like to visit her old haunts on Great Neck, Long Island before the adoption goes through. She'll surely jump at the chance for a nice cross-country train ride with some of her society friends."

"Then, my dear Mr. Rathbone," Karloff said, raising his glass of lemonade to propose a toast, "I think it's safe to say the game, to quote the Great Detective, is definitely afoot."

Rathbone jumped to his feet excitedly. "So it will be just the two of us against a sinister adversary!"

"Steady on there, Basil. We're looking for a murderer, not going on a fox hunt."

Basil began pacing, his blood on fire with anticipation. "Ah, but it is like a fox hunt, dear fellow! For although our murderer is clever, he or she has made one fatal mistake!"

"What mistake?"

"Because the front office has gone to such extraordinary lengths to keep the matter quiet, only those directly responsible will know the murder even took place! So, logically, amongst the immediate cast and crew, only you, me, and our killer should have any knowledge about the matter."

"Yes," said Boris, thoughtfully. "If a member of the cast or crew did it."

"Exactly! We must paint a picture of our potential killer, we must study his or her methods and track them down with only our wits to guide us!"

Boris rolled his eyes. All Basil needed at this moment was a deerstalker cap and a mackintosh.

"Well, Mr. Holmes," Boris said at last, "if I'm to be your Watson, I suppose I should ask you the obvious question. Just what sort of suspect are we looking for?"

Rathbone lit a cigarette and puffed thoughtfully as he continued to pace back and forth. "Let us begin with the obvious, for we must never overlook the obvious, Boris. I would think whoever did this is familiar with the inner workings of the studio system, and in particular, the seamier side of the publicity department. They had at least two or three weeks to formulate this scheme—"

"How do you figure that?" Boris asked.

"The note you described suggests a premeditated crime. You said the paper the suspect used felt odd. The edges were stiff, the paper smooth, and the topmost short edge felt as if it were a page torn out of a book. It *was* torn out of a book, my dear fellow. An autograph book with gilded edges!"

Karloff slapped his knee, chiding himself for not thinking of that. "Of course!"

Rathbone smiled. "Don't trouble yourself, Watson. Now, to continue. The *Son of Frankenstein* set has become the most visited set on the Universal lot. And when you have visitors—"

"You give out autographs! That explains my signature. What else do we know about this person?"

"They're familiar with the laboratory set. They knew how to activate the Strickfaden equipment. They must also be intimate with Martin Murphy's habits. Otherwise, how would they have delivered the letter to him?"

"We also know something else," Boris said.

"Yes?"

"Whoever did this can imitate Rowland's voice. Jack thought Rowland was calling me back to the set."

Rathbone stopped his pacing and stood motionless for a moment, puffing on his cigarette. "Yes, that's one possible theory. There is another, though."

"What might that be?" asked Boris.

"That our prime suspect, in fact, *is* Rowland V. Lee."

The ringing of a telephone came from inside the house, giving Boris a start. He got up and said, "I guess that will serve as our dramatic musical punctuation."

Rathbone chuckled. Then an alarming thought occurred to him. "I hope it isn't about Dorothy."

"Good heavens, you're right," Boris said, hurrying inside.

While Boris answered the phone, Rathbone sat back in his chair and sipped his lemonade, working out the details of his theory about Lee's guilt. Rathbone's meditations were interrupted with a shout from Boris. "Basil, come here, quickly!"

Rathbone jumped up like a shot and hurried into the house. "Is it about Dorothy?" he asked, concerned.

**"When the murderer confesses before you've even gotten your feet wet, where's the challenge of being a detective?"**

"No," Boris whispered, covering the mouthpiece while listening intently to whoever was on the line. He gestured for Rathbone to join him as Boris removed his hand from the mouthpiece. "Yes, Bela. Yes, I'm listening. Uh, Bela, I have a bit of a bad connection, could you repeat what you just said?"

Boris tipped the receiver so Rathbone could eavesdrop.

On the other end of the line the unmistakable voice of Bela Lugosi trembled with anxiety. "I say again, I did it! I killed him! I killed Murphy! You must come at once! I cannot live with his blood on my hands!"

Rathbone gave Boris a look of astonishment. "Do you think he means it?" Basil whispered.

Covering up the mouthpiece again, Boris replied, "Believe me, Basil, if Bela wants me to set foot in his house, it's deadly serious." He uncovered the mouthpiece and said, "Uh, I say, Bela, Basil is here. He'll keep you company while I change. You just keep talking."

Boris handed Rathbone the phone and hurried upstairs. Rathbone put his ear to the receiver in time to hear Bela complain, "No, Boris! Rathbone will only tell me more of his boring war stories! Don't give the phone to him!"

Rathbone suppressed the urge to chuckle. "Don't worry, old fellow," he said to Bela. "I'll restrain myself. Now, exactly how did you murder Martin Murphy?"

"I cannot discuss this on the phone! I can only unburden myself to someone face to face! Boris must come over to my home and hear my confession! I have to tell someone of my sin or I shall go mad!"

"Would you mind if I came along?" Rathbone asked.

There was a long silence on the other end of the line. Basil could imagine Bela weighing the pros and cons of the request. Finally Bela agreed, albeit reluctantly, "Yes, it is right that you also hear about my horrible crime, too, since both of you have witnessed it."

This last line perplexed Rathbone. "What do you mean by that remark?" he asked.

Boris came downstairs wearing slacks, a white shirt, and a jacket. Having hastily finished buttoning his shirt, Boris grabbed the receiver before Rathbone could hear Bela's reply.

"We'll be right over," Boris said and hung up. He looked at Rathbone and asked, "Well, what do you make of that?"

"I don't know, old chap," Basil said, looking a trifle irritated. "You hung up before I had a chance to find out."

"We'll find out when we get there," said Boris.

"Yes, I suppose you're right," Rathbone sighed, taking on a hang dog expression.

"Why the long face? Sad for Bela?"

"Well, yes, of course, partly," Basil ventured. "Only—."

"Only what?"

Rathbone shrugged, looking very downcast. "When the murderer confesses before you've even gotten your feet wet, where's the challenge of being a detective?"

Boris rolled his eyes for the second time that morning.

"Come on, we'll take my car," Karloff said.

**Who Framed Boris Karloff?**

## Chapter Eight

### 27 November 1938, 10:44 a.m.

1938 had been a particularly rough year for Bela Lugosi. Before winning the role of Ygor, the ex-bogeyman had suffered through a long period of unemployment. The birth of his son Bela, Jr. on January 5 was both a joyous event and one of bitter humiliation. Bela was too poor to pay the hospital bill. The Motion Picture Relief Fund stepped in to take care of the expenses. That was bad enough for a proud man like Bela Lugosi. But things became unbearable when Louella Parsons, whose husband was a doctor on the relief board, made this fact public in an article titled, "Bela Lugosi Jobless."

As a further result of the horror film drought, the actor forever associated with Count Dracula soon found himself without a castle to haunt. The finance company foreclosed on Bela's bomb-proof, earthquake-proof colonial mansion stronghold at 2227 Outpost Drive in the Hollywood Hills. Bela was forced to move his young wife Lillian, his new son, and the dogs to a rented house at 3714 Lankershim Drive off Cahuenga Boulevard in the San Fernando Valley—not even a half-mile away from Universal City, a detail hardly lost on Basil Rathbone. He made mention of it as Boris Karloff parked his dark blue Buick convertible in Bela's driveway.

"He's all but a stone's throw away from the scene of the crime," Rathbone said, lacking only a Meerschaum pipe and a Persian slipper. "Bela cut short his session with Jack Pierce, no doubt giving himself time to kill Murphy, frame you, and hurry home so he can use his wife to establish an airtight alibi. Poor Lillian, she marries a man old enough to be her father, and now to be used in this way. Tragic, quite tragic."

"Yes," said Boris as he drummed his fingers on the steering wheel. He gave Rathbone a cautionary glance. "Listen, Basil, I'm sure you're aware that you seem to irritate Bela for some reason."

"Bela doesn't look very kindly on you either, old boy."

"Perhaps, but he did ask me to be here. If we're to get a lucid confession from him, well, why don't you just let me do all the talking, eh?"

Rathbone shot Boris an imperious look. "Well," he said, obviously insulted, "why should I go in at all? I could just wait out here and sun myself."

"Now, don't be like that. You know what I mean. Just don't start acting like—," Boris searched for the right words, "well, like Holmes about to apprehend the culprit. Bela deserves his dignity."

"Need I remind you that if he did commit the crime, he is the very cold-blooded assassin that tried to frame you."

"Yes, I know," Boris sighed. "Although I deplore what Bela did, it still doesn't keep me from seeing why he might have done it. His cut-rate salary, Murphy's insulting remarks, his bitterness about refusing *Frankenstein*: I can see why Bela might have used me the way that he did, turning the role of the Monster against me as poetic revenge, you might say."

Rathbone leaned his elbow on the ledge of the passenger door and propped his cheek against his fist. "Yes, I suppose I do see your point."

"What I'm trying to say, Basil, is, well, just let Bela do all the talking. He says he wants to confess, so by all means, let him."

"Very well," said Rathbone, taking on a cavalier attitude. "I promise I won't say a word to antagonize him."

"Oh, and Basil—about Lillian—."

"What about Lillian?" Rathbone asked, nonchalantly.

"I know she hurt your feelings with that remark she made—."

"Oh, that," Rathbone said with a dismissive wave. "I've forgotten all about it."

"I remember how you reacted when you saw it in print."

Rathbone shrugged. "All in the past, I assure you."

"She called you a cold fish."

Basil's eyes flashed with wounded pride. "She called US a couple of cold fish!" He quoted the article word for word, with bitter, biting sarcasm, "'Basil Rathbone, verrrry Brrrritish. He's a cold fish, and Karloff is a cold fish. Bela, who is actually very warm, can't tolerate either of them!' Indeed!" He folded his arms petulantly, brooding for a moment, before abruptly changing his manner to nonchalant. "The matter is all water under the bridge."

"I hope so," Boris said. He was about to get out of the car when he turned to Rathbone. "You know, there's just one thing that bothers me about this whole situation."

"Just one thing? And what might that one thing be?"

"How could Bela imitate Rowland V. Lee well enough to fool Jack Pierce?"

Rathbone had to think about that one. "Yes," he said, bemused, "Mr. Lugosi doesn't easily pass for an Ohio native," referring to Rowland's home state.

With that discrepancy firmly in mind, Boris and Basil approached the front door and Karloff rang the bell. Inside the house, barking dogs answered the buzzing doorbell. Moments later, the door was opened by a tall, dark-haired beauty holding four excited wolfhounds at bay. Whatever Lillian Lugosi's past sentiments about her husband's co-stars may have been, she now showed only gratitude. "Thank God you're here," she said. "Bela shut himself away in his study and won't tell me why! He hasn't eaten. He hasn't slept. Please, you've got to do something or his health will be ruined!"

Over the barking, Boris said reassuringly, "Not to worry, my dear. I'm sure we can get this whole thing sorted out."

"Yes," Basil said, "we 'verrrry Brrrritish' people are rather good at this sort of thing."

"Basil," Boris cautioned.

"Thank you," Lillian said. She turned to the wolfhounds and commanded, "Quiet! Now go in the kitchen!"

The dogs obeyed, scampering quickly out of sight.

Rathbone whispered to Boris, "I see she picked up Dracula's affinity for wolves."

Lillian escorted them into the living room where a huge portrait of Bela in full Dracula regalia dominated the scene. The painting looked terribly out of place in the small middle-class home and would have been better suited gracing the mantle on one of Jack Otterson's massive gothic sets. On the opposite wall was another portrait of Bela, life size, with Bela dressed in a Prince Albert suit. There was certainly no denying whose house this was.

Toddling around in his walker was Bela, Jr., occasionally bumping into the coffee table or the sofa. The baby stopped his explorations and looked up at Karloff. Bela, Jr. gurgled and smiled, which was certainly a more positive reaction than his near hysterics was when he posed for a publicity picture with Boris while in full Monster makeup.

Lillian led Boris and Rathbone down the hall to the door of the guest bedroom Bela had turned into a private study. She knocked on the door and said in an imploring tone, "Bela, darling, Boris and Basil are here to see you. Please, Bela, my love, open the door."

After a few moments, Lugosi unlocked the door and opened it a crack. Like the tragic, tortured soul from a story by Edgar Allen Poe, Bela peaked through the crack with one bloodshot eye. Only upon visual confirmation that Boris and Basil were present did he open the door all the way and bid them admittance.

"Gentlemen," he said, looking very haggard and unkempt, "please come in."

Lillian paused at the door and ran her fingers through Bela's mussed up hair. "Can I get you anything to eat, Bela, dear?"

"No, thank you, my darling, nothing," he said.

She turned to Boris and Basil, "What about for you? Can I offer you anything to eat?"

"Nothing for me," said Boris politely.

"As for me," Basil said with a smile, hands in his pockets, his feet planted in a dramatic stance, "I think I fancy a plate of cold fish."

Lillian, obviously missing the meaning of the remark, merely looked confused. "So you'd like some tuna salad, perhaps?"

Boris sighed and gave Basil another cautionary stare as he said, "Thank you, no, my dear, we're fine."

Bela asked Lillian to leave them alone so they could talk. He closed the door after her and gestured for his guests to sit on the divan. The study smelled of stale cigars and had books piled up everywhere, some still in cardboard boxes. Over the divan was the infamous nude portrait of Clara Bow, the "It" girl with whom Bela had shared a tempestuous affair during his early Broadway appearances as the vampire Count. It was quite obvious from the oil painting that the "It" girl certainly wasn't shy about showing "it." Against another wall stood a four-drawer filing cabinet filled with photos covering most of Bela's long career. An ashtray on the cabinet was filled with cigar butts.

Bela pulled up a chair and buried his face in his hands, overcome by great sorrow. "Thank you for coming," he said, looking up finally, wringing his hands. "I'm not sure how much longer I can live with this terrible guilt."

"Yes," said Boris, putting a comforting hand on Bela's shoulder. "Perhaps it's time you let it all out. Unburden yourself, and, afterward, if you like, Basil and I can escort you to the police station where you can make a signed confession."

"Police," Bela said. "Bah! What can the police do? This is bigger than the police."

"Well," Basil interjected, "they are better equipped to handle homicide cases than we, old boy."

Lugosi gave Rathbone a venomous look. Boris leaned over to Basil and whispered from the corner of his mouth, "Basil, what did we talk about in the car?"

"So sorry, old man, I forgot myself."

"Go on, Bela," Boris said invitingly.

"But where to begin?" Bela said, looking into Karloff's eyes, grasping Boris' comforting hand. "I knew I had killed Murphy when I came back on the lot Thursday morning for 6 a.m. call. I went to Jack Pierce to be made up for the day's work, and that is when I was told that Murphy was dead and there would be no filming until Monday. I was told he died of a heart attack in his office. And then I knew, I knew that I had killed him."

Boris and Basil exchanged confused looks. "Come again?" asked Boris.

"Wednesday night," Bela continued, "I wanted to have it out with Murphy, but his office was dark and his studio cart was in his parking space. The other offices next to Murphy's office, they were dark, too. So everybody must have gone home, I thought. But no, I realize now that Murphy was dead on the floor. So, the next day when I hear Murphy is dead, I don't believe that Murphy is dead, so I go to his office in the morning to see. That is when I saw the moving men taking Murphy's furniture away. They were loading everything onto a truck. I knew then for sure that I had killed him."

Basil crossed his arms and asked in as patient a tone as he could manage under the circumstances, "I'm sorry, old chap, I'm a trifle confused. Just exactly how did you kill Mr. Murphy and when?"

Bela looked intently at both his guests and said, "You know how and when, you were there when I did it!"

"When you did what?" Boris asked.

"When I put the evil eye on Murphy," Bela said, in all seriousness.

"When you did what?" asked Rathbone.

Bela's eyes flashed with anger. "The evil eye! You saw! I spat at the floor and cursed Murphy!" His eyes became sullen and remorseful. "It is a thing that runs in my family. My grandmother, she had Gypsy blood, and taught me well, but she warned me not to use it, that it is a blessing and a curse. And she was right. Now I am condemned to wander in purgatory for all eternity for using the dark forces to kill my enemy."

Boris rubbed the bridge of his nose and tried to fathom what he just heard. "You mean to say THAT is the confession you wanted to make? That you killed Murphy with a Gypsy curse?"

"These things," Bela insisted, "are very strong. You are not Hungarian, so you cannot understand."

Boris and Basil exchanged looks and suddenly burst out laughing.

Bela eyed them narrowly, hurt at first, and then just insulted. "You would laugh at a condemned man? A man who pours out his heart and soul in confession of his sin?"

Boris tried his best to regain his composure. He put his hand on Bela's knee and said, "We're sorry, Bela, really. It's just we're relieved that you're not a murderer."

"Yes," said Rathbone, still chuckling. "You see, Murphy was murdered, but not by a Gypsy curse. Someone tried to frame Boris for the crime and we're trying to solve it ourselves."

"You mean to say," said Bela, "that another man killed Murphy?"

"Yes," said Boris, now fully recovered. "He was murdered late Wednesday night."

"Electrocuted," added Rathbone. "Or killed by the proverbial blunt instrument. The cause of death is still yet to be determined."

"I found Murphy's body on the laboratory set," Boris explained, "and now the studio is trying to hush it up. The heart attack is part of the cover-up."

Bela shot up to his full six-foot height and began raging. "So, some murderer would dare to make a fool of Bela!" He shook his fist furiously at the air. "Make me think I had cast a Gypsy curse when all this time it was just a man! I will make him pay when I find him!"

"When *you* find him?" exclaimed Rathbone.

Bela looked at Rathbone with annoyance. "Very well, when *we* find him! All the time you want top billing!"

Boris tried to reason with the Hungarian. "Bela, you can't join our investigation. Think of your wife and child. Basil and I are taking steps to protect our families, but if you come along, Lillian and Bela, Jr. will be placed in deadly danger."

"BAH!" Lugosi scoffed. "A Lugosi fears nothing! We have guns in every room in the house! Our dogs guard our bedroom doors! I fear no danger! Lillian fears no danger, too! Burglars, we fear, yes. That is why the dogs and the guns. But danger, NO!"

He shot a look at Rathbone. "You have war stories, Rathbone. Like I say before, Bela has war stories, too. Do you think Bela had to fight in the war? NO! In Hungary, actors didn't have to fight. But Bela fought! I was in the ski patrol!" Bela strode to the filing cabinet, pulled open a drawer and produced a purple velvet case. "I was wounded and awarded the Hungarian equivalent of the Purple Heart!" He opened the case and proudly displayed the medal. "A Lugosi fears no danger!"

Rathbone was genuinely impressed. "I had no idea."

Bela snapped the case shut and put it back in the filing cabinet. He gave his guests a challenging look and said, "So I will join you on your investigation! It will be the three of us against this coward who dares to make a fool out of Bela." After a pause, he added as an afterthought, "and who framed Karloff."

Boris turned to Rathbone. "What do you think, Basil?"

Rathbone considered the matter a moment and said, "A Sherlock Holmes with *two* Watsons. Whatever would Mr. Conan Doyle say?"

Bela said, "He would say, the game, it is afoot!" He held out his hand, much the way Rathbone had done on the set Wednesday night. "So, what do you say, gentlemen? All for one?"

Rathbone smiled and put his hand on Bela's. "Yes, indeed. All for one."

Karloff put his hand on Rathbone's making a triple pact. "And one for all."

Bela smiled and said, "I have Lillian make us sandwiches and coffee!"

## Chapter Nine

## Too Many Watsons

The sleuths gathered in Lugosi's living room for what Basil Rathbone called a "skull session."

"'Skull session!' Bela said to Karloff, "A perfect name for a meeting with ghouls like us, eh, Boris?"

After Lillian put Bela, Jr. down for his nap she brought out a serving tray with a plate of tuna salad sandwiches and coffee and asked if she might sit in.

"Of course, my dear," said Lugosi with a grand gesture. "You can be a Watson, too!"

"*Three* Watsons?" Basil sighed, looking rather despairingly at the food offering.

Karloff smiled and shrugged while Lugosi gestured at the sandwiches. "Eat, gentlemen. Lillian tells me you specifically asked for tuna salad."

Boris whispered, "Really, Basil, it's your own fault."

Rathbone ignored Boris' remark, poured himself a cup of coffee and took his place before a blackboard that had been rolled out from Bela, Jr.'s room. Because it was a child's blackboard, it was only three-feet high with painted toy blocks bordering the edges. Not exactly what Sherlock Holmes might have found to be the most dignified of writing slates.

"This part of the skull session," Basil explained, "is called, 'What do we know?' By listing all the pertinent facts, we can study each in turn and formulate a hypothesis. So, what do we know so far?"

"Murphy is dead," offered Bela.

Rathbone cast the Hungarian a bilious look.

"Well, he is, isn't he?"

Basil sighed. "Very well, I suppose we can start with the painfully obvious."

Karloff smiled. "Never overlook the obvious, Basil."

Rathbone eyed Boris narrowly, then bent down to the blackboard and wrote, "Victim: M. F. Murphy, Production Manager—Dead," then straightened up and asked everyone, "What *else* do we know?"

Before anyone else could answer, Bela said, "Someone has killed Murphy, but we don't know who."

Basil chewed his lower lip and arched an eyebrow. Bending down to the level of the blackboard again, he wrote, "Victim was murdered—by whom?" Turning back to the group, Rathbone looked imploringly at Karloff. "Boris, anything to add?"

"We know whoever did it knows the studio system, is familiar with the operation of Kenneth Strickfaden's machines, and whoever the murderer is, called Jack Pierce at his makeup studio pretending to be our director."

"Or it really was our director," said Basil as he got on bended knee this time and wrote the heading, "Suspects" and then Rowland V. Lee's name. "Our director certainly has a very strong motive for killing Murphy. He knows the studio system and how the equipment works." Next on Basil's list was James Whale. "James Whale is also a likely suspect. Like Lee, Whale knows the studio system and because he directed the two previous *Frankenstein* films—."

"—He would know how to operate Strickfaden's machines," Karloff said grimly. "I still can't believe it." He looked up at Rathbone, his dark eyes flashing. "Basil, if you only saw how winded James was when he and Jack helped me back into my costume. James had to support himself by leaning on the makeup table."

"The makeup table?" Rathbone asked, arching an eyebrow. "If he used the makeup table for support, Whale must have put his cane down somewhere first."

"He didn't have his cane," Boris said casually, then realized the significance of that fact.

"Exactly," Rathbone said, pointedly. "The cane is the perfect blunt instrument of opportunity."

Bela looked from Boris to Rathbone. "Wait," he said with a smirk, "are you suggesting that our clever assassin is a sissy boy?"

"The facts would seem to bear that out," Rathbone said.

Boris leaned back, looking particularly grim as he recalled, "Come to think of it, I do remember James occasionally exhibiting a rather—sadistic pettiness." A look of sadness crossed his face. "I've never told anyone this story, but—it happened on the set of *Frankenstein*. I suppose James was jealous of all the attention the Monster was getting. Well, for whatever reason, while we were shooting the scene where the Monster carries Frankenstein up the hill to the windmill, James insisted that I actually carry Colin Clive over my shoulder and up the mountain set. It was a long shot so we could have used a dummy, but James insisted I really carry Colin. We shot take after take, over and over again. I've had chronic back problems ever since."

"So," said Rathbone, "'sissy boy' or not, Whale might indeed be our murderer." He wrote the next name on the list of suspects.

"Jack Pierce!" Boris exclaimed. "Why Jack?"

"Murphy felt Pierce was 10 years out of date, remember? What if he and Pierce had a falling out? What if he told Pierce that one of his assistants would be replacing him as the new Chief Makeup Artist? You know Jack's temperament."

"The life mask!" Boris said with realization.

"What?"

"Jack rogue's gallery was missing a life mask. He said the nose had been chipped and he was going to cast a new one. What if—."

"What if it had been broken during a brawl with Murphy? Good," smiled Basil, adding "missing mask" to his list of facts on the blackboard. "We also know from testimony provided by Cliff Work and Eddie Mannix that Murphy was murdered in his office." Drawing a rough blueprint on the blackboard, he said, "Now, if memory serves me correctly, Murphy's office is part of a block of offices. He shares the first floor with his assistants and secretarial staff. An outside staircase leads to the second floor terrace. There we have temporary office space as well as space for staff writers. Murphy's office is, if you'll pardon the expression, dead center. There are three means of egress; a front door leading to the street, the window to the right of the front door, and an inner door connecting his office to a hallway. This gives him access to all the other offices on his floor as well as the back stairs leading to the second floor."

Bela looked skeptical. "But you said Murphy was killed by Pierce in the makeup studio, not at his office."

"True," Rathbone said. "But there may have been two confrontations. One in Pierce's studio and the last one in Murphy's office where the fatal blow was dealt. Of course, the missing mask could mean nothing. In real life, unfortunately, not everything is a clue connected with the murder. But for the moment, we'll look at the missing life mask as circumstantial evidence. Now, you testified that on the night of the murder, all the offices were dark, including Murphy's office."

"Yes," said Bela.

"What time was this?"

"I went right to Murphy's office after I left the set. So sometime around 10 o'clock."

"And," said Boris, "according to you, Murphy's studio cart was parked out front."

"Yes, it was," Bela insisted.

"Basil, if blood was found in the back of the cart, that would suggest the studio cart was used to take Murphy's body to Stage 7. But the cart was still in front of Murphy's office at around 10 o'clock. I found the body at 11:15, which begs the question, when was Murphy killed?"

Lillian asked, "When was the last time you saw Mr. Murphy alive?"

"Around 2:30 or thereabouts," said Rathbone. "He left Stage 7 with James Whale and the studio publicity photographer."

"So he might have been killed anytime between 2:30 and 10 or 11 o'clock, right?"

"So it would seem," said Basil.

"You're just assuming the body was taken to the soundstage after 10 o'clock. Maybe Mr. Murphy's body was hidden there earlier and placed on the operating table just before the killer called Jack Pierce."

"Ah, excellent," Rathbone exclaimed. "The killer could have hidden Murphy's body on the set while the cast and crew were eating in the commissary during either the lunch or dinner break."

Boris nodded in agreement and said, "The laboratory set has all sorts of nooks and crannies where a body might be hidden. For instance, under the cushion at the bottom of the sulfur pit."

"Or the well built into the floor that's supposed to lead down into the family crypt. It's covered over by a huge cement lid. Remember, Boris? The scene where the Monster is strapped to a plank and hauled up with a block and tackle?"

"How could I forget," Boris smiled, remembering how the whole crew, even the stagehands, helped get him ready for the shot.

"A perfect hiding place for a corpse." Basil smiled at Lillian and gave her a gracious bow. "Thank you, Madame. That was a capital notion."

Lillian smiled excitedly like a party guest winning a parlor game.

"The photo of Murphy and Whale that appeared in the newspaper might give us the clue we need to at least estimate a time of death." Rathbone stood up and rubbed his knee as he looked around the living room. "Bela, do you have the Thursday paper about?"

"We threw it away with the chicken bones," Bela said.

Lugosi got up and went to the kitchen where he dug the paper out of the trash. It was stained with chicken grease but Murphy's photo and the obituary were legible enough. Rathbone took the paper and searched his pockets, then realized he wasn't making a Sherlock Holmes movie and wouldn't regularly carry a magnifying glass. "You wouldn't happen to have a magnifying glass about, would you, Bela?"

"In my study."

Bela came back with an ornate brass magnifying glass. Taking the instrument, Rathbone held the paper up to the light and squinted at the photo of Murphy and Whale.

"Whale is wearing a wristwatch, but the newspaper photo is too small to make out the time." Basil folded up the paper and set it down on the coffee table with the magnifying glass.

Bela grabbed the paper and his magnifying glass and shouted at Rathbone. "That paper has been in the garbage! Don't put that on my nice coffee table!" He gave Rathbone a searing scowl as he sat back down, then turned his attention to the newspaper photo, studying it with the magnifying glass.

Boris said, "It wouldn't hurt to ask James about the time. Or maybe we can get hold of the original negative and have the picture blown up."

"No need for that, Boris," Bela said as he held up the newspaper. "I know when the picture was taken. It was taken in the late afternoon, just before sunset."

"You seem awfully sure of yourself, Bela," said a skeptical Basil Rathbone.

"And for good reason, Mr. Detective," Bela said sarcastically, pointing at the photograph. "You can see the light from the window in their brandy glasses."

Rathbone was taken aback. He grabbed back the paper and the magnifying glass and examined the photo again. "By George, he's right. What a fool I am!"

"For once, I agree with you," Bela smirked, taking a cigar from the humidor on the coffee table and leaning back and crossing one leg over the other with a superior air. "And because the window faces west, we know it is a setting sun, so it has to be he is alive in the late afternoon."

"He's right again!" Rathbone smiled, impressed with Lugosi's powers of observation.

Bela said to Lillian, "Maybe it should be me who plays Sherlock Holmes in the next movie."

Rathbone turned to the blackboard, sighed, then bent down and made notes as he spoke. "All right. Now we know Murphy was still alive in the late afternoon, which would put the time of death anywhere between say, roughly 4:30 to anytime before the body was discovered on the set. So let's say 4:30 to 10:30 p.m. So the body was hidden during the dinner break. Bela, you said that you saw a moving van taking Murphy's furniture away on Thursday morning."

"Yes, I did."

"Did you see any markings on the truck?"

"There were no markings. It was just a truck like any truck you see on the lot."

Rathbone considered this. "That rules out Salvation Army. So we can surmise that the furniture was taken away by a Universal Studios truck."

Boris said, "Or by a truck disguised as a Universal Studios truck."

"Very good," Rathbone nodded and wrote, "Moving Truck—from studio?" on the blackboard.

"But why take all the furniture?" Bela asked as he struck a match and lit his cigar.

Boris reached in his pocket for a packet of cigarettes. He looked to Lillian and asked, "Do you mind?"

"No, please," she said.

Rathbone considered Bela's question. "I believe Mr. Mannix was after the bloodstained carpet. Taking away all the furniture would seem to the casual observer merely the natural outcome of Murphy's death." Rathbone straighted up and studied the blackboard, rubbing his lower back as he pondered aloud, "But where did they take the furniture?" He wrote the question on the blackboard.

"Is it really that important that we know where the furniture is?" asked Boris.

"With so little physical evidence to go on, a bloodstained-carpet fiber would be nice."

"Speaking of blood, why didn't the killer wash the blood off the backseat of Murphy's studio cart? The murderer would have had plenty of time."

"Remember, old man," Basil said, "the killer's objective was to incriminate you."

Bela hissed scornfully.

Rathbone gave Lugosi a hard stare. "All right, Bela, you have something to say?"

"That blood in the back of the studio cart makes no sense! The killer tries to frame Boris with a note and his fingerprints on the lever. That I can understand. But then this man, this genius, he leaves evidence that Murphy was killed elsewhere and in some other way and that the body was moved? What are we supposed to think? That Boris is framing himself? What killer would be that stupid?"

"It was exactly those mistakes that convinced Cliff Work of Boris' innocence, and why Work brought in Eddie Mannix to cover things up. The perfect crime beautifully orchestrated."

"So," said Bela, "we have three of these suspects, Whale, Rowland, and Pierce. That's one suspect for each of us."

"For each of us?" Rathbone exclaimed.

"Of course, for each of us," Lugosi insisted. "We each take a suspect and interrogate them, we cover more ground that way."

"It does make sense, Basil," said Karloff.

"All right," said Rathbone. "We'll draw names from a hat."

"I'll get my hat!" Bela hurried into his bedroom and came back with his favorite Homburg. Rathbone wrote out the suspect's names on three slips of paper, folded them, and placed them in the hat. Lillian held the hat up and Bela reached in first.

"Wait," said Rathbone, "why should you get first pick?"

Bela scowled at Rathbone. "It is my house and it is my hat!"

Rathbone relented and Bela pulled out the first slip of paper and opened it. He scowled and crumpled the paper up. "Bah! I have drawn Jack Pierce."

"Oh, lovely," Basil said, reaching in the hat. "You and Pierce react like fire and petrol."

"Well, who do you have, Mr. Big Shot?"

As Boris took the last name from the hat, Rathbone opened his slip of paper and read it. "Looks like I'll be interviewing James Whale."

Boris tossed his slip back into the hat, not bothering to read it. "I guess that leaves me with Rowland V. Lee."

"Good," said Bela, "now all we need to do is each of us meet with our suspects. We go today."

"No, no, no," Basil said. "That wouldn't be wise."

"Why not today?" asked Bela, imperiously. "Today is as good a day as any. It is Sunday and we take the killer by surprise, maybe!"

Boris said, "We haven't arranged for our spouses' safety yet."

Bela eyed Karloff narrowly, then relented. "Yes, I see your point."

"Besides," said Rathbone, "I believe our first responsibility is to attend Murphy's funeral this afternoon. We might pick up a clue if we keep our eyes open. The culprit may want to gloat over Murphy's coffin."

With a sweeping gesture, Bela said, "Then we all go. Four pairs of eyes are better. One of us might see something the others miss."

Rathbone nodded. "Then it's settled. We'll arrive separately to avoid suspicion. Later, we'll all meet at the gentlemen's club where Julian Walker works. While we wait, we can compare notes about what we observed at the funeral."

Bela looked to Karloff. "Who is this Julian Walker? Why are we meeting him?"

"That's a rather long story," Boris said. "But he will be instrumental in keeping Dorothy safe."

"I see," said Bela as he took a puff of his cigar. "What is the name of the club, Boris? And where is it?"

"It's a private club in the Hollywood Hills," said Karloff. "A place called Mae's. Ever hear of it?"

"Mae's?" Lugosi exclaimed. "Have I ever heard of it!" He roared with laughter and slapped his knee. He nudged Lillian and said, "You will have to stay with Bela, Jr. while we men go. Rathbone can pick me up and take me there."

Basil gave Lugosi an aloof stare. "And what time should I pick you up, m'lord?"

Lugosi's demeanor instantly switched from a laughing rogue to an imperious Hungarian nobleman. "7:30," Lugosi commanded, then turned to Karloff, chuckling again. "Boris, have you ever been to Mae's?"

"No. Have you?"

Lugosi laughed even louder.

Rathbone glared at the Hungarian impatiently. "All right, what's so funny?"

"You will see," Bela said with a mischievous leer. "Tonight you will both see what it is I find so funny. But I tell you this, Mr. Detective, bring lots of money!"

Lugosi began to laugh again. The raucous laughter woke up Bela, Jr.

## Chapter Ten

## 27 November 1938, 1:22 p.m.

**Hollywood Presbyterian Hospital, 1300 Vermont Avenue**

Boris paid a visit to Hollywood Presbyterian Hospital after changing into appropriate funerary attire and before going to the mortuary. The five-story medical facility was built in the palatial style of a Spanish grandee's hacienda with rounded archways, alcoves, a balcony, pink adobe walls, and red clay roof tiles. Boris parked his convertible in the lot across the street. Up in Dorothy's private room on third floor maternity, Sara Jane was wrapped up in hospital blankets like a papoose and resting in her mother's arms. Dorothy would have appeared pale and tired had she not applied some makeup. According to the chart hanging from the foot of her hospital bed, Dorothy was still running a fever. She looked up at Boris and asked, "Goodness, why are you dressed in black?"

Boris took Sara Jane in his arms and indicated his clothes with a nod; "Basil, Bela, and I are going to Martin Murphy's funeral." Looking down at Sara Jane, he said, in a voice all adults seem to use when talking to babies, "Yes we are. We're all going together."

Dorothy smiled wanly. "It's certainly an improvement over what the papers said you wore on your first visit."

Boris gave Dorothy a wry grin. "Oh? Didn't fancy the Monster, eh?"

She studied his face. "Is something wrong, Boris? You seem, I don't know—tense."

Boris wanted to tell her everything, but knew now wasn't the time. He was about to make an excuse when a deliveryman in a green jumpsuit with

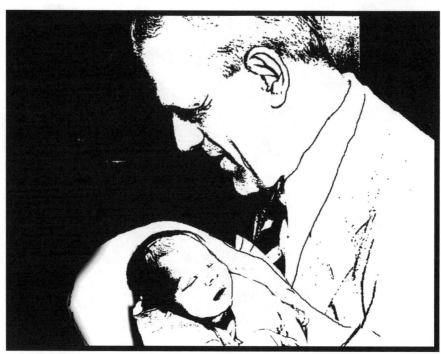

**"I think she has my eyes."**

"Brewster Florists" printed on the pocket knocked on Dorothy's open door. "Mrs. Nolan?" he asked, indicating the floral arrangement he was carrying.

"Next door," said Dorothy.

"Sorry," said the deliveryman. He was about to leave, then stopped short, having caught a glimpse of Boris. With eyes bright with recognition, he asked, "SAY, aren't you—?"

Boris stood there rocking Sara Jane and said, rolling his eyes, "Yes, I'm Boris Karloff."

The deliveryman put the flowers down on Dorothy's serving table and pulled a notebook and pen from his back pocket, holding them out expectantly. "Say, can I have—?"

Boris was about to hand the baby to Dorothy so he could scribble his signature, then thought better of it. He indicated Sara Jane and whispered, "Maybe later."

"Oh!" the deliveryman said. He put the pad and pen back in his pocket and picked up the arrangement, winked and flashed Boris the OK signal and shouted, "Gotcha!"

"Shhhh," Boris whispered, rocking Sara Jane to sleep.

"Oh, sorry," the deliveryman whispered back and tiptoed out of the room.

"Poor Mrs. Nolan," Dorothy sighed.

Dwight Kemper

"Who's Mrs. Nolan?"

"A lovely lady diagnosed with—cancer," she said, whispering the last word. "They can't do anything for her. She's been hanging on until her baby could be born. Now that he has, well—They expect her to die any day now." Dorothy gave her husband a searching look. "But let's not change the subject. What's bothering you? I've never known you to refuse a fan an autograph."

"I'm just worried about you, dear," Boris said, feeling it was only a partial lie, since he really was concerned. "How are you feeling?"

Dorothy smiled and shrugged, "Well enough, I suppose. I will be glad to be out of here, though." She indicated flowers displayed on the windowsill. "Speaking of flowers, Basil and Ouida Rathbone sent those. Aren't they lovely? I had to fight with the nurses to keep them there. Some old wives tale about flowers taking oxygen out of the room."

"Obviously the nursing staff doesn't do much gardening," Boris said, gently rocking Sara Jane. "I think she has my eyes."

"And your coloring," Dorothy smiled.

Boris smiled back. "I say, Dorothy, I've been thinking—."

"I *knew* there was something wrong. Thinking about what?"

Boris tried to be reassuring. "Oh, there's nothing wrong. It's just, I think you need a private nurse to look after you."

"Why?"

Boris tried to look nonchalant. "I don't know, just to see you've got everything you need."

"Boris, I have nurses here at the hospital that do that." She held up the cord that buzzed the nurse's station. "See? I just push this and instant room service."

"They can't watch you all the time, though."

Dorothy gave Boris a suspicious look. "Why would they need to do that? I just have a little infection."

"Well," said Boris as he looked out the window to avoid Dorothy's suspicious gaze, "I'd feel better if you were looked after properly. Nice view, by the way."

"What's nice about the Emergency Room driveway?"

"Uh, the palm tree. Anyway, I'm in the process of hiring a nurse through an agency." Boris started walking the floor with the baby. He stopped pacing and looked pleadingly at Dorothy. "Please, dear, just to humor me?"

Dorothy studied Boris carefully. Finally she said, "Very well, Boris, if it will make you feel better, hire a private nurse. But really, I'm doing just fine."

Boris faced the window and said to his daughter, "Now mummy will be taken care of properly, won't she, Sara Jane? Yes, she will." He could feel Dorothy's suspicious gaze burning into the back of his neck.

**Who Framed Boris Karloff?**

## Chapter Eleven

## 27 November 1938, 2:03 p.m.

### Edwards Brothers Mortuary, 1000 Venice Boulevard

The Edwards Brothers' mortuary was called the Colonial Mansion for good reason: The Southern Gothic domicile could have easily passed for the Selznick International Studios mansion. Boris Karloff stood just inside the doorway of the mortuary. He had a commanding view of the "A" list Hollywood mourners coming up the porch steps, although the word "mourners" seemed strangely inaccurate to describe the general feeling coming from the gathering crowd. The atmosphere was more that of a Hollywood premiere than a funeral service. A red carpet had been rolled out and crushed velvet red ropes strung on either side to keep autograph-seekers and reporters at bay. Mourners in name only were smiling and happily chattering away, pausing occasionally to strike a pose for newspaper photographers and scribble in the odd autograph book. Then they resumed their filing in, pausing to sign the guest book lying open on the stand in the foyer before taking their seats in the chapel. As Karloff studied the faces of the smiling, milling throng of black suits, dark dresses, sunglasses, and bonnets, he couldn't help feeling like he had been left out of some enormous private joke. Some of the attendees were rather startling. Walt Disney, Jack Warner, and Louis B. Mayor were just some of the executives in attendance. Boris had no idea Martin F. Murphy was so well connected. But by far the most startling thing about the funeral could be seen beyond the foyer in the Edwards Brothers' chapel. The decidedly unburned body of Martin F. Murphy was stretched out in his coffin in lacquered repose with a veritable bounty of floral wreaths displayed around him.

Dwight Kemper

Karloff scanned the arriving mourners for any signs of his cohorts. Jack Pierce and his wife Blanche came up the red carpet, causing not the slightest stir of interest from the spectators or the reporters. Jack and Blanche stepped into the foyer and paused while Jack signed the guest book. Pierce handed Blanche the pen and as he did, looked up and appeared shocked to see Boris.

"Oh, uh, hello, Boris," the makeup artist said politely, but with a nervous tremor in his voice.

"Hello, Jack," Karloff said with a smile. "Hello, Blanche."

"Boris," Blanche said, "I'm sure Mr. Murphy would be very glad to see you here. And congratulations about your baby girl."

"Thank you, Blanche," said Boris politely. He turned to Pierce and noticed a bruise on the makeup man's right cheek. He also noted the flesh colored makeup that had been hastily applied to conceal it. "That looks nasty," Karloff said, pointing at his own cheek.

Pierce touched his cheekbone and smiled nervously. "What, this? It's nothing. A guy, he stopped short in front of me. I hit the steering wheel, is all."

"I see. I take it you didn't apply the makeup to yourself."

"Of course I did. Who else?"

"It's just that you didn't do a very good job covering it up."

"I had to, you know, improvise."

"It's my pancake makeup," said Blanche.

"I would have preferred greasepaint," said Pierce. "But you gotta use what you got."

"Speaking of makeup," said Boris, nodding in the direction of the coffin. "Even from here I can see how natural Murphy looks. Did you have a hand in that, Jack?"

"Me?" said Pierce, obviously flustered. "Uh, no. I only make live people look dead, not dead people look live."

"You know, Jack, you ought to find out who made Murphy up. A makeup artist like that would be an excellent addition to your staff."

"What's so special?" asked Pierce with a nervous shrug. "I mean, it was just a heart attack." His eyes darted around, as if trying to find a way to escape. "Not like the makeup man had to do extensive work." He pointed and said, "Oh, I see Conrad Veidt over there. We haven't seen each other since *The Man Who Laughs*. Excuse me, would you, Boris?"

"Of course."

Karloff watched Jack hurry his wife over to the pew where Conrad Veidt was seated. After studying Pierce a moment longer, Boris returned his attention to the arriving mourners. That's when Boris spotted Cliff Work and his wife coming up the walk. Work clutched at his stomach the instant he saw Karloff; no doubt his ulcer acting up.

"What are you doing here?" Work asked pointedly.

"Same thing as you, my dear Mr. Work," Boris said, effecting innocence. "I'm here to pay my respects."

Work growled, "You were supposed to stay home and play tennis."

"You suggested cricket," Boris corrected.

"Whatever! The point is you're supposed to be anyplace *but* here!"

"A high-profile star like myself not attending the service? Now how would that look? After all, I know how you feel about bad press."

Work glared at Boris then turned and asked his wife to find them both a seat in the chapel. Once he and Karloff were alone, said with a heavy sigh, "Okay, I can't make you leave but for christssake try to keep a low profile, will you?"

"Not an easy task," smiled Karloff, "considering what an apparently high-profile funeral this has become."

"Murphy was a man well respected in the industry."

"So it would seem," Boris remarked as more attendees filed past, amongst them such Hollywood notables as Wallace Beery and Greta Garbo. Nodding in the direction of the coffin, Karloff said casually, "Murphy looks remarkably well turned out, especially considering how he looked earlier. Mr. Mannix's handiwork, I suppose?"

Work clutched his stomach again and said, "Mannix—and special effects." He grabbed Karloff's arm and whispered in his ear, "Look, it's a dummy. The real body's already at the crematorium. Just don't let on when you pay your respects."

"And where might Mr. Mannix be?" Boris asked innocently.

"He's at the crematorium doing what I hired him to do—make this problem go away."

"Like a good and loyal Bulldog should."

Work gave Karloff a hard stare. Mrs. Work caught her husband's eye as she waved to him from the seat she had saved. "I gotta go," Work said, giving the missus an acknowledging wave back. "Pay your respects if you have to, just make sure you don't stir up any trouble. You got me?"

"I got you," Boris said with a nod.

Work joined his wife for the service.

Outside cries from photographers of "Look this way, Mr. Rathbone! This way, Mr. Lugosi!" announced the arrival of Basil Rathbone with his wife Ouida and Bela Lugosi with Lillian on his arm. Approaching Boris, Rathbone said jauntily, "Lovely day for a funeral, wouldn't you agree, Mr. Karloff?"

"Indeed, Mr. Rathbone," said Boris.

Ouida gave Basil a playful slap on the arm. "Really, Basil, you're just dreadful." She shook Boris' hand and smiled, "Congratulations on your new baby, Boris. How is Dorothy doing?"

"She's well, Ouida," Boris said politely. "Well enough under the circumstances, anyway."

"Did she get the flowers we sent to her room?"

"They were lovely, thank you."

"When she comes home and feels up to it, you must both come have dinner with Basil and me!"

"We'd be delighted," said Boris. He studied Ouida's beaming pretty face. "You seem quite chipper, if you don't mind my saying."

"Dear Basil had the most wonderful suggestion," she said, hugging Rathbone's arm. "I'm to take a trip to the East Coast with some friends. It will be so nice to see the old homestead on Great Neck again."

"It's all arranged," Rathbone said, giving Boris a knowing smile. "I'll be dropping Ouida off at Central Station this evening."

"Basil's being so impetuous!" Ouida gushed.

Bela glared at Rathbone. "Don't forget you are driving me to—"

"YOUR PERSONAL APPEARANCE," Rathbone interrupted quickly. "I'll be there in plenty of time to pick you up."

Ouida looked from Basil to Bela, then gave her husband an arch look. "I thought Lillian drove Bela to things like that."

"Uh, she does, only, uh—." Basil faltered and looked imploringly to Lillian.

"I have to stay home with Bela, Jr.," said Lillian.

Basil smiled nervously. "Yes, so I'm helping Bela by driving him to the midnight spook show." Looking to Bela he said, "Right, Bela?"

Lugosi scowled, obviously not thrilled with the cover story. Nevertheless he said, if begrudgingly, "Yes, Rathbone is taking me to the spooky show tonight."

Ouida eyed her husband suspiciously. "If I didn't know better, I'd think you were sending me away so you boys could get into some bit of mischief."

"Mischief? Hardly," Boris lied. Attempting to change the subject, he pointed at the guest book. "I say, Basil, have you had a look at this?"

"The guest book?" Basil said, jumping at any diversion. "No, I haven't." He flipped through the pages and became genuinely interested. "I say, Ouida, look at these signatures. I had no idea Murphy was so popular with the *crème de la crème* of Hollywood."

"Oh?" Ouida read over her husband's shoulder. "I say, you're right! Why, it's a veritable who's who."

"Rather strange, wouldn't you say?" asked Boris.

"Very," said Basil.

Bela asked Lillian to help Ouida find a seat for them.

When the trio was alone, Basil breathed a sigh of relief. "That was close."

"A spook show?" Bela said with indignation. "Did you have to make it a spook show? Bela would not be caught dead at a spook show!"

"It was all I could think of," said Rathbone. "It's your own fault. You and your big mouth!"

"Please, gentlemen," said Boris, "about this guest book."

"Yes," the Hungarian said, "the guest book could be our suspect list, wouldn't you agree, gentlemen?"

"Perhaps," Rathbone said, regaining his composure. He scanned the signatures and indicated Rowland V. Lee's. "I see our director is here."

Bela nudged him aside and flipped through the pages. "Whale's signature is not here. Maybe that is significant, yes?"

"No," said Boris. "James has a morbid fear of funerals. Colin Clive's funeral service was held in this very mortuary and James couldn't bring himself to attend."

"Yes," Rathbone said, "and coincidentally, just as Murphy will be, Clive was cremated at the Rosedale Crematory."

"So what?" asked Bela.

"There was a bit of a scandal. The Rosedale Crematory lost Colin Clive's ashes. Rumors further allege that this was only one of many such incidents of carelessness."

Boris looked grim. "Now I see why Mannix chose that particular crematory. If Murphy's ashes should disappear, no one would suspect foul play."

"Just mismanagement," said Rathbone.

"Apparently, Mannix is supervising the actual cremation this very minute."

Bela looked past the entrance of the chapel to the body lying in state. "That isn't the body?"

"Work insists it's a dummy," said Karloff.

Rathbone's eyebrow arched. "It will be interesting to see if the likeness is as striking close up as it appears to be from a distance."

"In fact, I noticed that Jack acted very guilty when I mentioned how nicely I thought the body was laid out. I think he might have fabricated it. And you should have heard the story he gave me about a bruise I noticed on his cheek."

Bela shot Karloff an accusing look. "You questioned Pierce? I was to question Pierce!"

Boris shrugged. "Sorry, Bela. He saw me standing here and started talking to me. If it makes you feel any better, he made excuses to get away from me."

Lugosi scowled. "We drew names from my hat and you take my suspect away!" Lugosi folded his arms and stared Karloff down. "I want to change suspects! I want YOUR suspect! It is only fair!"

Dwight Kemper

"Be reasonable, Bela. I didn't ask Jack for his whereabouts on the night of the murder. That's really what you, as an investigator, want to know anyway. I'm sure he won't open up to me any longer."

"I don't care. Do you see me going around and questioning *your* suspect?"

Rathbone pulled Lugosi aside. "Do keep your voice down, old boy."

"I still want Karloff's suspect," Lugosi insisted.

"Basil," said Boris, taking on the role of peacemaker, "if Bela wants to switch suspects, I say let him. It really doesn't matter."

"See," nodded Bela. "If it doesn't matter to Karloff, why should it matter to you?"

"Because," Basil explained patiently, "if what Boris said is true, Pierce won't give answers to his inquires anymore. You're really the only one who might get Pierce to open up. In fact," he said, in a moment of inspiration, "you irritate Pierce so much, he just might crack and reveal an important clue just because you make him so angry."

Lugosi mulled that one over. The glare of the vampire Count sparkled in his eyes. "Yes, I do like to make Pierce angry. It is good that I question him."

"Now here's what you do," Rathbone said as he put a conspiratorial arm around Lugosi's shoulder. "See where Pierce goes after the service. Be his shadow! If Pierce goes to the cemetery, you follow in the funeral procession. Wherever he goes, you go! Then, when you get a chance, casually walk up to Pierce and engage him in conversation. Lead him to talk about the night of the murder."

"What about Lillian?" Lugosi asked. "She is my Watson, she must do something."

"Have Lillian chat up Blanche, keeping her out of the way while you make your move on Pierce. See if you can find out who really called Pierce that night on the phone. Be the puppet master, Lugosi. Pull the strings."

"Yes," said Bela, excited by his task. "I'll pull the strings!"

At that moment a familiar bullet-riddled Rolls Royce pulled up the mortuary drive and stopped in front of the red carpet. With practiced timing, the chauffeur got out and trotted around to the rear door and waited for the reporters to have their Graflex cameras ready. Then, as shutters clicked and flashbulbs popped, out stepped Mr. and Mrs. Lionel Atwill. Louise Atwill was the ex-wife of Douglas MacArthur and had been a stunning woman back in her day. Now she was hugely fat and stuffed in a girdle. She strode up the red carpet on Lionel's arm. As they entered the foyer, Pinky smiled warmly at Karloff and company. "Hello, gentlemen," he said, cheerfully. "Here for the festivities?"

Rathbone smiled. "Only you would find a funeral festive."

"Why should we fear death, Basil? Isn't death the great equalizer, after all?" Pinky surveyed the mourners taking their seats, giving them his patented leer. "Look at them. They're all here for just one reason: they're celebrating the fact that they're still alive. They've cheated death for yet another day."

"Now, Pinky," Mrs. Atwill chided. "Do restrain yourself. I'm sure these fine gentlemen would be absolutely appalled by your rhetoric."

"Oh, nonsense, Louise," Pinky said with a dismissive wave. "I'm not upsetting you fine gentlemen, am I?"

Bela smiled Dracula's smile and said, "There are worse things to fear — than death."

Atwill chuckled and gave Bela a playful jab to the arm. "That's the ticket! Give Death a jolly laugh and say to hell with him!"

Mrs. Atwill patted her husband's arm and said apologetically, "You really must forgive Pinky. He's so excited these days following this new murder trial."

"A most gruesome case!" Pinky said. "It rather makes Dr. Crippen look tame by comparison! I'll have to tell you three all about it!"

Rathbone smiled politely. "Perhaps another time."

Boris pointed to the chapel. "If we're going to view the body before the service starts, we'd better hurry."

"Very well," Pinky said with a smile. "But do remind me to tell you all about it later. You simply must hear the, uh, gory details! Especially the acid baths!" The plump actor chuckled and stroked his trim mustache thoughtfully with his index finger. "I can't wait to tell Rowland! He simply won't believe it! When Rowland says the case is implausible, I'll use his favorite saying against him," and in a fairly good impression of Rowland V. Lee, Atwill said, "It's suspension of disbelief!"

Rathbone's nostrils twitched. "I didn't know you could do impressions."

"Oh, it's nothing, really," Pinky said humbly. "You pick these things up."

As Boris, Basil, and Bela watched Mr. and Mrs. Atwill take their seats, Rathbone commented, "There goes the proverbial red herring, gentlemen."

Bela frowned at Rathbone. "What is this with you and fish? First you want my wife to make tuna salad and now you talk about herrings!"

"Let's join our wives and then pay our respects," Rathbone said to Bela good-naturedly. "I'll explain it to you later."

It was like a scene from a Universal horror movie. As an appropriate organ dirge played in the background, each attending mourner filed past and said his or her good-byes. The widow Murphy was first in line. She was a vision of black crepe and veils, as any Universal Studios heroine bedecked in a costume designed by Vera West might be. As reporters focused their cameras,

Dwight Kemper

**"Only you would find a funeral festive."**

the widow Murphy reached under the veil to dab her eyes and kissed a gloved hand that she extended to the cheek of her late husband. An explosion of flash bulbs caught the moment. Boris wondered if the dummy felt strangely stiff to Mrs. Murphy or if the body had been modeled from a pliable material. As Boris got closer to the body he couldn't help marveling at the workmanship. Like any genuine body lying in state, Murphy's dummy had that waxy, made up look of a Madame Tussaud's figure. Murphy's dummy was stretched out in quiet repose, its head resting on a satin pillow, the body swallowed up in the crumpled satin lining and a quilted coverlet. The hands were folded over its chest, giving the dummy the look of a man only sleeping. It wore a gold ring and its nails had been buffed to a high polish. Boris leaned in closer to study the face. It was a perfect likeness. Boris could see every line and pore. The muscles were relaxed, the eyes closed, reminding Boris of the many life masks displayed in Jack Pierce's makeup studio. Could it be that this perfect likeness was indeed one of Pierce's life masks? Then Karloff remembered the missing life mask in Pierce's rogue's gallery. Had a cast of Murphy's face occupied that space? If the missing mask were Murphy's life cast, why would Murphy submit to such a thing? Sitting for a life cast was far from pleasant. Unless this was a death mask! Could Jack Pierce have cast this face directly from Murphy's dead body before it was taken to Stage 7 and burned to a crisp?

Who Framed Boris Karloff?

Someone poked Boris in the back. It was Jack Warner. "Come on, Karloff. Give the rest of us a chance, will ya?"

"Oh," Boris said absently. "Sorry."

The funeral service was like any other. The minister gave a sermon that had little to do with the guest of honor. There were hymns sung and prayers spoken.

After the service, the pallbearers carried Murphy's coffin to the waiting hearse. Cliff Work was one of those pallbearers, along with Lionel Atwill, Wallace Beery, Spencer Tracy, Jack Warner, and Clark Gable. They carried the coffin reverently down the mortuary steps as a dozen photographers captured the moment with a barrage of popping flashbulbs. The funeral procession motored off toward Rosedale Cemetery as Rathbone and Lugosi joined Boris out in the foyer.

"Are you all right, Boris?" Rathbone asked.

"As well as can be expected," Karloff said, still thinking about the body.

"Remember, gentlemen, we meet at Mae's tonight, say, 8 o'clock?"

"Yes," chuckled Lugosi. "8 o'clock at Mae's." His mercurial temperament switched from jovial to stern as he stared Rathbone down. "Don't forget, you're picking me up at 7:30."

"I'll gladly drive you," Rathbone said, eyeing Lugosi narrowly, "if you will you kindly tell me what is so blasted funny."

"Not now," Bela said with a sly grin, indicating their approaching spouses. "The wives, they might hear." In a voice dripping with innuendo, he added, "You find out tonight."

Rathbone ignored Lugosi's remark and switched his attitude from daring sleuth to loving husband. As he escorted Ouida to their car, Rathbone chatted her up with inconsequential small talk. Lugosi smiled at Lillian and said, "Now you become my Watson." He added with a whisper, "Here come our suspects," indicating Jack and Blanche Pierce as they approached. Aloud to Jack Pierce, he said, "Going to the cemetery, Pierce?"

Jack turned to answer and spotted Karloff. He kept an eye on Boris as he said to Bela, "Uh, yes, I am. Are you?"

Bela seemed annoyed that Pierce was paying more attention to Karloff. The proud Hungarian grabbed Pierce's shoulders and forced the man to return his gaze. "We will go to the funeral together, you and I, and our wives." Jack stood cowering and transfixed like a rabbit caught in the gaze of a wolf.

"How about you, Boris," Pierce asked, still staring at Lugosi. "Are you going, too?"

"I'm afraid I can't, Jack," Boris said. "I have other matters that need my attention."

"You come with me," said Bela, insistently, hypnotically. "Lillian and I, we follow you down—in my car!"

"Uh, okay," Pierce nervously agreed.

Bela Lugosi escorted Jack to his car while Lillian and Blanche followed after them. The scene evoked images of Bela in the role of Dracula dominating the fly-eating Renfield, while Lillian was Dracula's faithful Bride awaiting her chance to feast upon Blanche's jugular vein. It was at that moment that Boris was taken completely unawares as a hand gripped his shoulder and a menacing voice intoned, "That's it, Boris. Take your last look."

Boris wheeled around, his fist poised for a fight. Rowland V. Lee jumped back, startled, raising his hands to protect his face. "Whoa! Sorry, there, Boris! I didn't mean to startle you like that." He pointed at the funeral procession driving slowly down Venice Boulevard. "I only meant take your last look at *Son of Frankenstein*, for christssakes. You know, now that Murphy's out of the picture and everything."

"Sorry about that," Boris said, chagrinned. "You did rather give me a bit of a start there." He looked back at the procession of cars as they turned the corner down South Union Avenue toward West Washington Boulevard. Jack Pierce's car was joining the procession. Bela's car followed closely behind with Lillian driving.

Boris gave the director an encouraging smile. "Don't worry about the picture, Rowland. I doubt the head office wants to see the money they've already invested go to waste."

"Yeah, maybe," Rowland said. "Depends who they get to replace Murphy." There was a decided look of uneasiness about him. "I need a drink. How about it? I'm buying."

"Why, yes," said Boris, seizing the opportunity. "I could use something myself. And I promise to refrain from any fisticuffs."

"That's a relief," Lee said with a smile. "Look, there's this little hole-in-the-wall bar up on West 9th Street called Tony's. I'll meet you there. I got something I want to get off my chest."

In a moment of wicked humor, Karloff said enigmatically, "The plot thickens."

"Huh?"

"Nothing. Where did you say this bar was?"

## Who Framed Boris Karloff?

## Chapter Twelve

## 27 November 1938, 3:05 p.m.

Rowland V. Lee waited under the awning outside Tony's Bar and Grill as Boris joined him. "I hear this joint is kind of a dive," Rowland said apologetically, "but it's usually pretty quiet this time of day. Just one word of warning, though."

"This place can be pretty rough?" asked Boris.

"Yeah, on your stomach. The gaffer who told me about this place warned me not to eat the chili."

As they entered, it struck Boris that American bars in the late afternoon are lonely places. The customers at Tony's sat around the bar, quietly nursing their drinks, not looking at each other, not talking to the bartender because they weren't drunk enough yet to list their troubles. A hooker sat on one of the barstools. There were a couple of call girls sitting together in a booth against one wall. It was obvious from their demeanor that all three working girls were "off the clock" and didn't want to be bothered. There were a couple of pool tables but no one was playing. It was nothing at all like the communal atmosphere of an English pub, to be sure. That is, until a celebrity like Boris Karloff shows up with a friend.

The waitress nearly hyperventilated when she recognized him. "Oh my Gawd! Boris Karloff!" she gasped. "Tony! Everybody! Look! It's Boris Karloff!"

A dozen people suddenly sprang to life and rushed up to meet Boris.

"I just LOVED you in *The Raven!*" one hooker squealed excitedly. "That Wakeman guy you played was so—forceful!"

This gave Boris pause as he remembered some of the "forceful" things that character did.

Another girl giggled, "I've seen *Frankenstein* a hundred times, I swear, a hundred times! Those bolts in your neck really send me!"

"Oh, and those eyes!" a third hooker said, "I love those heavy-lidded bedroom eyes!" Her own eyes brightened as she requested, "Come on, Mr. Karloff, give us a Monster growl? Please!"

This amused Boris no end. He never thought of the Monster as a sex symbol. "Well," he thought, "to each her taste." Out loud he said humbly, "Why, thank you, my dear. I'd be delighted." He grimaced, taking on the Monster's gruesome visage and let out with his guttural trademark, "RAAARR!"

All three call girls giggled and applauded. The rest of the gathering cheered.

Tony, the rotund pug-faced owner, took Boris' hand and shook it vigorously as he said, "It's a pleasure havin' you in my joint, Mr. Karloff! Just wait till I tell the Missus."

A man with a three-day growth of beard pushed past Tony and said, "I just got out of stir, Mr. Karloff." He extended his hand. "I just want you to know, we guys in the pen saw youse in *The Criminal Code*, and me and the other boys thought youse was great! What youse did to that lousy stoolie was too good for 'im!"

Another man, a giant with a broken nose and a cauliflower ear, said, "That guy Galloway you played can bunk wit' me anytime!"

Boris shook their hands and smiled. "I'm glad you all enjoyed it. But really, gentlemen, Galloway wasn't meant to be the hero."

The waitress pushed through the gathering crowd and pleaded, "May I get your autograph, please, Mr. Karloff?" She offered Boris her pad and pen. "I'm your biggest fan! Sign it, 'To Rhonda, you kill me!'"

Boris prepared to make an inscription, then hesitated. After a moment's pause, he decided a personalized autograph was fairly safe, particularly on a waitress' receipt book. Nevertheless, he made the salutation a less incriminating, "With every good wish, Boris Karloff."

She took back her pad and said, "Gosh, thank you, Mr. Karloff!" She looked at Rowland V. Lee and asked, "Are you anybody?"

"Nah," said Rowland. "I'm nobody. Listen, could we just sit in the back and be left alone?"

"Sure." She turned to the crowd and said, "All right, you guys, settle down and give Mr. Karloff some room to breathe!"

There was a mutual groan of disappointment. Boris felt for them and assured everyone that once he'd concluded his business with Mr. Lee, he'd gladly sign autographs.

The giant with the cauliflower ear wiped away a tear and said, "Gosh, what a swell guy!"

Boris and Rowland were taken to a corner booth in the back. Rowland ordered a beer and Boris a whiskey sour. After they were served their drinks the waitress left them a bowl of beer nuts to snack on and then kept her distance. Occasionally when a regular wandered in, she would point out Boris and show them the autograph she just got. "But they want to be left alone," she would add. "I think the other guy's his agent or something."

Boris tried to read what was written on Rowland's face. The man definitely looked troubled about something, but seemed hesitant to say what was on his mind. Boris decided to break the ice. "You said you had something to get off your chest?"

Rowland took a sip of his beer and after a long pause finally said, "Boris, there's something screwy about this whole set up."

"I'm not sure I know what you mean, Rowland."

"The funeral, the way Murphy died. It just doesn't add up."

"How so?" Boris asked.

"They said he died of a heart attack and somebody found him dead in his office. Well, I know for a fact that that's a lot of bull."

"Really?" said Boris, trying to look nonchalant as he sipped his drink.

Rowland took a handful of beer nuts and started popping them in his mouth. He sat chewing nuts and remained silent.

"Rowland, what is it?" Karloff asked, hoping to get him talking again.

"I went to Murphy's office. You know, after we wrapped for the night. I was mad, Boris. I was taking it out on you, Basil, Bela, and the crew and that was wrong. I was going to give the guy who really deserved it what he had coming to him."

This was beginning to sound like a confession. Boris remained composed but interested. "What happened?"

Rowland fell silent and grabbed another handful of beer nuts and started popping them again. He drew in a deep breath and let out a long sigh and said, "I saw the light on in Murphy's office." He hesitated, looked away a moment, then looked intently into Karloff's eyes as Boris took a sip of his drink. "I saw the light on. So I marched right in and I let him have it."

Boris would have reacted with a classic spit take, except he inhaled his drink instead of exhaling and nearly choked in the process.

"Boris? Are you okay?" Rowland stood up and reached over to pat Karloff on the back as the actor went into a coughing fit. At exactly the same instant, Rhonda hurried over and trying to be helpful started slapping Karloff on the back, too.

"Are you okay, Mr. Karloff?" slap, slap, slap. "You want some water?"

The giant with the cauliflower ear shouted, "Somebody call a doc!"

Boris shook his head and cleared his throat. "Thank you, no. Everyone, really. My drink just went down the wrong way."

Rowland glared angrily at the waitress. "Will you please leave us alone?"

Boris gave her a reassuring smile and said, "Really, my dear. I'm all right now. Thank you, though."

"Okay," said Rhonda. "But if you need ANYTHING, just you let me know."

"We will," Rowland glowered. "Now beat it."

Once they were alone again, Boris composed himself and asked, "So, um, as you were saying, you, um, 'let him have it?'"

"Oh, I wanted to, all right. Only Murphy wasn't there."

"But the door to the office was unlocked?"

"Yeah."

"The door was unlocked and the light was on, but no one was there?"

"Murphy wasn't there but Whale was."

"Oh? What did James have to say?"

Rowland sipped his beer and said, "He wasn't in any condition to say anything. He was passed out on Murphy's couch. Boy, he must have really tied one on. I tried to wake him but he wouldn't budge."

Boris nodded. "Yes, I imagine he must have been quite out of it, considering how much he probably drank before arriving at the studio. After you tried to wake him, then what did you do?"

"Yeah, well, I took a blanket Murphy had draped over the back of the couch, you know, one of those Mexican blankets, and kind of tucked Whale in for the night. He looked sort of chilly."

"So you're the one who—" Boris said, then caught himself. "I mean, is that all you did?"

Rowland shrugged. "Pretty much. I just turned off the light and left Whale to sleep it off in peace."

"Tell me," Boris ventured, "did you see anything—I don't know—anything *unusual* about the office?"

Rowland gave Boris a searching look. "Unusual like what?"

Karloff thought to himself, "Like a bloodstain on the carpet?" Out loud he said, "Was there any evidence of a brawl? You said you thought the heart attack story was 'a lot of bull.' I'm still not sure what you meant by that."

"Nah," Rowland said. "Nothing like that. The place was neat as a pin except for an ashtray full of cigar butts on the coffee table and two half-empty brandy snifters sitting on Murphy's desk. Oh yeah, and a third empty snifter tipped over on the rug by Whale. His clothes stank with liquor."

Boris wondered about this detail. He didn't remember smelling brandy on Whale's clothing when the director visited Jack Pierce's makeup bungalow. Then again, Boris' nostrils were filled with the smell of coffee, chemicals, and the waxy odor of the grayish-green greasepaint on his own face. For the time being, Boris was willing to accept Rowland's story. "I must say you do have a director's eye for detail," Karloff remarked.

"I remember about the snifter on the rug because it added to the impression I got looking at Whale. There was something familiar about the way Whale looked."

"Familiar in what way?"

"The way he was out cold like that. The last time I saw a guy looking like that was back in the army when a buddy of mine was slipped a Mickey Finn. But that's crazy, right? I mean, who'd want to slip Whale a Mickey?"

"Who indeed," Boris pondered.

"Oh, yeah, and that's not all. There was some kind of crap on the doorknob that came off on my hand. Whatever it was, I wiped it off on my pants. Made a hell of a mess. You know what my dry cleaner said it was?"

"No."

"Greasepaint."

"Greasepaint?"

"Yeah. Only at the time I didn't know it was greasepaint because it sure didn't smell like greasepaint."

"What did it smell like?"

"I don't remember, I just remember it just smelled funny. But what I want to know is, how the hell did greasepaint get on Murphy's doorknob?"

The minute Boris heard the word "greasepaint" he came to a sudden realization and exclaimed, "Pierce!" under his breath. He hadn't realized he had said it aloud until Rowland asked pointedly, "What about Pierce?"

Boris recovered himself and said casually, "Oh, probably Murphy had Jack in his office, you know, to call Jack on the carpet about that whole Technicolor thing. Jack's hands are always stained with greasepaint or some other muck."

"Yeah, I guess." Rowland chugged the last of his beer and slammed the glass down.

A notion came to Boris. "Which one, by the way?" he asked.

Rowland gave Karloff a puzzled look. "Which one what?"

"Which doorknob was the greasepaint on? The inside doorknob or the outside doorknob?"

"Oh, well, I didn't notice the doorknob being sticky when I first came in. I remember feeling something greasy when I tried to leave, so I think it was on the inside doorknob."

"Interesting," said Boris as he absorbed this particular detail and its possible implications. "I wonder how Jack was able to enter the office without getting the outside doorknob messy, too."

"Good question, Boris. But I have an even better one. When the hell did Murphy have this heart attack of his? I sure as hell know Murphy wasn't in his office around 9:30 on Wednesday night and his office was cleaned out the next morning. So when did he die? And who the hell found him? If Whale woke up and found Murphy dead, we'd have all heard an overblown account of it straight from Whale himself. That guy can't keep his trap shut about anything."

"True," Boris agreed.

Rowland smiled wistfully as he said, "Hey, you know what these nagging questions remind me of?"

"No, not really."

"Well, to prepare for *Son of Frankenstein* I screened the first two movies, right?"

"Yes. And?"

"Well, now don't get me wrong, I mean, Whale is a genius, to be sure, but, well, you have to admit, he was always kind of foggy on the details. You know, like, in *Frankenstein*. Frankenstein's friend Victor tells Frankenstein that Dr. Waldmen's body was found in the watch tower. But we never find out who found the body! See what I mean? Murphy being found dead by an anonymous somebody is just like that. If I didn't know better, I'd say Whale directed Murphy's death. I mean, that's crazy, right?"

Karloff became pensive. "Possibly," he said.

"Anyway, what about the funeral today? Murphy was a goddamn Studio Production Manager, not Rudolph Valentino! Why all the Hollywood bigwigs?" He looked at his empty glass and asked, "You up for another round?"

Boris looked at his watch. "I think I have time."

"Got plans?"

"I'm, uh, meeting friends for dinner later."

## Chapter Thirteen

## 27 November 1938, 3:15 p.m.

**Angelus-Rosedale Cemetery, 1831 W. Washington Blvd.**

At Rathbone's urging, Bela was to become Jack Pierce's shadow, and damned if Bela didn't take that suggestion to heart. Then again, Bela Lugosi was always one to take direction a little too literally. Bela stood beside Pierce at the Rosedale Crematory as the casket containing the alleged mortal remains of Martin F. Murphy was placed on the conveyor belt. Bela stood next to Pierce two hours later at the outdoor catered reception as the urn supposedly containing Murphy's ashes was presented to his grieving widow, still a vision in flowing black veils. Bela was close by Pierce's side as Mrs. Murphy laid the urn to rest in its columbarium at the Rosedale Mausoleum. And, of course, Bela, with Lillian on his arm, tagged along behind Pierce as Jack and Blanche headed for their car parked along the cemetery road with the other cars waiting in the procession. It was well past sundown and Bela motioned for Lillian to keep Blanche distracted as the Hungarian came up behind the nervous makeup man. This was the last straw for Jack Pierce. Jack had no sooner reached for the handle to the car door than he wheeled around quickly and shouted, "WHY DO YOU KEEP FOLLOWING ME?"

"Was I following you?" Bela asked, effecting an air of innocence that was less than convincing. "I have merely been paying my last respects to Mr. Murphy."

"No," Pierce insisted. "You been following me since the funeral service! Everywhere I turn, there you are!"

"Jack, Jack, Jack," Bela said, placing a sympathetic hand on Pierce's shoulder. "This funeral has obviously been a great strain upon your nerves. Your state of mind, it concerns me. Perhaps there is something to get—," he hesitated as he tried to remember the actual phrase, then said, "—something to get up off of your chest."

"Never mind my chest," Pierce said, glaring at Bela with his beady eyes, "just get off my back!" He looked around for his wife and spotted Blanche chatting pleasantly with Lillian. "Blanche, we going now!"

"Jack, remember," Bela's hand tightened around Pierce's shoulder as the Hungarian's hypnotic gaze bore down upon him, "those things we think are forever buried can rise again to haunt us."

With a quick, insistent gesture, Pierce broke Lugosi's hold on his shoulder and motioned for Blanche to get in the car. As he climbed into the driver's seat and slammed the door, Pierce said, "I don't know what it is that's gotten into you, Lugosi, but you just leave Blanche and me alone." He started the car engine and said, just before pulling away, "I don't wanna see you until 5:30 makeup call tomorrow morning. No phone calls! No any thing! NOTHING!"

As Jack pulled away, Bela heard Blanche say, "Why, Jack, that wasn't a very nice thing to say. What's gotten into you lately?"

Together Bela and Lillian watched as Jack and Blanche Pierce drove out of sight. "Well, Bela, my darling," Lillian said as she took Bela's arm, "there goes our suspect. I guess we weren't very good Watsons."

Bela straightened up and gave his wife a scowl. "I am not a Watson! I am a Sherlock Holmes! If Sherlock Holmes had been presented on the Budapest stage, it would be Bela who would have played him!"

"On the stage, that may be true. But in real life, we have learned nothing, my darling."

Bela was about to respond when Clark Gable and Spencer Tracy passed by. Gable said to Tracy, "...guess he just got too big for his britches."

"Yeah," remarked Tracy, "for however long he could keep those britches on."

They laughed together and were immediately followed by Howard Strickling and Louis B. Mayer, who were also on their way out. Bela overheard Strickling, who was known to stammer when he was nervous, say to Mayer, "S-s-so w-what d-d-do we d-d-d-do n-now, b-b-boss?"

"What do we do?" said Mayer. "We get ourselves a Bromo Seltzer and breathe a sigh of relief, is what."

Bela and Lillian watched Strickling and Mayer and the other Hollywood notables get into their cars and drive down the winding palm tree-lined road leading out of the cemetery.

**"…guess he just got too big for his britches."**

The Lugosis stood silently together on the cemetery road. Bela looked very natural standing there in the dark, illuminated by passing car lights, tombstones rising up behind him on lush green plots. After a long while Bela turned to Lillian and finally admitted, "I'm afraid, my dear, you are right. We have learned nothing."

Dwight Kemper

**Chapter Fourteen**

**27 November 1938, 8:45 p.m.**

**Mae's, Somewhere in the Hollywood Hills**

Boris Karloff paced back and forth under the *porte-cochere* of the 14-room mansion that allegedly housed the private gentlemen's club called Mae's. He paused to look at his watch and noted the time.

"Where on earth can they be?" he said under his breath. It wasn't like Basil Rathbone to be late.

The front door was opened by an attractive coffee-colored maid wearing a short black uniform with a lace apron and cap. She noticed Boris waiting under the *porte-cochere* and asked, "May I help you, sir?"

"I'm waiting for my friends," Boris explained.

"Would you care to wait for them inside, sir?"

"Thank you, but I think I'd rather wait out here."

"Suit yourself, sir," she said with practiced gentility.

As she turned to close the door, Boris said, "I say, miss, there is one thing you can do for me, if it isn't too much trouble."

"It's Della, sir. And how may I serve you?"

"Is Julian Walker here tonight?"

"Julian Walker?" Della remained polite, but was obviously somewhat taken aback by the request. "So, it's Julian you want to see?"

"It's a private matter."

Della smiled demurely. "Everything here at Mae's is a private matter, sir. We're very discreet. But you'll still have to see Miss West first."

"Miss West? Do you mean Mae West?"

**"Where can they be?" Boris wondered as he waited for Rathbone and Lugosi.**

"Of course, sir. This is Mae's." With a curtsey and a smile Della closed the door, leaving Boris quite stunned.

A pair of shining headlights illuminated the scene. Basil Rathbone pulled up under the *porte-cochere* and waved Boris over. "Sorry we're late, old man," he said, and nodded in Lugosi's direction. "I'm afraid his Majesty kept me waiting while he donned his regal raiment."

Lugosi, wearing a top hat and black dinner jacket gave Rathbone a withering scowl. "I like to dress well. Is that a crime?"

"No," sniped Rathbone, "but keeping me waiting like a schoolboy on prom night is certainly bad form. I arrived at precisely 7:30, as you requested. I didn't even get a chance to see Ouida's train off."

"Bah!" said Bela. "My wife kept you company while you waited. You should be honored she would even speak to you!"

"Now see here—"

"Oh, please, gentlemen," Boris interrupted, "at least you're both here now. Park the car and let's go in."

After Rathbone parked his car next to Boris' convertible he reached under the seat and produced three folded newspapers. "It seems the funeral made the late edition in several Los Angeles papers. Perhaps a closer examination of the photographs might reveal something we may have missed."

"A capital idea," said Boris. As they approached the front door, he asked, "I say, Basil, did you bring a magnifying glass?"

Rathbone froze in his tracks. He exclaimed, "BLAST! I knew there was something I had forgotten!"

Dwight Kemper

Bela smirked and reached into the inner pocket of his dinner jacket. "Bela the detective, he always comes prepared," and produced his brass magnifying glass that he offered to Rathbone with an arrogant air obviously meant to infuriate.

Lugosi got the reaction he wanted. Rathbone huffed disagreeably as he took the magnifier. Only after a long moment to regain his polite composure did Rathbone utter an unconvincing, "Thank you."

"Don't be mentioning it," Bela said with mock graciousness.

Rathbone arched an eyebrow as he reached for the doorbell. Boris intervened. "Before we go in, I think you ought to know there's something rather peculiar about this place."

Bela smiled and said, "More than you know, my dear Mr. Karloff. It would be well if you both let me do all the talking."

"Oh, really," challenged Rathbone.

"Really," Bela said. "I am a man of the world and know my way around." He gestured at the button. "If you will allow me?"

Rathbone stood aside and let Bela ring the doorbell. Della answered with her usual efficiency and polite manner. She smiled at Boris. "I see your friends have finally arrived, sir." She beamed when she recognized Bela. "Hello, Charlie! Welcome back, sir."

"Charlie?" Boris and Basil exclaimed simultaneously, giving Lugosi disbelieving looks.

"It is my, how do you say it? My alias!" Lugosi explained, then smiled at the girl. "We would like to speak to Mae about one of her employees. A Mr. Julian Walker."

Della smiled. "Oh, yes." She looked over Bela's shoulder and said to Boris, "I gave Mr. Walker your message, sir. He's entertaining in the dining room just now but invites you to join him after he finishes his next set. He said he'll gladly talk and have a drink with you, but that's all he's interested in. I hope you don't mind."

"That is precisely what we were hoping to do, thank you," said Boris.

"I do apologize for the way I behaved earlier. It's just we don't get many of your kind here, if you don't mind my saying."

Basil crooked his eyebrow. "Our kind? What do you mean by that remark? You don't get many British gentlemen here?"

Della curtsied. "I do apologize, sir. I didn't mean to offend you. What you three do in the privacy of your room is really none of my business."

"In the privacy—?"

Indicating Bela, she added, "And Charlie being a regular, well, I never suspected—."

Bela glowered at Boris and Basil. "Why does she say these things?"

Rathbone smirked, "You're the 'man of the world,' you tell us."

Bela glowered accusingly at the maid. "Why do you say these things? What kind of man is this Julian Walker?"

Della curtsied again. "Again, I do apologize, gentlemen. I've obviously offended you. I assure you, we're not at all judgmental here at Mae's. Julian just isn't *that way*, is all."

"What way?" Bela turned to Rathbone. "What way is she talking about?"

Della noted the newspapers tucked under Basil's arm. "And those really aren't necessary, sir. We expect the sheets to get messy and change them regularly."

"What?" Basil exclaimed, completely baffled. "Now see here—"

"Please, sir, if you'll follow me to the library, Miss West is expecting you."

After exchanging puzzled looks, the three men stepped over the threshold and entered the world of Mae's. On his part, Boris felt as though he were stepping out onto a soundstage. It was the way the place was lit that created this impression. The rooms were aglow in a half-light. Strategically placed spills cast mysterious shadows on the red patterned wallpaper, creating a distinctly theatrical ante-bellum atmosphere.

But what really gave the actor pause seemed to appear out of nowhere at the top of an impressive flight of red-carpeted stairs. She moved like a wraith, a lovely platinum blonde with finger-waved hair and thinly drawn eyebrows. She descended from the darkness at the top of the stairs in a filmy evening gown and floated down like a white flame. She paused at the bottom of the stairs and smiled coquettishly at Boris who instantly recognized her and grabbed Rathbone's arm. "Tell me I'm not imagining things," he said as he drew Basil's attention to the gossamer vision who wafted past and through an archway. Boris' eyes nearly popped out of his head as he exclaimed, "That was Jean Harlow!"

Della looked over her shoulder and said, "In the flesh, sirs."

"But—it can't be Jean Harlow! Jean Harlow's dead!"

"We know she's dead, sir. But Miss Harlow is still very popular and our guests still request her."

"Request her?" Rathbone exclaimed, more annoyed than mystified. "Just what sort of establishment is this?"

"You are the great detective," Bela smirked. "You figure it out."

The maid led them into a richly furnished paneled library illuminated by a fire burning in an ornate fireplace. The occupant of a large armchair and matching footstool could be plainly seen in a large ornate gold-leaf framed mirror hanging over the mantle. She was a buxom blonde in a glittering Gay Nineties gown with a plunging neckline. She radiated raw sexuality from every pore.

Dwight Kemper

**"I figured yah was switchin' teams, if yah catch my drift."**

"Miss West," said Della, "these are the gentlemen who have business with Julian Walker."

Mae reached for an oversized brandy snifter resting beside her on a small end table. Frankenstein's Monster could have imbibed from that glass. Mae swirled the amber liquid around and smirked as she gave her three guests' reflections the onceover. "I didn't know yah boys swung that way." Indicating Bela, she added, "Especially 'Chollie' here. Up to now yah always preferred dames."

Bela stormed over to her and said, staring her down, "I *do* prefer dames, still! Just what are you trying to say about Bela?" then quickly corrected himself, "I mean, about *Charlie*."

"Well," said Mae, giving him a knowing half-smile, "around these parts the only reason anyone asks for anyone is for a little of the slap and tickle. And seeing that Julian is the way he is, I figured yah was switchin' teams, if yah catch my drift."

Lugosi knitted his brows, looking to Boris and Basil for an explanation. "I do not understand. What is this drift I am supposed to catch?"

Karloff and Basil took the Hungarian aside as Boris explained; "I think, to use one of your own quaint expressions, she thinks we are 'sissy boys.'"

"ME! A sissy boy?" Lugosi raged, casting Karloff an affronted glare that could penetrate a London fog. "Just who is this Julian Walker?"

"Well," Boris ventured to explain, trying to find the right way to express it, "he—impersonates ladies."

"He does what?"

"He's a transvestite," said Rathbone.

"What is that?" asked Bela.

"A man who likes to dress in women's clothing," Boris muttered uncomfortably.

"But," Rathbone explained, "even though he likes to wear women's clothes, he likes to sleep with women."

"That is crazy!" exclaimed Bela. "What woman would sleep with a man dressed like a woman?"

Boris shrugged. "I suppose you could ask Julian."

"If Julian Walker sleeps with ladies why would Mae think I am a sissy boy?"

"I suppose because," said Rathbone, "transvestites are easily mistaken for drag queens, who ARE homosexual."

Bela stormed up to Mae's plush throne. "Supply me with a woman," he demanded. "NO! I want THREE women, any three women! I will show you which way Bela—I mean, CHARLIE, which way Charlie swings!"

Leering suggestively Mae nodded her approval. "Now that's the 'Chollie' I know." She reached for a button mounted on the small end table and pressed it three times. Right on cue, three ladies entered the library, the living images of Lana Turner, Barbara Stanwyck, and Joan Crawford.

Rathbone whispered to Karloff, "There's your explanation for Jean Harlow's ghost. It's not only Miss West who's a lookalike. The ladies who work here are all simulacra of famous actresses."

"You rang, Miss West?" asked "Lana Turner."

"Mae West" rose from her throne and addressed the stars. "Evenin', ladies," said Mae, "'Chollie' is here to see yah," indicating Lugosi. "Mmmm, and he says he can handle all three of yah at once. Now that I'd pay real money to see."

"Not only lookalikes," Basil remarked to Boris, "but call girls as well. Apparently Mae's is a most unique bordello."

"Good evening, my dears," Bela intoned in his classic Dracula delivery as he took a step forward, gazing hungrily at the ladies.

Boris stepped in to block Lugosi's way. "Bela, we don't have time for this. Besides, you're a married man."

"We get us a lot of married men," Mae said as she primped before the mirror.

"Boris is quite right, Bela, old boy," said Rathbone. "In your haste to prove your manhood, don't forget our reason for being here." He addressed Mae. "We want to hire Mr. Walker for a job that requires his talent for disguises."

"As a bodyguard," Boris added, quickly.

She draped her arm on the mantle and said, "If yah wants to hire Julian, yah'll have to go through me. I guess yah could say I'm his agent."

Karloff conceded the point. "That seems reasonable."

Mae told Della to escort the three ladies out so she could conduct business. Once they were alone, Mae invited her guests to join her by the fire. She sat down, put her feet up and said, "All right, gen'lemen, gimme the lowdown."

Boris said, "To begin with, I'm Boris Karloff."

"I know who yah are," Mae said, sipping her brandy. "All three of yah are pretty recognizable."

"Well, I've recently received a number of threatening fan letters and my wife is laid up in hospital. I want Julian act as a bodyguard and impersonate a private nurse."

Mae sat quietly and pursed her lips while absently swirling around the amber liquid. Finally, she said in full character, "Yah can have Julian for $250 a day. Make all checks payable to 'Billie Bennett' and I'll give him his cut after I deduct my 10 percent."

"Who's Billie Bennett?" asked Boris.

"I'm Billie Bennett," Mae said. "I'm just part of the window dressin', and very nice window dressin', I am, too. So like I said, the fee is $250 a day."

Rathbone intervened. "That's rather steep, wouldn't you say?"

"Maybe," said Billie Bennett AKA "Mae West," "but yah gotta remember that yah'll be takin' Julian away from me for the next two weeks. He supervises hair, makeup, and wardrobe. Yah don't think I just hire Lana Turner or Barbara Stanwyck lookalikes off the street, do yah? If yah ask me, $250 a day is gettin' off mighty cheap, but I'm bein' generous because," and she finished her sentence with a breathy lilt, "I'm a BIG Boris Karloff fan." She gave Boris a flirtatious smirk. "Perhaps yah might wanna come up and see me some time."

Boris stepped back but remained polite. "Miss Bennett, although I do appreciate the invitation, I'm afraid I must decline. However, I do accept your fee for Mr. Walker's services."

Billie Bennett obviously wasn't used to rejection. Her come-hither look turned quickly cold. She pushed the button on the end table.

Moments later, Della appeared at the library door. "Yes, Miss West?" she said.

With a decided chill in her voice but still in character, Mae said, "Take these gen'lemen to meet Julian."

"Yes, Miss West," the maid curtsied and gestured for the men to follow. "This way, please."

**Who Framed Boris Karloff?**

## Chapter Fifteen

### Julian/Julie

### Mae's, Somewhere in the Hollywood Hills

Della led the three gentlemen into a long and impressively furnished dining room that was lit with the same illusion preserving half-light as the rest of the establishment. The only other light source came from votive candles at each of the small tables where clientele sat with their actress lookalikes, enjoying their drinks and listening to the music. Two coffee-colored maids, each wearing the same identical black uniform and white apron and caps, were taking dinner orders or serving drinks.

At the far end of the dining room, a handsome ebony-colored man with short straightened hair and a pencil thin mustache accompanied "Alice Faye" on the grand piano while a tall black man stood beside the blond actress and played sax. As the pianist's nimble fingers played lightly over the keys he flashed the new arrivals a pleasant smile and a nod.

Pausing at the entrance, Boris whispered to Rathbone, "I say, isn't that Teddy Wilson at the piano? And the chap playing the saxophone, that's Lester Young!"

Rathbone gave the pianist and sax player a jaundiced-eyed look. "One could say they at least *look and play* like Teddy Wilson and Lester Young."

Bela indicated "Alice Faye" with a nod. "I take it that woman isn't really a woman?"

Basil studied the singer and was noticeably impressed. "You were right, Boris. Mr. Walker is indeed a remarkable female impersonator."

Bela shook his head disapprovingly. "I don't know how you know him, Boris, but you would never catch me associating with a man who wears women's clothing."

Della led the party to a table with four chairs. She whispered and nodded in "Alice Faye's" direction, "Mr. Walker will be with you after this song, sirs. If you're hungry, I can get you the house menu. Can I get you anything to drink?"

Boris ordered a vodka tonic, Rathbone a gin and tonic on the rocks, and Bela a Manhattan.

Rathbone, always one to get to the point, spread the newspapers out before them and said, "We ought to get down to business while we wait."

Boris said, "We may as well wait for Julian to join us. The song will be over in a few minutes."

"Besides," added Bela, holding the votive candle over the newspapers and squinting, "the light in here, it is too dim to see anything."

"Very well," sighed Basil, putting the newspapers away. He asked Bela, "How did your interrogation of Jack Pierce go?"

"I learned nothing," Bela scowled. "He shut up as tight as an oyster."

"Clam," Karloff corrected.

"That, too."

"I was able to question Rowland," said Boris. "From what he told me it would seem Pierce has good reason to keep his mouth shut."

"Oh?" said Rathbone.

"There was no bloodstain on the rug at 9:30 but there WAS greasepaint on the INSIDE doorknob of Murphy's office. I suspect Jack may have paid Mr. Murphy an unexpected visit."

"There was greasepaint on the inside doorknob, but not the outside doorknob?" Rathbone said thoughtfully. "Curious."

"Furthermore, it appeared to Rowland that Jimmy Whale had been drugged. Oh, AND—" Boris added excitedly, "there were THREE brandy snifters, so there must have been a third guest. Perhaps Pierce?"

"Or the owner of the mysterious monogrammed handkerchief," Rathbone said as his eyebrow arched and he steepled his fingers.

"BAH!" scoffed Bela. "Always you look for the most dramatic explanation! The photographer was there taking pictures. So the photographer was offered a drink. As the Americans say, 'Big deal.'"

"I doubt the third party was a lowly photographer," said Rathbone, deep in thought. "Obviously it was another executive."

"Perhaps it was Cliff Work," posited Boris, his eyes growing wide with excitement. "What if Cliff Work was covering up his OWN murder? Suppose HE killed Murphy?"

"A pity we don't have the glasses," Rathbone sighed. "If we had the glasses, we could lift their fingerprints. Then we'd have some actual physical evidence to work with instead of a lot of guesswork. Witness testimony is often so unreliable. But such is the life of the amateur detective."

"Speaking of witness testimony," said Bela. "Did you speak to *your* suspect yet?"

"I had to take Ouida to the train station, remember? Not to worry. I'll speak to Mr. Whale just as soon as I come up with a reasonable excuse for an audience."

"Oooo," Bela mocked. "That should be easy for you, the Great Detective. Just become Whale's shadow. Be the puppet master. Pull the strings! BAH! Your advice got me nowhere!"

Basil glared at Bela.

Hoping to change the subject, Boris asked, "So, uh, Basil, what train is Ouida taking?"

Ignoring the Hungarian, Basil said, "She's taking the *City of Los Angeles*. She'll arrive in Chicago at 12:15 p.m. Central Time on the 29th," he said, sounding very Sherlockian as he rattled off the timetable from memory, "then take the *20th Century Limited* leaving La Salle Street at 4 o'clock. She'll arrive in New York on Wednesday morning at Grand Central Terminal at 9 o'clock Eastern Time."

As they talked, Lester Young took center stage for the instrumental portion of the song while "Alice Faye" leaned against the grand piano and smiled seductively. She, or rather, *he* was a perfect likeness of Miss Faye, the bouncing blonde curls, the red lips and arched eyebrows. A glittering diamond ring was displayed on her, or rather, *his* delicate hand. The form-fitting dress showed not a single betraying bulge; every curve was womanly. The musical solo gave way to her next refrain as she sang,

"Oh, you nasty man.

"Taking your love on the easy plan.

"Here and there and where you can

"Oh, you nasty man—."

Della came back with their drinks on a silver platter. As she set them down on a coaster, Karloff remarked, "I'm really quite impressed with Mr. Walker's talents."

"Indeed, sir," Della agreed as she cast a come-hither look in the musical trio's direction. "In fact, Julian looks good enough that I'd like to have a piece of him myself."

The three men did a double take.

"Can I get you folks a menu?" she asked.

"Um, no, thank you," said a stunned Karloff.

"Enjoy the show, sirs." Della curtsied and left to get other drink orders.

Lugosi broke the stunned silence. "Maybe there is something to this dressing like a woman to attract women."

Rathbone snickered and nudged Boris. "Oh, yes, he's such a 'man of the world.'"

After "Alice Faye's" number the dining room filled with muted applause. "Take five, boys," she said to her musical accompaniment and sashayed over to Boris, Basil, and Bela's table. The three gentlemen, forgetting that this wasn't really a woman, instinctively rose for her. "Alice Faye" smiled and slinked past them to another table and sat down with two gentlemen.

"Now what was *that* all about?" remarked Rathbone.

Boris could only shrug.

Teddy Wilson stepped up to their table and pulled out a chair. "Evenin', Boris. Been a long time, ain't it?" the colored man said in a distinctly Liverpoolian accent.

All three men stood with their mouths agape as "Teddy Wilson" sat down and reached into the inner pocket of his jacket with his white-gloved hand and produced a packet of Camels. "So, I 'ear you wanna 'ire me for a job. So who do I have to kill?" He lit his cigarette and extinguished the match by waving it in the air. He noticed the look of shock on the three men's faces and said, "I was only jokin' about 'avin' a bloke killed."

Basil broke the stunned silence. "You mean, YOU'RE Julian Walker?"

"Teddy Wilson" flashed a set of pearly white teeth that shined brightly in contrast to his dark skin. "The one and only."

Bela eyed the impersonator narrowly and said to Karloff, "You didn't say he was a colored man!"

"He isn't," said a very flustered Boris Karloff. "Or at least, I didn't think he was."

"God, blimey," exclaimed "Teddy Wilson" AKA Julian Walker, "ain't you three a sight."

Suddenly, another Teddy Wilson, the real Teddy Wilson, entered the dining room and paused to pat his lookalike on the back. "Thanks for covering for me, Julie."

"Don't mention it, Ted. Thanks for sittin' for me little experiment."

"Anytime, man," Teddy Wilson said.

As Teddy sat at the piano and began playing Thomas "Fats" Waller's "Ain't Misbehavin,'" Julian turned back to the three gentlemen who were still standing dumbstruck. "Will you blokes sit down," chastised Julian, pulling off his white gloves to reveal a pair of delicately tapered Caucasian hands with nails painted in red polish. "And close up your mouths before a fly buzzes in."

The three men took their seats as Boris said, "That's the most remarkable makeup job I've ever seen."

"What, this?" Walker said, indicating his face. "Foam rubber and a dab of spirit gum, mate. That's all it is."

"I'd have to concur with Mr. Karloff," Rathbone said, picking up the votive candle and holding it up to Julian's black face. "Unless the light in here adds to the effect, you could pass for Teddy Wilson's identical twin."

"All part of the process," said Julian as he puffed away on his cigarette. "Ted let me make a mold of 'is face and from that I fabricated the pieces. It's the pores in the skin that's the convincer. People may not be conscious of pores, but sense if they ain't there."

Bela looked more annoyed than impressed. "I thought you said he dresses like a woman! Was that just a lie to make fun of Bela? He is not a woman impersonator. He is a minstrel man!"

Julian smiled, hunched forward and whispered to Bela, "If it 'elps any, not only 'ave I painted me nails, I'm wearin' a pair of pink silk knickers and black stockin's right now."

Bela recoiled. "It doesn't help. Stay away from me."

"I do apologize for my friend's behavior," said Boris. "This is all a bit much for Mr. Lugosi to absorb."

"Nah, I ain't offended," said Julian with a dismissive wave. "Look, finish your drinks and let's go downstairs where I can take this makeup off and we can have a bit of a chin wag. I'll even give you a behind-the-scenes grand tour, if you like."

"Now that," remarked Basil Rathbone, "should be most illuminating."

## Chapter Sixteen

## The Grand Tour

### Mae's, Somewhere in the Hollywood Hills

In the backstage area down in the basement, Julian explained, "We get costumes from all the big pictures." He was still disguised as Teddy Wilson as he conducted a tour of the clothing racks. "Western Costume Company, M-G-M, Twentieth, even Universal Studios." He pulled a glittering gown off the rack and held it up to his chin, admiring his reflection in a full-length mirror. "For instance, this 'ere gown was worn in a Busby Berkley number. Looks good on me, don't you think?"

Boris and Basil remained politely taciturn, while Bela sneered contemptuously.

"Yeah, you're right," Julian said studying his reflection more closely. "It ain't me color."

He hung the dress back up and led them into the fitting room. With a grand flourish, he indicated a kneeling heavyset woman pinning up the hemline on "Marlene Dietrich's" dress. "And this old rat bag—," he began, only to have the fake Marlene Dietrich, who was standing on a chair and reading a copy of *Variety*, look up from her magazine and glare at him. He said to her, "I don't mean you, luv, I meant the OTHER rat bag." He tried to give the old Jewish woman a kiss, only to be pushed away.

"Ahhhhh, don't come near me while you have that junk on your face!" she said.

"You love it," Julian chided. "Just call this dear sweet old lady 'Mrs. Nussbaum,' you know, like in Fred Allen's bit 'Allen's Alley.'"

"Charmed, Mrs. Nussbaum," said Boris graciously.

"She's a bit of a frump," Julian joked. "But we love her anyway."

The seamstress wagged a finger at Julian and chided, "Don't go sweet talking me, Mr. Sticky Fingers. I know you've been stealing all the silk underwear."

In the hairdressing and makeup department, an effeminate voice shouted sarcastically, "You call that a foundation? This is a bordello, deary, not a funeral parlor!"

"Uh oh," said Julian. "They're at it again."

Julian led the way as a second voice retorted, "What about that rat's nest hairdo? Really, honey, you should just let the poor girl stick her finger in a light socket."

"This here is 'Damon' and that's 'Pythias,'" Julian said, indicating the two beautifully made up young men working on a call girl. "They're the 'ouse makeup man and 'airdresser, respectively. They're on me staff and the best in the business. Just ask either of 'em. As for Janet 'ere," he said, indicating the lookalike Janet Gaynor, who, like "Marlene Dietrich," had her nose buried in a Hollywood gossip magazine, "she's doin' a bit of bonin' up."

"Hello," she said, and returned to reading her magazine as the two stylists busied themselves with her hair and face.

"All the girls are required to know every bit of gossip about the actress they're impersonating. Right, deary?"

"Uh huh," "Janet Gaynor" said absently as she turned to the next page.

Damon looked up from what he was doing and spied the visitors' reflections in the makeup mirror. He dropped his makeup brush and put his hands to his mouth in utter star-struck astonishment. "Oh my god! Boris Karloff, Basil Rathbone, and Bela Lugosi!" He turned to face them and gasped, "Look, honey, it's really them!"

Pythias looked up from his work and joined his lover in abject admiration, frantically fanning his face with his hand to keep from fainting. "Oh, God, Mr. Lugosi, I must have seen *Dracula* 57 times! Those eyes just DO something to me!"

Bela wasn't quite sure how to accept the compliment. After a moment of awkward silence, he ventured a simple, "Thank you."

Damon was practically on his knees before Boris Karloff. "PLEASE, Mr. Karloff, could you introduce me to Jack Pierce? He's my IDOL!" He gave Miss Gaynor a scowl of disdain. "All I ever get to do around here is make women look *beautiful*. Just once, I'd like to make someone look like a fiend!"

Pythias sniped, "Judging from this poor girl's makeup, honey, you've got your wish."

"Why you bitch!" said Damon as he grabbed a bottle of conditioner and prepared to clobber his lover over the head with it.

With the ease of a former soldier practiced in hand-to-hand combat, Julian quickly disarmed Damon. "Now, now, boys. Not in front of the company." He discarded the bottle. "I got private business with me guests, so off it, the three of you."

Once the door was closed and Julian was sure his staff was out of earshot, he turned to Boris and asked, "Now, what can I do for you?"

Boris said, "My wife is in hospital and I've received a number of threatening obsessed fan letters. I need someone to look after her. I naturally thought of you."

Julian sat down before the makeup mirror and grabbed the bridge of his nose and then peeled off the first of several foam rubber appliances, exposing lily-white skin. "Yeah, we get fans like that around 'ere sometimes. Every room has a panic button, just in case. So you want me to look after the Missus, eh?"

"Exactly."

"Not to worry, Boris," Julian said as he peeled back the forehead piece. "I can lick anybody my size and then some."

"But she isn't to know you're a bodyguard."

"Yes," Rathbone interjected. "We want you to pose as a private nurse and remain in character the whole time. Dorothy is to suspect nothing."

"Not a problem, mate," Julian assured them as he slowly peeled away a pair of fake lips and a chin piece. "'Ell, I even have a nurse's uniform that will suit the situation just fine and dandy. A little fantasy number I snagged for meself a while ago."

"Of course," Karloff noted, "that means you'll have to act as though you actually were a private nurse, which would include things like changing dressings and so forth."

Smearing cold cream on his face, Julian said, "Easy as pie, mate. I was a field medic. If I can 'andle 'ead wounds and missing limbs, I can surely take care of your Missus right enough."

"Excellent," said Boris with satisfaction. "We'd like you to start right away."

"Tomorrow mornin' okay?" Julian asked as he wiped off the last of the brown makeup.

"That would be splendid," said Rathbone, fascinated by Julian's sudden transformation from a black man to a Caucasian transvestite. Rathbone put the newspapers down on the makeup table and examined one of the discarded foam rubber pieces. He asked, "Is this a technique you invented?"

"Nah," said Julian. "There's been a bunch of us makeup men tinkerin' around with the foam rubber formula. But just between us, I'm the best there is. I get plenty of opportunity to experiment 'round 'ere."

"Really?" Basil said. "There's no one else in the field that's your equal?"

"Not in my opinion," Julian said examining his face for any makeup he might have missed. "And I ain't the only one who thinks so, neither. The late Mr. Martin F. Murphy 'imself would 'ave told you likewise."

"Martin Murphy?" Boris exclaimed. "You knew Murphy?"

"'Ere, do you think I want to spend the rest of me life workin' in a fancy 'ollywood bordello?" He turned away from the mirror to address Boris. "I've got ambition, mate. I showed Murphy me portfolio and told 'im I could make you up in 'alf the time it takes Jack Pierce. 'E seemed to go straight for it. Murphy even let me use 'im as a guinea pig, so I could demonstrate me technique."

Basil's eyebrow crooked and his nostrils began to flare. "How very interesting. What exactly did you do for this demonstration?"

Julian shrugged. "It took a couple of days. The first day, I cast Murphy's life mask, then made some foam rubber appliances and 'ad 'im come back the next day so I could do a bit of special effects makeup on 'im."

Boris asked, "And was he impressed?"

"Blimey, yes! Mr. Murphy said 'e was sold on the whole thing and wanted me to be the new 'ead of the makeup department at Universal. Imagine that, me the new Jack Pierce. 'E said all that was needed was to tie up a few loose ends and I was in."

"Loose ends like firing Jack Pierce?" Boris asked.

"Yeah, I guess." Julian looked guilty as he said, "Personally, I didn't fancy bein' the reason for Pierce gettin' the sack. I mean, 'e's a legend, ain't 'e? But Murphy was dead set on 'irin' me." He shrugged and turned back to the makeup mirror. "Too bad Murphy kicked the bucket like 'e did. Me career as a studio makeup artist went right up the spout when 'e croaked."

Rathbone gave Boris and Bela a haughty smile as he proclaimed, "Means, motive, and opportunity, gentlemen."

Julian gave their reflections a quizzical frown. "What's that supposed to mean?"

"Oh, nothing," Basil said, hastily. "Um, what became of Murphy's life mask? Might we see it?"

Julian shook his head. "Don't know what 'appened to it. Somebody must 'ave knicked it. Pity about Murphy," he added, looking dejected. "I could never be just a staff makeup artist, not with the way Pierce feels about me technique.

I 'ear 'e growls at you if you even mention foam rubber. So, I guess I'll be stuck 'ere for a bit. Mind you, it's not a bad job as jobs go. The Dragon Lady can't say enough good things about me and the girls love me, in every sense of the word." He shrugged the matter off and said, "Anyway, not to worry, Boris. The Mrs. Karloff is in good 'ands and won't suspect a thing."

Suddenly, a red light bulb mounted over the mirror began to flash. The flashing coincided with a buzzer.

"What is that?" asked Basil.

Julian jumped up, his jaw set. "That's Mae's panic button." The crash of overturning furniture came through the basement ceiling. "Come on, you can watch me throw a bloke out!"

The sound of breaking glass filled the stair hall. Julian, Boris, Basil, and Bela pushed through the gathering throng.

Julian hurried to Della and asked, "What's the story, luv?"

"I-I don't know," Della insisted. "This drunken crazy woman pushed right past me like she knew exactly where Miss West would be!"

More breaking glass, a scream, the shattering of something very costly, then the drunken woman's threats came through loud and clear, "Tell me where he is or I'll cut your throat with this, you lousy whore!"

Bela smirked. "Someone's wife looking for her husband, I think."

"Perhaps," Rathbone suggested tauntingly, "Lillian decided to follow us in your car."

"She wouldn't dare," Lugosi said confidently, then his expression grew less confident as more sounds of violence came from the library. "At least, I don't think she would."

Julian bolted into the fray, obviously ready for anything. Whatever he saw in the library made him stop dead in his tracks. Furniture was overturned, vases and statuary smashed to pieces, the large over-mantle mirror was reduced to jagged shards of broken glass glinting on the lush carpet. Mae was wielding a brass fireplace poker while the intruder, a very attractive brunette who looked as if she hadn't slept in several days, had grabbed a large jagged piece of broken mirror and held it like a dagger. Julian took one look at the crazed intruder and exclaimed, "LEGS!"

The brunette briefly took her eyes off Mae and squinted drunkenly at Julian. Her expression changed from demonic fury to sudden recognition as she exclaimed, "Julie? Is that you?"

"It's me, baby! I don't mind tellin' you, you look like you've seen better days."

Mae looked from the intruder to Julian and growled, "What the hell is this, old home week? Throw the bitch out!"

"Ahh, she's 'armless," Julian said with a dismissive gesture. "This 'ere is Toni Lanier, the dame with the million dollar legs. We toured together with the Ziegfeld Follies." He smiled, holding out his hand. "'Ere, luv," he said, "gimme the broken glass. We wouldn't want you cuttin' yourself, now would we?"

"Legs" looked from the shard in her hand over to where Mae stood ready to strike. "I will if SHE puts the poker down."

"Mae?" Julian scolded.

"I ain't leavin' myself defenseless around that psychopath!" Mae raised the weapon over her head.

"MAE!" Julian said sternly. "Put it down or I'll take it from you!"

"Mae West," or rather, Billie Bennett, looked from Julian to "Legs" and back to Julian. After a tense moment she exclaimed, "Ah, what the hell!" and tossed the poker aside.

Julian looked expectantly at "Legs." He said, "Come on, luv. Give it to Julie."

A tense moment passed, then "Legs" caved and handed Julian the shard. She broke down and sagged to her knees and started crying. "Where is he, Julie?" she sobbed. "Where's my Eddie?"

"He ain't been around here since Friday," Mae said with venom. "I tried to tell her that and she wouldn't believe me!"

"I KNOW she's lying," the woman sobbed. "Eddie's been gone for four days! He got a phone call late at night, somebody calling in a favor. He said he'd be back but he never came back! Eddie would never leave me that long without calling, not my Eddie!"

"Er, excuse me," Rathbone interjected. "Am I to understand that you are Eddie Mannix's wife?"

The woman sniffed as she wiped her eyes. As Julian helped her to her feet, she said, "I'm Eddie's girl." The instant Toni's bloodshot eyes spotted Boris, they grew bright with renewed fury. She lunged forward and shrieked, "YOU KNOW WHERE EDDIE IS! TELL ME, YOU BASTARD! I KNOW YOU HAD SOMETHING TO DO WITH THIS!"

Julian tackled her. "Take it easy, 'Legs,'" he said, getting on top of her and trying to pin her down, "let's not get all in a tizzy again!" He straddled Toni's midsection and got a firm grip on her wrists.

She struggled to free herself. "I KNOW YOU KNOW SOMETHING!" she screamed at Boris, "TELL ME! TELL ME!"

Julian looked up at Karloff. "You'd better say somethin' fast, mate."

In as soothing a voice as he could muster Boris said, "Mr. Mannix was last seen at the Rosedale Crematory earlier this afternoon. I didn't see him there myself, but I was told that's where he was by a very reliable source."

"There, you see?" Julian said to the woman struggling under him. "Eddie was all right earlier today. Why, I wouldn't be at all surprised if 'e's 'ome right now waitin' on you and wonderin' where his Toni is."

Toni stopped her struggling and looked imploringly up at Julian. "Do you really think so?" she sniffed, sounding like a lost little girl.

"I do, indeed," Julian said with confidence. "Now if I let you up, do you promise to behave? That means no more tantrums, no more threatening people with broken glass, and definitely leavin' the boss lady alone. Do you promise?"

"I promise, Julie," Toni nodded wearily. "I promise."

Slowly, Julian let go of Toni's wrists, then very slowly got up from on top of her and offered his hand to help her to her feet. Toni looked embarrassed as she tried to fix her tangled hair and smooth out her torn dress. She looked chagrinned at Boris and slurred, "I'm sorry for the way I acted."

Boris smiled. "That's quite all right. No harm done."

Julian put his arm around Toni's shoulder and hugged her. "Come on with me, luv, Auntie Julie will find you some new duds."

Mae glowered at Julian. "Oh, REALLY? That dame turns my library into a garbage dump and you wanna give her the pick of MY costumes?" She gestured wildly at the debris all around her. "Who the hell is gonna pay for all this? Why, I oughta have the cops lock that bitch up and throw away the key!"

"I wouldn't do that, if I was you, angel," Julian cautioned.

"And why not?"

"This 'ere's Eddie's girl. And if that ain't reason enough, you know the blokes Eddie 'angs out with. If they 'ear you've been nasty to Toni, well, it might not be too 'ealthy 'round 'ere for you."

Upon hearing this, Mae's whole demeanor changed. She smiled and tittered nervously and picked at her fingernails, "Oh, well, any friend of Eddie's is a friend of mine. Uh, Julian, (hee, hee) why don't you take Toni down to the wardrobe department and let her find somethin' nice. It's on me." She forced a smile.

Julian gave Mae a friendly smile back. "Now that's the generous Mae I've come to know and love." He chucked Toni under the chin. "So, what you say, angel? We go down and do a bit o' shoppin', eh? We wouldn't want Eddie to see you lookin' like this, would we?"

Toni smiled drunkenly. "No. I wanna look nice for Eddie."

"Then that's what we'll do, baby. We'll make you look swell for Eddie. I'll get Damon and Pythias to do up your 'air and makeup while we're about it. You'll be a real stunner, you will!"

"Okay."

"'Ere we go, then," he said, leading the intoxicated Miss Lanier out of the library.

Mae waited for Toni to be well out of earshot before she reverted back to her usual cast iron self. She glowered at Karloff and his friends and said,

"I don't know what the hell you have to do with all this, but I think it's time you boys scrammed outta here."

Rathbone took Boris' arm and said, "I couldn't agree more. Thank you for your hospitality."

"Just get the hell out. You heard me, HIT THE ROAD!"

"Good evening," said Boris. He and Basil departed.

Bela lingered a moment.

Mae started picking up the pieces and found an unbroken statuette and was about to put it back on the mantle when she noticed Bela still standing there and said, "Well, what the hell are you waitin' for?"

After the most pregnant of pauses, Bela said hopefully, "I come back next Saturday, yes?"

Mae violently threw the only remaining piece of unbroken bric-a-brac at Lugosi. "GET THE HELL OUT AND DON'T COME BACK!"

Bela ducked just in time. He looked back at where the statuette smashed against the wall and turned and said to Mae, "That's all right, we talk later."

Bela exited, leaving Mae to rage in private.

## Chapter Seventeen

## The End to a Perfect Evening

As Boris and Basil left the club, Boris said, "Well, what do you make of all that?"

"I don't know," said Rathbone. "Obviously whatever Eddie Mannix was hired to do took a great deal of arranging if he hasn't been home since that morning in Cliff Work's office."

"Yes," said Boris. "Unless something's happened to Mannix, too."

"Indeed," Rathbone said, lighting a cigarette and pausing to think. "It wouldn't be in the killer's best interest for Mannix to disappear. Quite the reverse, in fact."

"Or Julian is right and Mannix is home waiting for Miss Lanier to put in an appearance."

"Precisely," said Rathbone, puffing away thoughtfully. "One detail that strikes me as interesting, though, is why would Eddie Mannix, right in the middle of a cover up, visit a brothel?"

"Mae said he was here Friday night."

"Yes, but why?"

Bela, who had just come up behind them, said, "You English obviously don't understand a man's appetites. It doesn't matter what a man is doing, when he wants a woman, he wants a woman!"

"Yes, that must be it," Rathbone said, rolling his eyes. "How stupid of me."

"Or," Bela said with a shrug, "he was here to steal the life mask."

Rathbone gave Bela a double take. "What did you say?"

"That Walker, he said he didn't know what became of the life mask he made of Murphy. Maybe it was Mannix who stole it to make the dummy we saw at the funeral."

Rathbone turned to Karloff and smiled. "By Jove, I think he's hit on it!"

"But what about the mask missing in Jack's studio?"

Rathbone puffed on his cigarette and paced furiously. "We know from what Rowland said that there was no blood on the carpet at 9:30 p.m., BUT there was greasepaint on the inside doorknob, meaning Pierce was there at some point!"

"And," Boris said, "we know from what Julian told us that Murphy was going to fire Jack and replace him with Julian."

"PRECISELY!" Rathbone declared dramatically. "Now, couple that with the broken life mask in Pierce's studio. Murphy visits Pierce at the studio and tells him he's to be sacked—."

"AH!" exclaimed Lugosi. "So Pierce strikes Murphy with the mask and kills him!"

Boris thought for a moment and shook his head. "How did little Jack Pierce," he held up his hand to Pierce's approximate height, "drag Murphy's body back to his office and THEN use the studio cart to take the body to Stage 7?"

"And," interjected Lugosi, "what about the blood on the carpet?"

"Gentlemen, please!" said Rathbone, gesturing like a cop halting traffic. "One thing at a time!" After a pause, he said, "I suggest we convene at an all-night diner. Perhaps an examination of those photographs in the newspapers—" He stopped abruptly and looked under his arm and patted his jacket pockets. "Blast and thunderation!" he raged.

"What's the matter?" asked Boris.

"The newspapers!" He looked back at the mansion and said with annoyance, "I'm an idiot! I must have left them down in the makeup room!" He was about to go back when Boris grabbed his arm.

"I really don't think it would be wise to go back just now, Basil. Leave them. We can always pick up more copies at a newsstand."

Basil seemed hesitant, but relented. "I suppose you're right. It's just the Scotsman in me doesn't relish the loss of 15 cents."

"Besides," said Bela, "it is getting late and Boris and I, we have 5:30 makeup calls."

"Yes," Boris said, checking his watch. "It's nearly 11 now. The studio will be sending a car for me at 5 a.m. and I really need to get some sleep."

Bela started and glowered at Karloff. "The studio sends for you a car?"

Karloff realized he had let the cat out of the bag and tried to soften the blow. "Well, it's more of a taxi, really."

"They send for you a car and Bela has to have his wife drive him to the studio every day?"

"Well, you DO live close to the studio."

"Oh, yes," the Hungarian sneered, "you are so far away. You're only 20 minutes from the studio!" Bela crossed his arms and knitted his brows. "We will speak no more of this matter! Bela is very upset and will have a word with—well, whoever new is now in charge of studio production!"

Basil looked from Boris to an angry Bela Lugosi and shook his head. "All for one, and one for all, indeed."

**Chapter Eighteen**

**28 November 1938, 4:00 a.m.**

**Rude Awakening**

The telephone awoke Boris with a start. He fumbled for the receiver. "Hello?" he asked, still in a daze.

"Good morning, Mr. Karloff," a young woman's voice said. "This is the Universal Studios switchboard with your 4 o'clock wakeup call."

Boris suddenly remembered where he was. He was back on "The Farm." It was early Monday morning and time for him to get ready for work. "Oh, yes," he said to the operator. "Thank you."

"The studio car will be by to pick you up at 5 o'clock, sir."

"Thanks. I'll be ready."

He hung up the phone and threw the covers off. He had time for a quick bath, a cup of coffee and his version of an instant breakfast, namely a glass of orange juice with a raw egg floating in it. As he downed his juice with a quick gulp he saw the headlights of the studio car pass by the front windows. He threw on a jacket and grabbed the morning paper lying on the welcome mat.

A black sedan with the motor running was waiting in the driveway. Boris locked the front door to his house and got into the backseat of the sedan. "Good morning, Wally," he absently said to the driver as he opened the newspaper. When Wally didn't answer, Boris looked up and noticed someone was sitting next to him in the backseat.

And that someone was holding a gun on him.

Dwight Kemper

"Pleased to meet you, Mr. Karloff," the gunman said pleasantly.

Boris quickly reached for the car door handle only to have the gunman stick the barrel in the actor's ribs. "Uh, we'd appreciate it if you didn't run off just yet," the gunman said. He was a sharp dresser. His dark hair was slicked down and parted on the right. His long face, pointed chin, and chiseled features seemed vaguely familiar.

The driver, who definitely wasn't Wally, peered over the front seat. He had a mashed down nose and a long scar on his left cheek, reminding Boris of a Dick Tracy comic strip villain. In a voice like coarse sandpaper, the driver asked the gunman, "Where to now, boss?"

"Where the hell do you think, dummy? Santa Monica pier and step on it."

As the black sedan pulled out of the driveway the real studio car was coming up the road. Boris watched helplessly as the sedan drove past the studio car. He looked out the back window, feeling a bit like a dog being taken out to the country to be abandoned. He sighed and turned to the gunman. "I assume I'm being taken for what you chaps call 'a ride.'"

The driver said, "Yeah, a ride to the pier."

The gunman rolled his eyes and said, "He means the other kind of ride." To Karloff, he said, "Relax, it ain't that kind of ride. The boss just wants a word with you."

"And who might the 'boss' be?" asked Boris.

"Jack Dragna, and he can't wait to meet you."

Boris had read about Jack Dragna, head of the California crime syndicate.

"And you are?" Boris asked the gunman.

"Call me Ben, Ben Siegel," the gunman said. "Some guys call me 'Bugsy,' but not to my face, if you catch my drift. You know why they call me 'Bugsy,' Mr. Karloff?"

"Your hobby is entomology?"

"It's 'cause I love killing people. I really get a 'bang' out of it." He chuckled hysterically and said, "A bang out of it! Get it?" He quickly reverted to a more conversational tone as he said, "See, when I kill a guy, people say I get this look in my eye. Some guys say it's kind of a crazy, wild look. So they call me 'Bugsy,' get it?"

"I get it, yes."

Siegel nodded in the direction of the driver. "The driver there is Benny, Benny the Blade."

"Nice to meet yah," said Benny the Blade. He produced a jackknife and flicked it open, then flicked it shut and put it back in his pocket. "I'm a real fan, Mr. Karloff."

**"Uh, if it's all the same to you, I'd kind of like your autograph now. Later might not be too good."**

"Yeah," said Siegel. "We're both big fans, Mr. Karloff. See, I got me a bunch of Hollywood connections. George Raft and Cary Grant, they like to pal around with me. I'm invited to all the Hollywood parties. Of course, sometimes I have to duck out of a good party to make a hit."

"Must be inconvenient," Boris said.

Siegel reached into his pocket and produced a pad and pen. "Being that I'm a big fan and all, could I have your autograph?"

Karloff looked askance at the gunman. "Perhaps on the way back."

"Uh, if it's all the same to you, I'd kind of like your autograph now. Later might not be too good."

"I see your point." Boris took the notepad and poised to scribble his signature.

"Make it out to Ben Siegel. That's 'S,' as in 'Sam,'-i-e-g-," Bugsy spelled out, the whole time watching Karloff write out the inscription, and while keeping the actor covered with the revolver.

## Chapter Nineteen

## 28 November 1938, 7:02 a.m.

Boris was taken to Santa Monica pier where Siegel escorted him at gunpoint to a waiting water taxi. Sitting patiently in the back of the water taxi, both held at gunpoint by equally well armed and tough looking gunmen, were Bela Lugosi and Basil Rathbone.

"I see they've extended an invitation for a ride to all three of us," Boris said, sardonically.

Bela gave his "escort" a vicious scowl. "I should have been immediately suspicious when I was told a studio car was waiting for Bela!"

"Same ploy for you too, Basil?"

"Actually no," Rathbone said, matter-of-factly. "I was about to drive myself to the studio when this fine fellow popped up from my backseat." He indicated the gunman to his left.

"Mickey Cohen," the squat, dark haired tough said. He was as sharply dressed as Bugsy Siegel but seemed quite a bit rougher around the edges. "Nice to mee'cha."

Siegel joined them at the rear of the water taxi. "Well ain't this something? We got Frankenstein, Dracula, and Sherlock Holmes. Been a while, Rathbone."

"You know each other?" Boris asked.

Rathbone said, "I met Bugsy previously under less trying circumstances on the set of *The Hound of the Baskervilles*. My co-star Wendy Barrie introduced Siegel to the cast and crew."

**"Don't worry, it's a high class operation and if you're real cooperative, maybe we'll let you guys kill some time playing blackjack and chuck-a-luck."**

"Yeah, that Wendy," Siegel said, "nice ass. Now, if you'll be patient, gentlemen, we'll be on our way."

"To where?" asked Boris.

"To a little place we have anchored about three miles off shore. Don't worry, it's a high class operation and if you're real cooperative, maybe we'll let you guys kill some time playing blackjack and chuck-a-luck." Laughing wildly, he added, "Better to kill time than get killed, eh?"

Boris and his companions looked uneasily at each other as the water taxi pulled away from the dock. They sped out beyond the breakwater and past the legal limit of the anti-gambling forces to an anchored ship—a refurbished brigantine. *REX* was conspicuously painted on the hull of the ship in huge block letters.

Rathbone leaned in and whispered to Karloff, "An off-shore gambling ship. Under other circumstances this might be a pleasant outing."

The water taxi pulled along side the *REX* where it was tied off and the three celebrity guests were taken to the main office and an audience with Jack Dragna. Tony Cornero, the mobster responsible for converting the 41-year-old brigantine into a gambling ship, and two imposing bodyguards flanked Dragna. They all wore tuxedoes and looked very spiffy. Bugsy Siegel and Mickey Cohen joined Dragna and Cornero as Dragna said, "Have a seat, gentlemen."

Boris and company sat down in plush, high-backed, leather-bound chairs. The gray-haired, jowly Jack Dragna opened a box of Cuban cigars and offered them to his "guests."

"Care for a smoke, gentlemen?"

Bela reached for a cigar, only to have Rathbone slap his hand away. "Not now," he chided.

Dragna shrugged, took a cigar for himself and sat down in Cornero's chair. "Now, I suppose you're wonderin' why I've asked you fine gentlemen to join me here today."

Karloff smiled weakly, keeping an eye on Siegel. "The thought had crossed our minds, yes."

"Well," Dragna said as Cohen produced a lighter and lit Dragna's cigar, "it's like this, see? It's around 2 o'clock in the morning and I'm in a nice deep sleep when I get a phone call. And who should it be but 'Legs' Lanier. She's all hysterical about Eddie Mannix. It seems Eddie's been kind of—missing and Toni, that's 'Legs' Lanier, anyway, Toni's been real upset because he hasn't been home in four, now comin' on five days."

"I seem to recall hearing something or other about that," said Rathbone.

"Yeah," Dragna said, rolling the cigar around in his mouth and absently swiveling back and forth in the chair. "So anyway, Toni, she says somethin' about a picture in the newspaper."

Right on cue, one of the flanking tough guys produced a newspaper and handed it to Dragna. Dragna opened it up and said, "In fact, THIS newspaper." He folded the paper over, displaying a large photograph of Martin F. Murphy lying in state and his wife planting a kiss on his cheek with her hand. "She tells me she thinks that Eddie Mannix is dead and this picture proves it." He leaned forward and held the paper up for Boris, Basil, and Bela to see. "Uh, do any of you see anythin', I dunno, anythin' funny about this picture?"

Rathbone studied the photograph and shrugged, his eyebrows raised innocently. "Not particularly."

Dragna leaned back and tossed the newspaper on the desk. "To tell you the truth, neither did we. Just between us, I sometimes think Toni's a little nuts."

Bela was about to say something when Rathbone shushed him.

"Anyway," Dragna went on, "like I said, we didn't see nothin'. That is, until Toni told us what to look for."

He opened the middle desk drawer and produced a magnifying glass. Dragna handed Basil the newspaper and the magnifying glass. "Check out the ring finger on the dead guy."

Rathbone studied the picture closely.

"That's Eddie Mannix's ring," said Dragna.

Karloff took the magnifying glass and the newspaper. The details were fuzzy, but Boris definitely recognized the ring as the same ring on Eddie Mannix's finger back in Cliff Work's office.

Dragna leaned in. "Now, you tell me how Eddie's ring winds up on the hand of a dead guy that ain't Eddie Mannix. Toni gave that ring to him. It meant a lot to Eddie. He'd rather cut his own finger off than lose it and it's on the finger of a dead guy. Toni wants to know how come and so do I."

"I'm sure we don't know," said Rathbone.

"Okay, I'll give you that," said Dragna, leaning back in his chair. "Now, I guess you guys are wonderin' why we invited you here today?"

"I suppose because we were at Mae's Brothel last night and ran into Miss Lanier while she was, shall we say, upset about Eddie's disappearance?"

"Good answer," Dragna said. "But that ain't it. At least, not the whole reason."

Bela ignored Rathbone's warning look and answered, "Because we were at the funeral of that man in the picture?"

"That's partly it, too, but still not the whole answer." Dragna snapped his fingers and another tough guy reached into his pocket and produced what appeared to be a page torn out of a notepad. Dragna displayed the page. Heavy shadings of graphite revealed writing impressions scribbled on a previous page. Very clearly visible at the top of the lines of scribbling were block letters that spelled the name, "KARLOFF."

"Now," Dragna said, "guess what this is."

"Not a clue," said Rathbone.

"This was taken out of a notepad that Eddie keeps in his bedside table in case he gets a call and has to do a job. Now, Toni, who does a lot of readin', especially Raymond Chandler novels, she got the idea to rub a pencil on the page left on the notepad after Eddie tears off the top page. And YOUR name, Mr. Karloff, is at the top of the list. Along with other nasty words like 'ambulance' and 'dead body.'" He gestured with his cigar, indicating the three of them. "And since you guys have been seen together a lot lately, well, I felt it was my duty to find out what the hell's goin' on."

Dragna got up and leaned forward. "And before you open your yaps, let me remind you that Eddie 'The Bulldog' Mannix is a very dear friend of mine. Now, if you guys are keepin' any secrets from me, like what happened to Eddie, all I can say to you, Mr. Karloff, is that you better come clean and talk. Because if you don't start fillin' in a few of the blanks, there won't be enough left of you for Dr. Frankenstein to bring back to life again. You got me?"

"Clearly," said Boris. "Well, to begin with, someone tried to frame me for murder."

"Whose murder?" Dragna asked suspiciously.

Rathbone said, "The late gentleman in the newspaper, Martin Murphy. Mr. Mannix was called in to fix the matter."

"So instead of Eddie making the problem disappear," Dragna said, "Eddie disappeared." He smirked. "So what's that got to do with you guys sneakin' around all over the place and askin' questions?"

Bela said, "We are solving the case ourselves! The three of us are great detectives!"

Dragna smiled. "Listen, boys, I'm not an unreasonable man. Hell, if you guys wanna play 'I Love a Mystery,' who am I to discourage you?" He nudged Mickey Cohen and Bugsy Siegel. "Right, guys?"

"Right, boss," said Siegel. He and Cohen opened their jackets to flash their shoulder holsters and the guns in them.

"So," said Dragna, "you guys got any leads?"

Rathbone shrugged. "Nothing concrete, only speculation."

"But you guys must suspect somebody."

Bela gestured grandly. "We have many suspects. But some of them, they are not talking."

"That's no problem," Dragna said. "You give us a list and WE'LL get the answers. We got our ways of makin' guys talk."

"That's what we're afraid of," said Rathbone.

Dragna frowned. "So you don't wanna play ball?"

Affecting a calm demeanor, Basil said, "It would be irresponsible of us to accuse anyone willy-nilly."

Dragna leaned back and smiled. "It sounds to me like you guys are assumin' the responsibility of solvin' this case all by yourselves. Am I right?"

Reluctantly, the three sleuths nodded.

"Okay, fine. Leave no stone interned. But remember this. We wanna know what happened to Eddie. And we wanna know real soon."

"How soon?" asked Bela.

"Well," Dragna said, looking to Cohen, "Eddie's been missin' for five days now. Right, Mickey?"

"Right, boss."

"And me, being a business man, I believe in motivation." Dragna's steely gaze zeroed in on Basil. "Now Mickey here tells me the lovely Mrs. Rathbone is on a train with some pals for a little holiday on Long Island Sound. Nice place, too, I understand. Real exclusive like. Which, by the way, was real smart, you know, gettin' the little lady outta town so she'd be outta harm's way. The same thing with Mrs. Karloff at the hospital. The queer in the nurse's uniform, a real nice touch."

Karloff was shocked. "How did you know about—"

"Hey, we got our ways," Dragna said, smiling. "Now, seein' that Mrs. Karloff's a new mother and I have a thing for motherhood, her, we'll leave alone, and the baby, too. We don't go after kids. Same reason we'll leave Mrs. Lugosi and Bela, Jr. alone. Babies, motherhood, and apple pie. You gotta respect that." He turned to Siegel and Cohen. "Right boys?"

"Definitely, boss," said Siegel. "A kid needs their mother."

"Right," said Dragna. "But Mrs. Rathbone, she don't got no kids. And she's on a train."

Basil started to rise defiantly, only to have one of Dragna's men force him back into his seat.

"I mean, railway platforms, *very* dangerous places. Somebody could accidentally shove Mrs. Rathbone onto the tracks."

The blood drained from Basil's face.

"The *City of Los Angeles* pulls into Chicago on Tuesday and when Mrs. Rathbone changes over to the *20th Century Limited* and it leaves La Salle Street at 4 o'clock, she's gonna have company." He turned to Siegel. "Hey, Bugsy, who'd you get to meet Mrs. Rathbone in Chicago on Tuesday?"

"Pittsburgh Phil Strauss."

"Oh, he's good." He smiled warmly at Rathbone. "Pittsburgh Phil is Murder, Incorporated's top assassin—59 notches on the grip of his piece."

"A notch for each kill," added Siegel. "But Phil's got a thing for even numbers."

Dragna chuckled. "Ah, Siegel, you kill me!" He paused to take a drag on his cigar and blew a couple of smoke rings. He flicked the white ashes into a glass ashtray and smiled darkly. "I got certain friends that hang out at a certain 24-hour candy store in Brooklyn called Midnight Rose's. They wait there to get calls about doin' certain jobs, like rubbin' a bum out. This time, it'll be a call from me to go to call off the hit on your wife. So if they don't get the call, there ain't gonna be nobody on the platform to meet up with my buddy Phil when the train pulls in Wednesday morning. And if that happens," he clapped his hands together, crushing the lit cigar between them. He rubbed his hands together like a boy pulverizing dried autumn leaves. Dragna held out his open, blackened palms. "Mrs. Rathbone makes an even 60 notches."

"You wouldn't dare," snarled Rathbone.

"Try me," said Dragna.

Boris whispered, "This isn't the time for bravado, Basil. He has the upper hand."

"Listen to Mr. Karloff and you'll stay healthy," said Dragna. "And so will your wife."

He reached into his jacket and produced three business cards, which he gave to Mickey Cohen to give to his guests. "When you're ready to name a name, gimme a call, anytime, day or night. I'll take care of the rest."

Cohen handed out the cards as Dragna stood up and offered the chair to Tony Cornero. "That concludes our little meetin'. If I was you, I'd put on my Sherlock Holmes hats and start lookin' for a bad guy." He smiled and looked to his gang. "Present company excluded."

The mobsters began to laugh.

Boris, Basil, and Bela were in a less than laughing mood.

**Chapter Twenty**

**28 November 1938, 8:33 a.m.**

On the *REX*'s promenade, Seigel escorted his guests back to the boat launch and the waiting water taxi. Only the most astute individual would have noticed that the pocket where Siegel kept his hand had a distinctly gun-like bulge.

"There, you see," said Siegel, as chipper as a hungry shark that smelled newly spilled blood, "the boss is a very generous guy. Now, if it had been me, I'd have just plugged one of you guys to get the other two properly motivated." He poked Lugosi in the back with the muzzle of the hidden gun. "Probably you, Dracula. I'll bet compared to these two guys, you're nothing but a lousy sidekick. Comedy relief from the get-go."

Gun or no gun, Bela had his pride. He turned on Siegel furiously. "BELA LUGOSI IS NOBODY'S SIDEKICK!"

Karloff grabbed Lugosi's arm. The angry Hungarian wrenched his arm free and growled, "Keep out of this, Karloff! This does not concern you!" Lugosi glared at Siegel. "I am not afraid of you! YOU, you talk so big because you have a gun! I spit on you and your gun!" Lugosi let fly with two well-aimed balls of spit that hit both of Siegel's eyes. "A gypsy curse I put on you!" Lugosi declared.

Siegel blinked, breathing heavily, returning Lugosi's menacing glare with his own look of mounting rage as he pulled a monogrammed handkerchief from his breast pocket to wipe his eyes. Boris noted the monogram "B.S."

Lugosi stood there, immovable, his arms crossed defiantly. "I dare you to shoot me now!"

Siegel's face flushed red, his muscles tensed. After a nerve-wracking moment, he flashed a good-natured grin. "Gypsy curse!" he chortled as he patted Lugosi's face. "You know, I like you! You gotta lotta guts!"

Boris and Basil let out a sigh of relief as Siegel threw his arm around Lugosi's shoulder and escorted them to the boat launch. Once on shore again, Mickey Cohen took them back to Rathbone's car parked along the Pacific Coast Highway. They waited until Cohen was well out of sight, then Rathbone turned on Lugosi. "What kind of stupid, pig-headed, hare-brained, addle-pated stunt was THAT! You could have gotten us killed!"

Lugosi shrugged. "It seemed like the thing to do. You are not Hungarian, so you cannot understand."

"You listen to ME!" growled Rathbone. "This has become a deadly serious matter. I won't allow you to do ANYTHING to jeopardize my wife's safety. Do you understand?"

"What do you mean it 'has become' a serious matter? Hasn't this always been a serious matter? We are trying to find a killer, after all."

Rathbone's face transformed from a mask of rage to one of regret. He sighed heavily, turned to face the ocean and sagged defeated against his car.

Boris put a reassuring hand on his shoulder. "Basil, it's not your fault."

"He's right, Boris," Rathbone admitted. "Up until this moment our investigations have meant little more to me than a jolly puzzle to solve. If Ouida dies because of my cavalier attitude, I—I shall never forgive myself."

Boris tightened his grip. "I know, Basil. Quite frankly, I've found your 'cavalier attitude' a marvelous morale booster."

Bela kept his distance, but said encouragingly, "And look at what so far we have accomplished. We have learned much and only need a few more pieces to the puzzle."

"That's the problem," said Rathbone. "It's not a puzzle at all. We have so few clues, not even a trace of actual physical evidence. It's all hearsay."

Bela grimaced. "Oh, BOO HOO! My wife, she is right, you two are a couple of cold fishes!"

"I beg your pardon!" Karloff exclaimed.

Lugosi wagged his finger in Rathbone's face. "You, you yell at me for acting recklessly, yet it was I who faced evil and spat in his face, and here I am, alive and have my honor intact! You English, BAH!" Mockingly he said, "Ooooo, my wife, she will die. Boo hoo. Feel sorry for me."

Rathbone glared at Lugosi. "How dare you!"

Lugosi got in his face. "Be a MAN, damn you! A man fears no danger! You say you faced danger on the battlefield dressed as a tree to spy on the

Dwight Kemper

enemy? That was very 'cavalier,' was it not? What sane man would dress like a tree in No-Man's Land? It is crazy, no? Yet you got what you went after because no sane man would do such a thing and you took the enemy completely by surprise!"

"Well, I—" Rathbone said, falteringly.

"And YOU," Lugosi said, turning his ire on Boris. "It was YOU who said this was a matter of honor in the first place! And you were right! This killer, whoever they may be, is a coward who hides from us. But we shall win, and do you know why?"

"Why?" asked Boris.

"Because we have honor and we are doing what no sane man would do! So I say to you both, be cavalier! Face our enemy with good humor and determination! For we are in the right and the Fates will smile upon us!"

Rathbone blinked, and looked to Boris, who was equally dumbstruck. "My god, that was—."

"Yes?" said Lugosi, bravely confident.

"—The most utterly *ridiculous* thing I've ever heard."

"WHAT! How dare you!"

"Utterly ridiculous, and yet, so true!"

Lugosi gave Rathbone a searching look. "So, does that mean you agree with me or not?"

"By Jove, I DO agree with you, you melodramatically inclined lunatic!"

Boris looked from Lugosi to Rathbone. "Basil, are you sure you're feeling all right? You're under a lot of pressure."

Rathbone grabbed Karloff's shoulders and let out a high-spirited, and to Boris' mind, somewhat over-played yelp of defiant laughter. "My dear Boris! I feel absolutely invigorated! Quite in my prime again!" He grabbed Karloff and Lugosi in a rousing group hug. "We *shall* defeat this villain, whoever or wherever he may be! All three of us!"

Boris stood there a moment, not sure how to react to Rathbone's renewed sense of vigor. He said quietly, "If you think we have a chance, Basil, I guess I'm with you."

"I don't think, my dear Boris! I know!" said Basil.

Karloff thought to himself, "I don't think you know, either."

"Let's get back to the studio," said Basil.

"If you think you're up to driving," said Karloff.

"I've never felt more alive!" Rathbone's eyes shone with purpose. "On the way back we can conduct a skull session. To quote Mr. Dragna, 'we shall leave no stone interned.'"

Bela said, "Perhaps it would be better to call for a studio car to pick us up?" hoping to finally ride in one.

## Who Framed Boris Karloff?

## Chapter Twenty-One

### 28 November 1938, 9:20 a.m.

### Along Route 66 Heading Toward Los Angeles

"We should focus our mental powers on one fact at a time, gentlemen!" Basil exclaimed, driving a bit too fast, weaving in and out of traffic, rattling off minutiae at a furious and overly dramatic pace.

Karloff sat up front with Basil. "Did you notice Siegel's handkerchief? James had the same handkerchief that night in the makeup studio. Do you suppose Siegel killed Murphy?"

"I'm sure Siegel has his role in all this, to be sure. For instance, point one! Jack Dragna knew everything! The train Ouida was on, about your wife, about Julian Walker, everything! How did he know?"

From the backseat, where Bela had the privilege of feeling chauffeured, the Hungarian said, "Maybe it could be that this Dragna has sent Siegel to spy on us."

"Dragna seemed genuinely concerned for Mannix's welfare," said Boris, who flinched every time Basil skirted around another car. "If Siegel is involved, he's probably working behind Dragna's back. I say, Basil, I know we're late, but can't you drive a trifle more within the speed limit?"

"Oh, certainly, certainly," Basil said in quick, clipped intonations.

"Maybe," posited Bela, "Walker told them."

Rathbone shook his head. "Not a man with his war record! And Walker knew nothing about Ouida's train. No, there is only one other possible explanation. The dining room, the basement, in fact, all of Mae's Brothel, is bugged!"

Karloff said, "That makes sense, I suppose."

"The next question, gentlemen, MOVE DAMN YOU!"

Basil leaned on the horn and swerved around a pokey road hog, then sped down Route 66 at full speed.

"Regarding the problem of Eddie Mannix," he continued calmly, "what is the significance of Mannix's ring on the dummy corpse of Martin F. Murphy?"

"Well," said Boris, gripping the armrest, "I've been giving that a great deal of thought." Boris was nearly thrown against the dashboard when Rathbone slammed on the brakes to avoid colliding with a slow-moving truck. A sharp, burning pain stabbed at Karloff's lower back. "All right, Basil, that does it! Either drive more carefully or I'm taking the wheel."

Rathbone looked dazed. He smiled nervously at Karloff. "Yes, so sorry, old man. I don't know what's come over me. If you really don't mind driving, I'll take you up on your suggestion."

"Good. Now pull over—carefully!"

Basil pulled the car over and he and Boris switched places. As Boris signaled and merged into traffic, he said, "Now, as I was saying, if Eddie Mannix stole that life mask from Julian on Friday night, and he gave it to Jack Pierce to fabricate a dummy, that means Jack needed someone else's hands to cast the dummy's hands. The most convenient model would have been Eddie Mannix."

Rathbone considered this. "So, what you are proposing is that Eddie Mannix wore his ring during the casting process."

"AH!" exclaimed Bela. "That makes sense! For was it not Dragna who said Mannix would never part with that ring because of what it meant to him?"

"Exactly," said Karloff. "Which means the ring in the photograph is a copy made from that mold."

"So where does this leave us?" asked Bela. "Is Mannix dead or alive?"

Rathbone was silent a moment, then a gleam came into his eyes. "We have one of three possible alternatives, gentlemen. Either Eddie Mannix is in hiding for some reason, or Mannix is being held against his will, OR—" he said, pausing dramatically.

"Or? Or what?" Bela glowered. "Stop already with the pregnant pauses and just spit it out!"

"Toni Lanier may have been right all along. Mannix is dead and the body in the coffin wasn't a dummy at all, but Eddie Mannix wearing foam rubber makeup applications similar to the kind used by Julian Walker for his impersonation of Teddy Wilson!"

"Dear lord!" Karloff gasped. "Do you really think so?"

"There's only one way to be absolutely certain."

"How?" Bela asked.

"Bela," Rathbone inquired, "were you there for every step of the cremation?"

"Not every step, no. But I was there as the coffin was placed on the conveyor belt and it went to the oven. We were taken to an outdoor reception where we ate and people talked. It took over two hours for the ashes to be made ready. They gave to the widow an urn that was supposed to have in it the ashes. I saw with my own eyes the Widow Murphy place them there in the mausoleum in a little vault set in a pillar with other little vaults. They looked to me like safety deposit boxes in a bank."

"So, logically, if the body they cremated was a dummy, then the ashes in the urn are composed of whatever material the dummy was made from. Which would suggest that Eddie Mannix is still alive."

"That is," said Boris, "assuming they didn't substituted Murphy's cremains for the dummy's. They still had to dispose of his body, after all."

"True. If what Cliff Work said was true, Murphy's body was being cremated while the rest of us were attending the service. A dummy would have turned to ashes in mere moments. Bela said the funeral party had to wait the necessary two hours for the Widow Murphy to put the urn in its final resting-place. That suggests that a human body was being cremated. Wouldn't you agree?"

"Or the body was a dummy and they waited the required two hours before bringing out the ashes to create the illusion of a real cremation."

"Ah, but if the body they cremated belonged to Eddie Mannix, and the ring he wore was the actual gold ring, then the urn will no doubt contain the melted gold of the ring and the stone from the setting, identifying those ashes as Eddie Mannix's. Agreed?"

"Not necessarily," Boris pointed out. "It's my understanding that noncombustible things like jewelry are removed from the ashes and disposed of later."

"In a properly run crematory, perhaps. But remember there are scandals of mismanagement associated with the Rosedale Crematory; therefore it is unlikely they would follow proper procedure. That means the evidence we need is waiting for us at Rosedale Cemetery."

"Waiting for us?" Boris frowned. "Basil, what are you suggesting?"

"Isn't it obvious? Tonight, gentlemen, we shall exhume those ashes and see for ourselves if that body was a mere fabrication, or Martin Murphy, or if it was indeed Eddie 'The Bulldog' Mannix!"

Now it was Karloff's turn to slam on the brakes. He pulled over to the side of the road. "Basil, have you gone mad?"

"On the contrary," Rathbone insisted, "I think I'm being most reasonable."

"You want us to sneak around in the middle of the night and break into a mausoleum? That's illegal!"

"So is murder," Rathbone said, folding his arms and giving Karloff an arched look of defiance. "If committing a harmless act of grave desecration will insure my wife's safety, then damnation, I shall break into the vault by myself if I have to!"

After a long pause, Boris sighed heavily. "I can't let you go alone."

"CAPITAL!" Rathbone proclaimed, holding out his hand. "Then it's all for one!"

Boris gave Basil a hard stare as he switched gears and merged back into traffic. "Basil, let's not do that anymore, shall we?"

From the backseat, Bela said excitedly, "I shall bring the lanterns!"

## Chapter Twenty-Two
## 28 November 1938, 10:30 a.m.
## Universal Studios

After Boris parked Basil's car in Rathbone's private space, the three of them commandeered one of the studio carts waiting at the entrance to the parking lot. Bela checked the backseat carefully.

"What are you looking for?" Boris asked, taking the wheel.

"Blood. Around here, you cannot be too careful."

They were tooling down the broad avenue between soundstages; Basil was seated next to Boris, arms folded, deep in thought, puffing on a cigarette, reminding Karloff of a Sherlock Holmes illustration by Sidney Paget straight from the pages of the *Strand Magazine*. Finally, Basil said, "Rowland is going to pitch a fit."

"I know," said Boris. "But we can't tell him what really happened."

"Why not?" asked Bela.

"Because," Basil explained, "if we tell them we were kidnapped by gangsters, we'd have to tell them why."

Boris pulled up to Stage 7. "We have to keep our investigation a secret."

"So where have we been?" asked Bela.

Stepping out, Boris said with a shrug, "We'll just have to make up a cover story."

"I'm sure we'll think of something," Basil said confidently.

They hurried onto the laboratory set. Apart from a working "ghost light" the stage was completely dark. Boris felt a strange sense of *déjà vu*. The sound of sweeping broke the eerie silence as a balding man in his early 40s with a hairbrush mustache stepped out of the darkness pushing a broom. The unassuming stagehand wore a checkered shirt and coveralls. He looked up with a start and gawked at the three actors. "Mr. Karloff, Mr. Rathbone, Mr. Lugosi! Gee, you guys gave me a fright." He smiled and added, "But I guess that's what you're best at, isn't it? Where'd you come from?"

"I came from Lugos, Hungary," declared Bela. "So what is it to you?"

"We were unavoidably detained," Rathbone said. "Has shooting wrapped for the day?"

"Oh no," said the stagehand. "Mr. Lee and the crew are over on the Phantom Stage, shooting some interior shots with Mr. Atwill and Miss Hutchinson." In a stage whisper, he added, "Mr. Lee was fit to be tied."

"Yes, I can imagine," said Boris.

The stagehand went over to the telephone. "I guess I can call Mr. Lee and tell him that you're here. Well, just as soon as I tell the prop warehouse not to bother sending that truck."

"Truck?" asked Rathbone.

"To take away the fluoroscope," the stagehand said, gesturing at the device as he dialed. "Now that you're finally here, I'm sure Mr. Lee will want it."

Boris snapped his fingers. "The prop warehouse!"

"Well, sure," the stagehand said with a shrug. "That's where all the props are kept."

"Don't tell Rowland we're back just yet," Boris said, grabbing Basil and Bela each by the arm and rushing them toward the exit.

"Sure thing, Mr. Karloff," the stagehand called after them. "Whatever you say."

Outside the soundstage Basil wrenched himself free of Boris' grip. "What ever has gotten into you?"

"Why did you rush Bela out like that?" Lugosi said.

"I'll explain on the way," Boris said, getting in the studio cart and gesturing for his companions to do the same. Boris made a sharp turn to the left and headed down the avenue that led to the prop warehouse. "Basil, if you were going to hide a tree, where would you hide it?"

"Where would I hide a tree?" Rathbone said, nonplussed. "What does that have to do with anything?"

Boris rolled his eyes impatiently. "The furniture in Murphy's office, Basil. The truck Bela saw. What if it was a properties truck? If you wanted to lose office furniture with incriminating evidence on it, the best place to lose it is—"

"—with a lot of other furniture," Basil said, finishing Boris' thought. "And that's where you would hide a tree!"

"In the prop warehouse?" asked Bela.

"No, my friend. In a forest."

They pulled up to the huge prop warehouse, allegedly the largest in Hollywood. Inside a riot was in progress. Assistant directors, stagehands, and underlings of every description were crowded around the desk of a very harassed warehouse manager. He wore a sweat-stained brown fedora and a look of exasperation.

"ONE AT A TIME!" the manager barked over the mob. "ONE AT A TIME!"

"Where's our ambulance?" complained an assistant director.

"Nevermind his ambulance, what about our hearse?" asked a stagehand. "Our director's having fits!"

"Forget his hearse," another assistant demanded. "What about our coffin? We can't shoot a funeral scene without the goddamn coffin!"

The rotund manager pulled a rag from his back pocket and mopped his face. "We're doing the best we can but yelling at me won't get those properties to you any faster."

"What kind of a deal is this?" grumbled another. "This never happened before!"

"We checked the inventory but things ain't where they're supposed to be. I've got my boys working on it right now. Now get outta here!" The manager herded the angry mob towards the door.

"But we need that ambulance pronto!"

"We found the ambulance a couple of hours ago. You'll get it as soon as the motor pool gives it the once over. Now beat it, all of you. The rest of you will get your stuff as soon as we find it. OUT!"

He slammed the door, leaning against it and breathing a sigh of relief. He wiped his face again and returned the rag to his back pocket. It was then that he noticed Boris, Basil, and Bela. "Hey, what are you guys doing here?"

"I'm sorry to disturb you," Boris began. "I'm—"

"I know who you three are. I don't see what your beef is with me. We sent that fluoroscope over to the *Son of Frankenstein* set this morning, just like Mr. Lee wanted."

"We're not here about that. We were wondering about furniture delivered here last Thursday morning."

"We get deliveries every day," the warehouse manager said as he waddled to his desk. He took a cigar from his shirt pocket, bit off the end and spat it out. "There's stuff coming and going all the time. The question is," he said, striking a match on an upright Egyptian coffin, "what's it to you?"

Basil stepped forward. "The furniture we're inquiring about came from Martin F. Murphy's office."

"Oh," the manager said, taking off his hat respectfully. "The feller with the heart attack." Putting his hat back on, he asked, "What makes you think his furniture was delivered here? Office furniture is handled by a whole different department."

"True," said Boris. "But the furniture may have been delivered here by accident."

"Well, I ain't surprised," the manager said with a scowl. "Somebody's been messing around with my filing system. When I find out who, heads will roll, you mark my words!"

"So there is missing a coffin?" asked Bela.

"A real nice one, too," said the manager. "From one of your pictures, Mr. Lugosi. From *Dracula*." He went to a bank of filing cabinets and began searching through his records. "They'll just have to make do with another coffin."

"About the office furniture," asked Boris. "We're particularly interested in an Oriental rug."

The warehouse manager's fingers nimbly danced over file folder index tabs. "Mr. Karloff, we got hundreds of Oriental rugs. If it was delivered here by accident, that rug is as good as lost. You could search here for months and never find it."

A frightened workman ran into the office. "Dan! Dan! You gotta come upstairs quick!"

"Did you find those missing props?" the manager asked, still looking through his files.

"No, but—"

"Now see here, Lou," Dan said, pulling out a folder. "I'm only interested in the props on the list I gave you. Now go back and look for 'em."

"Listen, Dan," said Lou, swallowing hard, grabbing the manager's arm.

"Say, what's gotten into you? You look like you seen a ghost."

"I was upstairs lookin' for the props when I smelled somethin' bad. I thought that maybe it was a dead rat. But it wasn't no dead rat."

Rathbone smiled wryly. "What was it? A dead body?"

"No, sir, Mr. Rathbone," said Lou. "It was three dead bodies, Dan. Upstairs, under the stunt dummies."

"Have you been hitting the sauce again? I warned you about that!"

"I swear to you, Dan, I ain't touched a drop, but I sure want a slug now, and you're gonna want a slug or two yourself when you see them. All three of 'em got holes in 'em like Swiss cheese. It's horrible."

Boris stepped forward and demanded, "Take us there now!"

The second floor was filled to capacity with furniture, hand props, swords, guns, and statues of every shape, size and description, rack upon rack, row upon row. A sickly odor hung heavily in the musty air as they approached the area where the stunt dummies were stored. It was a smell that Basil Rathbone's wartime experiences had made him intimately familiar with. It smelled like death. Two other warehouse employees had managed to get the bodies out from under the stunt dummies and had laid the bodies out on a tarpaulin; a bloodstained blanket covered each corpse.

Rathbone smacked his open palm with his fist. "They disturbed the crime scene! The fools!"

"Steady on, Basil," said Boris.

Lou joined the two other workers and gestured at the bodies. "What are we gonna do, Dan?"

One of the other workers said, "We gotta call the police."

"Now let's not be too hasty," Dan said, wiping his face. "We'd better tell the front office first. They might have their own ideas about how to handle this."

Basil pushed his way through the small huddle of men to get a better look at the bodies. The manager blocked his way. "Sorry, Mr. Rathbone, but I think maybe you fellas ought to leave. We can take it from here."

Lugosi brazenly pushed the manager aside. "Out of the way! We are here to investigate!"

"Come again?" said the manager, scratching his head.

Rathbone said, "Don't mind him. He's researching a new role and taking it a little too seriously."

"Even so," said Boris, "we might spot something important."

"Sure," said the manager with a shrug. "If you say so." To Lou, he whispered, "Get Mr. Work on the blower."

"Sure thing, Dan."

Basil handed a notepad and pencil to Boris. "Take this down, will you, old chap?"

Pencil poised to write, Boris said, "Ready."

Lifting up the edge of the first blanket, Basil said, "The first decedent is male; dressed as an ambulance attendant, approximately 25 to 30 years old with dark hair." He looked up at Boris. "Multiple gunshot wounds to the head, chest and abdomen." He dropped the corner of the first blanket and moved to the second body.

The manager tapped his foot impatiently. "Now look here, you guys, you ain't the police. You ought to leave things be for the cops."

"Bah!" said Lugosi. "You have already disturbed the evidence by moving the bodies. What harm can Rathbone do now?"

Dan flinched and stepped back. "I'm just sayin' is all."

"The next decedent," Rathbone said, "is also male, about 35 to 40, with brown hair. He, too, is dressed as an ambulance attendant and has similar gunshot wounds." He rolled the body on its side and pulled back the collar of the uniform top. "The uniform is studio costume department issue." Rolling

Dwight Kemper

the body back over, he looked up at the manager. "Did I hear you correctly before? You found a missing ambulance?"

"Yeah. So we did."

"Where did you find it?"

"Behind one of the soundstages. It was covered over with a tarp. Clean as a whistle, though."

Rathbone nodded, then returned his attention to the first two bodies. "I'd say they were both shot with a .38 caliber weapon, either a pistol or a service revolver. Did you get that, Boris?"

"Yes."

Lifting up the blanket on the third decedent, Basil said, "The last victim is also male, wearing a Universal Studios security guard's uniform." He held the blanket edge higher to see the victim's waistline. "He's wearing a gun belt, but the holster is empty." He looked up at Karloff. "Perhaps the missing gun was the murder weapon."

"Basil, let me see his face."

"Brace yourself, Boris. It isn't pretty." Rathbone exposed the victim's face. Boris' own face turned deathly gray.

"Oh my God," he exclaimed in a whisper. "I know that man!"

"You knew Smiley?" asked Dan.

"Smiley? Uh, yes," Basil lied. "Dear old Smiley was a frequent guest on our set. An ardent admirer."

Looking grim, Boris said, "He'll be missed."

"Yeah, Smiley was a decent guy, all right. He'd stop by during his rounds and cat nap on one of the sofas."

Bela gestured at the bodies. "They must have been killed elsewhere and hidden here afterward. There isn't enough blood."

Basil covered the security guard's face with the blanket and stood up. "I agree." Smiling at the manager, he said, "Well, I think we'll turn this matter over to you, sir."

"Thanks, Mr. Rathbone. Don't worry, we'll take care of everything."

"I'm sure that you will." Gesturing to his companions, Basil said, "Boris, Bela, let's leave these men to their work."

"Oh, and Mr. Rathbone," the manager said.

"Yes?"

"Let's just keep this to ourselves. We wouldn't want to start any rumors."

"Rest assured," said Basil, "we won't gossip."

"Yes," said Bela. "Mummy is the word."

"'Mum's the word,'" corrected Boris.

"That, too."

**Chapter Twenty-Three**

**28 November 1938, 10:57 a.m.**

**Stage 28**

On the Phantom Stage where the Castle Frankenstein interiors had been erected, a full camera crew was awaiting their marching orders on the library set. Seated by the fireplace at a table set for tea were Josephine Hutchinson wearing one of Vera West's gowns and Pinky Atwill in his police inspector's uniform. Beneath the uniform, Atwill's right arm was encased in a metal framework that gave his extremity the look of an artificial prosthesis.

Looking down from a full-length portrait hanging over the mantel was Colin Clive as Baron Heinrich von Frankenstein. He wore a tie, tails, and a sash. He was posed with a small laboratory table on which was arranged exotic scientific glassware. Clive's somber expression was nothing compared to the exasperated look Rowland was giving Josie as he stood between the actors and listened to his actress complain. Josie was gesturing at a page of typed screenplay. "Really, Rowland, these lines—"

Lee shrugged. "What's wrong, Josie? The lines sound fine to me."

"Just listen to this." She cleared her throat and read aloud, "He came to lunch looking gray as a ghost and I could see he was on pins and needles so I suggested he go out into the open air for a while. But just as soon as his problem is solved he'll be as gay as a lark again." Josephine looked imploringly at her director. "Just how many clichés CAN Mr. Cooper squeeze into one paragraph, do you suppose?"

"COOP!" Rowland shouted to the screenwriter.

"Yeah?" Willis Cooper asked as he typed. He sat at a card table stationed in a corner of the soundstage. As he pecked away furiously on a studio typewriter, he puffed on a huge cigar.

"Josie doesn't like your dialogue."

"Josie can kiss my ass," Cooper growled. "And tell your staff to quit monkeying with my typewriter."

"Huh?"

"Yeah, back on Stage 7. I get up to get something and I come back and look at the page and the goddamn sentence doesn't line up right. Somebody messed with the carriage."

"Who the hell cares? You're not being graded on neatness!"

"Or politeness," Josie said with a huff.

Pinky, sporting a monocle, his dark hair slicked down, his mustache framing one of his patented smirks, exuded oily villainy. "Well, the prodigals have returned."

All eyes turned to look at the truant actors.

Lee roared, "WHERE THE HELL HAVE YOU GUYS BEEN?" Rowland's face was flush with rage.

"Sorry, Rowland," Rathbone said.

"We were just on Stage 7," Boris explained. "A stagehand told us where you were."

"We were," Bela said, "unavoidably detained."

Lee rubbed his temple where a vein was visibly throbbing. "It's almost 11 o'clock!" Lee's voice was literally bouncing off the soundstage walls. "I couldn't shoot my laboratory scenes! The only actors I had on hand were Josie, Pinky, and—that other guy!"

He jabbed a thumb in the direction of an actor standing off to the side dressed as a Tyrolean servant. "I've had Cooper re-write this scene six times just so we had stuff to shoot! But it's still only three pages! You better have a DAMN good reason for being late!"

Bela crossed his arms and gave Rowland an angry scowl. "It is the studio's fault we are late!"

Boris and Basil gave Bela a double take.

Crossing his own arms, Rowland returned Bela's scowl. "How the hell is your being late the studio's fault?"

Boris was about to say something when Lee held up his hand. "Please! Don't bother. I don't care why you three were late. Just get the hell over to Jack Pierce and get into your costumes, then come back so we can get some film in the can! Is that asking too much?"

"Right away, Rowland," said Rathbone.

"This won't happen again," promised Karloff.

Just then Cliff Work stepped onto the set with a very eager Peter Mitchell. The former studio publicity photographer was wearing a new gray business suit.

Work smiled at the director. "Morning, Rowland."

"Whatever it is, Cliff, can it wait?" Lee said, glowering at his stars. "We're kind of behind schedule." He frowned at Mitchell. "No pictures today, kid."

Work said proudly, "You better talk real nice to this young man. The head office has big plans for him."

Lee looked archly from Mitchell to Work. "What the hell are you talking about?"

"It's a shame about Murphy's heart attack and all, but it's time to move on." Work patted Mitchell on the back. "Mr. Rowland V. Lee, meet Universal Studio's new studio production manager."

Boris, Basil, and Bela exchanged looks of mute astonishment. Josephine gasped. Atwill snickered.

Mitchell's young eyes shined brightly. "And don't worry, Mr. Lee, everybody! I'm behind *Son of Frankenstein* 100 percent!"

Rowland V. Lee's reaction would have been deemed unsuitable by the Hayes Office and censored. Cliff let it slide good-naturedly. "Aw, don't be that way, Rowland. You'll get used to the idea. M-G-M had Irving Thalberg."

"Good-bye, everybody!" Mitchell said as he waved enthusiastically.

"Come on, son," Work said. "I'll show you around the executive wash-room."

"Golly!" Mitchell effused as they left the soundstage.

Josephine chose that moment to shake her script page in Rowland's face. "About the dialogue," she said.

Lee gazed heavenward. "Talk to Cooper about it, baby. I need a Bro-mo."

Josie looked imploringly at Boris and handed him the page. "I mean, Boris, just look at these lines!"

Karloff scanned the paper casually, then noticed something that made him grab Rathbone's shoulder. Rathbone glanced at the page and shrugged questioningly. Boris took Basil aside and said, "The type," he whispered, pointing at the words "needles" and "solved." "The "d"s, they have breaks in them like in the note!"

"The note that lured Murphy onto the laboratory set?" asked Rathbone, taking the page and glancing over at Cooper. The writer was getting an earful from Josie.

Lugosi joined them. "What are you two whispering about without Bela?"

Rathbone hesitated a moment. "We'll tell you if you promise not to do anything—impulsive."

Bela gestured dismissively. "I promise. Now, what is going on?"

Rathbone, albeit reluctantly, showed Lugosi the page of dialogue. "If Boris is right, this was typed on the same typewriter used to forge the incriminating note found in Murphy's hand."

"I see," said Bela, examining the page. "So this is evidence, yes?"

"Yes," said Boris. "Now, all we have to do is find out where Cooper got that typewriter."

"Yes," said Rathbone. "But we don't want to tip our hand so we'll have to be subtle about it."

Lugosi shouted, "Hey, Cooper! Where did you get that typewriter?"

Cooper looked away from Josie. "The writer's bullpen. Why?"

"I was just wondering. Who gave it to you?"

"The new production manager. Do you wanna know where I get my cigars, too?"

Rathbone snarled at Lugosi. "You promised not to do anything impulsive!"

"That wasn't impulsive. That was practical. So now we know the typewriter came from this bullpen."

Boris nodded. "Which is in the same building as Murphy's office."

Suddenly, Rowland V. Lee joined their conclave, holding a fizzing glass of water and Bromo seltzer. "WILL YOU GUYS GET OVER TO MAKEUP ALREADY!"

"Right away, Rowland," said Basil.

As they hurried to Jack Pierce's makeup studio Rowland exclaimed, "JESUS! Those guys are worse than directing the goddamn Marx Brothers!"

**Who Framed Boris Karloff?**

**Chapter Twenty-Four**

**28 November 1938, 12:10 p.m.**

Behind the wheel of the studio cart, Boris said, "Why do you think those men in the prop warehouse were killed?

Rathbone was jotting in his notepad. "Obviously they were victims of what is commonly referred to as a 'Mob hit.'"

Bela said, "But where does that leave our investigation?"

"It leaves us with more questions than answers." Rathbone tapped his notepad. "Not to change the subject, but about our excursion in the cemetery this evening—I've been making a list. We'll need crowbars, maybe a hammer and chisel, oh, and perhaps a ladder for climbing over the wall."

"Oh, yes," Karloff sighed, shaking his head. "Wouldn't do not to have a ladder handy."

"I'll bring the ladder. I think there's one in my garage."

Lugosi said, "I already said I would bring the lanterns."

"Three torches will suffice."

"But lanterns are safer."

Rathbone sighed. "I meant *electric* torches. Americans call them flashlights."

"Flashlights? They are no good. Flashlights are boring. Lanterns, they create a better mood for the scene."

"Bela," Boris said, "this isn't a movie we're making. We're going to break into a mausoleum for real."

Rathbone looked up from his notepad and asked, "What else do you think we'll need, Boris?"

"To get our heads examined! This whole plan is ridiculous."

"We need the physical evidence," Rathbone insisted.

"Isn't it true that the criminal always returns to the scene of the crime? Perhaps the killer's conscience will get the better of him and he'll break into the mausoleum and take the urn. If that happens, it will prove the ashes in the urn aren't Murphy's, and if they aren't Murphy's ashes, then logically, they must belong to Eddie Mannix."

"But we'd have to keep the mausoleum under surveillance 24 hours a day."

"Not necessarily. If we place a wax seal on the plate covering the niche containing the urn and if that seal should be broken—"

"—then," Rathbone said, finishing Boris' thought, "we'd know if the urn had been tampered with. Hmm, that's really quite clever. Still, that whole 'killer returning to the scene of the crime' thing is just a melodramatic myth. There's no guarantee the tomb will be disturbed before Ouida's train reaches New York."

"Maybe we can turn up the heat, as they say in the movies."

"Speaking of heat, there's Jack and he appears to be fuming."

Pierce's steely gaze was set upon them as Boris pulled up to the curb. "HEY! You guys get in here so we can start! All of you! NOW!" Pierce stormed back inside, shaking his head.

"He's in a lovely mood," said Rathbone.

Bela nodded. "He was like that before. At the funeral he was, as the Americans say, 'all wound out.'"

"Wound *up*," Karloff corrected.

"Wound up, wound out, what's the difference?"

Rathbone's eyebrow arched with excitement. "By Jove, I think I've got it!"

"Got what?" asked Bela.

"A brilliant notion for making the criminal return to the scene of the crime."

"I don't understand," said Boris.

"You will, my friend! You will! Just follow my lead. And, Bela, just be yourself."

"What is THAT supposed to mean?" Bela asked, not sure whether or not to be insulted.

"You'll see," Rathbone said confidently. "To quote the immortal Bard, 'Conscience doth make cowards of us all!'"

## Chapter Twenty-Five
### 28 November 1938, 12:32 p.m.

Inside the makeup studio, Boris, Bela, and Basil sat with makeup capes tied around their necks. Because of the time crunch, Pierce had conscripted his three assistants, Otto Letterer, Sam Kaufman, and Bill Eally. Naturally Pierce, assisted by Letterer, took on the responsibility of making up Karloff. Kaufman was applying yak hair and the rubber-crooked neck to Lugosi, while Eally applied the smart, pencil-thin mustache and red-based makeup to Basil Rathbone.

"I say, Jack," Boris said, nodding toward Pierce's rogue's gallery where a plaster life mask filled the once empty space, "I see you've cast a new copy of the missing bust."

"Oh, yes," said Rathbone, leaning forward to note the new addition. "Why, it's Henry Hull!"

"Sure," said Pierce, gluing down Karloff's rubber forehead piece. "I made that cast of Henry for *The Werewolf of London*."

"Good thing you still had the mold handy," Karloff remarked.

"Me, I never throw away nothing. Once I make a mold I keep it safe in case I need to make new masks."

"Safely under lock and key here, I suppose," Rathbone remarked.

"Some, the newer ones, here, yes. The other ones, the older ones, I keep at home. Blanche, she's all the time after me to throw them away. I tell her, 'you don't throw away your children.'"

"You'd better be careful, Jack," Boris cautioned as Letterer attached the scar that ran along the Monster's left cheek line. "One of these days Blanche might get it into her head to do a bit of spring cleaning."

"She wouldn't dare," Pierce insisted, mixing the gray-green makeup base. "Besides, the molds I keep in the garage. I got the only key to the cabinet. She don't go near it."

"I say, Boris," Rathbone said with a casual air. "Not to change the subject, but wasn't that a lovely service for Murphy yesterday afternoon?"

"Yes," Boris said, "indeed it was."

"I particularly liked the way Murphy was presented," Rathbone commented. "I'm sure his wife greatly appreciated the painstaking effort taken by the makeup artist. Wouldn't you agree, Bela?"

"Oh, yes, indeed," nodded Bela as Kaufman singed Lugosi's fake beard with a hot curling iron. "And the widow, very lovely, or so I could tell from her figure, which was very nice." He used his hands to inscribe a busty figure in the air. "Her face, I could not see under the veils, but I am sure it was very nice, too."

"The widow?" remarked Kaufman, looking puzzled. "What widow? Murphy was divorced."

Pierce glared angrily over at his assistant. "Shut up, Kaufman, and keep to your work. Or would you like maybe to inventory my life mask molds?"

"Was he divorced?" remarked Karloff, genuinely surprised. "His ex-wife was practically beside herself with grief."

Rathbone shrugged under the makeup cape. "Perhaps the divorce was an amicable one."

"That's not what I heard," Letterer snickered.

"Oh?" asked Rathbone, eyebrow crooked.

"I heard she found Murphy with a starlet on his casting couch. They were in a compromising position, you might say. His ex took him for a fortune."

Pierce showed his upper teeth, as he growled, "No talking. We don't have time for talking!"

"On the contrary," remarked Rathbone, "I just love a bit of juicy gossip. Do continue, Mr. Letterer."

"Well—," Letterer began.

Pierce glared at Letterer and held out his hand. "Stippling sponge!" His voice was tinged with menace.

"I heard she remarried," Kaufman said. "A Broadway producer, I think. Anyway, she moved to the East Coast."

"How touching," said Rathbone. "To think that she would travel all this way just to bid her ex-husband good-bye." Then he added innocently, "But wasn't that a wedding ring I saw on Murphy's finger?"

"Wedding ring?" asked Kaufman.

"Yes," said Rathbone. "Gold with a brownish stone."

"Tiger-eye," said Karloff.

Kaufman shrugged. "I don't really remember ever seeing Murphy wearing a ring, especially not like that."

"Oh?" said Boris. "He was definitely wearing a ring, a very distinctive one. The stone was carved into the relief of a Spanish Conquistador. You can see it very plainly in the newspaper photographs."

Rathbone nodded. "I imagine it was custom-made."

"Not so, Basil," Karloff corrected. "I remember seeing a stone just like that once before."

"You have? Why where might that have been, Boris?"

"Hmm," Boris said, faking deep contemplation, "now where did I see it? AH! I remember now! Eddie Mannix had a ring exactly like that."

"You mean Eddie Mannix over at M-G-M?"

"The very same," said Karloff. "I understand it was given to him by the young lady he's presently seeing. What was her name?"

"Oh, I think I know," said Rathbone, snapping his fingers, pretending to recall the name. "Now, what was it? It's a mannish sort of name. Tommy, Terry, no, TONI! Toni, uh, LANIER! Toni Lanier."

"Nice legs," Lugosi commented, recalling Toni in her torn dress.

Boris said, "I understand she and Mannix are quite the item and that ring symbolizes their feelings for each other."

"Really?" Basil said in mock surprise. "What a strange coincidence that Murphy and Miss Lanier should choose the exact same design for the stone."

"Of course," said Bela, "now that Murphy has been cremated, there is now definitely only one such ring like it still in existence."

"Not necessarily," pointed out Rathbone as Eally combed and parted his hair. "The stone is probably still intact and resting with the ashes in Murphy's crypt."

Boris nodded. "You know, it's funny that you should mention Eddie Mannix. I understand Jack Dragna has been looking for him."

"Jack Dragna, the mobster?" asked Bela, overacting innocence.

"I heard that Mr. Dragna thinks that something *untoward* has become of Mr. Mannix."

Boris looked directly into Pierce's eyes. "I certainly wouldn't want to be the poor soul who knew about Mannix and didn't say anything about it."

"You know who I would not want to be, Karloff?" asked Bela, casting Pierce an equally significant look.

"No, Bela, who?"

"The poor makeup man who prepared Mr. Murphy's body for cremation. Because of the body wearing the same ring as Mannix, the mobsters, they might think the makeup man was, how do you say the word—?"

"An accomplice?" suggested Karloff.

"YES! Was an *accomplice* in Mannix's murder."

"I see your point," Karloff nodded solemnly. He turned to Pierce. "How are you coming there, Jack?"

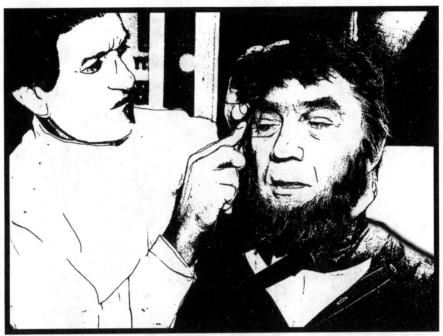

**"You know who I would not want to be, Karloff? The poor makeup man who prepared Mr. Murphy's body for cremation."**

Jack's hands were visibly shaking. "I—I just have to apply the mortician's wax to the eyelids and you'll be ready for the costume."

"I say, Boris."

"Yes, Bela?"

"If Dragna and his men DID suspect those ashes in Murphy's crypt belonged to Mannix, what do you think they would do about it?"

"Oh, I imagine they'd break into the crypt and look for the stone."

"Indeed," said Rathbone. "If you'll pardon the pun, the gangsters will leave no stone *interred*."

Boris and Bela chuckled. Boris said, "Oh, that is droll, Basil. You are a wit."

Eally removed Rathbone's makeup cape and said, "You're ready for wardrobe, Mr. Rathbone."

Rathbone got up and examined his face in the makeup mirror and smiled. "My goodness, is my face red." He waved at his co-stars. "I'll see you chaps on the set."

"We'll be along soon, Basil," Boris said as Letterer took on the task of gluing on the drooping eyelids. Boris gave Pierce a look of concern. "Are you all right, Jack? You look awfully pale."

"Me?" Pierce said, his voice cracking with obvious anxiety. "I'm fine. I'm just fine. Now let's get you into the costume." He gestured to Letterer and growled, "And no more talk about ex-wives or gangsters or nothing."

## Chapter Twenty-Six

## 28 November 1938, 8:46 p.m.

## Stage 7

Rowland V. Lee had worked hard on getting a good bit of footage in the can. Scenes were shot of Wolf von Frankenstein taking the Monster's heart rate and blood pressure, recording his lung capacity, and even conducting a fluoroscopic examination of the Monster's heart ("Bullets!" proclaimed Cooper's overblown dialogue. "Two bullets in his heart, and he still lives!"). After retakes and reverse angles and more retakes, all was now ready for the last big shot of the night: the "Monster's Revival" scene.

Karloff was strapped down on the operating table. Lugosi's Ygor stood at the Monster's bedside. Rathbone was stationed next to the operating table, manning the control box for the Strickfaden apparatus. He was quite a sight in surgeon's smock, rubber gloves, lead apron, and goggles.

Sitting behind the camera in his folding chair, taking it easy reading the newspaper, was the lanky, hawk-nosed Edgar Norton, who was dressed in his butler costume.

Pierce was on set, too, hovering nervously in a corner next to Boris' Monster chair.

Sound supervisor Bernard B. Brown sat behind his control box, listening on his headphones and taking sound levels while little Donnie Dunagan, who played Wolf von Frankenstein's son, Peter, sat on his lap. The boy knew today's scene involved lots of sparking machines and noise and he wanted to watch. He begged Brown to give him the headphones so he could listen. Brown complied and put his headphones over the boy's tiny ears.

While Robinson checked the lighting and Lee got fresh pages of dialogue from Cooper, Rathbone nodded in the makeup man's direction. "Look at Pierce," he whispered to his companions, "he's as jumpy as a cat."

Pierce was obviously trying to look busy as he fiddled nervously with the jars and brushes he kept in his portable makeup kit.

Bela smiled mischievously and waited for just the right unguarded moment to shout, "HOW'S IT GOING, JACK?"

Almost simultaneously, Donnie screamed and pulled off the headset while Pierce started and spilled the contents of his makeup kit. "DON'T DO THAT!" the makeup man shrieked.

"Yeah," Brown scolded. "What are you trying to do? Deafen the poor kid?"

"Oh, please let me listen again," the boy pleaded. "I like listening."

While Donnie put the headphones on again, Rathbone suppressed a chuckle. "Now we'll let Pierce's imagination do the rest. Tonight we'll go to Rosedale Cemetery and prepare the columbary."

The Monster ogled Basil incredulously. "You don't seriously think Jack is going to try and break into that crypt by himself?"

"Perhaps not, but I suspect Jack *will* tell whoever's behind this scheme about our little conversation and that person will take appropriate action."

Bela smiled through his crooked false teeth. "Perhaps we should bring with us a pair of binoculars?"

"An excellent idea," Rathbone agreed.

"I have a pair of sport glasses," said Karloff.

Brown, now wearing his headphones again, announced, "Sound ready!"

Robinson said, "Camera ready!"

"Get over here, Norton," said Lee as he handed Rathbone and Lugosi their lines.

Bill Hedgcock took a grounding strap from the control box. "Norton, pull up your pant leg so I can get this around your ankle."

"Yes, sir." Norton bent down and did as he was told. Hedgcock pulled Norton's sock down and made sure the insulating strap touched the skin firmly. He stood up and said, "Okay."

Rowland nodded and addressed his cast. "This is the big scene where Wolf tries to revive the Frankenstein Monster. Now, Boris, you just sort of twitch your face while the electricity goes through you. Edgar, when Boris wakes up and sees you, he's going to growl at you. We'll be doing several pick-up shots and point-of-view shots of you grabbing a scalpel and threatening the Monster with it, so please be sure to use the same hand each time."

"Yes, Mr. Lee," Norton nodded.

"It's Rowland," Lee corrected. "I told you to call me Rowland."

"Sorry, Mr. Lee. But since I am playing a butler, I prefer to remain in character by addressing you as Benson would."

Lee rolled his eyes. "Sure, whatever works for you." Turning to Lugosi, he instructed, "Now, while Wolf tries to revive the Monster, you begin to worry about your friend here. You grab his hand while the electricity is going through him and you get a big shock. Hold his hand and, you know, go kind of spastic like you're being electrocuted." He grabbed Boris' wrist and demonstrated what he wanted. "Got it?"

"Yes," nodded Bela. "I have it."

"Uh, Rowland," Boris ventured.

"Yes, Boris?"

"Speaking of being electrocuted, I haven't had a strap put on me yet."

"You don't need one," Lee insisted.

"Since when?" asked Boris with vivid memories of Murphy's lifeless, unmoving body sizzling on the very same operating table.

"Since always," Lee insisted. "Kenny had this operating table especially rigged. The whole thing will keep you grounded."

"I rather doubt that."

"Seriously, Boris. There is no way in hell this rig could hurt you."

"The director of *The Mask of Fu Manchu* told me the same thing. Kenny Strickfaden assured me I'd be safe, but I told him if he was so sure of himself, he could do the scene in a Fu Manchu mask. On the first take, Strickfaden was shocked and thrown back about five feet. So please don't tell me I'm perfectly safe when I know I'm not."

"He's quite right, Rowland," Basil said, backing up his co-star. "I think we're playing with Fate here."

Rowland looked like he was ready to throw something. Instead he took a short breath, counted to 10, and said, "Tell you what, even though we're running REALLY late, and I can't imagine why we are, if I get on this table and PROVE to you that it's perfectly safe, can we PLEASE get on with this thing?"

Boris hesitated. "I'm really not sure you should."

"Boris is right," said Rathbone. "It might be dangerous."

"Get off the table," Rowland insisted.

"But—," Boris began.

"Get off the goddamn table!" The director undid the Monster's straps and cranked the operating table to an upright position. "Get off! NOW!" Reluctantly, Boris did as he was told and held his breath while Rowland, with the assistance of Hedgcock and special effects man John P. Fulton, got into position for the demonstration. "Okay, I'm strapped in. I got a metal buckle on my belt. Now, if this wasn't safe, I'd be a goner, right?"

"Definitely," Boris said with visible apprehension.

"Okay, Rathbone, throw the switch."

Basil's hand hesitated over the toggle switches. He looked from Bela to Boris and back to Lee.

Rowland had just about had enough. "Throw the goddamn switch, already!"

Rathbone held his breath and shut his eyes. Donnie Dunagan leaned forward in Bernard Brown's lap, eyes wide with anticipation. Basil flicked the first switch that set the Jacob's ladder and radio tubes going. The ladder buzzed and flickered spectacularly, the radio tubes pulsated. The display elicited squeals of joy and applause from Donnie. Rathbone reached for the final toggle switch but couldn't bring himself to throw it.

"Oh, for christssake!" Lee grumbled as he reached over and pulled the control box closer. He flicked the switch himself, bringing "Meg Senior" to full, brilliant, crackling life. Although the electric arcs were firing at the electrode mounted behind him, Lee himself remained unharmed. After a few tense moments he looked over at Boris and shouted over the noise, "Okay, satisfied?"

"I'll bet you wouldn't feel so secure if that arc of electricity hit your belt buckle."

Rolling his eyes, Rowland asked Hedgcock, "How about it?"

"Is there any metal next to your skin?" Hedgcock asked. "You know, over your skin but not touching? Any gaps could create a spark and burn you."

"No. I don't think so."

"Just to be on the safe side." Fulton tore off a piece of cardboard being used to mask a spot lamp. He folded it up and stuck it in Lee's pants. Then, while keeping one hand on the operating table to stay grounded, he took a screwdriver from his tool kit, attracted the arc to the metal tip, and then touched the tip to Rowland's belt buckle. The arc now passed harmlessly between "Meg Senior" and Lee's belt buckle.

"Well?" Lee asked Boris.

Boris was dumbstruck. Seeing nothing amiss, Karloff finally nodded resignedly and shouted back, "Yes, Rowland, I guess I'm satisfied."

Lee told Rathbone to shut the machine off and, as Fulton and Hedgcock helped him off the operating table, the director said, "Okay, now that that's settled, can we PLEASE shoot this and wrap for the night? While we're young!"

After Boris was strapped back onto the table and cranked back into a prone position, he whispered over to Basil and Bela, "What do you make of that?"

Bela could only shrug.

Rathbone said, "I'm not sure what to think. Yet."

Bela looked the operating table over. "A monkey may have been thrown into the works, perhaps."

"Monkey *wrench*," Karloff corrected.

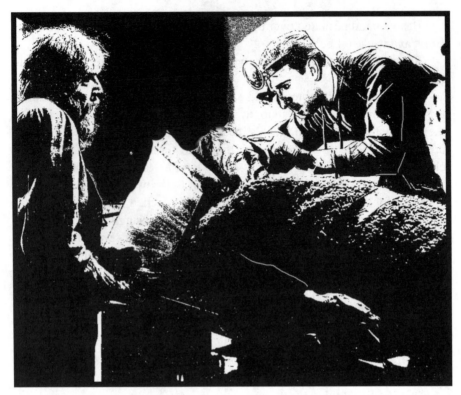

**"Monkey, monkey wrench, either way, maybe it was sabotaged by the killer."**

"Monkey, monkey wrench, either way, maybe it was sabotaged by the killer."

Rathbone considered this. "Which would suggest a highly specialized knowledge of the apparatus."

Boris looked concerned. "You're not suggesting it was Fulton or Hedgcock?"

"They *are* thoroughly familiar with the apparatus."

Lee called to Robinson, "ROLL CAMERA!" To Brown, "ROLL SOUND!" To the actors, he shouted the all-important, "ACTION!"

The rest of the night's shoot came and went without incident, much to the relief and bafflement of the three amateur sleuths.

Dwight Kemper

## Who Framed Boris Karloff?

### Chapter Twenty-Seven

### 29 November 1938, 1:34 a.m.

### Angelus-Rosedale Cemetery

Boris parked his convertible one street over from Venice Boulevard. He and Basil got out of the car while Lugosi, who had been holding onto the ladder on the ride over, got out of the backseat with three "boring" flashlights.

The Hungarian wore a black-knitted cap, a black shirt, and a pair of black pants. He had also smeared burnt cork on his face. Boris wore his white cricket uniform while Rathbone, looking rather fetching in his white tennis wear, grabbed the ladder and reached in the backseat for a plumber's satchel.

"Boris, did you bring your binoculars?" asked Basil.

"They're right here," said Boris, reaching into the glove box and pulling out a pair of Bausch & Lomb sport glasses in a leather carrying case. He slipped the small binoculars in his pocket.

Bela gestured at their costumes. "I still say you two are dressed all wrong. Look at Bela. Bela is ready to sneak around in the dark. And you two, I don't know what you are dressed for."

"Believe me, Bela," Rathbone explained, "if we look like celebrities, the police, if they should come upon us, will treat us like celebrities. You on the other hand, look like a burglar and could arouse their suspicions."

Lugosi sneered, "I look like a burglar because burglars do not want to get caught!"

"No more arguments," Rathbone said as he gave Boris the ladder and put the satchel down on the sidewalk. He opened it, pulled out a service revolver and offered it to Boris. "I thought you might need it, just in case."

"No, thank you," said Boris. "I'm not very good with firearms."

Rathbone shrugged, checked to make sure the safety was on, and then stuck the gun in his pocket. Lugosi indicated the bulge. "If Karloff doesn't want it, why not give the gun to Bela?"

Rathbone said, "No offense, but I don't want to chance you shooting off anything more lethal than your mouth."

"Very funny," Lugosi glowered. "I would like to see YOU fire a rifle while skiing down a Hungarian mountain slope, Mr. Big Deal Celebrity Marksman."

"No gun," Rathbone said firmly. He took up the satchel, shouldered the ladder and together they sneaked along the north wall of the cemetery.

Lugosi asked, "Why do we not first check to see whether the gates are unlocked?"

"Because the gates ARE locked," Rathbone insisted.

"How do you know unless you check to be sure? There are gates by the crematory on Normandie Avenue, and the front gates are on Washington Boulevard. Either of them, they could be unlocked."

Boris looked over his shoulder. "The gates are there to keep out intruders."

Bela smirked. "Keep out intruders who do not carry around with them a ladder, you mean."

The brick wall surrounding Rosedale Cemetery was seven-feet tall in some places, while other sections were nine feet tall with wrought-iron fencing along the top ending in nasty-looking iron spikes. Rathbone picked a section of the wall that was flat on top and leaned the ladder against it. Setting one foot on the rung, Rathbone paused and said with a smile, "I haven't climbed up a ladder since I was but a mere slip of a lad playing the title role in the Stafford Players production of *Romeo and Juliet*."

He stuck his flashlight in his back pocket and then climbed up the ladder while Boris held it securely. Peering out over the top of the wall, Rathbone called down in a whisper, "The coast is clear." He pulled himself up and sat on top of the wall. "Hand me up the tools."

Boris grabbed the plumber's bag and felt a sudden twinge of sharp pain in his lower back. He grunted and dropped the tools. "Bela," he whispered, "you'll have to give me a hand." He waited for Bela to answer, but heard only the sound of distant traffic and chirping crickets. Bela was nowhere to be seen. "Basil," he called up, "Bela's gone. Do you see him anywhere?"

Rathbone looked around. "*Now* what has he gotten himself into?" Shaking his head in frustration, he said, "Well, we can't wait for him." He motioned to Karloff. "Hand me the tools."

Boris sighed and braced himself for the inevitable pain. He grabbed the plumber's satchel, heaved it up and winced as burning sharp pains shot down from his lower back into this right leg. "Quick," he said in a strangled gasp. "Take the bag!"

Basil grabbed the satchel and dropped it inside the cemetery, then asked, "Are you all right?"

Not wanting to let on that he was in pain, Boris said, "Don't worry. I'll be all right."

"Here, I'll help you up." Basil offered his hand.

Karloff took Basil's hand and waited for the pain to subside. Then he slowly climbed up while Basil kept him steady. With Rathbone's help, Boris sat on top of the wall, moving very slowly, wincing as he did, feeling very much like an old gaunt Humpty Dumpty.

"How does that rhyme go?" said Boris, looking down. "All the King's Horses and all the King's Men?"

"Are you sure you're up to this?"

Karloff nodded. "I'll be all right, Basil."

"Very well." Rathbone stood up and grabbed the ladder and placed it on the other side of the cemetery wall. "Come on, old chap," he said reassuringly as he helped Boris get to his feet and onto the ladder. "Easy does it. Just don't look down."

Rathbone watched as Boris made his slow and careful descent, then climbed down to join him. While Boris leaned against the wall, Basil hid the ladder behind the shrubbery, and then together they sneaked between the rows of grave markers.

The mausoleum was a cement structure built to resemble an Egyptian tomb. The sign on the lintel read, "Angelus-Rosedale Mausoleum and Columbarium." As they hurried up the three red-carpeted steps, Boris asked, "What do you suppose happened to Bela?"

"Oh, I don't know," Rathbone said as he reached in his back pocket for the flashlight. "Maybe he changed into a bat and flew over the wall."

Boris and Basil shined their flashlights through the iron gates guarding the entrance to the mausoleum. The window at the far end reflected back the flashlight beams. Inside were a marble bench and a couple of ornate wooden chairs. The walls of the mausoleum were lined with brass marker plates and flower holders. The columbaries were set in pillars and marked with smaller brass plates.

Staring intently into the tomb, Boris asked, "Which one of those has Murphy's ashes, I wonder?"

"If Bela were here, he could tell us."

Peering over their shoulders, Bela said, "It is in the pillar there."

Karloff and Rathbone wheeled around with twin looks of panic, shining their lights in Lugosi's face.

The Hungarian smiled with obvious satisfaction. "Now, Karloff, we know which of us is truly the master of horror."

"WHERE THE HELL—," Rathbone began, then switched to a hushed whisper, "where have you been?"

"And," asked Boris, "how did you get in here without the ladder?"

"How do you think?" declared Lugosi. "I walked in through the gate. You English, everything you do has to be so complicated."

Karloff looked at Rathbone. "A fine couple of graverobbers we are."

Basil nodded in mute agreement and then realized something. "Wait a minute. Why would the gates be unlocked at this time of night?"

Bela pointed to the far side of the cemetery. "There are groundskeepers who are waiting for the police. I heard them say something about an exhumation."

"You HEARD them?" exclaimed Boris.

"And they didn't see you?" asked Rathbone.

"Yes," said Bela. "It is funny, but when you are dressed in black, other people, they tend not to notice you."

"Wait a minute," said Boris. "Did you hear what grave they're exhuming?"

"They didn't say. Just that a grave is to be exhumed."

Rathbone craned his neck, searching the grounds for any signs of someone approaching. "We may only have a few moments!" He pulled on the mausoleum gates. "Locked."

Noting the twin locks, Boris asked Rathbone, "Do you know how to pick a Yale lock?"

Basil shook his head and sighed. "This isn't the time for subtlety, I'm afraid." He put the tool bag down and pulled out a crowbar.

"Or," said Bela, jangling something in his hand, "you could use the keys."

"The KEYS?" Basil gasped.

"Where did you get the keys?" asked Boris, shocked.

"From the information booth." Bela handed the ring of keys to Rathbone. "Again, when you are dressed in black—,"

"Yes, I know," Basil grumbled, taking the keys. After a couple of tries he found the key that opened the gates. "Quickly," he said to Lugosi, "show me Murphy's columbary."

"His what?"

"The niche where his ashes are kept. Boris, you be the lookout!"

"Right," whispered Boris.

Inside, Lugosi pointed at the topmost repository. "His ashes are there."

Basil dragged over one of the chairs and set his tool bag down on the marble bench. He rummaged around in the bag and produced a box of sealing wax candles and a box of matches. As Rathbone climbed onto the chair and lit the candle, Bela held the flashlight. "So you think the police are coming to get Murphy's ashes?"

**"How do you think? I walked in through the gate. You English, everything you do has to be so complicated."**

"A bit too coincidental, wouldn't you say? An exhumation at this hour?" Rathbone held the candle close to the crevice of the columbary door. The melting wax seeped into the crevice.

"What Bela wants to know is," said Lugosi, mindful of any unexpected noise, "who was the woman pretending to be Murphy's widow?"

Rathbone shrugged as he worked. "Valentino has his mysterious Woman in Black, so why not Martin F. Murphy? Perhaps she was that starlet caught on Murphy's casting couch. Really, what difference does it make?"

"No difference. Only now it makes sense what Gable said to Tracy."

Rathbone looked down and gave Lugosi a searching look. "What are you talking about?"

**Who Framed Boris Karloff?**

"After the funeral. I heard them, they were talking."

"This is the first time you said anything about this. What exactly did they say?"

"It was nothing, just that Murphy could not keep on his pants. He sleeps with starlets, so that is what they must have meant."

"All right, the wax is in place. Let's get out of here." Rathbone climbed off the chair and returned it to the corner and grabbed his tool bag. "Let's go."

As they emerged from the mausoleum, Rathbone asked Boris, "Did you see anyone?"

"Nothing yet."

"Good." Rathbone locked the mausoleum doors. "Let's hide behind those grave markers over there."

Hiding behind the gravestones, they sat huddled and waited. Rathbone asked Lugosi, "Now, what was this business about Gable saying something to Tracy?"

"Something about Murphy being too fat for his pants and not keeping the pants on. Like I say, it was nothing."

Boris looked askance at Lugosi. "'Too fat for his pants?' By any chance could they have said, 'Too big for his britches?'"

"Pants, britches, what's the difference?"

Rathbone said, "Did they mention Murphy by name when they said this?"

"I don't think they did. Maybe. I don't remember."

"Think, Bela. It's important."

After thinking a moment, Bela said, "No, I don't think so."

Boris asked, "Did you overhear anything else?"

Lugosi shrugged. "Something Mayer said to Strickling, it wasn't important."

Rathbone said, "Let US be the judge of that. What did they say?"

"The food at the outdoor reception, it must have disagreed with them. They said something about breathing a sigh of relief and having a Bromo seltzer."

Rathbone and Karloff exchanged looks.

"What?" asked Bela, irritated about being left out of something.

"It's a conspiracy," said Rathbone at last. "Gable and Tracy weren't talking about Murphy, they were talking about Eddie Mannix!"

"What are you talking about?" asked Boris, extremely confused.

"Don't you see, gentlemen? Eddie was the intended victim the whole time! Now, follow my logic: Eddie Mannix, being the best fixer in Hollywood, would be the custodian of Hollywood's darkest secrets, right?"

"Right," said Boris.

Dwight Kemper

"And he has friends in the syndicate we know will go to any extreme to avenge Mannix's death if anything should happen to him, right?"

Boris' eyes brightened. "Right!"

"So let us suppose certain people high up in Hollywood got it into their heads that Mannix was going to blackmail them, and THAT inspired this rather convoluted murder plot!"

Lugosi peered over his grave marker. "Quiet, someone, he is coming."

Two police cars and a L.A. County coroner's wagon drove slowly past. The procession moved further down the road to the Western side of the cemetery where a backhoe was waiting.

Rathbone's voice was filled with disappointment. "They're here to exhume some other body." He sat back down and leaned against the headstone.

Bela continued to watch the procession. "Then why are they stopping at that open grave?"

"What open grave?"

"The one over there," Lugosi said, pointing.

Basil and Boris peered out over their respective markers and saw, illuminated in the headlights of the cars, men dressed as police, but taking bodies *out* of the coroner's wagon and depositing them *into* the open grave. Hanging suspended over the hole on a chain hooked to the extended arm of the backhoe was a cement grave liner.

Bela said, "Doesn't 'exhume' mean to dig up?"

Basil kept his eye on the scene while holding his hand out expectantly. "Quick, Boris, your binoculars!"

Putting the sport glasses to his eyes, Basil adjusted the focus, then paused to consult his wristwatch. "It's almost 2 o'clock. A bit late for a burial, wouldn't you say?"

"What do you see, Basil?" Karloff whispered.

"They've just deposited two bodies and now they're dragging a third one out of the coroner's wagon. The bodies are wrapped up in winding sheets and tied up with twine." Basil smiled triumphantly. "Gentlemen, I believe we've just stumbled upon a cemetery acting as a dumpsite for Murder, Incorporated."

Suddenly the sleuths were caught in the blinding beams of two flashlights. Before either Boris or Basil could stop him, Bela smiled at the mysterious figures dressed as policemen and said, "Good evening, officers. I am Bela Lugosi. This is Mr. Basil Rathbone and that is Mr. Boris Karloff. As you can see, they are here to play tennis and cricket. As for Bela? I am dressed strangely, I admit, but would either of you care for our autographs?"

The policemen, two very tough-looking customers who never said a word, grabbed the three actors and, while one cop kept the trio covered with a gun, the other patted each man down. He found Rathbone's gun and gave the actor a chastising finger wag. Confiscating the service pistol, the two cops took Boris, Basil, and Bela to a well-dressed man wearing a fedora who was supervising the nighttime operation. He was medium height, with dark hair. His demeanor was coldly pleasant as the actors approached the grisly scene.

"Evening, gentlemen," he said. "Kinda late for a game of tennis, ain't it?"

The first cop handed over Rathbone's gun. "They came packing heat."

The well-dressed man took the weapon. "You shouldn't carry a thing like this around. Somebody could get hurt." He dropped the pistol into the open grave just as one of the groundskeepers was about to drop in the third body. The man said, "Hold it a second." The groundskeeper hoisted the body up. As the well-dressed man addressed his prisoners, he pulled back a portion of the winding sheet covering the corpse's face. "I hear you guys like to poke your noses in where they don't belong." He made sure the dead man's face was fully illuminated in the beams of the police car headlights. Boris immediately recognized the dead man as "Smiley" Jenkins, the Universal Studios security guard. "This is what happens to guys who get too nosy."

The well-dressed man motioned to the groundskeeper, who dropped the body into the open grave. With a beckoning gesture, the man invited the three amateur detectives to look into the hole. Boris reluctantly peered over the edge and saw the three sheet-enshrouded bodies piled atop each other. Basil's gun had landed on one of them. The backhoe started up. Karloff moved away from the grave. While two other "policemen" jockeyed the massive slab of concrete, the mechanical arm slowly lowered the cement grave liner into the hole. In a few moments the grave liner completely covered the evidence.

"Tomorrow," said the well-dressed man, "there'll be mourners and a minister and a coffin and nobody will be any the wiser."

Bela said, "I thought you used coffins with secret panels for disposing of bodies."

Basil glared angrily at the Hungarian. Boris held his breath as the well-dressed man smiled.

"In case of exhumation, this way is better," he said. "Nobody ever looks *under* the grave liner." With a chilling look of significance he said again, "Nobody."

One of the cops stabbed a thumb at the actors. "What do we do with them, Mr. Roselli?"

Mr. Roselli smiled. "I think we made our point. Besides, Mr. Work would be awfully upset if he didn't have his stars to finish the picture." He patted Karloff's cheek with mock affection. "Loved you in *Criminal Code*, by the way." He tipped his hat. "Escort these fine gentlemen to their car and then make sure they get back to the studio. I'll let Mr. Work know they're coming."

## Chapter Twenty-Eight

### 29 November 1938, 3:20 a.m.

"They're all yours," said one of the "policemen" as he shoved Karloff onto Cliff Work's couch, while the other cop dropped the tool bag on the floor with a noticeable clank next to Rathbone.

"Thanks," Work said with a heavy sigh. Once again, he was half dressed and wearing a bathrobe. After the policemen left, Work looked imploringly at the three men. "What the hell were you guys doing in a cemetery? Don't you get enough of that kind of stuff just making our movies?"

"Well, if you must know—," Rathbone began.

Work held up his hands. "Forget it, forget it. I don't care what the hell you were doing. But I'm telling you this: if I didn't need all three of you to finish *Son of Frankenstein*, I would have let you guys rot in jail."

"In jail?" exclaimed Bela, still in cork and burglar wear. "I would have preferred jail to being harassed by those felons!"

"Mr. Roselli sends his best regards, by the way," added Boris.

Work pulled open the drawers of his desk and began his ritualistic lining up of pill bottles. "John owed me a favor. He's very big in Hollywood."

"Very big with the mob, too, I expect," said Rathbone as he took a seat next to Boris.

"Hey, he's legit," Work said, popping the first pill and taking a swig of water. "He used to be Harry Cohen's bodyguard over at Columbia Pictures. Now he runs the stagehand's union."

"HA!" Lugosi scoffed. "The stagehands, they get time and a half for moving the bodies, I suppose."

Work glared at Bela as if seeing him for the first time. "What the hell are you made up for?"

"Never you mind what it is I am made up for!" the Hungarian said sternly. "What is your connection to a criminally run cemetery? We demand to know!"

Work put his hands to his ears like the "hear no evil" monkey. "I don't know anything about a cemetery! I didn't hear a word!" He grabbed another bottle and began shaking blue pills into the palm of his hand. "John Roselli owed me a favor and said he could take care of—trouble found in the prop warehouse. And that's all!"

The three actors exchanged knowing looks. "Cliff," said Boris, "I don't know what you're involved with, but why do you need Mr. Roselli when you already have Mr. Mannix taking care of things?"

Work's eyes nearly bugged out of his head. Gesturing at Bela and Basil, he said, "You told THEM about Eddie Mannix? What the hell part of 'keep a low profile' don't you get, Karloff?"

"So we know about Mannix," said Lugosi. "Pull yourself together, man, and answer Karloff's question!"

Work gulped the pills down and took swig of water directly from the pitcher. His face took on the expression of the mask of tragedy. "You know, calling in a favor to Eddie Mannix is a big deal. Once you call in the favor, that's it. There're no more favors. So I had to call in Roselli."

Boris asked, "When did you see Mr. Mannix last?"

Work grabbed another bottle of pills. "What the hell do you care?"

"Believe me," said Basil. "We care a lot."

"Well, if you must know, the last time Eddie and me talked was Sunday. He was taking care of things at the crematorium." He grimaced at Karloff. "I'll bet you told them about THAT, too."

"When did the cremation actually take place?" asked Boris.

"I don't know, around 7 or 8, I don't remember. Eddie made special arrangements with the funeral parlor. They have a history, I guess."

Boris smiled. "Yes, we saw the kind of history Mannix and the cemetery people must share."

"Why all the questions?"

Boris leaned forward. "Stop pretending that you don't know what I'm talking about. We saw bodies from the warehouse being buried UNDER someone else's grave by Mr. Roselli and those 'policemen.' We also think Mannix might be in danger, if he isn't dead already."

Work was visibly shaken. "In danger? Dead? What are you talking about?"

"Just what was the master plan, Cliff? How many people were involved with the cover-up and how many of them had to be silenced?

"Silenced? Are you nuts?"

"On the contrary," Rathbone said, rising defiantly. "I examined those bodies myself. It was obvious those men in the warehouse were executed. If you don't want to join them in Rosedale Cemetery, you'd better tell us what you know. Let's start with Murphy's cremation. Where was Murphy's body kept? Obviously not at the city morgue or the funeral parlor."

Work sweated like a stool pigeon getting the third degree. "Okay, well, if you must know, we kept Murphy's body on ice here at the studio. Eddie got a hearse from the studio motor pool. He and Pierce drove the body over to the crematorium." He reached for another bottle of pills, sighed and put the bottle down. "It's funny that you should mention about Eddie being in danger. After it was all over I was gonna treat Eddie and Toni to a night out at the Brown Derby, you know, to thank him. Eddie never called. He just took a powder and I haven't heard a peep since. I figured he was just laying low."

"Didn't you ask Miss Lanier about Mannix's whereabouts?" asked Boris.

"Hey, I don't talk directly to Toni. Nobody talks directly to Toni unless they want to find themselves dead. Eddie's got one hell of a temper and he's the jealous type."

Rathbone grabbed the desk lamp and turned the shade so the light shined in Work's eyes. "What time was the dummy delivered to the funeral service?"

Squinting, Work said, "Pierce was supposed to have it ready that morning."

"So Jack *was* the one who made the dummy?"

"Who else? He did a good job, too. Even if he didn't make the mask."

"Who did?"

"I dunno, one of his assistants, maybe? Eddie took care of those details and I don't ask too many questions." He looked at the actors narrowly as he returned the lamp shade to its original position. "Unlike what you three have been doing. Why are you guys even involved in all this?" He froze in mute horror, his jaw dropping with sudden realization. "Oh, Jesus H. Christ! Rathbone, you only PLAY a goddamn detective! Are you telling me you guys are really trying to investigate Murphy's death? Where are my heart pills?" Work grabbed his chest with one hand and rummaged through the drawers of his desk with the other.

"You don't take heart pills," Boris pointed out.

"Oh yeah," Work grabbed a pencil and jotted on his desk calendar, "Ask the doc for heart pills." Throwing the pencil down, he leaned back and wiped his hand down his sweating face, reminding Boris of comedian Edgar Kennedy and his "slow burn" routine. "Boris, look, I know how strongly you feel about

Murphy's death, but this ain't a mystery novel. In a mystery novel it's always just one guy with a clear motive, and all the clues point to just that guy. But this is real life. The killer could be ANYBODY in Los Angeles with no motive at all. For all we know, some crazy bastard nobody ever heard of just sneaked onto the lot and Murphy was just in the wrong place at the wrong time."

Rathbone's eyebrow arched with significance. "I don't happen to agree."

"Look, Rathbone, I'm just trying to protect the Studio's assets and like it or not, Karloff here is a BIG studio asset. So enough already with the Sherlock Holmes and Watson crap, huh? You're actors, so go out and do what we goddamn pay you to do, for christssake. ACT! And leave the detective work to Dick Tracy." Work gestured at the plumber's satchel. "Now get that thing out of here."

Rathbone consulted his watch. "My makeup call isn't until 6. What am I supposed to do until then?"

"Read a goddamn magazine or take a nap. Why the hell do you think we give you guys your own studio bungalows?"

Bela stiffened with indignation. "They get their own bungalows? Bela has to share his bungalow with Atwill and that little Dunagan boy!"

Work's face turned three shades of purple. "Just get outta here!"

Rathbone picked up his plumber's satchel. "Come along, Bela. You can clean up in my bathroom."

"Bela should have his own bathroom!"

As Rathbone herded a fuming Lugosi to the door, Boris said, "I'll be along shortly. Mr. Work and I have things to discuss." He closed the door after them.

Work waved Boris away dismissively. "Get out of here, Boris. We're done."

With his hand still on the doorknob, Karloff said, "Tragic thing, what happened at the prop warehouse."

"Forget it ever happened." Work gulped another handful of pills.

"I wish I could forget, Cliff," Boris said, returning to the couch. "But things aren't that simple."

Work leaned back in his chair. He sighed and gazed heavenward, exasperated. "You wanna tell me why?"

Boris indicated the line of pill bottles. "I hope you have lots more of those, Cliff. I think you're going to need them."

## Chapter Twenty-Nine

## 29 November 1938, 4:10 a.m.

## Basil Rathbone's Private Bungalow

Basil was talking to Lillian when Boris walked into the studio bungalow. She was standing by the bathroom door holding a wooden clothes hanger. Basil was straddling a chair smoking a cigarette, leaning his forearms on the backrest, and looking quite casual for a man describing what had transpired at Rosedale Cemetery.

"Then they brought us back to the studio and here we are."

"You're all lucky to be alive," said Lillian, frowning with concern. "I think it's time you went to the police."

"We can't," Basil insisted. "Ouida's life hangs in the balance."

"Hello, Lillian," Boris said. "What brings you here?" He looked around the room. "Where's Bela, Jr.?"

"Bela wanted a change of clothes. And my neighbor is watching the baby. I feel terrible imposing on her like this, but Bela insisted."

Basil shook his head. "Really, Bela," he shouted through the door. "What's the point of changing out of your burglar gear? You're only going to have to change into your costume when Jack gets here."

From behind the bathroom door, Lugosi called back, "I don't want Jack to see me in black face! Is that Karloff out there?"

"I'm here, Bela," Boris called back.

"What did you talk to Work about?"

"I'll tell you when you're dressed."

Boris looked at his watch. "Where is Jack? I stopped by the makeup studio and it's locked up tight."

Rathbone shrugged. "Maybe he's running late." He took a drag of his cigarette. "I say, Boris, what *did* you talk to Work about?"

Bela stepped out of the bathroom in time to hear Boris say, "I told Cliff about Dragna."

Bela froze in the act of adjusting his necktie. "You did what, Karloff?"

The blood drained from Rathbone's face. "Are you mad?"

Boris held up his hands. "Hear me out, both of you."

"Hear you out?" Basil dismounted the chair and threw down his cigarette. "Work may have orchestrated everything! He obviously has mob connections!"

"I don't agree," Boris insisted.

"Who brought Mannix into all this? Who arranged to have those bodies disposed of? Who called in a favor to this John Roselli?"

Boris sat on the edge of Basil's makeup table. "Cliff didn't orchestrate Murphy's death, but he may have given us the one clue we needed to prove who did."

"What clue?"

"After I told Cliff about Dragna's involvement, he told me that Roselli's been extorting millions of dollars from all the major studios."

"Extorting them how?"

"His power over the stagehands union. If the studios don't pay up, Roselli makes sure the stagehands slow down production. I think Roselli murdered Murphy, or hired thugs to do it, and he used our stagehands to plant Murphy's body on the set. I think you're right, Basil, about Eddie Mannix being lured into a trap. And the culprit is John Roselli."

"The stagehands?" Bela scoffed. "That is like saying that the butler did it."

Rathbone's eyes flashed with excitement. "No, Bela, I think Boris might just be onto something." He began to pace the floor, hands in his pockets. "And you're quite right. Stagehands *are* the butlers of the movie industry. They're expected to be everywhere. No one pays attention to what they do, particularly if they're transporting what looks like a stunt dummy to a soundstage."

"AND," Boris said, "a stagehand would know how to operate the Strickfaden machines."

"Precisely!" Basil searched his pockets and found Jack Dragna's business card. He rushed to the telephone on the makeup table and grabbed the handset.

Boris grabbed Rathbone's hand before he could raise the handset to his ear. "What do you think you're doing?"

"Calling Dragna. You've solved the case, Boris. Now we have someone to accuse."

Dwight Kemper

Boris took the handset from Rathbone and hung it up. "We're going to need hard evidence to convince Dragna about Roselli's guilt."

"Why?"

"Because according to Cliff, Roselli is Dragna's righthand man."

"What?"

"Roselli works for Dragna."

Bela frowned. "Wait a minute, Karloff. If Roselli works for Dragna, why would Roselli kill Mannix who is Dragna's friend?"

"I think Roselli killed Mannix precisely *because* Mannix was Dragna's friend."

"And possibly his protector," said Basil.

Boris said, "I think Roselli wants to unseat his boss and take over the Hollywood Mafia."

Rathbone folded his arms and considered the matter. "We definitely need hard evidence to convince Dragna."

"We have the typewriter," said Bela.

Rathbone shook his head. "We can't prove that typewriter wrote the incriminating note. Mannix burned the evidence. Besides, there's nothing about the typewriter that links it to Roselli."

Boris sighed. "If only we had the glasses from Murphy's office."

Basil shook his head. "How ironic. Mannix aided in committing his own perfect murder."

Lugosi gestured at the front door. "There might still be evidence in the prop warehouse. I say that we go and we find it."

Rathbone said, "Assuming the evidence is still there, it will take weeks to find it. We don't have that much time. Ouida's train arrives in Chicago at 10:15 this morning."

"Standing around here, we will never find anything." Bela fell silent for a moment, then indicated his wife with a dramatic gesture. "We send Lillian to find the evidence we need!"

Boris cast a sideways glance at Lugosi. "What makes you think Lillian will have any better luck finding Murphy's furnishings than we would?"

"Lillian can find anything! Bela constantly loses his cufflinks, his tiepin, and his socks. Lillian, she knows just where to find them. She is uncanny!"

Lillian patted her husband's arm affectionately. "That's a little different, my darling."

"Nonsense," Bela insisted. "You are a Watson, too! A Watson should help find the clues."

Basil gave a gesture of resignation. "I suppose if you're game, Lillian, it couldn't hurt for you to try. However, it would also be helpful if at some point today you visit Rosedale Cemetery to look for any signs of tampering in the columbarium."

"I'll be glad to."

Lugosi beamed. "AH! It is settled then!"

The telephone rang and gave everyone a start. "Rathbone here," Basil answered. He listened intently to the party on the line. "Dear God, when?"

"What is it, Basil?" Boris asked, only to have Rathbone curtly hush him.

"I see," said Basil. His expression grew graver with every moment. "Yes," he said finally, "Boris and Bela are right here. We'll be there immediately. Good-bye." He hung up. "That was Otto Letterer. Jack Pierce won't be in today. His assistants will be making us up."

"Pierce isn't here?" asked Bela.

"Is he sick?" asked Boris.

"He was rushed to Encino General and they transferred him to Hollywood Presbyterian."

"My God," Boris exclaimed. "What happened?"

"Letterer didn't go into details. But it sounds like Pierce met with foul play. The police are involved."

Boris sat brooding a moment, then said, "Why would they transfer Jack to Hollywood Presbyterian Hospital?"

Rathbone shrugged. "Letterer didn't say. Better surgery, perhaps."

"I hope that's the only reason," Boris said.

**Chapter Thirty**

**29 November 1938, 7:15 a.m.**

**Stage 7**

"They're here," Fred Frank told the director when Boris, Basil, and Bela arrived on the set in costume.

From his director's chair, Rowland called out, "Okay, everyone! Gather around! I got an announcement!"

Everyone looked up from what they were doing. John P. Fulton was checking the blanks in the chambers of two prop guns, George Robinson was checking light levels, Bernard B. Brown was checking sound levels, and Willis Cooper was beating the keys of his typewriter. Waiting patiently behind the cameras were Josie, Pinky, little Donnie Dunagan, Donnie's mother, and Emma Dunn. Emma played little Peter's nanny, Amelia. Donnie was in light blue pajamas for his "Monster Kidnaps Peter" scenes and was holding onto Emma's hand.

"Come on, come on," the director commanded, picking up a large fishbowl and motioning everyone over. "We don't have all day and this is important. Okay, in case you don't know, Jack Pierce is in the hospital."

Josie frowned. "I was so upset when I heard. Does anyone know what happened?"

"Last night burglars broke into his house out in Encino. The police think they were trying to steal his car. Pierce, I guess, tried to stop them. You know Pierce, five foot six of pure dynamite. Anyway, those bastards roughed him up pretty bad."

The cast and crew murmured amongst themselves. Donnie looked up at Emma Dunn and his mother. "What's a bastard?"

Emma softly hushed the boy while Mrs. Dunagan gestured for her son to pay attention.

"Is Blanche all right?" asked Boris.

"No one knows where Blanche is. Neighbors heard the car speeding away from the scene."

"Oh my!" Josie exclaimed. "Do they think she was kidnapped?"

"That's the way it looks. The police are on the lookout for Pierce's car right now." Rowland held up the fishbowl. "Anything you guys can spare for Jack, I'm sure he'd appreciate."

Peter Mitchell chose that moment to arrive on the set, filled with boyish enthusiasm. He stepped into the middle of the circle of cast and crew. "Hello, fellas! What's doin'?"

Lee looked reproachfully at Mitchell. "We're taking up a collection for Jack Pierce."

"Gosh, why?"

"You're in charge of production. Didn't they tell you?"

"Tell me what?"

Boris explained, "Jack was sent to hospital. Thugs broke into his house and assaulted him."

Rathbone added, "We're taking up a collection for Jack. His wife Blanche has been kidnapped."

"Not that Jack knows about it," Lee said. "He's got a concussion." He turned to Boris. "I guess it's a pretty safe bet you don't have your wallet on you."

"On the contrary," Boris said, reaching into the sleeve of his costume. "Eally told me you were planning to take up a collection, so I came prepared." He pulled out a $20 bill and dropped it in, adding an apologetic, "Excuse the greasepaint."

Rowland smiled. "At least we'll know which bill is yours."

"My turn," said Basil, reaching into the pocket of his two-tone tweed jacket and producing his billfold. "Here you are, Rowland."

Rowland held out the bowl. Rathbone deposited two $10 bills. He happened to notice the fingerprints smeared all over Karloff's $20. He glanced over at the worktable where several bottles of chemicals called for in the original script were haphazardly arranged.

"It just might work," he muttered aloud.

Lee gave Basil a searching look. "What just might work?"

"Oh, just thinking out loud."

Lee shrugged and held out the fishbowl for Lugosi, who apparently was only going to put in five dollars. The Hungarian grimaced, pulled an additional $20 out his wallet and put it in.

"Thanks, boys," Lee said, and offered Mitchell the fishbowl so he could make a donation.

"Golly, I'll gladly pitch in." Mitchell dug into his pocket and pulled out a dollar and dropped it in. "There you go."

Lee looked at the dollar. "Gee, boss, can you spare it?"

Josie put in a 10 and held the bowl while Emma held up Donnie, who dropped in his 50 cents along with $10 from Emma.

"Excuse me, Mr. Karloff!" A stagehand was standing by the telephone and gestured at the handset. "Sir, it's for you!" It was the same meek-looking stagehand Boris had seen sweeping the floor earlier.

Karloff excused himself and approached the stagehand as the man whispered, "It's Mrs. Lugosi."

"Thank you," said Boris, reaching for the phone.

"Mr. Karloff, I know it's not my place to say anything, but—" The stagehand glanced nervously at Bela. "Why does Mrs. Lugosi want to talk to you and not to her husband?"

Boris put his hand over the mouthpiece and leaned in close. "She's going to give me Bela's secret recipe for Hungarian goulash." He put his finger to his lips. "Shh. Bela's very protective of it."

"He won't hear anything from me."

The stagehand scurried off as Boris put the handset to his ear. "Hello, Lillian," he said. "How goes the search?"

Lillian whispered into the prop warehouse telephone. "Mr. Rathbone was right. Even with a whole army helping me look, it would still take days to find anything."

Another voice was heard on the line. "Is everything all right, Mrs. Lugosi?" Karloff recognized the warehouse manager's voice.

"Thank you, yes," Lillian said.

"Anything else I can do to help you?"

"No, I'm fine, thanks." After a moment, Lillian said to Boris, "He won't leave me alone."

"Did he try to stop you?" asked Boris, concerned.

"Just the opposite. I guess he has a thing for brunettes. He can't do enough for me."

Boris did his best not to laugh.

"What should I do?" Lillian asked. "I'd like to keep looking but I don't want to impose on my neighbor any more than I have to."

"Why don't you call it a day. Before you go home, visit Rosedale Cemetery and see if anybody tampered with the crypt."

"Okay. This is Lillian Lugosi, secret agent, over and out."

Chuckling to himself, Boris cradled the handset. He was about to return to the huddle of actors when John Fulton grabbed the telephone and exclaimed, "Ew! Boris!"

Boris saw Fulton rubbing his hands on a rag, and then wiping out his ear. He looked at the rag and gestured at the green makeup stains. "You should wipe off the telephone when you're in makeup. Or at least warn a guy. Yuck!"

"I'm terribly sorry, John. Next time I'll—" Boris froze in mid-sentence. He looked down at his hand and over at the telephone as Fulton wiped the greasepaint off the handset.

Fulton noticed the expression on Karloff's face. He gestured at his own face. "What's the matter? Didn't I get it all?"

"Yes," said Boris, absently. "You got it all."

Boris remembered when "Smiley" the security guard used the very same telephone. Boris was so self-absorbed that he barely noticed Lionel Atwill bumping into him.

"Oh, excuse me, Lionel," Boris said.

"My apologies, old man," Pinky said, magnanimously. He waved at the director. "Don't forget me, Rowland." Using his "good hand," which was his left hand, since his right was clad in the "wooden arm" rig, he bent his right arm at the elbow, an action that elicited a ratcheting sound from the joint. Atwill reached into his back pocket and pulled out his wallet, placing it in his gloved right hand. He deftly extracted two $20 bills, which he dropped into the bowl. Taking back the wallet with his left hand, he returned the wallet to his back pocket, then used his left hand to put his right arm down at his side.

"Here's a 50," said Cooper, dropping his donation into the fishbowl. "Maybe I'm not as much fun to watch as Pinky, but it's the thought that counts."

Rathbone motioned for Boris and Bela to join him by the sulfur pit. Now well out of earshot of the rest of the company, Rathbone whispered, "What do you think really happened at Jack's place?"

Bela frowned behind Ygor's gruesome features. "You think this Roselli is behind it?"

"Possibly," Rathbone said. "But why would Roselli kidnap Blanche when killing her would have been easier?"

"Perhaps he did," said Boris. "Roselli might be preparing her final resting place at this very moment."

Basil shook his head. "Why kill Blanche and leave Jack alive? That doesn't sound like the way Roselli operates."

With a sly look, Lugosi said excitedly, "IF what Work said is true, then Pierce was with Mannix as they took Murphy's body to the crematorium. What Bela wants to know is why would Mannix need Jack along for the cremation? He's a makeup man. So, it seems very obvious to Bela who is the killer." Dramatically, he declared, "It was Pierce!"

Peering over the crowd of cast and crew, Lee shot Bela an irritated look. "Yeah, it was Pierce who got beat up! What the hell do you think I've been talking about all this time?"

"Sorry," said Rathbone, giving the director a apologetic wave. "We've been reminiscing about poor Jack. I asked Bela, uh, who was responsible for that very startling makeup Conrad Veidt wore in *The Man Who Laughs*, and just as he said, it was Pierce."

"Oh," Lee said, nodding. "Okay." He gestured at a large greeting card on Cooper's card table. "When you get a minute, everybody sign the card and we'll send that along with a nice gift basket or something."

Back by the sulfur pit, Boris shook his head. "Jack's a bit of a curmudgeon, but a murderer?"

"Bela does have a point," said Rathbone. "What about the makeup on the inside doorknob to Murphy's office, eh? That's clearly evidence that Jack was there!"

"That reminds me," said Boris. "It's a detail that I had forgotten about until just now."

"What detail?"

"The security guard who found me with Murphy's body. He called the studio police from that telephone over there. There was something on the handset that he wiped off on his trouser leg. It might have been greasepaint."

Bela said, "Well, that proves it then."

"I don't know," Boris said skeptically. "I just can't see little Jack Pierce overpowering Eddie Mannix. My money is still on John Roselli."

"We don't know how Mannix died, remember," Rathbone insisted. "Jack could have stabbed or shot him when Mannix's back was turned. But if John Roselli is involved, he'd get other people to do his dirty work for him. Maybe one of the stagehands."

Bela nudged Rathbone. "Or maybe it was Siegel and Cohen who put Pierce in the hospital and they killed Mannix and Murphy."

Karloff let out a frustrated snarl and lurched toward the sulfur pit.

Basil smiled wryly. "Getting into character, Boris?"

"All this theorizing is getting us nowhere. We still need hard evidence and there simply isn't any. Which reminds me, Lillian just called. She couldn't find anything at the warehouse."

"I wonder," Basil said thoughtfully, "if I could pay someone to push Pittsburgh Phil off the train platform first." He looked at Boris. "What do you suppose a hit man charges these days?"

Boris eyed Rathbone narrowly. "Basil, you're scaring me."

Rathbone shrugged. "As a last resort, of course."

Meanwhile, Rowland said, "Now, I want you all to do your best and do it for Jack. Jack would want us to finish this picture because he's a trooper. He's counting on you!" He clapped his hands together and rubbed them vigorously. "Okay, so let's get some film in the can!"

"That's right," said Mitchell, clapping his hands together, mimicking Rowland. "Let's do that!"

Lee gave Mitchell the fisheye, then sighed. "Let's set up for Ygor's big death scene." He joined his actors by the sulfur pit. "Uh, when you guys are finished reminiscing, we have a movie to make."

"We're done," said Rathbone.

Boris grabbed Basil's arm. "I hope you were only joking."

"Of course I was joking," said Basil as Fulton brought him a .38 revolver armed with blanks. Rathbone gave Boris a pleasant nod. "Now if you'll excuse me."

"Okay, guys, this way," said Lee, walking over to the front door to the laboratory. Basil and Bela followed as Lee explained the scene. "Basil, you have just left Inspector Krogh to kick Ygor off the estate. Now, Bela, you hear Rathbone enter the laboratory, so you hide behind this pillar with your blacksmith's hammer ready to clobber him. Got it?"

Fulton handed Bela a hammer with a rubber head. Bela hefted his hammer and made a few test strikes in the air. "Got it, I clobber Rathbone. Easy."

"No, you don't clobber Rathbone, you TRY to clobber Rathbone." Lee began acting out the scene. "Okay, Basil, you enter with gun in hand. You're cautious, you're not sure what's in here waiting for you. Maybe you'll find Ygor, or maybe you'll find the Monster. So you're scared, unsure of yourself. Got it?"

"Clearly," said Rathbone.

"Meanwhile," Lee said, taking on Lugosi's part, "Ygor is hiding behind the pillar here and he waits for Wolf to pass by. Bela, you come up behind Rathbone with your hammer at the ready and you strike—"

Bela hefted his hammer and smiled. "So, like I say already, I clobber Rathbone. Easy."

Lee glared at Bela impatiently. "—AND you MISS!" Pantomiming both parts, Lee switched to Rathbone's role again. "You see Ygor with the hammer, you get out of the way and kick Ygor against the operating table. Ygor recovers. He gets ready to throw the hammer at Wolf."

"And that is when I clobber him?" Bela asked hopefully.

"No," said Lee, pointing at Rathbone. "That's when YOU fire and kill Ygor! Any questions?"

"Not from me," said Rathbone.

"I know what to do," Bela insisted.

Lee nodded approvingly. "Good. We got a lot to shoot today and I want to get us back on schedule."

"Definitely," said Mitchell. "Mr. Lee, do you think we'll be done for the Christmas release?"

"Places," called Lee, sitting down in his director's chair, trying his best to ignore Mitchell hovering at his side.

Rathbone took his position on the other side of the laboratory door. Lugosi went behind the pillar and waited.

"Okay," said Lee, "Roll sound, roll camera, and—ACTION!"

Fred Frank held up the clap board, "*Son of Frankenstein*, production 931, Ygor Death Scene, take one."

The clapperboard clacked.

Rathbone cautiously entered the laboratory, his gun at the ready. Lugosi stalked him from behind the pillar, hammer at the ready. Lugosi made a lunge for Rathbone, they struggled, Rathbone pushed Lugosi away with his foot, and Lugosi fell against the operating table, then raised his hammer and made a second lunge for Rathbone. Rathbone fired two shots. Lugosi fell back against the table, gasped, and dropped to the floor. It was a very convincing death scene.

"Bang! Bang!" giggled Donnie, pretending to shoot Lugosi with his tiny index finger.

"PERFECT!" shouted Lee. "Cut! Damn, I'd say print that son of a bitch but I think we need one more for protection. Bela, Rathbone, back on your marks."

Rathbone did as he was told, but Bela remained motionless on the floor.

Lee shouted, "Come on, Lugosi. Get back to your goddamn mark, already."

Bela remained where he was. His breathing was shallow and a wet red spot was forming under him.

"Hey, Fulton! That's too much stage blood. The Hayes Office won't go for it."

**"Hey, Fulton! That's too much stage blood."**

**Who Framed Boris Karloff?**

Fulton looked confused. "I didn't rig Lugosi to bleed stage blood."

Rathbone stepped forward and looked down at his gun. "I thought the recoil was too strong!" He opened the cylinder of the gun and dumped the bullets into his handkerchief. Examining the rounds closely, he declared, "These bullets are real!"

"Like HELL they are!" Fulton stormed over and looked into Rathbone's hand. He looked up in shock. "Those aren't the blanks I used!"

Boris hurried over to Bela, much the way the Monster was meant to do when he came upon Ygor's prostrate form. Boris felt around Bela's abdomen and felt something wet. Looking at his hand, Boris saw it was covered with real blood. "Oh my God!" he shouted with shock and disbelief, "Bela's been shot! Someone call an ambulance! Somebody get me something to stop the bleeding!"

"Gosh," gasped Mitchell, who took one look at the rapidly spreading pool of blood and fell backward in a dead faint.

Josie screamed and Emma Dunn carried Donnie Dunagan off the set, followed closely by Donnie's anxious mother. Atwill hurried over with the handkerchief that he kept in the sleeve of his wooden arm. Boris took the rag and used it to apply pressure to the bullet wounds.

Bela smiled and whispered through his crooked Ygor teeth, "Turn me the other way, Karloff, so when I die, the camera, it—sees my good side."

## Chapter Thirty-One

## 29 November 1938, 1:20 p.m.

"You'll be fine," Rowland V. Lee assured Bela as the attendants strapped him to the stretcher. "We'll put you in the same room with Jack Pierce. If there's anything that'll motivate the guy to get well fast, it will be having you as a roommate."

Bela scowled weakly. "Oh, very funny. Big joke."

"I'll tell Lillian what happened," Rathbone said.

"I hope," the Hungarian whispered, "Lillian brings with her my silk pajamas. I refuse to wear hospital gown where my ass, it will stick out."

As the ambulance drove away, Rowland said, "Okay, let's get back to work."

"Do you seriously expect us to film after this?" Boris protested.

"Look," said Lee, "I'm not any happier about this than you are, but we HAVE to finish this picture. Bela's a trooper. He'd want us to go on."

"Don't give me that 'the show must go on' nonsense!" Boris gestured at Bela's blood all over the front of his Monster jersey. "Whoever loaded that gun with real bullets did it deliberately!"

"He's quite right," added Rathbone, hefting the handkerchief containing the bullets. "I've done my best to preserve the fingerprints on these shells. I think we should notify the police and begin an official investigation."

Mitchell, who had been revived by the ambulance attendants before Lugosi was taken to the hospital, stepped in and said, "Oh no! We can't involve the police! Mr. Work wouldn't like that!"

"Cliff Work be hanged!" Karloff growled. "There's been too much sneaking around already and *this*," he said, gesturing angrily at the red stain on the floor, "is the result." He leveled a hard stare at Mitchell. "And just where were you while the gun was being loaded?"

"Huh? What does that have to do with anything?"

Rathbone's eyebrow arched with suspicion. "Yes, rather a strange coincidence your being here today. Also, your sudden promotion as the new head of production is very suspicious."

"The head office said I had potential."

"As an assassin, perhaps. But as a production manager, you seem strangely unqualified."

"Yes, VERY suspicious, I'd say," Karloff said as he and Rathbone pressed forward. The two actors had the cowering Mitchell cornered against the very pillar Bela had just been hiding behind.

Mitchell grew pale. "Oh gosh! You don't think I—Ohh, oh gosh!" The blood completely drained from his face and Mitchell fainted again.

Lee ran over and cradled the kid in his arms, slapping his cheeks. Mitchell was out cold. The director looked up at Karloff and Rathbone, his eyes full of skepticism. "You think HE'S a murderer?"

Rathbone pocketed the handkerchief, bullets and all. "It does seem a trifle unlikely."

Boris searched the crew for anyone who looked suspicious. "Wait, where's the stagehand?"

"Which stagehand?" Lee said, leaving Mitchell to wake up on his own.

"The one who handed me the telephone earlier. Where did he go?"

"Oh great," Lee grimaced. "First you're accusing the kid and now we're looking for a phantom stagehand."

"Fulton was busy using the phone. A stagehand could have tampered with the guns when he wasn't looking!"

"Pretty soon we'll be pointing the finger at each other. It was just a goddamn accident."

Fulton gestured at the prop table. "Mr. Karloff is right. I left the guns on that prop table. Both those guns had blanks. I turned my back on those guns twice, once to make the phone call and once to contribute to the fishbowl. In fact, ANYBODY could have switched the blanks for live ammunition while that fishbowl was being passed around."

Rathbone nodded over at the prop table. "Did you check the other pistol?"

"Right after Bela was shot. Pinky's gun still has blanks."

Basil studied the prop table and thought a moment. "And Pinky's gun is a .45 while mine is a .38. Two distinctly different weapons." He cast Boris a significant look. "It would seem .38 is a very popular caliber."

Boris contemplated the bloodstain on the floor. "Which means Bela was the intended target." He returned Rathbone's gaze. "Possibly by the same person who—" he stopped himself from mentioning the bodies at the prop warehouse.

Lee looked from one actor to the other. "Who what? What are you talking about?"

Rathbone looked accusingly at the director. "We're working without a script except for whatever dialogue Willis Cooper writes on the spur of the moment." He turned his gaze on Cooper.

"Hey, don't look at me," said Cooper, holding up his hands. "I've been over here with the typewriter the whole time."

"Not while the fishbowl was being passed around," Rathbone pointed out, then returned his attention to Lee. "Only YOU knew the content of today's scenes."

"Oh, so now I'm the big bad murderer, eh?" Lee scoffed. "The call sheet says very clearly that Wolf is supposed to shoot Ygor. And why would I want to shoot Bela? I've been fighting in Bela's corner ever since day one of this production. And more importantly, why the hell would I do anything to jeopardize my shooting schedule?"

"I can think of one good reason," Rathbone said, his words filled with significance.

"Oh yeah? Like what?"

"I think I'll keep that to myself until the police arrive."

Lee waved dismissively. "Fine! Call the goddamn police if it will make you feel better." He pointed at Rathbone's jacket pocket. "You better let me have those bullets."

Rathbone put a protective hand on his pocket. "I'll only give these over to the proper authorities. Chain of evidence and all that. You understand."

Rolling his eyes, Lee grumbled, "Oh, brother."

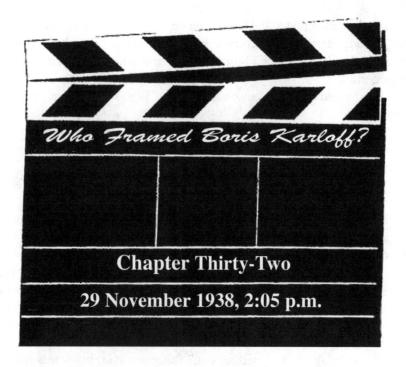

## Chapter Thirty-Two

### 29 November 1938, 2:05 p.m.

The police arrived in due course. After taking everyone's statement, and after asking Boris and Basil for their autographs, and after Rathbone handed over the handkerchief filled with bullets, the police said they'd file a report.

"If Mr. Lugosi doesn't pull through," said the investigating officer, "we'll turn this over to homicide. Until then, we've done pretty much everything we can do."

"Say," said Mitchell, indicating the pool of blood without actually looking at it, "is there any reason we can't mop up that blood and finish filming?"

"We have everything we need," the cop assured him.

Basil looked skeptical. "Aren't you going to call the crime lab and take pictures?"

"What for? According to your camera man, you got it all on film." The cop turned to Lee. "Send us a copy when you get the dailies developed."

"Don't worry, I'll get the film to you right away."

"No hurry," said the second officer. "Like we said, we don't have a homicide case until there's a homicide."

After the police left, Lee turned to Rathbone. "There? Satisfied, Mr. Sherlock?"

"I suppose," said Rathbone.

"Good. Boris, get yourself over to wardrobe and put on a fresh jersey."

"Yes," said Mitchell, trying to effect authority. "I promised the head office we'd get a lot of work done today."

Karloff gave Mitchell and Lee a hard stare. "What's the matter? Don't you boys want to exploit the fact that I have real blood on my clothes?"

Lee considered this a moment, but rejected the idea. "The censors might think it's too gruesome."

If Boris had been a violent man, he might have given Lee a punch in the mouth. He did, however, manage to deliver a very withering stare.

Lee's face softened. "Look, I apologize. I'm all focused on finishing this picture and it's kind of thrown my perspective out of whack. Between you and me, I'm worried about Bela and I'm scared to death."

Mitchell looked worried. "But we HAVE to get this picture ready before Christmas or the head office will fire me for sure!"

"All that aside," Lee said, rolling his eyes, "we have to get back on schedule or the head office may say screw it and shut us down for good! Besides, I really think Bela would want us to finish the picture. His work as Ygor could be the start of a whole new career for him. Come on, Karloff, you know I'm right."

Boris didn't like the idea, but had to agree with Lee's argument about Bela getting a new start. "All right, Rowland," he said, albeit begrudgingly, "I'll get over to wardrobe and we'll make a picture."

"I'll drive you," said Rathbone.

As they left the stage, Boris said, "Did you get the feeling the police weren't interested in pursuing this case?"

"Very much so, which is why I decided to withhold a couple of bullets for my OWN analysis." He patted his pocket, then got behind the wheel of the studio cart. "I also borrowed a few items when no one was looking." He gestured behind him. "They're in the backseat."

A broad smile crossed the Monster's face as he took the passenger seat. "Good thinking, Basil."

As they headed off toward wardrobe, another studio cart came up from behind them and drove alongside, keeping pace with the actors. "Afternoon, boys," said the driver.

"Siegel!" exclaimed Karloff.

Ben "Bugsy" Siegel signaled for the actors to pull over. Still sitting behind the wheel of his cart, he said, "Say, was that a cop car I just saw?" The gangster jerked a thumb toward Stage 7. "And an ambulance before that?" He looked at the bloodstain on Boris' jersey. "Gee, I hope you didn't have any, uh, accidents on the set today."

"What are you doing here?" said Rathbone.

"Mr. Dragna felt you boys needed motivation, so he says to me, 'Bugsy,' he says, and the boss is the only one who can call me 'Bugsy.' 'Bugsy,' he says, 'maybe those guys need better motivation.' So I came here to motivate you."

Karloff glowered with menace. "Did you have anything to do with what happened to Bela?"

Siegel smiled and shrugged. "What? Did something happened to Dracula?"

Rathbone leveled a hard stare. "Mr. Lugosi was shot by a prop gun that had real bullets instead of blanks."

Siegel smirked. "Aww, that's too bad. You know, you actors gotta be more careful with your firearms."

"So you *are* behind this!" Karloff snarled, getting out of the cart.

"Hey, like I said, I ain't Dragna. I got my own ways to motivate you guys."

Boris tensed his fists. "You psychopath!"

Rathbone leapt from the cart and grabbed Boris' arm. "Steady, Boris."

Siegel smiled. "Flattery won't get you nowhere."

"I take it," said Rathbone, "that you also had something to do with Jack Pierce and his recent assault out in Encino."

"Boy," Siegel said, sarcastically, "this movie you're making is having all sorts of hard luck. Yeah, that might also explain why Pierce and Lugosi were ever so conveniently taken to the same hospital where Mrs. Karloff is staying. It's a 'Gypsy curse.'"

Rathbone's grip on Boris' arm was the only thing keeping Karloff from making a lunge for Siegel's throat.

"Hey," Siegel said with a smile, "you know the perfect cure for Gypsy curses? I got a feeling that if maybe you finger a guy, any guy, as Mannix's killer, the jinx will go away."

"I see," said Rathbone. "So you want a name and it doesn't matter whose."

"Dragna's the one all bent out of shape about Mannix. Me? I couldn't give a damn. In fact, now that M-G-M is out one Vice President, maybe I can get Mayer to consider me as the new Hollywood fixer. See, I got what you call, aspirations. I want to be a big man in show biz."

Rathbone flashed a waggish smirk. "Is that a confession? Did you kill Mannix?"

"Believe me, if I knocked off Mannix, I'd make sure that everybody knew about it. Killing Eddie would be a real reputation maker with the guys back home, if you catch my drift."

Boris said, "IF you lived to enjoy it."

"Yes," said Basil, "I don't think Jack Dragna would be very appreciative."

"Well, there is that. But, uh, no, I ain't the guy. But, listen, Rathbone, you better name ANOTHER guy real soon." Siegel's eyes widened with mock astonishment. "Say, and I know just the guy!"

Dwight Kemper

"Oh, you do."

"Sure I do. I heard you met him already, a guy by the name of Roselli. I think he might have done it. Maybe I can even help you convince Dragna that he's the guy."

"How accommodating of you."

"Hey, I'm only trying to help. Because right about now your wife is riding on the *20th Century Limited* with Pittsburgh Phil on her tail. At 9 o'clock Wednesday morning she'll be standing on the Grand Central Terminal platform and good old Phil will be right behind her—9 o'clock, New York time, that's your deadline, emphasis on dead."

Now it was Boris' turn to hold Rathbone back.

With a wave and a cheery, yet menacing, "Tootle-loo," Siegel stepped on the accelerator and drove away.

Basil watched as Siegel's studio cart turned the corner.

"Mr. Karloff."

"Yes, Mr. Rathbone?"

"I have the very distinct feeling we are being had."

## Who Framed Boris Karloff?

## Chapter Thirty-Three

### 29 November 1938, 2:20 p.m.

"You want to be a what?" asked Rowland V. Lee.

"The treasurer," smiled Rathbone. "After all, you will be busy all day filming Boris' scenes. My stuntman will be substituting for me in the scene where Boris' stunt double is knocked into the sulfur pit. So, it seems only logical, since I have some free time, that I should deal with the business of buying Jack and Bela a nice get-well basket."

"I sure can't argue with that," Lee said.

Rathbone took the fishbowl of money. "Now, uh, before I toddle off, who contributed what? I wasn't paying attention."

"What the hell difference does it make?"

Rathbone flashed Lee a disarming smile. "Oh, no reason. Uh, but it's only proper form for the treasurer to keep a record of these things."

"God, you English guys and your 'proper form,'" the director sighed as he scratched the back of his head, trying to recall events. "Okay, uh, Pinky chipped in two 20s, Coop a 50, oh, and our fearless production manager, 'Henry Aldridge,' he chipped in a buck. Josie and Emma both put in a 10 spot. Donnie dropped in two quarters. As for the crew, let's see—."

Rathbone took out his pad and made notes of the names along with the denominations each of cast and crew contributed to the fishbowl.

"Anyone else?" Basil asked. "What about that stagehand Boris mentioned?"

"Honestly, I don't remember a stagehand."

Dwight Kemper

Rathbone put away his list. "I think I have everything now."

"Where are you going for the gift baskets?"

Rathbone looked up absently. "I'm sorry, what gift baskets?"

Lee sighed and pointed at the fishbowl. "The ones you're going to buy Pierce and Lugosi."

"Oh, those. Uh, there's this lovely florist's shop around the corner from the studio. I thought I'd go there."

Lee nodded in agreement. "Yeah, I know the place. Good choice." He turned to address Karloff, who was in a freshly dusted jersey stained with nothing more sinister than fuller's earth.

"Oh, Rowland," asked Rathbone.

"Yeah?"

"Uh, what was your contribution?"

Lee slapped his forehead. "Oh, Jesus! I was so busy getting money from everyone else I damn near forgot!" He pulled out his wallet and dropped in a 50. "Thanks for reminding me."

"Torn on the right corner," Rathbone mumbled to himself.

"Huh?"

Looking up, Rathbone smiled. "Oh, your bill is torn at the right corner."

"I really don't think the florist shop will care."

Rathbone chuckled. "No, of course they won't. How silly of me."

Basil hurried to leave when Lee called, "Hey, Basil!"

"Yes, Rowland?"

Lee grabbed the get-well card signed by the cast and crew, and now made out to both Jack Pierce and Bela Lugosi. "Don't forget the card."

"Oh! The card, yes, how forgetful of me." Rathbone grabbed the card by one corner and placed it very carefully into the fishbowl. "Not to worry, Rowland. This money is in good hands."

Lee flashed Basil an irritated look. "You're going to buy two gift baskets at a goddamn florist shop, not take secret communications across enemy lines."

Rathbone chuckled nervously. "Of course not."

Boris was watching all this with growing bewilderment. He caught Basil's eye and shrugged and mouthed, "What are you up to?"

Rathbone held up his hand and wiggled his fingers and mouthed back, "Fingerprints."

Lee glanced back at Basil just in time to see him wiggling his fingers. "Yeah, Basil, bye-bye now!"

Basil quickly put his hand down and took his leave as Lee turned his attention back to Boris. "Okay, now where were we?"

**"Any news yet about Bela?"**

"Any news yet about Bela?" asked Boris, really not in a playacting mood.

"I asked the doctor to call the set when Bela gets out of surgery—or the alternative."

Boris sighed heavily. He and Bela occasionally had their differences, but deep down he liked and respected the man.

"Okay," Lee said, starting again. "This is the big scene where the Monster tears up the laboratory. You found Ygor shot by Wolf von Frankenstein and you're mad, you're real mad."

Boris looked grim under the makeup. "Really, Rowland, I require very little motivation for this scene, considering."

Lee looked into Boris' sad eyes. "Oh yeah. Well, consider this scene a way to get all that emotion out. You come out of the pit there," Lee pointed to a circular opening in the laboratory floor covered by a large hinged lid made of what appeared to be heavy cement. The lid had a heavy iron ring at one end and a winch and windlass arrangement for raising and lowering it. "You come out of the pit, grab the lid and shove it closed, growling with rage. Then you start throwing things into the sulfur pit: machines, the operating table, kick the stool in, whatever suits your fancy."

Boris looked questioningly at the operating table. "Rowland, I have a bad back, remember. I could hurt myself lifting that thing."

"It's not the same table. That one's made of balsa wood. Even I could lift it. In fact, all the other machines around the pit are hollow props." Lee pointed at the worktable. "The table there is the only thing kind of heavy. All I really want you to do is upturn it. If you don't think you can do it, we'll forget it and find some other way for you to discover little Peter's storybook."

Boris tested the weight of the table. "I think I can handle it all right."

"Great!" Lee looked around the table at the various flasks and beakers and racks of test tubes. He frowned and called out, "Hey, Gausman!"

Set decorator R.A. Gausman was sitting on a stool behind the camera. He looked up from his racing form and said, "Yeah?"

"Didn't there used to be a microscope here?"

"There's supposed to be. Isn't it there?"

"No. And where are some of the chemical bottles that were here? And the small beaker?" Scratching his head, Lee wondered aloud, "Where the hell—?"

## Chapter Thirty-Four

### 29 November 1938, 2:20 p.m.

In the makeup bungalow, Otto Letterer was at the sink cleaning brushes while Sam Kaufman was taking an inventory of Jack Pierce's life mask molds.

Letterer looked over at Kaufman and shook his head. "Sam, why are you bothering with that? Pierce just gave you that job for being a wise guy and Pierce isn't here."

Kaufman shrugged. "Yeah, but Jack's in the hospital. It just seems disrespectful not to do it."

Basil entered carrying the fishbowl full of money and a microscope. Bottles of chemicals were clinking around in his jacket pockets as Letterer looked up and said, "Hello, Mr. Rathbone. I didn't know you were finished for the day."

"I'm on a break," Rathbone said, looking for a table to work on. "Is anyone using this makeup table?"

"No, go ahead," said Kaufman.

Rathbone cleared away a workspace and set the microscope and fishbowl down. As Basil emptied his pockets of bottles containing iodine crystals, calcium chloride, and potassium bromide, as well as a small beaker or two, Kaufman spotted the fishbowl of money and reached into his pocket. He was about to drop in a $5 bill when Rathbone saw him and shouted, "NO!"

Kaufman jumped back in shock. "What? Why? I just wanted to pitch in for Jack."

"So sorry, old man," Rathbone apologized. "It's just I have everything just so. When I'm finished, then you may contribute to the fund, by all means."

"What are you doing?" asked Letterer, washing out a makeup sponge.

"An experiment," Rathbone said, looking around for supplies. He indicated a coffee cup containing various sizes of makeup brushes. "May I?" he asked, as his hand poised over a brush well suited for fingerprint dusting.

"Sure," said Letterer, now watching with interest.

Rathbone searched the makeup tables. "Do you happen to have any cellophane tape?"

Kaufman opened a drawer and handed Rathbone a dispenser. "Anything else?"

"A white index card, perhaps?"

"I think there may be some in Jack's desk here." Kaufman searched around and found some. "What next?"

"Tweezers?"

"Right here."

"A stick of charcoal?"

Letterer handed him one of the sticks of charcoal used to sketch proposed makeup designs.

"And a knife, and, uh, a sheet of paper or two, if you please."

Kaufman found the objects Rathbone requested and watched closely as Basil worked. Using the knife, Basil scraped the charcoal stick over one of the sheets of paper until he had a pile of fine black powder.

"Hey, it looks like you're gonna dust for fingerprints or something."

"Very astute, Mr. Kaufman," smiled Rathbone as he worked. He reached into his pocket and produced his handkerchief with the two bullets he had kept for himself. "Now," Basil said, "let's hope our suspect didn't use gloves."

Holding the bullet jacket with the pair of tweezers, Basil dipped the fine ends of the makeup brush in the black powder and lightly played the brush over the flat end of the bullet casing.

"This must be done delicately," Rathbone remarked as he twiddled the brush lightly over the case head.

Slowly, very slowly, a thumbprint began to emerge.

"Now we're getting somewhere," Rathbone said, smiling with satisfaction. He displayed the bullet and said to the two makeup artists, "That, gentlemen, is what we in the detective game call, a 'latent print.'" He unspooled a small piece of cellophane tape and pressed the sticky side against the black thumbprint. Peeling the tape away slowly, Rathbone managed to lift a perfect print that he then transferred to one of the index cards. Taking a pen from his pocket, Rathbone jotted down, "Thumbprint—Bullet casing."

"Now, comes the hard part," Rathbone said, using the tweezers to pick up the dollar bill contributed by Peter Mitchell. "Getting readable prints from paper money."

"Are you going to dust the money?" Letterer asked.

"It's not going to be quite that easy, I'm afraid," Rathbone smiled. "I'll need some of those empty jars you have in that cabinet there." He went to the sink and filled a beaker with about 100 milliliters of water. "We'll see if I really am a Sherlock Holmes after all."

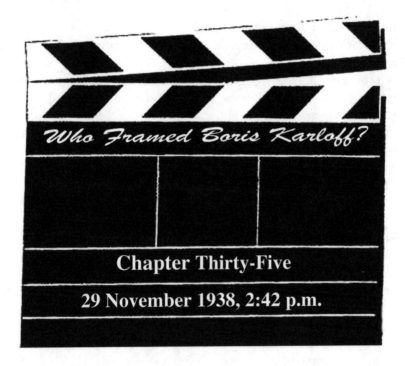

## Chapter Thirty-Five

## 29 November 1938, 2:42 p.m.

"ACTION!" shouted Rowland V. Lee.

Frankenstein's Monster emerged with a growl of fury from the opening in the floor of the laboratory set. He grabbed the supposedly heavy cement lid and slammed it down over the pit. The Monster looked around for other things to smash. He grabbed the straps on the operating table and hurled it into the sulfur pit. He kicked a stool in. He grabbed a hollowed out Strickfaden machine and raised it over his head and growled. In went the prop, followed by other apparatus and furniture. As each thing the Monster threw in hit the pad at the bottom, the grip in the well ignited a series of flash pots to create the illusion of boiling sulfur consuming the laboratory's scientific flotsam and jetsam. The crew and the director marveled at Boris' stunning performance. They were all completely unaware that what they were watching was the actor playing the Monster really consumed by rage and frustration. The days of worrying about Dorothy and the baby, about Bela, about Ouida Rathbone, his anger directed at Ben Siegel, all of it was coming out as one huge monstrous tantrum.

Finally came the moment when the Monster was to upturn the worktable, then look down and discover little Peter's storybook. Boris growled, grabbed the end of the table. The table upended spectacularly in a crash of smashing lab glass.

Boris looked down for the storybook.

He blinked, started, reached down and picked up not a child's storybook, but a bamboo cane.

It looked like Jimmy Whale's cane.

There was a smear of greasepaint as if someone with makeup on his hands had gripped the tip of the cane.

"CUT!" Lee shouted. He turned to Robinson and asked, "Did that goddamn cane get in the shot? I swear to God, if that thing screwed up such a great take—"

"The cane was out of picture," Robinson assured the director. "We can always cut just as the Monster looks down and do an insert shot of his hands holding the book."

"Thank God."

Boris examined the cane. The greasepaint was a mixture of reds and browns and blacks.

There was something else, a familiar odor.

He sniffed the end of the cane.

He detected the smell of bacon fat.

Lee looked up and watched Boris sniffing the end of the cane. "Uh, Boris, if you're through with that cane, I'd like to get the scenes with you and Pinky in the can."

"All right," said Boris, taking the cane to his Monster chair and hooking it to one of the armrests.

Fulton handed Atwill his gun. "Here you go, Pinky. This time I triple checked the chamber."

"I hope so," Pinky said, taking the gun and sticking it in his military holster.

"Okay," said Rowland, "this is the scene where Inspector Krogh shoots the Monster."

## Who Framed Boris Karloff?

## Chapter Thirty-Six

## 29 November 1938, 3:02 p.m.

Rathbone studied a row of a dozen glass jars. Inside each jar was paper money suspended from the lid by a small piece of cellophane tape.

"The reaction usually takes two or three minutes," Rathbone explained.

Kaufman had taken a break from inventorying Jack Pierce's life mask mold collection to watch Rathbone work. Each jar contained not only the paper money but also a thin layer of iodine crystals.

"The iodine vapors," Rathbone explained, "react with the fingerprint oils, which are absorbed into the paper."

"Let me know what comes up," Kaufman said, returning to his work.

Letterer continued to watch as a series of purple-brown colored prints began to emerge on each paper bill. "But how are you gonna tell who's prints are whose? Money is passed from hand to hand all the time and must collect a lot of prints."

Rathbone watched the jars keenly. "I'm hoping only the most recent prints will emerge. If worse comes to worst, I'll dust the fishbowl for control prints. I hope I won't have to do that. I don't have a lot of time."

Mitchell's prints were ready. Using the tweezers, Rathbone removed the dollar bill from the lid of the jar and dipped it in the beaker containing a solution of calcium chloride and potassium bromide mixed with water.

"This solution," Rathbone explained as he worked, "will fix the fingerprints."

**"That was disappointing."**

"Oh," said Letterer. "Kind of like when you're developing pictures."

"Exactly."

Using the microscope, Basil compared Mitchell's alleged prints to the print taken from the bullet casing.

They didn't match. In fact, none of the prints on the bill matched.

"That was disappointing," Rathbone mumbled.

"Anything wrong?" asked Kaufman, over by the storage cabinet.

Looking up from the microscope, Rathbone said, "No, not really. It's just part of me was really hoping this one person was somehow connected to all this."

"Connected to what?" asked Letterer.

"Trust me, you don't want to know," said Rathbone, taking the print of Bela Lugosi, just for comparison's sake and checking Lugosi's pattern of double loops with the distinctive central pocket and the line of a scar that distinguished the print from the bullet casing. Definitely not a match.

Kaufman pulled out a cardboard box and looked inside. He compared his checklist to the mold in the box. "Hey, Letterer, is this one of your molds? It's not marked."

"Couldn't be one of mine," Letterer said, peering into the box. "I always etch the name of the subject on the back of the mold." Taking the mold and looking it over, he added, critically, "This must have been a real rush job, you can see some of the burlap backing coming through the plaster."

Dwight Kemper

Kaufman took back the mold and held it up to the light. "Maybe I can make out the face."

Rathbone wasn't listening. He was too preoccupied with his fingerprint identification. So far there were no matches. Josie Hutchinson was in the clear. So, too, was Emma Dunn, not that Basil found that terribly surprising. John P. Fulton's print was also not a match. A great pity since Fulton was at the top of Basil's suspect list. So far, no one had even a remotely similar pattern of thumbprint. He slipped in another bill into the microscope and was about to compare the prints when he became aware of Kaufman and Letterer's conversation.

"Geez, this guy's ugly," commented Kaufman as he gave the mold and its subject a critical appraisal.

"He kind of looks like a bulldog," Letterer smirked.

The word "Bulldog" got Rathbone's attention. "Who looks like a bull-dog?"

"Whoever's face this is," Kaufman said, putting the mold back in the cardboard box.

"May I see that?" asked Rathbone, gesturing for the box.

"Sure," said Kaufman, who brought the box over and handed the mold to Rathbone. "Here, if you hold the mold up to the light just right, you can make out the imprint as a positive."

As Rathbone did as Kaufman instructed, Letterer gestured at the micro-scope. "Hey, Mr. Rathbone, can I have a look?"

"Yes, but don't change the focus, please." Basil tilted the mold to create the illusion of a three-dimensional face staring back at him from the negative mold. There was no doubt about it. The mold belonged to the life mask, or more likely, the death mask of Eddie "The Bulldog" Mannix. With a ray of hope, Rathbone examined the rough side of the mask and, sure enough, there were samples of what criminal scientists called "plastic prints," fingerprints imbedded in pliable materials like soap, butter, wax, or, as in this case, once wet and now hardened plaster.

Letterer squinted through the eyepiece of the microscope. "Say, these two prints kind of look alike," he said. "Especially the line running through it."

Rathbone put the mold back in the box. "Don't go anywhere with this," he told Kaufman.

"Where would I go?"

Rathbone took Letterer's place at the microscope. He compared the pat-terns of double loops, whorls, and central pockets, and more importantly, the outline of a scar.

This time, the patterns matched!

Rathbone pulled the bill out from under the microscope and read through the list he had compiled of paper money and the corresponding names of each contributor.

"My God!" he gasped. In a panic, Rathbone grabbed the cardboard box with the mold of Eddie Mannix's face and placed the rest of his makeshift lab in the box. "Excuse me," he said, indicating the mask mold, "I need to borrow this."

"No problem," Letterer said. "I doubt Pierce would care about a crude mold like that."

"Yes," Rathbone smiled nervously, "I imagine he wouldn't."

Basil dashed from the makeup bungalow, the rattling cardboard box tucked under his arm. He hurried out front but found the studio cart was gone.

"Damn!" he said, and took off down the studio road on foot, dodging actors, skirting racks of costumes being moved by stagehands to other stages, and was nearly run down by the inevitable studio cart. Rathbone ran in the direction of Stage 7, hoping he would be in time to prevent another possible "accident."

This time the intended victim was Boris Karloff.

## Chapter Thirty-Seven

## 29 November 1938, 3:10 p.m.

Donnie Dunagan climbed out of the sulfur pit with the Monster following him up the ladder. The grip in the well working the rising steam effects was in rare form.

"Here we are," Donnie said, extending a helping hand to Karloff's Monster. Karloff effected the look of a Monster with murderous intent visibly touched by a boy unafraid of him.

"CUT!" said Lee. He joined Donnie and Boris at the edge of the sulfur pit. "Great steam work, Arnie!"

"Thank you, Mr. Lee," the grip called up from the well. "But it's, Albert, sir."

"Whatever," Lee said, then turned to Karloff and Donnie. "Okay, Boris, here's the scene. You hear Josie and Emma banging on the door of the laboratory and you pick Donnie up because in your mind, the boy is yours because his father killed your friend."

Boris smiled down at the boy. "Ah ou aving fun, Donnie?"

Still holding Boris' green hand, the little boy smiled up at the Monster and giggled at Boris' mumbling speech.

"Uh, where's Pinky?" Lee said, looking for the actor.

"Right here, Rowland!" Atwill was standing off to the side, being worked on by Bill Eally and John Fulton. Eally had just strapped Atwill's right arm against his body and was buttoning the actor's uniform while Fulton checked the tear away prosthetic arm rigged to the actor's shoulder. As Eally worked,

Atwill was practicing drawing and aiming his gun with his left hand. After Fulton was satisfied everything was set, Pinky sauntered over to the director and displayed himself proudly. "How do I look?"

Lee nodded with satisfaction. "That looks swell! You can't even see your real arm."

Showing off with his left hand, Atwill began performing tricks with all the dexterity of a rodeo cowboy. "See? I've become positively ambidextrous!"

"I know, I know," Lee said, rolling his eyes. "Okay, quit fooling around."

Twirling the gun by the trigger guard, Pinky holstered the weapon and stood at attention. "Proceed."

"Okay, Wild Bill, when I give you the signal, you climb out of the pit, and confront the Monster. That's when Boris grabs your fake arm and rips it off like a turkey leg at Thanksgiving." He turned to Boris. "Just before you do, you put the kid down and pin him under your boot so he can't get away. Pinky will fire at you and all the time you'll be waving his arm around like a club. Got it?"

"Uh huh," nodded Karloff.

Lee got down on one knee so he could be at Donnie's eye-level. "As for you, you don't get scared until the big guy stomps on you with his foot. Then, when I tell you to you look up, you see your Daddy through the hole in the roof and call out to him, shouting, 'Daddy! Daddy!' Cry and give it everything you've got. Got it?"

"I'm this many years old," Donnie said, grinning and holding up four fingers.

Standing off to the side, Mrs. Dunagan coached her son. "Say, 'yes,' Donnie. Tell the nice director you understand."

"Never mind," Lee said, standing up. "I'll take what he just said as a 'yes.'" He turned back to Atwill. "We're doing a long shot first, then we'll break things down to close-ups and two shots. So be prepared to shoot Boris a lot."

"And I never miss," Pinky said, giving Boris a smile tinged with oily villainy.

Boris would have normally made a joke, but Atwill's remark only reminded him of what happened to Lugosi. "Wowand, any wor about Bewa?"

"Boris, look," said Lee, gesturing at the phone, "I told the studio switchboard to patch any calls from the hospital to the stage telephone. The call light hasn't flashed all afternoon. Believe me, Bela will pull through just fine. That guy's too much of a ham to die before we get his final close-up."

Boris tried to smile but his attention was focused on Atwill's holster. Enunciating as clearly as he could, he said, "Are we sure those are blanks?"

Pinky patted the holster. "Not to worry, Boris. I checked it myself and the gun hasn't been out of my sight since. But to put your mind at ease—," Atwill unholstered the gun, twirled it, took aim at the large laboratory mirror and fired. There was an explosion and a puff of smoke, but the mirror was intact.

"Whew," said Boris.

Bending his prosthetic arm at the elbow, Pinky presented the gun to Boris with military formality, handle first. "Care to inspect it yourself?"

"No. Et's okay."

Lee said, "Okay, now that we're all happy, can we please just shoot this thing?"

**Who Framed Boris Karloff?**

## Chapter Thirty-Eight

## 29 November 1938, 3:23 p.m.

Meanwhile, Basil Rathbone was contending with an unexpected obstacle: a herd of camels and a stubborn elephant. The handler was having trouble getting the menagerie onto a soundstage while Rathbone tried darting around the odorous obstacles. One of the camels became ornery and spat at him.

"Do you know a Mr. Lugosi, by any chance?" Rathbone glibly said the the grumpy dromedary as he hurried between the animals.

Free at last from the herd, Basil dashed forward and stepped right into a pile of elephant dung. His foot flew out from under him and he slipped and suddenly found himself going ass over teakettle, landing with a thud on the pavement.

The handler saw the whole thing and hurried over to help Rathbone to his feet. "I am so sorry," the handler said. "I hope you're not hurt." He picked up the cardboard box of evidence and dusted Basil off. "Rosie didn't mean nothin' by it. That's just the way it is with elephants. They're just like you and me. When you gotta go, you gotta go."

Grabbing the box back, Rathbone said, "That's not the first pile I've stepped in lately. Excuse me."

Basil took off at top speed.

Dwight Kemper

## Chapter Thirty-Nine

## 29 November 1938, 3:31 p.m.

"Places everybody," called Lee. "Camera ready?"

"Camera ready," said Robinson.

"Sound ready?"

"Sound ready," said Brown.

"Okay, roll camera! Roll sound!"

Fred Frank held up the clapperboard. "*Son of Frankenstein*, production 931, Krogh shoots Monster, take one."

CLAP!

"ACTION!" Lee called out, "Okay, Josie, Emma, bang on the door. You can't get in because the worktable is acting like a barricade. But you try to get in anyway!"

The actresses pounded furiously on the door.

"Okay, Boris, you hear the banging and grab the kid."

Boris did as he was told. The Monster reacted to the sound of intruders by picking up the boy and holding him possessively.

"Okay, Pinky, climb out of the sulfur pit!"

With a curtain of steam rising behind him, Atwill climbed out of the pit, his face creased with a look of urgency. He unholstered his revolver.

"Good, good," smiled Lee. "Okay, Boris, you see Pinky and you grab his arm."

Just as he had been instructed to do, Boris put the boy down and grabbed Atwill's fake arm. And, just as the Monster had done to Inspector Krogh when

**"STOP! CUT! CUT!"**

the police officer was just a boy, the Monster tore the fake arm out by the roots and wielded it like a club while Boris growled menacingly.

Atwill got down on one knee and prepared to fire the first couple of rounds before the stuntman substitution.

His finger squeezed on the trigger.

"STOP! CUT! CUT!"

Atwill and Boris froze.

Rowland leapt from his chair raging. "WHO THE HELL YELLED CUT?"

A breathless and rather smelly Basil Rathbone all but collapsed on the stage floor as he tried to catch his breath.

"Basil?" asked Boris. "Whus the mattah?"

"RATHBONE!" shrieked Lee, his face purple with rage. "Who the HELL do you think you are yelling CUT like that? Nobody yells cut but the director, and the last time I looked, I WAS THE GODDAMN DIRECTOR ON THIS PICTURE!"

Rathbone put the cardboard box of evidence down in his canvas chair and said, between gulps of air, "So sorry—old man—but you see—it's a bit of a long story—."

Lee opened the cardboard box and looked inside. He pulled out the mold and gawked at the rest of the contents. "What the hell? That's the microscope we're missing, and the chemical bottles and," he pulled out the money that had been tossed back into the fishbowl. "Why's the money covered with PURPLE FINGERPRINTS? Where are the goddamned gift baskets?"

Boris and Pinky joined them as Basil huffed and puffed with, "That's—a bit—of a—long story—too."

Atwill examined the money with some amusement. "Purple fingerprints. How festive."

Boris smiled with sudden understanding as he slipped in his dental bridge. "So that's what you were talking about! You were checking the money for fingerprints."

Rathbone nodded.

"Fingerprints?" exclaimed Lee. He sniffed the air. "What the hell is that stink?"

Taking a deep breath, Rathbone exhaled the words, "Elephant dung."

"Yeah, well the same to you," Lee growled. "Don't be such a smart ass."

"No, I *fell* in elephant dung."

"Swell, now we'll have to get you in fresh wardrobe." With hands on hips and breathing deeply to try to keep calm, the director added, "And just what the hell is this all about, anyway? Why did you stop the scene?"

"I will gladly tell you everything."

"Good."

"Just as soon as I have a word with Mr. Atwill."

"About what?" asked Pinky, who appeared greatly amused by the whole situation.

"Yeah," grumbled Lee. "About what? I need Pinky to RE-shoot the scene you just messed up!"

From behind the camera Robinson said, "That's not a problem, Rowland. We can cut just before Basil yelled cut and pick up Pinky in a close-up."

"Thank God for that," said Lee. He glared angrily at Rathbone. "You have FIVE minutes. Got me?"

Basil nodded. "I've got you."

As Basil gestured for Atwill to join him outside, Boris grabbed the amateur sleuth's arm and said excitedly, "Basil, I've found Jimmy's cane! It was under the worktable. It must have been there the whole time! It was an amazing stroke of luck!"

"Or it was planted there for you to find? We'll talk about it later. Why don't you join us? You'll find this interesting."

As Rathbone, Boris, and Pinky Atwill stepped outside, Lee sighed, "I shoulda taken up ranching in Montana." To the crew he ordered, "Okay, let's set up for a crane shot. Where's Bud? Oh, there you are."

## Who Framed Boris Karloff?

## Chapter Forty

### 29 November 1938, 3:37 p.m.

Outside Stage 7, Atwill pulled out a pack of cigarettes, shook the box, and used his teeth to select a smoke. He felt around in his pockets with his free hand and then smiled at Rathbone. "Do you have a light?" He nodded at the shoulder stump. "My real arm is somewhat incapacitated and I can't find my matches."

Instead of reaching into his pocket for a lighter, Basil remarked casually, "I only have five minutes, so I'll cut straight to the point." Whereupon Basil grabbed Atwill by the lapels, threw him back against the wall and shouted, "WHY DID YOU PUT LIVE AMMUNITION IN MY GUN?"

The coloring completely drained from Pinky's face until his complexion was anything but what his nickname suggested. "Rathbone, have you lost your mind?"

"Basil, no!" said Boris, about to intervene.

"Atwill's thumbprint was on the bullet!" Basil grabbed Pinky's free left hand and held up his thumb. "That scar leaves a very distinctive mark."

Boris stared in disbelief. "You mean HE'S the one responsible for Bela's accident?"

"Rather stupid of you really," Rathbone said to Atwill. "You've become so used to favoring your left arm that you instinctively held the gun with your gloved right hand and used your ungloved left hand to insert the live ammunition!"

Boris' face twisted into the Monster's look of mounting rage. He pressed forward angrily. "If Bela doesn't pull through—" was all he could muster.

"You're both mad! How could you think I had anything to do with it? It was an accident!"

"Oh really?" Rathbone turned to Karloff. "Hold him, Boris."

"With pleasure," Karloff growled.

"Wait! You can't do that!" Atwill protested as Rathbone grabbed the gun from Atwill's holster.

Rathbone cocked back the hammer and stuck the muzzle under Atwill's pudgy chin. "Now, if you didn't substitute live ammunition in THIS gun to shoot Boris, then there won't be any real harm done beyond a mild burn if I should pull this trigger." He made ready to do just that.

"Basil, wait," said Boris. "He already demonstrated that his gun contains blanks."

"Oh?" said Rathbone, looking directly into Atwill's eyes. "I'm gambling that at least one of these bullets is fatal." He poked the gun barrel deeper into Atwill's flesh. "I say, Pinky, ever play Russian Roulette? Why don't we have a go? Although I should warn you, I'll be playing it a bit one-sided."

Sweat beaded on Atwill's face as the actor squeezed his eyes shut. "NO! DON'T!"

Rathbone took the gun away and eased the hammer back. "I thought so. Now, tell us what you know, or you may have a rather nasty accident of your own. Who put you up to this?"

"Ben Siegel."

"Why?"

"To convince you that John Roselli was behind all this."

Boris glowered. "So we'd be looking for a crooked stagehand."

"And Roselli controls the stagehands union," smiled Rathbone. Leveling a hard stare at Atwill, he asked, "So Siegel's the mastermind behind the whole plot, isn't he?"

Atwill stiffened. "I'm not saying another word. You might threaten to kill me, but I know you wouldn't. But there are people who really would kill me if I should talk."

Rathbone levered his forearm against Atwill's Adam's apple and pinned him to the wall. "Are you so sure I won't kill you? I've killed men before, Atwill. Now talk!"

Between gasps, Atwill said, "I—can't—talk—with—your—arm—on—my—neck!"

"So you will talk then?"

Atwill nodded.

Rathbone released the pressure on Atwill's windpipe. Rubbing his throat, Atwill said, "This was all the moguls' doing."

"Moguls?" asked Boris.

"Mayer, Strickling, Disney, all of them, all the moguls from all the major studios. They all owed a debt to Eddie Mannix for keeping their dirty little secrets. Then the rumors began circulating that Mannix was going to resort to blackmail."

Rathbone nudged Boris in the ribs. "I TOLD YOU it was a conspiracy!" To Atwill, in a more threatening tone, he said, "Go on, keep talking."

"They couldn't just kill Mannix. He had too many connections with the Eastern syndicate and there would have been severe reprisals, so a plan was suggested by someone — it might have been Mayer, I'm not sure — but someone suggested a way to make Mannix disappear. It was felt that if Mannix disappeared while doing a job at a studio other than M-G-M, no one would come after Mayer or Strickling."

"How do you know any of this?"

"Because I'm the reason Universal Studios was chosen as the venue for killing Mannix. Mannix owed Cliff Work a favor for, well — let's say things became a bit dicey at one of my weekend tennis parties and Cliff intervened on Mannix's behalf."

"Ridiculous!" said Boris. "How much trouble could anyone get into at a tennis party?"

With a somewhat embarrassed and altogether shifty look, Atwill said, "Well, gentlemen, I use 'tennis party' to describe my afternoon sex orgies. My wife indulges my habits. You see, I have a rather insatiable sexual appetite and, well, at my 'tennis parties' there's very little tennis but a great deal of 'love,' if you catch on."

"Clearly," said Boris, looking at Atwill with distaste.

"So," said Rathbone, "Cliff Work is in on all this, eh?"

"No, Work knows nothing about this. That's why the whole murder had to be staged the way it was, framing a big star like Boris Karloff for the murder of a studio executive. Work would be forced to call Mannix and ask him to cover things up."

"So," said Boris, grimly, "Murphy was just the sacrificial lamb luring Mannix to his death."

"It would seem so," said Atwill.

"Now for the big question," Rathbone said. "WHO killed Martin F. Murphy in the first place?"

"I don't know. My part in the scheme was rather superficial."

"Doing what?" asked Boris.

"I arranged after a certain hour for the studio switchboard to reroute any calls coming from Stage 7 directly to a telephone where I was standing by."

"I see," Rathbone said, pressing forward. "So the call from the security guard was relayed to you, and then what?"

**"Go on, keep talking."**

"Actors from Central Casting were standing by in an ambulance supplied by the studio motor pool. They were to play out a scene for Eddie Mannix's benefit. They thought it was for a publicity stunt."

Rathbone glared narrowly at Atwill. "And then you shot them!"

"What? NO!"

"A dead body burnt to a crisp must have been rather hard to explain. There couldn't be any witnesses."

"No, no, they thought the body was just a dummy! A special effect!"

Rathbone grabbed Atwill by the lapels and shook him. "A special effect? Well, those three dead bodies were no special effect! They were shot with a .38! One of our prop guns is a .38! It doesn't take a Sherlock Holmes to put two and two together, Atwill!"

"I swear to you! My role was superficial! I only made a few phone calls and hired the actors!"

Boris glowered. "If your role was as superficial as you claim, how do you know all this?"

"It was all outlined in the memos."

"Memos?" asked Rathbone.

"Unsigned memos from the head office with complete instructions."

Rathbone said, "And where are these 'memos?'"

"I burned them. I had to. My secrets would have been leaked to the press if I didn't."

"And who killed Eddie Mannix?"

"I don't know that either. I do know that Jack Pierce was there when Eddie Mannix was killed. I know because Pierce had to confide in someone."

"So poor Jack confided in you. So why and when did Jack Pierce make a death mask of Mannix?"

"I didn't know that he had," Atwill said, genuinely shocked. "So that's what he meant by 'insurance.'"

"What?" asked Boris.

"Monday morning Pierce was a bundle of nerves. He wouldn't say why, but he said he might have to use his insurance to keep Blanche safe. That was on his mind all day yesterday, Blanche's safety."

Rathbone said, "And now Blanche is in the hands of the killer."

Boris looked to Basil. "So they tore Jack's house up trying to find Mannix's death mask."

"Which was no doubt fabricated to prepare the foam rubber appliances to transform Mannix's corpse into Murphy's corpse."

Atwill said, "Pierce must have told whoever killed Mannix that he had proof that Mannix was dead."

"Who put Pierce in the hospital?" demanded Rathbone. "Was it you?"

Atwill shrugged. "Hired thugs, I imagine."

Rathbone raised the gun menacingly. "Is there anything else you're not telling us?"

"I understand from Siegel that the Western syndicate isn't very happy with the way Jack Dragna is running things here in California. There's talk that he may be—replaced."

Boris nodded grimly. "And Siegel is trying to insure that he's the next big boss."

"Perhaps," said Rathbone. "But the next in line to succeed Dragna is John Roselli."

Atwill said, "The movie moguls are tired of the syndicate and they're particularly fed up with Roselli's extortion schemes."

"Yes," said Boris, "I heard about that."

"Siegel promised to make things easier for the moguls if they helped him get Dragna and Roselli out of the way." Atwill looked around nervously and added in a whisper, "But I can tell you that after the funeral things went decidedly wrong."

Rathbone smiled knowingly. "The funeral attended by the former recipients of Mannix's help?"

"It was a way for everyone involved to put the past behind us. At least that's what we were told. As it turned out, that wasn't the real story. Everyone who attended that funeral, everyone who had something to hide and who signed that guest book, we all got—blackmail letters."

"Blackmail letters? From whom?"

"We don't know. There's no return address. All the letters were typed but not signed. The letters were also soaked in gasoline to remove any fingerprints. But the message was the same for everyone: the sender claims to now possesses the material that Eddie Mannix had kept hidden. If we don't pay up, that material will be sold to the highest bidding gossip column. Either way, the blackmailer stands to make a bloody fortune."

"Emphasis on bloody," sneered Rathbone. "Do you still have the letter? If you do, I want to see it."

"I don't have it on me," Atwill insisted, but added with a sly look, "But I can get it for you, for a price."

"Our silence, I suppose," said Boris, whose face was flushed with anger behind his gray-green makeup.

"In a word, yes," said Atwill.

Rathbone smiled, "Do you seriously expect to get away with this? If Bela Lugosi dies, we'll see you're prosecuted to the full extent of the law. That is, assuming you survive the night."

Atwill cast Rathbone a look of disdain. "Is that a threat? Remember, Basil, you merely *play* a detective. And the police are well paid by the moguls to look the other way."

"Oh, I'm not referring to the police. I'm sure that once Mr. Siegel hears that Boris is alive and well, he'll prove to you just why they call him 'Bugsy.' He doesn't strike me as a man who forgives failure."

Boris smiled with extreme satisfaction. "Yes, Mr. Siegel will gladly accommodate your tastes at a very painful 'tennis party' of his own."

Rathbone flashed a gloating smile. "Unless, of course, you agree to cooperate in return for our help."

Atwill looked suddenly very nervous. "What can you possibly do to help me? Siegel is a very powerful man."

"Give us the letter," Rathbone said, "along with your signed confession naming names and I'll do my best to see you get immunity for turning State's evidence at the trial."

"A trial! You can't be serious! By the time either the moguls or the syndicate finishes rewriting history, no one will know any of this ever happened." With stubborn determination Atwill added, "No confession, but I will give you the blackmail note, IF you can really insure my safety."

"I can guarantee it."

"But how?"

"By letting you succeed in your mission."

Boris was taken aback. "I beg your pardon? Basil, his mission was to shoot me."

"Precisely," said Rathbone. "So what do you say, Lionel?"

Atwill looked confused. "You're going to let me really shoot Boris? I doubt Mr. Karloff will agree to that."

"Here, here," said Boris.

Rathbone patted Boris' hairy jersey. "This is Hollywood, after all. When an actor needs to do anything that's too dangerous to do themselves, what's the first thing they do?"

"Call their agents."

"Besides that."

Boris snapped his fingers. "They get a stuntman!"

"Rather convenient that we just happen to have one wearing a Frankenstein costume, eh?" Rathbone turned to Atwill. "We'll use Bud Wolfe to fake Boris' untimely death. I'll even arrange to have publicity photos taken of the 'tragic accident.' They'll be in the late edition of every Los Angeles newspaper. Siegel will read about Boris' demise, thus keeping you out of harm's way."

"You can't fake Boris' death forever. Eventually Siegel will discover the truth."

"Leave Siegel to me. By the time I'm finished with him, he won't be a problem anymore. But I warn you," Rathbone added darkly, "betray us, and I'll see there's a retraction in the next edition."

Just then, Peter Mitchell stuck his head out the door to the soundstage. "Hey, fellas! We got a picture to make."

Rathbone put on a pleasant demeanor. "We'll be right along. Mr. Atwill and I are working out a scene." Giving Atwill a significant look, he asked, "Right, Pinky?"

"Uh, yes. In that case, I'll bring you the letter later tonight."

"What letter?" asked Mitchell, insinuating himself into the meeting.

"A fan letter," smiled Rathbone. He pulled back the release pin on the gun and opened the cylinder, emptying the bullets in his hand. Rathbone then picked out the two live rounds and put them in his pocket. Reloading the blanks, he closed the cylinder and handed the gun back to Atwill. "Here you go. I'll double check the weapon before you fire it." He jerked his head toward the door. "Go on now. Off with you."

As Atwill returned to the soundstage Boris eyed Rathbone skeptically. "I hope you know what you're doing. Are you sure you can trust HIM?"

"Why can't you trust Mr. Atwill?" Mitchell asked innocently.

"On the contrary, Mr. Mitchell," said Basil, giving Boris a significant look. "I'm very sure we can trust Lionel."

Boris leaned in, trying to keep Mitchell out of the conversation. "You realize this means letting the cat out of the bag." He indicated the young studio head with a nod. "What if the killer is one of them?"

"I think," said Rathbone, suggesting with a gesture that they wander away from the eavesdropping young man, "that I can say with some certainty that Murphy's killer is NOT amongst the immediate cast and crew. BUT, I believe our clue-planting ally IS."

"How do you figure that out?"

Rathbone jerked a thumb in the direction of the soundstage. "Did you not just tell me you found Whale's bamboo cane in there?"

Not getting the hint, Mitchell was following them.

"Yes," Boris said, trying to ignore the lad. "But it could have been there since—since *that night*."

"With all that constant dressing and redressing of the set for long shots, close-ups, and the like? I doubt it. I think someone in there planted that cane just before you discovered it. Just like they did with the typewriter. They're just too afraid to come forward."

"Yes," said Boris. "A typewriter Mr. Cooper was given by *certain persons*." He jerked a thumb at Mitchell who was trailing after them like a bratty little brother. Mitchell smiled and waved. "So, Basil, how do we get our informant to reveal himself?"

"One problem at a time, Boris. First, let's get you killed."

"Yeah," said Mitchell. "That's the scene they're gonna shoot right now. Mr. Lee wants you back on the set, Mr. Rathbone. It's a really great scene, too." Mitchell acted the scene out with great enthusiasm. "You swing on a chain and knock the Monster into the sulfur pit! WOW!"

Ignoring Mitchell as best he could, Boris said, "Basil, about that. If that story about my death reaches the papers and Dorothy reads about it—"

"You let me worry about that. Meanwhile, I want you to go back to the makeup bungalow and get back into your everyday attire."

Mitchell looked disappointed. "What? You mean, you're gonna go home before the Monster dies?"

"The stunt double falls into the pit," Boris explained patiently. "I don't have to be there."

Rathbone tried to take Boris aside, but Mitchell kept close. "Wait for me over on the Phantom Stage." He looked over at Mitchell, then tried to ignore him. "I'll explain the rest when I see you later, but right now I want you to 'lay low,' as the gangsters are fond of saying."

"Very well, Basil." Boris turned to leave, then remembered he left the cane on the soundstage. "I better get that cane. I wouldn't want it to suddenly disappear."

"Don't worry about the cane. I'll see to it."

"It's hanging on the Monster chair."

"SAY!" said Mitchell, taking Karloff by the arm. "Since you're gonna get out of makeup anyway, why don't I show you my new office? It's swell!"

"I really don't have time," Boris said, politely, finding it difficult to release the boy's ardent grip. He looked to Basil. "Just be careful when you handle the cane. There's greasepaint on the tip. It might be an important clue."

"Good, and all the better to get fingerprints." Rathbone knitted his brows in thought. "Greasepaint, eh? Did you observe anything else?"

"Only that the greasepaint smelled of bacon fat."

"BACON FAT!" Rathbone exclaimed. He considered this a moment, then exclaimed triumphantly, "By Jove, THAT'S IT! The final piece of the puzzle! What an idiot I've been! And what a genius Bela is! He asked the right question all along, but I was too stupid to see it until just this second!"

"I don't follow you," said Boris.

"Neither do I," said Mitchell.

"Don't you see, Boris? We've been investigating what we thought was an Arthur Conan Doyle mystery, when all the while we've been caught up in the plot of an altogether different mystery writer!"

"Which mystery writer?"

With a sly grin, Rathbone said, rather enigmatically, "Agatha Christie!"

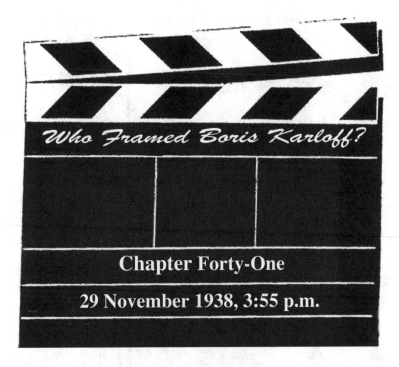

**Chapter Forty-One**

**29 November 1938, 3:55 p.m.**

As Rathbone ducked back onto the soundstage, Mitchell took Boris' arm and steered him to the studio cart.

"C'mon, Mr. Karloff," he said, eagerly. "I'll take you right over to the makeup studio after you see my office!"

Boris squeezed into the passenger seat. "I'd rather get this makeup off first, if you don't mind."

Mitchell got behind the wheel, looking crestfallen. "But I want to shoot you looking like the Monster."

"WHAT!" Boris exclaimed, ready to fend off an attack.

"I've got a camera with a squeeze bulb. I want to get a shot of us sitting on the couch."

"Oh," Boris said, relieved. "You mean take a picture."

"What else?" Mitchell stomped down on the accelerator. The cart jerked forward, then sped down the avenue toward the office block. "I want to pose us just like Mr. Murphy and Mr. Whale when I shot them."

Boris let out a sigh. "Considering recent events, could you use another word for taking a picture?"

"Gosh, you still don't think I had anything to do with Mr. Lugosi getting shot, do you?"

"No, not anymore."

"That's a relief. I'm your biggest fan. I was hoping we could, you know, be friends or something."

"The door's open...go right in!"

"If you really want to be my friend, let's make this brief. This isn't the most comfortable of costumes."

"Oh, don't you worry, Mr. Karloff. See? Here's my new office!"

They pulled into the studio production manager's private parking space. Mitchell helped Boris out of the cart and escorted him to the door.

"The door's open," he said with a magnanimous wave. "Go right in!"

Boris hesitated. He made an equally sweeping gesture. "You first." He wasn't taking any chances.

Mitchell shrugged and stepped into the office, then held the door open, beckoning Karloff inside. Boris lurched in and waited as Mitchell closed the door and hurried to the supply closet. He came out with a camera on a tripod.

Mitchell opened the legs of the tripod and positioned the camera. "Just sit over there on the couch, Mr. Karloff." He checked the focus. "I'll be right there."

Boris sat on the couch and waited. As Mitchell fiddled with the camera, Boris couldn't help feeling yet another sense of *déjà vu*. He looked around the office and at the couch he was sitting on and at the Mexican rug draped over the back of the couch and down at the Oriental rug with the large red stain on it.

"This is Murphy's furniture!" he exclaimed.

"Yeah, they had it all ready for me." Mitchell visibly shuddered as he looked around the room. "At first I was kind of, you know, creeped out using Mr. Murphy's furniture." He gestured at the red stain on the rug. "If I didn't know Mr. Murphy had died of a heart attack, that spot would really get to me. Good thing it's only fake blood."

Dwight Kemper

"Fake?"

"Sure. One of the makeup men told me it's just syrup and food coloring. He even had me taste it. Tastes like pancake syrup." He smiled shyly. "If that was real blood, I'd be out like a light. I left it there because it's kind of a conversation piece, you know?"

Boris got up to look closer at the stain and tested it with the toe of his Frankenstein boot. It was stiff and crystallized, not at all like real blood.

"It IS stage blood," Boris said. "I have to tell Basil." He headed for the door.

Mitchell was trailing a long thin hose with a squeeze bulb on the end to the couch. He looked at Boris imploringly. "Gosh, Mr. Karloff, I'm all set. This will just take a minute."

Boris hesitated, his hand grasping the doorknob. After a moment, he nodded begrudgingly. "Very well, Mr. Mitchell. I'll pose with you."

He was about to return to his place on the couch when something made him look back at the doorknob. It was stained with gray-green makeup. He looked down at his hand and then at the fake bloodstain.

"Makeup on the inside doorknob, but not on the outside doorknob," he muttered aloud.

"Huh?" asked Mitchell as he took his place on the couch formerly occupied by Martin Murphy.

"It's nothing, Mr. Mitchell," said Boris, taking his place where James Whale sat for his picture with Murphy. "Take your picture."

Mitchell took his place and posed exactly as Murphy had done the day of his death. Shaking off a sense of morbidity about the situation, Boris played along and tried as best he could to mirror Mitchell's pose. Mitchell squeezed the bulb and the flash went off.

The boy smiled from ear to ear. "Gosh, this was sure swell of you, Mr. Karloff!"

He got up and fiddled with the glass film plate, slapping the protective panel over the exposed negative and pulling out the plate.

"Tell me, Mr. Mitchell. How did you earn this promotion?"

The young executive shrugged. "To tell the truth, I dunno. One minute I'm just a still photographer, the next minute Mr. Work says I'm the new production manager. But you don't look a gift horse in the mouth, right?"

Boris smiled. "I suppose not." He got up and gestured at the door. "If you'll excuse me, Mr. Mitchell, I really do want to get out of this makeup."

Mitchell smiled warmly, hugging the exposed film plate. "Thanks again, Mr. Karloff. I'll make you a copy, if you like!"

"That would be—swell," Boris said with a smile.

## Chapter Forty-Two

## 29 November 1938, 6:20 p.m.

Boris was back in street clothes and passing the time playing a game of darts with himself on the Frankenstein Castle Library set on the Phantom Stage. He wasn't really concentrating on his game because he was too busy worrying about Dorothy and the baby.

Looking up at the portrait of Colin Clive, he sighed and said, "Colin, I sincerely hope that wherever your ashes happen to be, you're resting in peace, because these days the living are feeling anything but peaceful."

It was at that moment that Basil Rathbone finally arrived, jauntily swinging James Whale's cane. "Ah, there you are," Rathbone said, hanging up the cane on a dart imbedded in one of the wooden fireplace supports. "Before I report on your, uh, 'accident,' I have good news!"

"I could use some," muttered Boris.

"The hospital finally called. Bela is going to pull through just fine. He's being moved from the recovery room to his bed near Jack Pierce."

Boris smiled for the first time in hours. "Oh, thank heaven!"

"He's still groggy from the anesthesia, but I'm quite certain, knowing Bela, that very soon our Hungarian friend will be flirting with the nursing staff."

"No doubt."

"I thought that might lift your spirits a bit. Oh, and as for Lillian, she made her pilgrimage to Rosedale Cemetery earlier this morning."

"And?"

"The wax seal was intact," said Rathbone with a disappointed frown. "Pity. I was so certain the scene we played out for Jack Pierce's benefit would have goaded our killer into action."

"It did," Boris said grimly. "Only it wasn't the action you expected."

"You mean the assault and robbery?"

"Yes." Boris tossed another dart. "It seems very obvious to me. What did you do with Mannix's death mask?"

"Locked safely away in the boot of my car." In a more chipper tone, he added, "As for my latest plan, it's all going quite swimmingly."

"Oh?"

"Yes, indeed," Rathbone said, apparently overjoyed at his own cleverness. "The late editions of all the major newspapers will carry the following headline, 'Boris Karloff and Bela Lugosi in Near Fatal Shooting Accident.'" With a half smile, he added, "No doubt Bela will complain about getting second billing, seeing that he was shot first."

"*Near fatal* shooting accident? I thought the plan was that I was supposed to die."

"That was my original thought, yes, but then I decided a near fatal accident would suit the situation better."

"It probably won't suit Atwill at all. Siegel is sure to read about it and take action."

"That's exactly what I'm hoping. And don't worry about Atwill. He's cooperating, albeit reluctantly. I promised to keep him safe until this all blows over."

"How?"

"He's in my protective custody."

"What's that supposed to mean?"

"Don't trouble yourself about it, old man," Rathbone said with a dismissive gesture. "Anyway, the ambulance attendants didn't suspect a thing! It seems that one fellow in a Frankenstein costume looks pretty much like another."

"I see," Boris said, throwing another dart, which hit the floor. "Don't you think the hospital might catch on when they don't find a bullet wound anywhere or when they take the makeup off and find Bud Wolfe and not Boris Karloff?"

"I've taken care of that with a cover story that's been used quite a bit lately, namely that this was just a publicity stunt." Rathbone studied Karloff's technique of dart throwing and commented, "You know, for an Englishman, you're a terrible dart player."

"My mind isn't on the game." Boris walked up to the pillar, collected the darts, and returned to his pitching spot.

"And you should have seen Rowland!" Rathbone said.

"Oh?" Toss, toss, toss, and toss. Miss, miss, miss, and miss.

"The whole cast and crew, in fact," Rathbone said, stepping well out of the way of Boris' dart throwing. "They played their parts well. Why, even I was almost convinced Lionel Atwill had really shot you. By accident, of course, and all of it happened right in front of a stills photographer."

"Of course."

"And here's the interesting bit," Rathbone said, chuckling. "The publicity department ran with the whole story so that now you and Bela are the unfortunate victims of 'The Frankenstein Curse.'" Posing heroically before the darkened fireplace, he added with a haughty laugh, "Naturally, they have me again insisting there's nothing in it! I say, those writers in the publicity department are positively morbid!" Rathbone noticed Boris' mood and gave him an impatient frown. "All right, why are you acting so—I'm not quite sure what—but why are you acting that way? Oh, I know. You had to suffer Peter Mitchell's awe. How did that meeting go, by the way?"

Boris smiled mysteriously as he retrieved his darts. "I found out something that even you don't know, Mr. Holmes."

"About Mitchell's involvement? Capital!"

"Mr. Mitchell," said Boris, tossing his darts haphazardly, "is naïve and possibly an obsessed fan, but he's no murderer. I believe the moguls needed someone to sacrifice to the syndicate and Mitchell's promotion makes him look extremely guilty."

"Maybe he's only pretending to be naïve."

Boris cast Rathbone a jaundiced look. "No one is that good an actor."

"So, is that all you learned? You hinted that you had discovered something significant."

"I discovered two things. Firstly, how you can have makeup on the inside doorknob, but not on the outside doorknob. You don't leave makeup on the outside knob if someone opens the door for you."

Rathbone chuckled. "That was so obvious, it never occurred to me. And the other significant discovery?"

"I know where Murphy's furniture wound up."

Rathbone became galvanized with excitement. "You did? Where?"

"In the one place we wouldn't think of looking. The movers took the furniture out of Murphy's office and then put it right back."

"What?"

"Mitchell's office is furnished with Murphy's old furniture."

Rathbone was shaking with anticipation. "So, what did it look like? Was there a stain of any kind on the rug? WAS there a rug, or did they dispose of it?"

"The same rug was there and there was a stain. It was blood all right—stage blood."

"Stage blood!"

Dwight Kemper

"Mitchell left the stain there because he thought it would make a good conversation piece."

Rathbone slapped his knee dramatically. "That proves my theory!"

"I realize it's a Watson's lot to stand by ineffectually while the master setective dazzles us all with his clever wit; still I wish you'd be as forthright with me as I've just been with you."

Rathbone studied Boris with arms spread wide and and eyebrow crooked. "'Stand by ineffectually'? Aren't you being a trifle melodramatic?"

Boris gave Basil a hard stare. "Melodramatic? If Dorothy reads that story in the newspaper, she'll have a heart attack."

Rathbone waved dismissively. "Oh, I told you not to worry about Dorothy. She'll see for herself that you're quite all right when you visit her this evening."

"How am I going to do that? I'm 'laying low,' remember?"

"Only so a small circle of co-conspirators knows what's really going on."

"But *I* don't know what's really going on."

"I've been telling you what's going on. You are going to the hospital to lie in wait for the killer to kill you, or rather to kill Bud Wolfe, who will be in bed playing you. You'll be disguised as, I don't know, an orderly perhaps, or an intern. I haven't decided." He studied Boris a moment and wondered, "Perhaps a nurse. How do you think you'd look in drag?"

"Like a two-dollar whore," said Boris, rolling his eyes while retrieving his darts. "Just what makes you think the killer will show up tonight?"

"Siegel so much as told us that Pierce and Bela were taken to Hollywood Presbyterian because Dorothy is staying there. And with you staying in the same room with Bela and Jack, you'll be lined up like ducks in a shooting gallery. Or fish in a barrel. Your choice of metaphor."

"And what will YOU be doing?"

"I shall be questioning Mr. James Whale, apparently by the pool, over cocktails." Rathbone paused to consider that. "Rather unfair to you, when you stop to think about it. Anyway, if Mr. Whale can keep his hands off me long enough to answer a few questions concerning his involvement, I'm sure I'll be back in plenty of time for the, uh, festivities at the hospital. The killer will be arrested and his picture published in the newspaper."

"The newspaper?"

"Oh, I almost forgot. The publicity department is arranging for a reporter and a photographer from *The Los Angeles Examiner* to cover the story at the hospital."

"Are you completely insane?"

"I've never thought more rationally." Rathbone put his hands in his pockets and started pacing. "I still want to know Whale's involvement in all this." He stopped pacing and exclaimed, "Jimmy wasn't at the funeral!

Maybe it was a fear of funerals, or maybe he's the blackmailer sending those threatening letters."

Boris crossed his arms and gave Rathbone a knowing smile. "Basil, I think I know what you're really up to."

"I told you what I'm up to."

"Oh, yes, you told me. Basil, we already know that Siegel ordered Atwill to have Bela and me shot. So, logically, the man who will visit us tonight to finish the job will be Siegel."

"He practically confessed to killing Mannix, and there's the evidence of his monogrammed handkerchief in Whale's possession on the night of the murder, but that's beside the point."

Boris shook his head. "So that's it. You're setting a trap for Siegel. Even if he didn't kill Murphy, I don't see you crying tears over his death once Dragna gets hold of him."

"Siegel is only the accomplice," Rathbone said with a knowing smirk. "I not only know the identity of Murphy's killer, but who our mysterious informant is, the one who planted the cane and Cooper's typewriter."

"Mitchell gave Cooper the typewriter. Cooper said so."

"That's what our informant wanted people to think. In fact," he looked at his watch, "our informant should be joining us any minute."

"How did you find this person?"

"I didn't. He approached me. Listen to what he has to say. I promise you, Boris, on my word of honor, if you still haven't figured out the identity of the murderer by yourself after hearing what the informant has to say, I'll just flat out tell you. But that bit about Agatha Christie *was* a hint."

Suddenly there was a hesitant, tremulous knocking at the library doors.

"What was that?" asked Boris.

"I hear it, too. It sounds like a gentle tapping."

"Yes, as if someone were rap, rap, rapping on the library doors."

"If I'm not mistaken," said Rathbone, "I think that might just be our informant now."

"Or the Raven," said Boris, looking at the library doors in bewilderment. "Who on earth would knock on the doors instead of just coming around the stage flat?"

Rathbone smiled, "Our informant, of course." He called out, "Come right around the wall, Mr. Kirkwood! It's all right."

"Who's Mr. Kirkwood?" asked Boris.

Mr. Kirkwood peered around the flat, then stepped forward shyly.

"THAT," announced Basil Rathbone, "is Mr. Kirkwood."

Mr. Kirkwood said, rather meekly, "I didn't want to interrupt."

"That's quite all right, Mr. Kirkwood," Rathbone said, motioning for the man to join them. "I say, Boris, does this chap look familiar to you?"

Boris studied the man's face and suddenly realized. "Why, that's the stagehand with the broom, who—"

"—subtly suggested the idea about the prop warehouse," Basil said with a smile.

"I'm sorry about that," said Mr. Kirkwood. "I really thought they had hidden Mr. Murphy's furniture there. They did at first."

"Who is 'they?'" demanded Boris.

"The boys in the stagehands union. I guess when you started nosing around the warehouse, they thought of furnishing Mr. Mitchell's office with Mr. Murphy's furniture."

Rathbone said, "Like hiding the purloined letter."

"There wasn't any letter."

"It's a mystery story by Edgar Allan Poe. About an item hidden in plain sight." Turning to Boris, he said, "Our informant was right under our very noses the whole time. Uh, quite literally." Addressing the man, Basil said, "Do tell Boris what your job is on *Son of Frankenstein.*"

"I'm Albert. I do the sulfur pit effects." He added shyly, "I'm the grip who works the fan and the lights."

Rathbone said, "Why don't you tell Boris what you told me."

"About the cane and the typewriter?"

"Yes."

"Oh, it wasn't anything really," Mr. Kirkwood said, humbly.

"You're far too modest, Mr. Kirkwood," said Rathbone. "Tell Boris what happened. Start from the beginning."

"Well, it all started last Wednesday night. Mr. Lee was yelling at me about wanting more steam and so I gave it to him. Well, it's kind of hard to hear with the fan going anyway and the steam hissing so loudly, not that I mind, because, well, I actually find the noise to be rather soothing really and—"

Rathbone cleared his throat. "Maybe not QUITE the beginning. Could we jump ahead to what happened later that night, please?"

"Oh. Sorry. Well, to make a long story short, I fell asleep in the well."

"Until?" Rathbone said, coaxing Mr. Kirkwood along.

"Until something woke me up. The pit effects were all turned off so I guess Mr. Fulton forgot I was down there and left the soundstage dark and me all alone. Well, that is, until something woke me up. It was the machines on the set. They were all sparking and making the most frightful noises."

Boris said, "Did you see who started them up?"

Rathbone hushed Boris. "Wait, this gets better." Gesturing to Mr. Kirkwood, he said, "Tell Boris what happened next."

"Well, I climbed up the ladder to see why the machines were on and that's when it hit me."

"A realization?" asked Boris.

"No, a bamboo cane. Right here." Mr. Kirkwood displayed a knot on his forehead. "It knocked me right down the well. Good thing there was that pad at the bottom to break my fall. I was lying at the bottom of the well in a daze. And that's when I smelled it, this aroma of bacon frying, well not so much bacon frying but more like—"

"Barbecue?" suggested Boris.

"Why, yes, a barbecue. Not that I've ever been invited to one. The Laemmles had company picnics, but do you think anyone ever told me about them? No."

Rathbone cleared his throat. "Mr. Kirkwood, focus."

"Oh, sorry. Well, anyway, I decided to stay where I was. I mean, the soundstage is pretty scary at night with the lights off anyway, but when somebody hits you in the head with a cane, that's pretty scary all by itself. Well, then the machines stopped going and I heard a security guard telling somebody not to move. A man with a lisp said someone named Martin Murphy was dead and—"

"Yes, thank you," interrupted Boris. "I was there for that part."

"Maybe I should condense this a bit," said Rathbone. "He stayed hidden in the well and witnessed everything that transpired after you were taken to Work's office. He finally gathered enough courage to climb up the ladder again when he heard the ambulance sirens. And that's when he saw it."

"Well, now we're getting somewhere," said Boris. "What did you see, Mr. Kirkwood?"

"Well, the ambulance men came hurrying in with the stretcher and ran over to the operating table. That's when the man lying on the table sat up and said, 'About time you got here.'"

"The man on the table sat up?" exclaimed Boris.

"Why yes, he did. And, oh, Mr. Karloff, he was horrible looking. He was all black and brown and his clothes were all burned. He got up, got onto the stretcher and told the ambulance guys that when someone named Mannix arrived, to 'play it up big.' And something else."

Boris waited.

Mr. Kirkwood remained silent, but smiled expectantly.

"Well?" asked Boris.

"Sorry, I was waiting for you to ask me what he said."

Boris rolled his eyes. "All right, what did he say?"

"He said, and this is exactly what he said, he said, 'Take the note out of my pocket, I don't want to get anything on it.'"

Rathbone stood there with his arms folded, smiling, looking from Mr. Kirkwood to Boris Karloff, giving Boris an expectant look. "Well? Do you know who the killer is now?"

"The actor playing Murphy's corpse?" asked Boris.

Rathbone looked somewhat disappointed. "Oh dear. I was rather hoping you'd get it by now."

"Get what? Basil, all I'm getting is frustrated."

Rathbone turned to Mr. Kirkwood. "Mr. Kirkwood, while you were down in the pit, could you hear what was going on topside?"

"Well, the steam and the fan were off, but the machines were crackling and sparking and—"

"I mean after the machines were turned off. Could you hear things like footsteps, for instance?"

"Oh, yes, with the machines off I could hear footsteps."

"Did you hear any?"

"I did when Mr. Karloff left and later when the ambulance arrived."

"But did you hear any footsteps *between* those two events? Either footsteps or the sound of a body being dragged?"

Mr. Kirkwood thought a moment. Slowly, he said, "Uh, no. I didn't hear anything like that."

"Did you hear the windlass being used to open the round hole in the floor, the one with the big heavy cover?"

Mr. Kirkwood shook his head. "No, I don't remember hearing that either."

Rathbone turned to Boris. "All right! There you have it, the last clue! And just like Sherlock Holmes in 'Silver Blaze,' the clue is a noise that Mr. Kirkwood didn't hear, but should have done. NOW do you know who the killer is?"

Boris bellowed impatiently, "No!"

Now it was Rathbone's turn to get impatient. "But the cane, the grease-paint, the lack of noise between your exit and the arrival of the ambulance, and the burnt actor rising from the operating table. Agatha Christie, and all that. Oh, come on, Boris! It's so obvious. So ridiculously obvious that during our first skull session Bela asked the right question and I didn't even realize it at the time!"

"Basil, you promised you'd just tell me if I didn't guess it. So tell me."

Rathbone waved Boris off. "In a moment, in a moment. Don't you want to know about the typewriter and how the cane got under the table?"

"I assume Mr. Kirkwood planted the cane there, since he retrieved it from the well." Looking questioningly at Mr. Kirkwood, he asked, "But how did you get the typewriter?"

"Well," Mr. Kirkwood said, "Mr. Mannix got the stagehands, including me, to clear the furniture out of Mr. Murphy's office."

"The typewriter was in Murphy's office?" asked Boris.

"Yes, sir. Anyway, we loaded up the truck, and when they told me to make sure we got the typewriter, that's when I said, 'Albert, you better make sure that typewriter doesn't disappear.' See, I read a lot of mystery novels and I know that sometimes you can identify a typewriter by little imperfections in the type, and since they were making such a fuss about getting rid of it, I figured the typewriter was important."

Boris was confused. "But Mitchell gave Cooper the typewriter. Cooper said so." He turned to Mr. Kirkwood. "How on earth did you arrange that?"

"Nobody ever notices me. My mother calls me the 'Invisible Man.' I kept the typewriter and the cane with me down in the sulfur pit and just waited for my chance to plant evidence."

"But how did you know we were even investigating this case?"

"I didn't know, at first. But it sure looked like somebody was trying to frame you for something, so I figured you ought to know the truth. So I planted the typewriter."

"When did you decide to plant the cane?"

"When I heard the three of you discussing the case today." Shyly, he added, "No offense, but the three of you are pretty loud with all your whispering." He smiled at Basil. "Then when Mr. Rathbone told the rest of the cast and crew what the three of you were up to, and after poor Mr. Lugosi getting shot, well, I felt it was my civic duty to come forward."

Basil smiled, giving Mr. Kirkwood a pat on the back. "And a fine, up-standing citizen you are, too, my dear Mr. Kirkwood!"

Mr. Kirkwood smiled shyly. "Gee, like I said, it was nothing, really."

Boris tapped Rathbone's shoulder. "I say, Mr. Holmes?"

"Yes," Basil said with a smile.

"It's time you kept your promise. Who are we looking for? Who killed Murphy and who killed Mannix?"

Basil sighed. "Before I just come out and say it, let me just help you review the evidence." He counted off on his fingers. "There were no sounds of footsteps or the dragging of a body, which means, no attempt to hide a body. There was greasepaint mixed with bacon fat on the tip of the cane. We had Rowland himself very clearly demonstrate that when you're lying on the operating table, you're properly grounded. And, most important of all, when you described finding Murphy, you said you thought it was a dummy at first. You do remember that?"

"Yes."

"So the body on the operating table was still, it didn't move?"

"Of course not," Boris huffed impatiently. "The man was dead."

"Dead and had electricity coursing through his body."

"So?"

Basil threw up his hands impatiently. "Boris, haven't you ever seen that classic experiment with a frog's leg? The one demonstrating galvanic response by stimulating the muscles with a probe connected to a battery? My God,

Mary Shelley herself witnessed such a demonstration with a convict's cadaver. That's what inspired her to write *Frankenstein* in the first place! Dead or alive, Murphy's muscles ought to have twitched!"

Suddenly the realization hit Boris. "My dear Lord! That means, if the muscles didn't twitch, the body had to have been grounded! And if the body had been grounded, it couldn't have been burned!"

"And while lying down on the operating table, our murderer felt it was safer to use a non-conductive object to work the toggle switches on the Strickfaden control box. Something like—"

"—a bamboo cane!"

"Which, by the way, eliminates Rowland as a suspect, because he very clearly felt no hesitation about handling the control box while lying on the table."

"Of course!"

"And, finally, my dear Watson, what is the one convention that Agatha Christie is most famous for?"

Boris snapped his fingers. "That the killer is always the least likely suspect!"

"And in this case, who would be the least likely suspect?"

"The first murder victim!" Boris looked from Basil to the cane hanging from the imbedded dart. "Martin F. Murphy isn't the murder victim, he's the murderer, the murderer of Eddie Mannix!"

"EUREKA," Rathbone belauded. "Now, don't you feel so much better having worked it all out yourself?"

"But where has Murphy been all this time? How are we going to expose him without proof? And do you think we can convince Jack Dragna about this?"

"All very good questions, my dear Karloff. And I have no bloody idea. But I think I know who might." He sized up Boris with a searching look. "By the way, what size lab coat do you take?"

## Chapter Forty-Three

## 29 November 1938, 7:30 p.m.

### Hollywood Presbyterian Hospital, 3rd Floor

A crying man stood in the hall by the door to the suite next to Dorothy's. A nurse tried to comfort him.

"I know it hurts, Mr. Nolan," the nurse said. "But take comfort in knowing that your wife is at peace now."

"I know," Mr. Nolan sobbed. "She's been in so much pain. And at least I had a chance to say good-bye." Indicating the empty gurney, he asked, "Where are they taking her?"

The nurse said, "They're taking her down to the morgue. The mortuary will pick her up later. At least you have your son."

"Thank you," said Mr. Nolan. "Thank you for everything."

They heard running footsteps heading their way. A man wearing a black wig, mustache, and black horn rim glasses and dressed in a doctor's smock and lab coat with a stethoscope hanging around his neck, skidded to a halt before he collided with them.

"I do beg your pardon," said Boris Karloff.

"You should know better," the nurse scolded. "No running in the halls."

A reporter and photographer from the *Los Angeles Examiner* skidded to a stop behind Boris just as a doctor stepped from Mrs. Nolan's suite. He motioned Boris over.

"You must be the new intern," the doctor said. "We missed you on rounds this morning." He pointed inside the room at an empty gurney. "Take Mrs. Nolan down to the morgue."

Nonplussed, Boris said, "But the gurney is empty."

The doctor scowled disapprovingly. "Is this your first time on the floor? Of course it's empty, man. It's a morgue gurney. Now do as you're told."

Boris raised his wig revealing graying hair beneath. "I do apologize but I'm Boris Karloff, not an intern. Now if you'll excuse me, my wife needs me."

Boris left the flabbergasted doctor and hurried to Dorothy's bedside. Julian Walker, AKA Mrs. Julie Walker, RN, looked up from his knitting. He appeared to be just an older, yet still attractive, matronly woman with long gray hair pinned in a bun.

Boris took his wife's hand. "Darling, I hope you haven't been worrying too terribly much. I feel awful! As you can see, I'm quite all right!"

Dorothy looked at Boris like he had gone completely insane. "Why on earth are you dressed like that?"

"My, Mr. Karloff," said Julie, fingers nimbly working away on one of a pair of baby booties, "don't we look all mad doctor-like this evening. Tryin' to give your Missus a bit of a fright, are we?"

The reporter and photographer stood in the doorway.

"What a scoop!" said the reporter. "Karloff consoles wife before risking life and limb." To the photographer, he said, "Get a picture, Mike!"

"What's going on?" asked Dorothy, pulling her blankets up to her chin.

The photographer was about to take a picture when Boris reached out with his hand and covered the camera lens. "Would you both please wait for me in Bela and Jack's room?"

"But," the reporter protested, "Universal Studios promised us an exclusive!"

"And you'll get it. But not HERE!"

"Now, look," the photographer began, about to insist on taking a picture. Boris stood up and gave them both an intimidating look. The reporter nudged his photographer. "Yeah, we'll just wait in Bela and Jack's room. Come on, Mike."

"I'm with you, Johnny," said the photographer.

Once the press was out of sight, Boris returned to Dorothy's beside and took her hand again. "I was afraid you might have read about the accident."

"ACCIDENT?" Dorothy exclaimed. "What accident?"

"The article in the newspaper, of course."

"The paper didn't come this evening."

Mrs. Walker cleared her throat and reached into her bag of knitting. "Sorry, Mrs. Karloff, but I thought it best to keep it from you, considerin' your condition and all."

Mrs. Walker handed Dorothy the late edition with the blaring headline, KARLOFF AND LUGOSI IN NEAR FATAL SHOOTING!

**"Boris, if you don't tell me what this nonsense is all about—"**

Looking up from the paper, Dorothy cast her husband an accusing look. "Boris, if you don't tell me what this nonsense is all about—"

Boris opened his mouth, only to be silenced by Dorothy's raised index finger. "And don't tell me this is all a publicity stunt," she warned. "I'll have none of that. Sara Jane is scheduled to be home tomorrow morning with a nurse."

Mrs. Walker held up a freshly knitted cap and sweater. "Don't you think the little lady will be all nice and cozy in this outfit?"

Dorothy looked at the cap and sweater and gushed, "Oh, that is so sweet!" Then she shot Boris a stern look. "As I said, the nurse will be coming home with the baby and I won't have you frightening that poor woman with any more of your strange antics of late. Now, I want to know what you're up to and I want to know this instant!"

"Well, dear," Boris began, "if you really feel well enough." He cleared his throat, "By the way, I'll have to keep this brief because I need to be on the next floor so I can ambush a murderer."

Dorothy's eyes widened in astonishment. "WHAT?"

Mrs. Walker sighed. "Oh dear, those nasty obsessive fans. Might I be of any help to you, Mr. Karloff?"

"Just stay here and keep Dorothy safe." Giving his wife a worried glance, he added, "Uh, can you protect her from an assailant with a gun?"

"You can count on me, sir." Mrs. Walker picked up her bag and patted it confidently. "There's a bit more than me knittin' in 'ere, if you know what I mean."

Dorothy looked from Boris to her private nurse and back to Boris. "What are you two talking about? Ambushing murderers? Obsessive fans? Have you both gone completely out of your minds?"

Boris smiled wanly. "Sometimes it does seem that way. Did you say you wanted the WHOLE truth?"

"Every word of it!" Dorothy insisted.

"Very well," Boris sighed. "I suppose I should first introduce you to your bodyguard. Dorothy, this is Julian Walker. Julian, Dorothy Karloff."

Pulling off his wig, Julian smiled. "'Ello, luv. Don't be too upset, dear. I was a field medic, so you were always in safe hands."

Dorothy grew pale. "You mean, you're a—and you've been—and he—?"

A call light flashed at the nurse's station. Dorothy Karloff needed a sedative.

**Who Framed Boris Karloff?**

## Chapter Forty-Four

### 29 November 1938, 8:00 p.m.

#### James Whale's Villa, Pacific Palisades

Basil Rathbone rang the doorbell. Anna Ryan, James Whale's maid, greeted him. "Yes, sir," she said in a thick German accent.

"I have an appointment with Mr. Whale," said Basil.

"Mr. Jimmy is expecting you." She indicated the cardboard box Basil had tucked under his arm and the cane he was holding. "May I take from you your things, sir?"

"No, thank you. These are for Mr. Whale."

"I see," she said with a tinge of suspicion in her voice. "Yes, that is Mr. Jimmy's cane. He said he had *lost* it." Basil had the distinct impression that from the way she said, "lost" that the maid was accusing him of having stolen it. Her probing stare rested on the cardboard box. "You have for him his hat in that box? He *lost* that, too."

"No. But you're right. This is his cane. I'm returning it to him."

"I see." She stepped aside and said, "This way please."

She led Basil through the villa and out back to the patio at a very brisk pace, as if she feared lingering might give him a chance to make off with one of the knickknacks. She led him through a beautiful English garden, down a grassy slope and along a winding path. They came to a Greco-Roman studio with 20-foot high pillars reflected in a swimming pool. A naked young man, probably no more than 18, stood on the diving board trying to get a very pensive James Whale's attention by displaying his muscular physique. The lights around the pool gave the scene a surreal quality.

Whale sat under the umbrella of a poolside table. He wore a pair of silk oriental pajamas and was nursing a drink. On the table beside him were a half-empty bottle of gin, a bottle of tonic, a bucket of ice, and a burgundy drawstring bag.

"Come on, Jimmy," said the young man as he flexed his pectorals. "Watch me dive!"

But Whale paid him no mind. He sipped his gin and tonic and kept staring at the drawstring bag. He only looked up when the boy's dive splashed the director with a few drops of water. Whale threw a protective arm around the drawstring bag.

"Be careful, darling!" he said with a slurring delivery. "Do be careful!"

Anna paused by the pool and cleared her throat as Basil stood beside her. The boy climbed out of the pool and was about to join Whale at the poolside table when Anna's throat clearing made the young man aware of Rathbone's presence. The young man instinctively grabbed a towel and tucked it around his waist before taking his seat.

"Mr. Basil Rathbone to see you, Mr. Jimmy," Anna announced, rolling her eyes and avoiding the young man's gaze.

Whale looked up and smiled drunkenly. "AH! So delighted to see you, Mr. Rathbone!" As Whale made formal introductions, he gestured with the glass of gin and tonic, first at the young man, then up at Basil. "Young Mr. Christopher Dean meet Mr. Basil Rathbone; Mr. Rathbone, Mr. Dean."

"Wow," Dean said, "I didn't know you and Jimmy were—"

"We're not," Basil quickly interrupted. "This is purely a business call." He added with significance, "and private."

Dean frowned as James shooed him away with a gesture. "Now, now, don't pout. Mr. Rathbone and I have much to talk about. Go inside and have a bit of a lie down and I'll join you later. Maybe."

"Okay." The boy got up and let the towel drop as he pushed past Basil. "Nice meeting you," he said icily before following Anna, who had grabbed a robe lying by the pool.

"Please to put this on, Mr. Dean," she insisted before taking him back to the house.

When they were finally alone, Rathbone sat beside Whale and presented the cane. "Your cane, Jimmy. I've already made a complete photo record and fingerprint analysis of it and I thought I'd return it to you."

Whale took the cane and smiled. "Wherever did you find it?"

"Boris found it on the laboratory set. That cane, I've since discovered, has led a very adventuresome life since you last saw it."

"Boris didn't happen to find my hat, too, whilst he was about it?"

"I'm afraid not."

Whale sighed glumly. "Pity. That was my favorite hat."

"Where did you last see it?"

Whale smiled at Rathbone and chuckled. "The same place I THOUGHT I had left my cane—in dear Martin's office last week."

"Jimmy," Rathbone began, "I know a great deal about what happened that night, but not everything."

"No, I imagine not," Whale said, refreshing his drink. "Sorry, I'd offer you a drink, but I only brought the one glass. If you like, I could have Anna bring you something."

"I'm fine."

"No, I think you should have a drink." Whale grabbed a bell and rang for his maid. "Otherwise the ceremony would lack something."

"Ceremony? I don't underst—"

"ANNA!" Whale shouted impatiently. "Where the devil is that silly woman? ANNA!"

Anna came hurrying back down the path to the pool. "Yes, Mr. Jimmy?"

"Dear, please see Mr. Rathbone has a proper drink of something." To Rathbone he asked, "What's your poison?"

"Well, if you insist," said Rathbone. To Anna, he said, "Vodka tonic, please."

Anna nodded. Looking to Whale, she asked, "Anything more for you, Mr. Jimmy?"

With a tipsy shake of the head, he slurred, "No, I'm quite satisfied. Now do hurry along."

Anna did as she was told, hurrying back up the path.

Alone again, Rathbone said to Whale, "What ceremony are we talking about? A confession, perhaps?"

Whale giggled. He looked down at the drawstring bag and said to it, "Did you hear that, darling? He wants to hear my confession. How droll."

Basil studied the bag with some interest. "What is that?"

"The guest of honor, Mr. Rathbone," Whale said enigmatically.

"Guest of honor? Guest of honor for what, exactly?"

"For a proper sending off." He laid a gentle hand on the bag and sighed. "If I can gather enough courage to finally let him go."

Ten minutes later, Anna was back with a silver service holding Basil's drink and a plate of cucumber sandwiches. "I thought maybe you might want a little something," she said, serving the drink and plate. She stepped back and said, "Anything else, Mr. Jimmy?"

"Just see that young Chris is comfortable, my dear," Whale said. "Get him whatever he wants."

"Yes, Mr. Jimmy," she said, a hint of disapproval in her voice before returning to the house.

Whale rose drunkenly to his feet. Basil jumped up to steady him. Whale gestured his assurance that he was all right. "Let's raise our glasses, Mr. Rathbone, raise our glasses in a toast."

Basil decided it was best to humor him and did as he was instructed as Whale said, "To dear Colin Clive, my finest actor and my greatest love, may you now forever rest in peace." He added, as he raised his glass to his lips, "For no doubt I shall surely burn in hell."

He downed his gin and tonic and flopped back in his deck chair.

Basil gestured at the drawstring bag with his glass. "I take it THAT is Colin Clive?"

"His ashes, yes," said Whale, picking up the bag and holding it with a reverence usually afforded holy relics.

"I thought they were lost," Basil said as he sat back down.

"They *were* lost," Whale said, sighing and putting the bag back down. "They *were* lost." He looked up at Basil with bloodshot eyes displaying a hint of clarity behind them. "I say, Basil, have you ever done anything you greatly regretted?"

"I'm sure we can all admit to having done so, at least at some time in our lives. Have you?"

"Oh, yes," Whale sighed. "During my life, many things. Lately, a great deal more." He stared out beyond the pool to the English garden. "Do you think Colin would like to rest there amongst the flowers? Or should I stand on a cliff and let the winds carry him out to sea?"

"How did you come by them?" Basil asked, keeping his eyes on the drawstring bag.

"Oh, therein hangs the tale," Whale chuckled. "But where to start?" he said reflectively. "I suppose we should begin with Colin's death. June the 25th, 1937, the day Colin died, and he died alone, alone at Cedars of Lebanon Hospital, cause of death, pneumonia from chronic alcoholism." Looking down at his glass, he added, "Sadly, I find that gin only blurs, but never completely obliterates, the bitter memories that still haunt me." After a long, thoughtful pause, he said, "Funeral services on June the 29th, where his ashes were subsequently lost."

"How exactly did that happen?"

"Colin's wife Jeanne had forsaken him when she discovered that Colin and I were lovers. She didn't even bother to make the trip from London to attend the service. It was because of that, and my own weakness, that led to Colin's ashes getting lost in the shuffle."

"Your fear of funerals?"

Whale nodded. "Yes. I SHOULD have been there." He poured himself a glass of straight gin, no tonic. "I was supposed to be one of the pallbearers. The others were there to see Colin's coffin off on its final journey: Peter

Lorre, Alan Mowbray, everyone but the one who should have seen to it that Colin was properly looked after. Everyone but me." He looked pleadingly at Basil, tears forming in his eyes. "I wanted to be there. I tried to be there. I wore white for the funeral."

"The suit you wore Wednesday?"

"Yes. I thought if I avoided the trappings of grief I could overcome my fear of death." He scowled at the memory. "But I couldn't bring myself to do it. I got as far as the mortuary steps, then the fear took possession of me and I ran." He took a sip of straight-up gin. "They loaded Colin into the hearse and that was the last I saw of the man who meant everything to me."

"When did you first learn of the ashes having been mislaid?"

"Long after it was possible to locate them. The papers said his ashes had been sent back to England, and I believed them. Months later I got up the courage to write Jeanne and inquire after her husband's ashes. She told me she hadn't sent for them, and further, she would speak no more of Colin. Then came news of the Rosedale Crematory scandal. A call to the mortuary confirmed my worst fears. Colin's ashes had been lost."

Basil gestured at the bag. "Until now."

"Yes," nodded Whale. "Until now. Delivered yesterday morning by none other than Benjamin Siegel. For services rendered."

"What might those services have been?"

There was a chill in the night air. Steam rose from Whale's heated pool. Whale gave Rathbone a sly look. "Leading a lamb to the slaughter, the lamb being Eddie Mannix."

Rathbone studied the bag. "So you cooperated with Siegel and Murphy because Siegel promised you Colin Clive's lost ashes?"

"Sounds silly when *you* say it," Whale commented as he poured himself another straight gin. "But, yes. Mr. Siegel told me the crematory was a front for some gangster business and all the unclaimed ashes were in the basement. He said he had recovered Colin's ashes and would give them to me if I did him a favor."

"So who put Seigel up to all this?"

Smiling impishly, "Nobody put him up to it," Whale said. "It was all his idea."

"I thought the studio moguls—"

Whale shook his head. "It was all Siegel's idea. He became star struck. Oh, he just loves Hollywood and all the glitzy glamour that goes with it. He started charming the pants off the moguls and the panties off the starlets." Taking a sip of gin he mumbled, "When he wasn't beating someone to a bloody pulp, that is." Leaning in, Whale gestured for Basil to come closer and he whispered, "Siegel wants to head the West Coast syndicate, you see. Apparently Jack Dragna is all talk and little action. Do you know, he apparently makes threats he has absolutely no intention of following up on?"

"You don't say?" said Basil, hoping Whale was telling the truth.

"That's why the East Coast syndicate sent Siegel and a chap named Cohen out to California, to see exactly what was what."

"If Dragna was so ineffective, why didn't Siegel just kill him outright and take over?"

"Because of Eddie Mannix and John Roselli. Mr. Roselli is Dragna's second-in-command and extorting money from the producers. He's set to succeed Dragna and is very well connected. As for Eddie Mannix, the East Coast syndicate worshipped him! No, if Siegel ever hoped to rise in the ranks of Hollywood as the new crime boss, Dragna, Mannix, and Roselli would all have to be put down."

"So," Rathbone said, "Siegel arranged to have Mannix's reputation tarnished by ugly rumor and innuendo."

"The moguls, those rich, self-important bastards, wanted Mannix dead, but feared the wrath of Mannix's underworld allies."

"Then came Bugsy Siegel with a foolproof plan."

Touching the side of his nose with his index finger, Whale winked and said, "On the nosey."

"How was Siegel planning to get rid of Roselli?"

"He was going to make it look like Roselli put a contract out on Mr. Mannix. Mannix's friends would do the rest."

"Why did Siegel call upon you?"

Whale sat back and shrugged. "My association with Boris, I suppose. It also seemed a natural consequence considering the trouble Martin's been having lately with Lee's rather unorthodox directing methods."

"So, Murphy planned to fake his death with the assistance of Jack Pierce."

"Pierce made Martin up right in Martin's office. God, the poor man looked simply horrid."

Rathbone nodded, "That explains greasepaint on the inside doorknob. And with the stage lights off, the illusion would be most convincing."

Whale nodded. "Yes, it was a marvelous plan."

Rathbone reached down and opened the cardboard box containing the death mask mold. He handed it to James Whale. "I assume it happened either before or on the way to the crematorium, the murder of Mannix, I mean."

Whale took the mold and giggled, giddy from drink. "I've wondered how Mannix's face must have looked when Martin rose up from the dead to do him in." His giggling turned to tears as he cradled the mold in his lap. "And I helped to kill him."

"The studio cart with the incriminating bloodstain. Whose blood was in it?"

Whale recovered himself. "Blood?"

"Eddie Mannix claimed there was blood in the studio cart."

"So that's why Siegel was so damned insistent I lend Boris that cart. But why should I be so surprised? The man thinks he's a natural in show business. Siegel must have planted the blood after the fact."

"Siegel was on the lot that night?"

"In Martin's office while Martin made ready for his part in all this. We toasted our success over three glasses of brandy."

"Why did they drug you?"

"Drug me?" Whale broke into a sheepish grin and looked like a bad boy who had just been caught breaking his mother's favorite vase. "I drugged myself."

"You what?"

"Actually, I was hoping to drug Siegel. I was getting cold feet and the man scares me. I brought a vial of knockout drops with me in case things got out of hand and I needed to make good my escape."

"So you were faking being drunk that day?"

"God, no. I was definitely four sheets to the wind, toasting Colin's memory and trying to convince myself I was doing the right thing by him."

"Is that what you were doing on the Phantom Stage that day?"

"I heard they had a portrait of Colin there. I stopped by to beg his forgiveness for what I was about to do to insure his final rest."

"So, let me see if I understand you correctly. You got cold feet at the last minute and tried to drug Siegel?"

"I was so damn drunk I picked up the wrong bloody glass and was out like a light."

"Rowland said he found you unconscious on Murphy's couch at around 9:30 p.m. How did you wake up in time to complete your mission at 10:30? Did the drug merely wear off?"

"I wish it had," Whale said, wincing at the memory. "Siegel came back and found me still out like a light. He's the one who roused me, if you want to call it that."

"Rowland said he tried to wake you and couldn't."

"He obviously didn't use Mr. Siegel's method. Namely a quick punch to my dangly bits. That will wake you fast enough, trust me." Rubbing his cheek, he added, "Also a good slap to the face."

"That's when you got your nosebleed, I take it."

"Siegel was kind enough to lend me his hanky." Whale sighed wistfully and returned the mold to Basil. "I think Colin would have preferred the garden," he said, taking the drawstring bag. "There he can live again in fragrant growing things." He looked imploringly at Basil. "Care to help me give poor Colin his proper sendoff?"

With an understanding smile, Rathbone nodded. "Yes, I'd be honored."

Whale carried the burgundy bag to the garden as Basil followed. There amongst the rose bushes, Rathbone held open the drawstring bag while Whale reached in and produced a small cardboard box. He opened the box and pulled out a brown paper bag. Whale grabbed a handful of white soot. "I release you to the winds, dear lovely Colin. Be at peace at last!" With that, he flung out his hand and let the ashes fly. The soot filled the air and covered the roses, turning their red petals grayish white. Two objects dropped onto the grass.

"What are those?" asked Whale, his face and pajamas dusted white with human soot.

Rathbone bent down to pick up the objects. He examined them with a look of grim understanding. "It would seem, Jimmy, that when you make a deal with the Devil, you very often get burned."

Basil held out his hand. There in his palm were a lump of gold and a blackened tiger-eye stone with a relief carving of a conquistador.

## Chapter Forty-Five

## 29 November 1938, 8:40 p.m.

### Hollywood Presbyterian Hospital, 3rd Floor

The bedside telephone rang. Mrs. Walker quickly answered it.

"Dorothy Karloff's room, Mrs. Walker speaking."

Julian Walker was back in costume and instantly recognized the voice and gushed, "Oh, it's you, Mr. Rathbone! I'm sorry, sir, but the Mrs. Karloff is really in no condition to chat at the moment." Julian looked over at the unconscious form of Dorothy Karloff, resting comfortably, but insensate. "She's 'ad to be sedated."

"Sedated? Why? What's happened?" Basil was using the telephone in Whale's living room while nibbling a cucumber sandwich. He glanced over at the couch where James was clutching the now empty drawstring bag, laughing and crying at the same time. Anna and Dean were trying their best to console the director.

In the hospital room, Julian sighed and said, "Well, when Mr. Karloff told Dorothy about the whole sordid story she became a trifle—upset, you might say." Looking at Dorothy's sleeping form, Julian pulled his wig off and gave his hot scalp a good rubbing. "In a way, I'm rather glad to 'ave everythin' finally out in the open. I've never worn a wig for so long and it sure does get 'ot and itchy."

"I see," Basil said on the phone.

"'Ere," said Julian, "why didn't you folks tell me you was investigatin' that whole Murphy affair?"

"To be honest," said Basil, "James Whale was a prime suspect and we were afraid you might inadvertently give something away, being a close friend of his and all."

"Oh, Jimmy and me, we 'aven't spoken in years. Not since he learned I was strictly a lady's man, if you catch me drift."

"Yes, I think I do."

"The thing is, I could 'ave saved you blokes a hell of a time with all your pokin' about."

"How so?"

"Well, take the identity of the mystery widow, the woman in black who was at Mr. Murphy's funeral. I could 'ave told you who it was straight away."

"Well, don't keep it to yourself, man! Who was it?"

"It was Mae, all right."

"But how can you be so sure? The widow's face was never seen, either in person, or in any of the published photographs."

"From the picture in the newspaper. I recognized the dress the widow was wearin'. Mrs. Nussbaum made that dress for Mae just last week. It's a copy of a dress from some movie or other, I think it was a Vera West original."

Rathbone clutched the phone cord with excitement. "Of course! So Mae's Brothel *is* connected to all this."

"As Mrs. Nussbaum was doin' the fittin', Mae was all excited about 'er bein' involved in some 'big score' or other. At the time I wasn't sure what she was goin' on about, but now that Mr. Karloff mentioned that little blackmail scheme, I figured that was what she meant."

Basil began pacing excitedly with the telephone. "I'll wager Mae and Siegel are working together! And if Mae's Brothel IS bugged, she has wire recordings of client pillow talk!" His eyes brightened. "THAT'S how she was able to convince the moguls that Mannix was turning against them!" Chuckling, Basil mused, "So, Siegel plays both ends against the middle. On the one hand, he promises the moguls his protection, and then he uses Mae to bleed them dry with blackmail."

Back in the hospital room, Julian was cradling the handset between his chin and shoulder. "Rather clever, I must say." Walker sat in a chair and grabbed his bag of knitting, rummaging around until he found a nail file. "Anyway, is there a message I can give Mrs. Karloff when she wakes up?"

"No, but if you could tell Boris not to wait for me, I'd appreciate it. I think I'll pay a call to Mae's Brothel and confront Mae with what I know."

"I 'ope you're armed, Mr. Rathbone. Mae's been known to keep a derringer 'andy."

"Thanks for the tip," said Basil, then as an after thought, added, "Oh, and Julian, be prepared. I expect things will get rather nasty. Mrs. Karloff must be kept safe at all costs."

"Not to worry, sir," said Julian, reaching into his knitting bag and producing a loaded .45. "I'm ready for trouble and I'm a crack shot."

Back at the villa, Basil said, "Excellent."

He hung up the telephone and gulped down the last of the cucumber sandwich, then reached into his breast pocket, producing Dragna's business card. He dialed the number and waited. As the ring tone buzzed in his ear, Rathbone looked over at Whale.

The director stared sadly at the drawstring bag in his hands. "The irony both pains me and tickles me at the same time! Poor Colin. What a damn fool I've been. A fool for love."

There was a click on the phone. Basil said, "Hello? Mr. Dragna? Mr. Dragna, this is Basil Rathbone. I'm prepared to name the killer of Eddie Mannix. The killer is Ben Siegel. He's behind a plot to dethrone you as leader of the West Coast syndicate and Mannix was in the way. He was planning to frame John Roselli for the murder so you would eliminate Roselli. Yes, I'm absolutely certain of it. In fact, I'd stake my life on it." He paused to listen, then added grimly, "Yes, I'd stake my wife's life on it, too."

### Who Framed Boris Karloff?

## Chapter Forty-Six

## 29 November 1938, 8:45 p.m.

### Hollywood Presbyterian Hospital, First Floor Lobby

Siegel and Cohen entered the lobby of Hollywood Presbyterian Hospital. Ben Siegel's hair was slicked down with pomade. He was dressed in his finest double-breasted suit, a suit that was specially tailored to conceal any telltale bulge from his gun and shoulder holster. He was also wearing enough cologne to choke anyone within a 20-yard radius.

"You smell like a French whore house," grumbled Mickey Cohen, who wore his usual gray suit and brown fedora.

"Like you would know," said Siegel as they approached the information desk at the northwest corner of the lobby. A pretty nurse sat reading a Hollywood gossip magazine. Siegel leaned in and flashed his pearly whites. "Excuse me there, beautiful, my friend and me are executives from Universal Studios and we're here to visit Mr. Boris Karloff and Mr. Bela Lugosi. Can you tell us what room they're in?"

The nurse looked at the clock on the wall behind her. The time was 8:45. "I'm sorry, gentlemen," she said politely, "but visiting hours for the Isolation Ward ended at 8:30."

Siegel leaned in closer, giving the pretty nurse his most seductive leer. "Aw, come on, sugar. We're only late by 15 minutes. Are you sure you couldn't, you know, look the other way and let us up? Maybe I can arrange a screen test. We can maybe discuss it over dinner later."

The nurse recoiled and held her nose while waving the air with her magazine. "I'm sorry, sir," she said in a nasally tone. "But we're very strict about enforcing visiting hours." She began to cough and pushed her chair back. "Sorry, I'm allergic to perfumes."

"Now look, baby," Siegel began more earnestly, only to be interrupted by Cohen tapping him on the shoulder.

With a jerk of the head, Cohen took Siegel aside. "Will you just plug Florence Nightingale already."

"Hey, you don't just plug nurses. They're angels of mercy, for christssake. Besides," Siegel added, looking around the lobby, "we open fire in a hospital lobby, the cops will be down on our necks just like that." He snapped his fingers for emphasis.

"Yeah, well, it was your idea that we do the hit ourselves. Me, I'd have just hired a couple of goons."

"I tried that, didn't I? And Atwill screwed it up."

"That guy ain't a professional."

"Whatever! Remember, Mickey, if you want somethin' done right, you do it yourself."

"I don't see us gettin' in any quicker by bein' nice. And I don't think that dame likes you very much."

"Shaddap," Siegel growled, looking around the lobby for inspiration. "There's a way around this, just give me a minute to think."

Siegel took in the details of the lobby. An intern sitting on a bench was reading a newspaper. Orderlies, doctors, and nurses entered and exited the lobby through the elevator car situated to the left of the information desk and through the swinging doors leading to other parts of the ground floor.

A deliveryman entered the lobby from the street. He wore a green jumpsuit with "Brewster Florists" embroidered on the pocket along with the phone number. He was carrying a bouquet of flowers with a blue balloon floating above the arrangement with the words "It's a Boy!" printed across it.

He approached the information desk and winked at the pretty nurse. "Say, Daphne, I got me some flowers for a Mrs. Lois Danberry from her lovin' hubby."

"Okay, Lloyd." Nurse Daphne checked her records. "Maternity Ward, Room 315."

"Thanks, gorgeous. Say, are we still on for tomorrow night?"

Nurse Daphne smiled. "We sure are."

"Still off all day tomorrow?"

"No, I'm working seven to three. But I'll be ready by six."

"Then I'll pick you up at seven." He winked at her again and trotted over to the elevator, pushed the button, and waited. He flashed the nurse a smile.

Siegel grinned broadly and nudged Cohen. "That's it."

"What? Because she's already got a boyfriend, you think that's why you couldn't make time with that dame?"

"No, you dope," grumbled Siegel. "I just thought of a way to get upstairs and do the hit. Come on, we gotta find a payphone."

The intern on the bench lowered his newspaper. It was the disguised Boris Karloff. He waited for Siegel and Cohen to leave the building, then hurried through the door by the elevator and up the stairs.

## Who Framed Boris Karloff?

## Chapter Forty-Seven

## 29 November 1938, 8:55 p.m.

### James Whale's Villa, Pacific Palisades

Out in Whale's driveway, Atwill was waiting, not very patiently, in the front seat of Rathbone's car. He sighed and tried to lift his right arm, finding it rather difficult since Rathbone had taken the liberty of handcuffing his wrist to the armrest. He looked down at the manacles and sighed.

When Pinky saw Rathbone approaching the car, he said, "It's about time you got back!"

Basil got in and said a very cheeky, "Miss me, did you, darling?"

Pinky indicated the handcuffs. "Was THIS really necessary?"

"I promised to keep you in protective custody," Basil said, starting the car. "I didn't specify in what form that custody would take."

"You call THIS protective?"

Basil shrugged. "Perhaps more for my protection than yours. Then again, considering your extra-curricular activities, I should think you'd rather enjoy being handcuffed."

"Very funny," Pinky grumbled. "I gave you the blackmail note. What more do you want?"

"I want to know exactly where you are at all times."

Pinky sighed and watched out the window. "Where are we going now?"

"To a brothel," said Basil. Then added, "Don't get too excited. This is strictly for investigative reasons."

They drove along in silence for a while, then Pinky sighed and said, "I really had no choice, you know."

"I beg your pardon?" said Basil, keeping his eyes on the road.

"What I did," Pinky said regretfully. "I didn't want to do it, but Siegel left me little choice."

Basil crooked his eyebrow at Atwill. "My good man, a gentleman AL-WAYS has a choice. And apparently, sir, you are no gentleman. You ARE, however, either a very bad liar or a very stupid pawn."

"What do you mean by that remark?"

"You denied Siegel was the mastermind of this scheme. In fact, I've come to discover it's quite the opposite. Furthermore, he's also the one who arranged to have Billie Bennett, better known to her associates as Mae West, send you all those mysterious blackmail notes."

Atwill gave Basil a look of shock and disbelief. "You're lying! Why would Siegel—"

"Why wouldn't he? Siegel gets both your loyalty and your money." Basil gave Pinky a knowing and imperious smile. "And do you know the really funny bit?"

"I'm almost afraid to ask."

"You and your movie mogul friends in your selfish attempt to keep your dirty little secrets probably helped to murder the only man who was really looking out for your best interests."

"You mean Eddie Mannix?"

"Exactly. And, if we don't succeed in stopping him tonight, I fear Siegel will become a far greater threat to Hollywood than Eddie Mannix or John Roselli ever could be."

Thirty minutes later they reached the gates to Mae's Brothel. As they got closer, Basil could see the flashing lights of a dozen police cars parked around the estate and a cop guarding the front gate.

"A raid, do you suppose?" asked Pinky.

"I understand Mae pays hush money to avoid that sort of thing." Basil gave Atwill a cautionary look. "If you're entertaining any ideas about turning me over to the police, just remember that in the boot of my car is enough evidence to put you away for attempted murder. Do we understand each other?"

Atwill glowered at Rathbone, then gave him a capitulating nod. "Clearly."

As Basil pulled up to the gate, he rolled down his window and called the police officer over.

"Sorry, Mac," said the cop, approaching the car. "You'll have to turn back around. This whole place is a crime scene. Only ones allowed through are the police, the coroner's office, and the press." The cop shined his flashlight into Basil's face, and gasped. "HEY! Ain't you Basil Rathbone?"

"Uh, yes, I am," said Basil. Nodding to his passenger, he added, "And this is Lionel Atwill."

The cop shined his flashlight over at Atwill, who instinctively tried to wave with his right hand, then remembered about the handcuffs, so merely nodded a hello.

"Gee, Mr. Rathbone, the wife and me was just at an advanced screenin' of your new movie, *The Hound of the Baskervilles*! It was terrific! We said so on the preview card!"

Basil flashed the officer a pleasant smile. "Why, thank you. I take it you and your fine wife are fans of Conan Doyle's detective?"

"We sure are! Why, hell, readin' about Sherlock Holmes was the whole reason I joined the force. Wait till I tell the guys!"

"Uh, as it happens," said Basil, "I'm, uh, here to do some research on police work, uh, for the next Sherlock Holmes movie."

The cop scratched the back of his head. "But they ain't released the first one yet."

"Well, it's because of the fine response from movie audiences just like you that convinced 20th Century Fox to consider a sequel. I, uh, don't suppose the detective in charge of this case would mind if I, oh, uh, you know, kibitzed a bit?"

"Wait right here and I'll ask for ya."

The cop hurried back to his police car and called up to the house on the radio.

Atwill looked askance at Rathbone. "You don't seriously think they'll let you into a crime scene, do you?"

"Never underestimate the power of celebrity."

The cop came back and said, "You're in, Mr. Rathbone. Detective Ford is a big fan, too. Just go up the drive and park in the lot. They're waitin' for ya at the house."

"Thank you," said Basil graciously, then rolled up his window and drove up the winding drive to Mae's Brothel. "Easy as pie," he said.

"I suppose you expect me to wait in the car," Atwill sneered.

"I should think you'd want to avoid the company of police."

Inside Mae's Brothel, Basil discovered that half the L.A. police department must have attended the *Baskervilles* sneak preview. A uniformed officer took Rathbone to the library and introduced him to Detective Ford. The detective looked as though he had dressed quickly. His shirt was buttoned wrong, his jacket was open, and his tie was crooked. The homicide detective was contemplating the large crimson stain on the rug.

"Pleasure to meet ya, Mr. Rathbone." The gruff detective gave Rathbone's hand a friendly and painfully firm shake. He pushed back his fedora and frowned. "Too bad you ain't really Sherlock Holmes. I could really use a consulting detective right about now. This case is just plain screwy."

"Well," said Basil, with some forced humility, "perhaps I could be a sounding board. I take it the murder victim was Billie Bennett, alias Mae West?"

**"Did you check the walls and the ceiling for a secret panel?"**

Detective Ford was taken aback. "Wow! That's right!"

"I also take it," Basil said gesturing at the detective's attire, "that you are hastily dressed because you were, shall was say, roused out of bed."

Blushing slightly, Ford said, "Uh, yeah, undercover work, you know how it is. Say you really are Sherlock Holmes. Come upstairs. Maybe you CAN help with this mess."

As they passed through the stair hall, Della was sitting in a chair, wrapped in a blanket, sipping some coffee as a detective took her statement.

"He shot both Miss West's eyes out!" she sobbed, "It was horrible! He looked like the Invisible Man! He had a slouch hat, dark glasses, a scarf over his face! Just like the Invisible Man!"

In the second floor hallway, the crime unit was dusting fingerprint powder on a door camouflaged to appear as part of the wall.

Fred said, "After the killer shot Mae he made a beeline for this secret door with a mob hot on his heels. I heard all the racket and ran out to see what was going on." Ford led Basil by the arm into the apartment and over to the closet. "I saw the guy run in here and shut the door. When I opened the door, the guy was gone. Screwy, huh?"

Basil stepped in the closet and poked around. "Did you check the walls and the ceiling for a secret panel?"

"Yep. Like this." Ford joined Basil in the closet and used his fists to bang all around on the walls and the ceiling. "See? Solid."

"So if not the walls or the ceiling —," Basil shoved back the clothes hangers and examined the hanger rod more closely. "AH HA!" He pulled out his handkerchief, using it to grab the rod. Looking over at Ford, he cautioned, "You might want to take a few steps back."

Ford stepped out of the closet while Basil stood against the back wall and gave the hanger rod a counter-clockwise turn. A trap door opened, revealing a ladder and a hidden passage.

Ford gawked with amazement. "But how did you know?"

"Elementary," said Rathbone. "No one would think to examine the floor." Basil pointed at the hanger rod. "I deduced that the bloody glove print on the rod was made by the perpetrator when he grabbed it and turned it."

Ford glared at the crime scene detectives. "Didn't any of you guys see that handprint there?"

"Well, yeah," said one of the technicians. "We took pictures of it but didn't think it meant anything."

Arms folded across his chest, Ford growled, "So you didn't think it meant anything. That's just swell."

The lab crew was milling about a canopied bed. A portrait of Toni Lanier in her Ziegfeld Follies costume had been taken down revealing a wall safe over the headboard.

"Any prints yet?" Detective Ford asked.

"A lot of prints," said one of the investigators, "but girls are in and out all the time so that's no surprise."

Rathbone stepped over the trap door and out of the closet. "What about the picture frame and the safe?"

The investigator said, "The only prints we found belong to Eddie Mannix. The safe is empty."

"That makes sense. This is Eddie's room," Ford said. "The colored maid said the killer wore gloves."

"Interesting," said Rathbone, approaching the portrait. "The killer was in a hurry, and yet he treated this portrait with great care. It's propped against the wall instead of dashed to the floor. He also knew the combination to the safe."

"How do you figure that out?"

"Elementary. There was no time to crack the safe."

"Hey, I hadn't noticed that." He reached into his pocket for a flashlight and shined it down the trap door. "You feel like crawling around a secret hallway?"

Basil joined him and slapped the detective on the back. "Capital idea! After you, detective."

An investigator handed Rathbone a flashlight. The actor followed Ford down into the murk. The passageway was dusty and laced with drooping cobwebs. There were other ladders along the passage that obviously led into other bedroom closets.

"By Jove," Rathbone exclaimed with mounting excitement. "Mae was running her own version of a 19th-century panel house!"

"Panel house?"

"Yes! In the Old West, thieves would use secret panels to pick the pockets of customers whilst the young ladies kept the victims otherwise occupied." Shining his light up into the support beams, Basil noted cables running along the passageway. "I wouldn't be at all surprised if those cables led to a series of wire recorders. It's the perfect intelligence gathering set up! In fact—." He climbed up a ladder that led up to a tiny room. Inside the room was a camera on a tripod pointing at a window built into the fourth wall. The window was the size of a full-length mirror and gave a commanding view of an elegantly furnished bedroom.

Ford poked his head up, shining his flashlight around. "Is this another closet?"

"Even better!" Rathbone said. "This is a two-way mirror and this camera records all the naughty details."

"So that's why the guy musta plugged Mae. She tried to blackmail somebody who wasn't gonna stand for it."

"That doesn't explain about the safe," said Basil, climbing down the ladder.

"What about the safe?" asked Ford as Basil joined him back in the passageway.

"The perpetrator knew the combination to Mannix's safe. Your common variety blackmail victim wouldn't have had that kind of information. But I have a good idea who might."

"Oh, yeah? Who?"

Basil smiled at the detective. "Well, it's a bit of a long story, but I suspect Mae's killer is a man named Martin F. Murphy. I also suspect he murdered Eddie Mannix. What I don't understand is why Murphy killed Mae."

The secret passage led down to a flight of stairs and out a secret exit at the back of the house hidden behind a row of hedges. Shining his flashlight around the grounds, Basil discovered the grass littered with cast off clothing.

Detective Ford picked up a discarded wide brimmed hat. "Wow, maybe this guy *was* the Invisible Man."

"Or," said Basil, examining the bloodstained coat, "our perpetrator decided to change into fresh clothes." He pointed at the label sewn into the coat. "This coat came from the Universal Studios wardrobe department. Well, well—what do you know! It was previously worn by Claude Rains for *The Invisible Man*."

Detective Ford checked the brim of the hat. "Ditto the label in his hat."

Basil examined a discarded coat hanger. "Murphy must have grabbed one of Eddie Mannix's suits." He picked up a pair of discarded pants and examined the waistband. "According to this laundry mark, these pants belonged to someone with the initials 'M.M.' And Martin Murphy would have had access to the Universal Studios wardrobe department. That proves it. Martin Murphy *is* our killer."

"No kiddin'?"

"If Murphy killed Mae," Basil mused aloud, "that means he might also be after Siegel. And if Mae knew where Siegel was going, maybe Murphy persuaded Mae to tell him."

"What are ya talkin' about?"

"Detective, I think I know where your suspect can be found. If you would provide me with a police escort, we may catch our killer in the act of killing a killer."

"Come again?"

Rathbone hesitated a moment, then said with a smile, "To put it more simply, 'Quickly, Watson, there isn't a moment to lose!'"

"Okay, now THAT, I understand!"

## Chapter Forty-Eight

### 29 November 1938, 9:52 p.m.

### Laurel Canyon Boulevard to Hollywood Boulevard

The sirens of their police escort blared around them as Basil drove at full speed toward the hospital.

"Now let me see if I understand you correctly," said Atwill. "Your brilliant plan is to catch Siegel in the act of assassinating Boris and Bela?"

"To finish what you started, yes," said Basil, keeping his eyes firmly fixed on the road.

"And you don't think it's a problem that you've arranged to have a homicidal maniac like Bugsy Siegel open fire in a crowded hospital?"

Basil smiled confidently. "Your concerns are groundless. Mr. Siegel won't have a chance to open fire, of THAT I can assure you."

"What about Murphy? He's gunning for Seigel. At the very same hospital, I might add."

"The police will see to him."

Atwill shook his head. "Your overconfidence is only matched by your naïveté."

"Perhaps we should change the subject."

Indicating his handcuffed wrist, Atwill grumbled, "What do you suggest? A game of 'I Spy' to pass the time?"

Basil shrugged. "Why don't you tell me about the court case that fascinated you so much the other day. You said something about the facts being too remarkable to be believed. What did you mean by that?"

With a sigh of resignation, Atwill said, "Very well. It happened here in Los Angeles. This fellow named John Avery ran a boarding house to lure travelling salesmen to their deaths. It seemed Avery was inspired by an earlier case involving a mass murderer named H.H. Holmes."

"Who was H.H. Holmes?"

"A murderer who took in boarders attending the 1893 Chicago World's Fair. This Avery chap, like Holmes, had turned his boarding house into a veritable human abattoir. Rooms were airtight so poison gas could be pumped in while the victims slept. Bodies were taken to the basement where the bones were prepared with acid, then mounted and sold to medical schools."

"Quite ghastly," Basil said. "But hardly remarkable."

"Oh, but that wasn't the remarkable part. Avery had captured a traveling salesman named Ives, only Ives was playing dead."

"How did he escape the gas?"

"Wait, I don't want to spoil the story."

"So sorry."

"Ives played dead while Avery prepared to strip the flesh from his body. That's when Ives grabbed one of Avery's surgical knives and slit his throat."

"Jolly good! Serves the devil right!" Then a thought occurred to Rathbone. "Wait. If the murderer was killed by his victim, whose trial are you following?"

"This is the remarkable bit," Atwill said excitedly. "It turns out Ives was also a murderer! He slaughtered the ladies in his sales district with the very item he was selling door-to-door."

"He murdered them with a vacuum cleaner?"

"He was selling kitchen knives!"

"Of course, how silly of me," said Rathbone.

"And that's how Ives escaped the gas. Being a murderer himself, he suspected a trap and took precautions. And since Avery had set up such a remarkable murder factory, Ives impersonated Avery and kept on killing!"

"I see!" said Basil, now completely taken up with the story. "So the man they're trying for murder is Ives and not Avery."

"Exactly! Isn't that amazing! One killer kills another killer and then takes on that killer's identity! Truly remarkable! I dare say it couldn't happen again in a million years!"

Rathbone got a terribly sick feeling in the pit of his stomach. "Oh dear," he said as realization dawned.

"What's wrong?" Atwill said, studying Rathbone's worried face. "You look positively green."

"I have a very bad feeling a million years came and went very quickly." Jamming his foot on the gas, Basil sped ahead of the police cars. "We must make all possible haste to that hospital!"

## Chapter Forty-Nine

### 29 November 1938, 9:56 p.m.

**Hollywood Presbyterian Hospital, First Floor Lobby**

Two suspicious looking characters were loitering around the elevator, each holding up an open newspaper to hide their faces as Lloyd approached the information desk.

"Hello, beautiful!"

Daphne looked up from her magazine. "You're back again?"

"Yup. Got me two orders, one for Boris Karloff and the other for Bela Lugosi."

"Karloff and Lugosi, huh?" said Daphne, eyeing the two men by the elevator. She gestured at the arrangements. "Lilies? Aren't those for funerals?"

"Maybe it's a joke," Lloyd said with a shrug. "Then again, what ELSE would you get Karloff and Lugosi?"

"I guess." Daphne pointed up. "They're in the Isolation Ward on the second floor."

"Isolation Ward? But I thought—"

Daphne hastily interrupted him. "You heard me, Lloyd! The Isolation Ward, second floor!"

"All right, all right. You don't have to bite my head off."

"Now remember, Lloyd, just leave them at the nurse's station. No one but hospital staff are allowed in the CCU after 8:30."

Lloyd winked. "You got it, baby. Oh, and you better call security. There's a car out in the parking lot across the street with a stuck horn."

"Okay, I'll tell someone." Daphne picked up the phone and began dialing.

Lloyd nodded, hurried to the elevator, pushed the "up" button, and waited. There was a DING! The doors parted. As soon as Lloyd got in the elevator, Cohen and Siegel folded up their newspapers and followed, flanking the deliveryman on either side. The elevator doors closed just as Lloyd felt something poking into his back.

At the information desk, Daphne was already on the phone to hospital security. She eyed the closing elevator doors keenly. "This is Daphne Cole. Those two men are on their way up to the Isolation Ward right now. Be careful. They look like a couple of real troublemakers. They might even be armed." She paused to listen to the party on the other end of the line. She had to cover her free ear because the sound of sirens could be heard coming from outside. "You want me to call the police?" She looked outside and saw police cars turning into the Vermont Avenue parking lot. "It looks like somebody already did."

## Chapter Fifty

### 29 November 1938, 9:59 p.m.

#### Hollywood Presbyterian Hospital, Parking Lot

The tires on Rathbone's car screeched as he turned sharply into the hospital parking lot. With sirens blaring and lights flashing, the police escort had split up, some taking the patient-loading area at the main entrance, while others followed Basil's car.

Detective Ford shouted over the sound of whining sirens as Basil abandoned his car and dashed in the direction of the hospital. "Rathbone, have you lost your goddamn mind? HEY! Where the hell are you goin'?"

Coming to an abrupt halt, Basil turned and shouted, "If I'm right, this hospital is in far greater danger than I first suspected!"

"Well, gee, Rathbone, it's not like having a bunch of cops with you would HELP with that, now would it?"

Basil hesitated, realizing he was acting too hastily. "An excellent point, Detective."

A cop hurried up to Ford. "Hey, Lieutenant, do you hear that?"

Basil strained to listen. "I think I hear it, too."

The continuous blaring of a car horn filled the parking lot.

Ford scanned the lot. "Where the hell's that coming from?"

One of the cops pointed at a maroon Cadillac parked at the far end of the lot. "I think it's that car over there!"

They ran up to the car and looked inside. A woman's body was draped awkwardly over the steering wheel. She was bound and gagged and had fainted from exhaustion.

One of the cops used his nightstick to smash the driver's side window. He pulled the woman's limp body out of the car and laid her gently down on the black top. As the cop pulled away the tape covering her mouth, Basil leaned in and gave a gasp of alarm.

"My dear Lord!" he exclaimed. "That's Blanche Pierce! Jack Pierce's wife!"

The cop rolled her on her side and began working at the ropes tying her hands behind her back. "I'll have these ropes off in a minute."

Detective Ford turned to one of the other officers leaning over in the huddle. "Lewis, call dispatch and run those plates. Find out what sick bastard owns this car."

"Right away, Lieutenant!" Officer Lewis hurried to the nearest police car and got on the radio. "Car 17 to KGPL dispatch—."

"Is she alive?" asked Rathbone anxiously.

"She's breathing," the cop said as he loosened her clothing. "But she's been through a hell of a lot."

Ford stood up and glared down at the huddle of police. "Well, did any of you goddamn geniuses think to tell someone in the goddamn hospital to get a stretcher out here?"

It wasn't long before attendants from the Emergency Room hurried out to the parking lot with a stretcher. As they loaded Blanche onto the stretcher, Officer Lewis screeched to a halt and grabbed the hood ornament of the maroon Caddy for support, huffing and puffing, "I—ran the—plates—I got the owner's name—."

Rathbone said, "I already know his name."

Arms akimbo, Detective Ford grumbled, "Huh? How the hell could YOU know?"

## Who Framed Boris Karloff?

## Chapter Fifty-One

### 29 November 1938, 10:00 p.m.

**Hollywood Presbyterian Hospital, Second Floor**

Two doctors, a nurse pushing an elderly man in a wheelchair, a yawning intern, and a patient holding onto a portable IV stand were waiting for the elevator. The doors parted revealing a deliveryman holding two lily floral arrangements. Flanking him rather closely on either side were two well-dressed men with intense faces. The deliveryman and the two men stepped off the elevator in perfect synchronicity. What nobody noticed was the gun Cohen had in Lloyd's back or that Siegel had a painfully tight hold of the deliveryman's arm.

"Take us to Karloff and Lugosi," Siegel growled in the deliveryman's ear, "and don't screw with us."

"Yeah," added Cohen, "or Daphne's gonna need a new date for tomorrow night."

"I—I gotcha," stammered Lloyd, who was trying mighty hard not to pee his pants.

Siegel kicked open the doors to the dimly lit Isolation Ward and aimed his gun at the nurse's station. "HANDS UP, EVERYBODY!"

Cohen shoved Lloyd through the door and aimed at doctors discussing a case. "DON'T DO NOTHIN' STUPID AND MAYBE YOU'LL LIVE TO FLEECE YOUR PATIENTS!"

Everyone froze. Three doctors, one wearing a parabolic physician's mirror turned to cover his eye, all dressed in white tunics, stood together in one corner with their hands up. Hospital beds were lined up against the walls. Scattered around the unit were three parked gurneys and a folded wheelchair.

Dropping to the floor and crawling on his hands and knees, Lloyd screamed, "THEY MEAN IT! THEY'LL KILL US!"

"Cover the nurse's station, Mickey," Siegel ordered.

"Right."

While Cohen kept the nurses cringing behind the nurse's station, Siegel pulled Lloyd to his feet. "Get up, you asshole!"

The gangster dusted off the deliveryman's jumpsuit, all the while shaking his head like a frustrated mother. "Jesus! What if your girlfriend saw you crawling on your belly like that! If you're gonna die, die like a MAN!"

Cohen leveled his gun at a blonde nurse behind the nurse's station who shrank back against the huddle of other nurses. "YOU! Where's Karloff and Lugosi?"

The girl burst into tears and began screaming.

Cohen pulled back the hammer on his piece and took aim. "SHADDAP! Just POINT, for christssake!"

The shaking nurse pointed at three beds that had the privacy curtains drawn around them.

"Right," snarled Siegel, shoving Lloyd out of the way. "Keep 'em covered, Mickey."

"No problem," said Cohen, taking a step back and leaning against one of the parked gurneys. "And, Siegel—."

"Yeah?" said Siegel pausing by the first bed.

"Just plug 'em and then let's just lam outta here. No funny stuff, huh?"

"You got it," Siegel said, flashing his partner a mad grin of anticipation as he raised his weapon and jerked open the first curtain.

Siegel knew from the chart at the foot of the bed that the man sleeping with the top of his head peeking out from under the blankets was Bela Lugosi. Siegel began to laugh, his eyes gleaming with murderous lust as he leveled his weapon and said, in a very poor imitation of Bela's accent, "Good evening! And GOOD NIGHT!"

He squeezed off two shots at the torso.

He yanked back the next curtain hiding the bed of Boris Karloff. His sleeping form was likewise obscured under hospital blankets but the square head with the gleaming metal clamps made the occupant very obvious. Siegel shouted, "It's alive! But NOT FOR LONG!"

He pumped Karloff's body with two slugs of lead.

He tore away the curtain around the third bed and took aim at Jack Pierce's blanket-covered form. "Good night—uh—."

Unable to think of anything pithy to say, Siegel uttered a rather hesitant, "makeup—guy." Again, he squeezed the trigger and blasted Pierce with the last two of six shots.

He blew on the end of his smoking gun and returned the empty weapon to his shoulder holster.

One of the doctors, the one wearing the physician's mirror over his eye, shouted, "NOW!"

The padded tops on three gurneys were thrown back like coffin lids and three stuntmen armed with cowboy six-shooters leaped out and took aim at the stunned mobsters.

"REACH FOR THE SKY!" commanded Bud Wolfe.

A photographer from the *Los Angeles Examiner* jumped out from behind the huddle of nurses and popped off a flashbulb in Siegel's startled face.

Siegel spun around and squinted through blobs of blue and yellow spots floating before his eyes, trying to see who was threatening him.

Wolfe fired a shot at Siegel's feet. "I said, REACH!"

Siegel did as he was told.

Lloyd screamed and stuck his hands up, too.

Cohen was at a standoff with an extremely tall stuntman with a black mustache and a prune face and a second stuntman who was only a fraction of an inch shorter than his partner. The first stuntman pulled the hammer back on his piece and snarled in a deep gravelly voice, "Drop it, partner!"

Being a man who never said die, Cohen aimed at prune face and squeezed the trigger, only to have the gun shot out of his hand by the second stuntman. "Now reach for the sky," the stuntman said.

The gangster raised his hands.

At that moment, police led by Rathbone and Detective Ford burst into the room just as Ford announced, "EVERYBODY FREEZE! POLICE!"

Boris Karloff stepped forward as he removed his wig and physician's mirror. "Ah, it's about time you got here. As you can see, we have things well in hand."

"So we heard," said Rathbone.

"Yeah," said Ford. "We had to see it to believe it."

Boris looked puzzled as he peeled off his fake mustache. "How did you know?"

"The intercom," Rathbone explained. "Somebody must have hit the broadcast button by mistake."

"The intercom?" Boris exclaimed.

One of the nurses picked up the microphone by the callboard and looked at the switch. It was in the "talk" position.

"Oops," she said. "Sorry."

Wolfe pushed Siegel forward, keeping the gangster covered with his six-shooter. The stuntman clucked his tongue and said, "Robinson is going to be real upset when he sees what Siegel's bullets did to his Monster dummy."

Boris nodded. "Fulton won't be too happy about the bullet-riddled stunt dummies, either."

Rathbone surveyed the scene, looking somewhat disappointed. "But this isn't anything like I planned."

Boris took off his costume spectacles and said, somewhat apologetically, "I'm sorry, Basil, but your original idea was impractical and rather risky. But I WAS inspired by your tales of dressing up like a tree in No Man's Land. Instead of a soldier in a tree costume, I decided to employ three stuntmen disguised as empty gurneys."

Ford examined one of the gurneys as the police took custody of Siegel and Cohen. "But where'd you get the gurneys?" he asked.

One of the doctors said, "They're standard hospital issue."

"Yes," said the other physician. "When someone dies we don't want to alarm the other patients with the sight of a dead body being taken to the morgue."

"So," said the first doctor, "we hide the deceased in these gurneys. Then all the patients see are empty gurneys being wheeled around by orderlies."

Basil smiled at Boris. "Was this your idea?"

"Mr. Wolfe suggested I get hold of his two friends to assist us, while I proposed we use these gurneys for an ambush. Mr. Basil Rathbone, meet Mr. Glenn Strange."

"Howdy," said prune face.

"And Mr. Eddie Parker."

"Hello," said Parker with a wave.

Boris smiled and said, "They're stuntmen who also double as Western movie heavies. They're crack shots. Much better than I would have been."

Basil was impressed. "Where are Bela and Pierce?"

"Bela and Pierce are where they've always been—the medical surgical wing on the 4th floor."

"But why the Isolation Ward?"

"The ward was designed to be isolated from the rest of the hospital. That kept the patients and the hospital staff out of danger."

"But where are the Critical Care patients?"

One of the nurses explained, "The CCU has been closed for the past two weeks for renovations. Patients who would ordinarily be kept here have been sent to other hospitals."

Boris indicated the doctors and nurses. "At Mr. Wolfe's urging, I informed the hospital administrator about Siegel and Cohen's intentions and what we had in mind. These people all volunteered to help us with our little trap."

Ford said, "You mean, you guys were all in on this?"

The formerly crying nurse squealed delightedly and said, "GOSH! That was exciting! I always wanted a chance to show I could be an actress!"

"—Meet Mr. Glenn Strange—and Mr. Eddie Parker."

Cohen looked around in utter disbelief. "You mean, you guys were expecting us?"

"The whole time," Boris said with satisfaction. "I told the very charming nurse at the information desk to send anyone who asked for Lugosi, Pierce, or myself up to the Isolation Ward and to call security, who in turn would notify us."

Basil patted Boris on the back. "A brilliant plan! Using the gurneys was a masterstroke! This is truly amazing! I'm very impressed!"

Boris crooked his eyebrow. "You needn't sound so shocked."

"No, of course not," smiled Rathbone. "I only meant that—" He suddenly started with realization. "BORIS! This hospital is still in deadly danger! There's another assassin on the loose."

"Yeah," said Ford. "We found Jack Pierce's wife tied up in the guy's car." Nudging Cohen with the muzzle of his gun, he added, "And the guy's after you two."

"Yes," said Rathbone. "He's already killed Billie Bennett at Mae's Brothel."

"Good Lord," gasped Boris. "Who is it?"

"It's—" Basil began, only to be interrupted by a telephone ringing at the nurse's station.

One of the nurses answered the phone. "Hello?" She looked up in surprise and held out the handset to Boris. "It's for you, Mr. Karloff. He says it's very important."

Boris took the phone and said, "Yes? This is Boris Karloff."

"Hello, Karloff," said a familiar voice. "This is Eddie Mannix."

"EDDIE MANNIX!" Karloff gasped.

"MANNIX!" echoed Cohen, wide-eyed with shock.

Siegel shook his head in disbelief. "It can't be! Whoever's on the phone, that guy's a phony!"

"Eddie Mannix is dead!" Boris insisted.

Mannix chuckled and sneered, "You think you and Lugosi have a monopoly on comin' back from the dead? Nice little gag you played on Siegel and Cohen, by the way."

Boris looked at Basil. "He heard our accidental broadcast."

"Right now I'm upstairs," Mannix's voice was tinged with menace as he added, "keepin' your wife company."

"You leave Dorothy alone," Boris growled.

"Hey, she's just fine and sleepin' like a baby."

"What do you want?" Boris was all but choking the cord.

"All I want is Siegel and Cohen. We'll make the exchange in the hall outside your wife's room. No funny stuff, Karloff. I've been through hell and back and I ain't in a friendly mood. Just ask Pierce. That crumb tried to warn Siegel I was still alive and, well, he don't feel so good no more. You got five minutes."

CLICK!

Boris remained frozen in shock, staring into space, holding the handset to his ear.

Basil took the handset from Boris and hung it up. Boris finally came round and said, "Basil, it IS Mannix and he's got Dorothy."

"I know," said Basil. "Not about his taking Dorothy, but about Mannix being alive."

"But what happened to Julian? He was supposed to look after her!"

Basil looked gravely at this co-star. "Mannix must have killed him."

Turning to the handcuffed hit men, Boris said in a foreboding tone, "He wants Siegel and Cohen."

Siegel looked from Karloff to the cops flanking him. "Hey, you can't give us up to Mannix! We're under arrest. You have to take us in!"

"Yeah. You gotta," insisted Cohen. "It's the Law!"

Ford took off his fedora and scratched the back of his head, eyeing his prisoners. "Well, we really only have these guys on reckless endangerment and concealed weapons charges, and for shooting three movie dummies." He smiled slyly. "It's not like we got signed confessions or nothin.'"

Siegel said quickly, "Hey, we'll confess to whatever the hell you want. Just don't give us to Mannix!"

Ford looked at Boris. "Well, boys, I think that's gonna be up to Mr. Karloff to decide."

Boris glared at Siegel and Cohen. He lurched forward and grabbed Siegel's arm and said in a low, guttural voice, "You got Dorothy into this situation and you're getting her OUT!"

## Chapter Fifty-Two

## 29 November 1938, 10:18 p.m.

### Hollywood Presbyterian Hospital, 3rd Floor

Boris Karloff and Basil Rathbone stepped off the elevator with Siegel and Cohen. The gangsters had their hands shackled behind their backs. Rathbone was limping, using a metal cane for support.

Mannix stood at the far end of the hallway, one hand was wrapped tightly around the wheelchair handgrip where the heavily sedated Dorothy Karloff sat slumped. The other hand held a gun to the back of Dorothy's bowed head.

"Basil," Boris began to anxiously whisper, only to have Rathbone shush him. Boris looked from Siegel to Cohen, who both kept their heads down and wore fedoras, and then back at Mannix, who made a come hither motion with his hand.

"Send 'em over and I'll give you back your wife." He nudged the muzzle of his gun against the back of Dorothy's head. "And no funny stuff."

Boris looked anxiously at Dorothy, who was backlit against the light coming from her room. "You come forward with Dorothy," he said, "and I'll bring Siegel and Cohen."

"Fine," Mannix sighed.

Mannix slipped the gun into his shoulder holster, took the wheelchair grips and pushed Dorothy slowly down the hall. Basil continued to rely on his metal hospital issue cane as he and Boris looked Mannix in the eyes and urged their prisoners forward.

It was as they drew ever nearer that Boris noticed something odd about his wife. She had gray hair. Something also drew his attention past Man-

Dwight Kemper

nix to Dorothy's suite. There was movement under Dorothy's hospital bed. Someone was lying on the floor under the bed. And that someone appeared to have Dorothy's hair color!

"Uh, Basil," Karloff whispered. Rathbone would have none of it—he shushed Boris insistently, his attention focused on Mannix, and more specifically, on Mannix's gun hand.

As Mannix brought the wheelchair ever closer, Boris could see the figure in the chair was actually Julian in full drag, wearing Dorothy's housecoat! Dorothy's clever guardian opened his eyes and winked at Boris, then continued to play dead. Under the hospital bed, Dorothy began to groan and stir awake. Not realizing where she was, she sat up quickly and bumped her head on the steel frame.

"OW!" she said. "What in the world!"

Mannix's head twisted around to see where the sound came from. He spotted Dorothy crawling out from under the bed.

"What the HELL?" Mannix growled as he reached for his gun.

Julian grabbed the right wheelchair wheel rim and spun the chair around. The handgrips caught Mannix in the stomach. Julian used his body to flip the chair over backward. His feet flew up and kicked Mannix in the chin as he did a backward summersault to a standing position..

At the same time, "Cohen" and "Siegel" drew their weapons and shouted, "FREEZE! POLICE!"

Mannix growled with anger and raised his gun just as Dorothy staggered to the doorway of her room and shouted, "BORIS! What on earth is going on?"

Mannix leveled his gun at Dorothy, who screamed and froze to the spot. Julian raced to shield Dorothy.

Rathbone took up his metal cane like a fencing foil and saluted his opponent with a rousing—and to Boris' mind a somewhat overplayed—"WHAT HO!"

Mannix turned back to see Rathbone take an *en garde* stance, cane held parallel to the floor, lunging forward with the back leg, back foot completely flat, front leg moving forward at the same time, body kept at a 45 degree angle to his opponent. Before Mannix knew what hit him, Rathbone was thrusting his cane forward in a perfect *coup droit* that smacked the rubber tip of the cane into Mannix's gun hand, followed by a quick *dégage* that sent the gun flying to a corner.

"You son of a bitch!" growled Mannix, holding his hand. He retreated toward Dorothy's room. Julian slammed the door in his face.

"YEOW!" yelped Mannix.

Holding his now bleeding nose, Mannix dashed for the stairwell door with Rathbone and the police in hot pursuit.

**"What-Ho!"**

Basil paused in the stairwell as the footsteps of the running police officers echoed below and then came to an abrupt halt.

One cop shouted to the other, "Jesus, I think we lost him!"

Basil looked up and heard a door close. "Of course!" he said, and called down to the cops. "He's gone UP to the next floor!" and added, gesturing flamboyantly with his cane, "THIS WAY, LADS!"

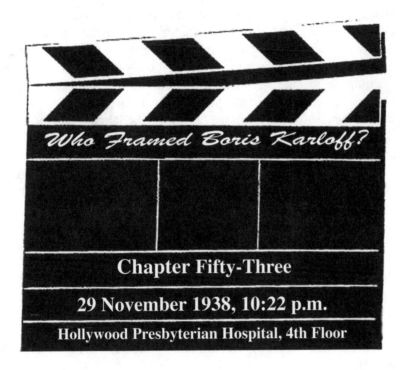

## Chapter Fifty-Three

### 29 November 1938, 10:22 p.m.

#### Hollywood Presbyterian Hospital, 4th Floor

Rathbone dashed up the stairs and through the door, ducking just in time to avoid a swinging fire axe blade. Mannix had removed the axe from a convenient glass wall case that might just as well have said, "IN CASE OF HAM ACTOR BREAK GLASS." With the blade of the axe now embedded in the doorframe, Rathbone, using what he had learned about fight choreography from fencing master Fred Cavens, elbowed Mannix in the breadbasket with his foil arm. With Mannix now doubled over in pain, Rathbone came back around with a rabbit punch to the face. Mannix reeled back and shook his head.

Nursing staff and orderlies came running to see what all the noise was about. Seeing Rathbone and Mannix fight it out, the hospital staff applauded, no doubt thinking this was a publicity stunt.

The pursuing cops were about to draw their guns when Basil said, "NO! He's mine!"

There was hospital hardware lined up along the hallway. Mannix grabbed an IV stand and swung it at Basil like a club. Basil ducked, ready for Mannix's returning swing at his legs. Rathbone countered this with an adroit leap as the makeshift weapon swung under him with a SWOOSH!

Again, a rapidly gathering audience applauded and cheered.

Mannix snarled furiously as he changed his grip and wielded the IV stand like a quarterstaff, swinging at Rathbone's head and body. Basil easily evaded the attack, and then took the offensive with a quick parry and a thrust, again knocking the wind out of Mannix with a direct blow to the breadbasket.

Mannix dropped the IV stand and held his throbbing stomach, turning and stumbling down the hallway to the nurse's station. Rathbone came at Mannix, cane cutting the air, chasing Mannix around the nurse's station and down the next hallway where Mannix came upon a parked wheelchair. He grabbed the empty chair and shoved it down the hallway at the lunging Basil Rathbone. Basil leaped just as the chair was about to make contact, placing his forward foot on the back upholstery of the chair and balancing with his rear foot on the edge of the seat upholstery. With a simple shift of weight, Basil flipped the chair backward and landed gracefully on the floor not missing a beat of his lunging attack.

Taking his *en garde* position again and smiling, Basil said, "Ah HA! Just as I said to Errol Flynn, you may be the guy that's going to win the lady, but I can kill you whenever I want to! And, sir, YOU are no Errol Flynn!"

Just then a nurse stepped out with a metal tray containing surgical hardware to be autoclaved. Mannix grabbed the unsuspecting girl with one hand and a scalpel from the tray with the other. He held the blade to her throat and warned, "Playtime is over, Rathbone! Back off or the broad gets it!"

The nurse cried and said, "PLEASE DON'T HURT ME! PLEASE DON'T HURT ME!"

"Threatening a woman!" Basil said, eyes flashing. "You, sir, are no gentleman!"

"Just back off, Robin Hood!"

"I played Sir Guy of Gisbourne!"

"WHATEVER! Just get outta the way!"

At that moment, Boris Karloff came up the stairway and ran in the direction of all the commotion. He stood behind a crowd of anxious hospital staff who were huddled behind Eddie Mannix. Rathbone spotted Karloff and decided to keep Mannix busy. "You'll never get away with this, Mannix!" Rathbone boasted. "The police have this place surrounded!"

Mannix rolled his eyes and said, "JESUS! Enough already with the cliché movie dialogue!"

Boris looked around for a weapon and then noted a nurse holding a glass syringe. He grabbed the syringe and took aim, launching the syringe like a dart. The syringe hit Eddie Mannix squarely in the right buttocks. He yelped in pain, dropping the scalpel and grabbing his buttocks. The captive nurse wheeled around and whacked Mannix across the face with the metal tray. Mannix fell against the wall and slid down to the floor, unconscious.

Rathbone grabbed the pretty nurse around the waist like Robin Hood rescuing Maid Marion. "Are you all right, young lady?"

The girl took one look into Rathbone's eyes, smiled and then swooned. Holding the girl's limp form, Basil grinned triumphantly at Karloff. "I've still got it," he said.

"Obviously," said Boris.

"Say, when did you become such a great dart thrower?"

"I told you, Basil, before my mind wasn't on the game."

From one of the hospital rooms, Bela emerged supporting himself with his IV stand while Lillian tried to get him back in bed. "Unhand me, woman!" Bela demanded. "I have solved the mystery! From Pierce's mumbling I know now that Murphy tried to kill Mannix and it is Murphy who is dead and Mannix who is alive!" He stopped abruptly when he spotted the unconscious form of Eddie Mannix. Bela's narrow glare shot accusingly at Boris. "DAMN YOU, KARLOFF!" he raged. "AGAIN, I AM UPSTAGED!"

"You're up and around!" Basil gasped.

"Of course I am! You are a terrible shot!" Bela gestured at his left side. "Your bullet only grazed me!"

Lillian tried to calm him. "Yes, darling. Mr. Rathbone is very bad at killing you. Now get back in bed!"

As Lillian shooed the protesting Bela Lugosi back to his room, Boris and Basil exchanged half-smiles.

Meanwhile, back in the parking lot, a very frustrated Pinky Atwill had finally gotten fed up with Rathbone's idea of protective custody. He rolled down the passenger window and stuck his head out, shouting, "Officer? Someone? Anyone? I'm handcuffed to the door! Someone get me out! Anyone? I have to go to the bathroom!"

No one was around to pay him any mind. Atwill sat back and sighed.

## Chapter Fifty-Four

## 24 December 1938, 2:32 p.m.

### Back Lot, Universal Studios

It was Christmas Eve and all work on the Universal Studios lot would traditionally stop at noon. Rowland V. Lee kept the cast and crew well after that to get the all-important exterior shots.

Boris Karloff was sipping tea and resting on his Monster chair while Julian Walker provided a quick touch up to his makeup. Lugosi sat in his canvas chair, puffing away happily on his cigar. Having survived a gunshot wound, the Hungarian felt an even greater kinship to old Ygor, the blacksmith who could not be killed.

Lillian was there with Bela, Jr. The baby was somewhat perplexed by his father's present appearance.

Dorothy was there, with Sara Jane in a baby carriage being rocked by a private nurse, who was a woman, a *real* woman, and you can bet Dorothy made certain of it.

Extras crowded the "Bahnhof Frankenstein" train station set where Basil Rathbone stood in a wide-lapel traveling coat and cloth cap along with Josie Hutchinson, resplendent in furs, and Donnie Dunagan in a coat and cap. Pinky Atwill, attired as Inspector Krogh, was looking none the worse for wear after being in Basil's "protective custody."

"Okay," said Lee, who was looking a bit ragged around the edges after spending several weeks trying to rush production. "This is the last scene of the picture. Unfortunately, it's not the last scene we're gonna shoot."

**"Why are you guys still here? Go the hell home, it's Christmas Eve, for christssake."**

"Oh, honestly," huffed Ouida Rathbone, bedecked in furs and jewelry. "Couldn't you just pick up where you left off after Christmas break? I want Basil to spend Christmas Eve at home with me."

"NO!" Lee insisted.

"Now, now, darling," said Basil. "I know you think you're my agent but—"

"I AM your agent," Ouida insisted. "And a very good one, too! Just WHO negotiated a marvelous contract with M-G-M for your first motion picture?"

"You did, darling. Nevertheless, the show must go on."

"HEY!" Lee shouted, "All eyes on the director!" When he was sure he had everyone's attention, he said, "NOW, the villagers are really happy because Wolf killed the big bad Monster."

Boris smiled and said, "At least until Universal resurrects him again!"

The cast and crew laughed, much to Lee's frustration. "AS I WAS SAYING!" Lee began through gritted teeth. "You're all happy that the Monster is dead and you're here to see the von Frankenstein's off on their farewell trip. That's when Basil says—."

"Cliff Work is here," said Basil.

"That's not your line!"

"No, but Cliff Work IS here."

Cliff Work got out of a studio car and stepped up onto the train platform. "Merry Christmas, everybody!" He looked somewhat perplexed as he surveyed the scene. "Why are you guys still here? Go the hell home, it's Christmas Eve, for christssake."

"Literally," quipped Basil.

"I mean," said Work, "it's not like you're gonna have this dog and pony show ready for Christmas Eve release like we wanted." He added with a dismissive wave, "So, a late January release will be just as good. Now, get the hell out of here."

Lee stared the cast and crew down. "DON'T GO ANYWHERE!" He glared at Work, "I'm gonna film the closing shot or know the reason why!"

"Okay, okay," Work said with a smile. "But, listen, I brought along a couple of special guests. HEY, EDDIE!" he called over to the studio car. "EDDIE! TONI!"

A chill went down Karloff's spine as Eddie "The Bulldog" Mannix, with his lady fair Toni Lanier on his arm, marched through the parting crowd like visiting royalty. They stepped onto the train platform and Eddie gave the crowd a good-natured wave and a hearty, "Hi, gang! Merry Christmas!"

Work announced, "Eddie and his girl was nice enough to come all the way from M-G-M to wish our three stars a Merry Christmas!"

"How, uh, delightful," said Basil, looking in Boris' direction for his reaction. Even from where he was standing, Rathbone could see Boris was less than thrilled.

Mannix nudged Lee in the ribs and said, "Say, mind if I borrow your stars a minute?"

"Uh, sure, Eddie," said Lee, begrudgingly. "Whatever you want."

"Thanks!" Eddie turned to Toni and gave her a big kiss. "Keep your motor runnin', doll face."

She turned away from him aloofly. "Don't you 'doll face' me, Edgar J. Mannix!"

"Aw, baby, you're not still sore about the ring, are ya?"

"It was a symbol of our love and you cremated it!"

"But I explained why I had to do it, sugar," Eddie said, pleading. "Aw, baby, have a heart."

But Toni would have none of it. "Go and talk to your friends. But believe me, for you it's gonna be a VERY cold Christmas."

Eddie sighed. He turned to Rathbone and grumbled, "Dames. Can't live with 'em, can't kill 'em. Most of the time, anyway." He gave Basil a good-natured slap on the back. "Well, let's get this over with."

Mannix escorted Rathbone off the platform. Together they joined Karloff, Lugosi and the wives. "Hello, boys! Ladies!" Eddie tipped his hat politely.

Lillian and Ouida remained aloof while Dorothy situated herself between Eddie and the baby carriage.

"Brrr," Eddie said, rubbing his hands together. "Kind of chilly around here."

"Did you expect a warm welcome?" Karloff snarled.

"I guess not," Eddie said with a shrug. "You wanna come over this way so the four of us guys can talk in private?"

"And if we don't?"

"You'll hurt my feelings."

Bela glowered at Mannix. "We will go, but BEWARE! Harm our families and Bela will put a curse on you that will make a grown man cry!"

Mannix laughed and grabbed Lugosi by the shoulders. "Siegel was right, you *are* a riot! Come on, let's take a walk."

Eddie led them out of earshot of wives, cast, and crew, then said in a low voice, "I guess you're all wondering why I'm walking around free and still have my job at M-G-M."

Boris scowled and said, "I'm more interested in why you think we care."

"Aw, now don't be that way," Mannix said. "I squared this meeting with Rathbone here so's there wouldn't be no hard feelings."

Boris shot Basil an angry look. "You KNEW about this?"

"Now, now," said Basil, trying to calm Boris by patting the actor's padded arm. "I saw no point in trying to avoid this meeting. Besides, Mr. Mannix has an interesting proposition."

"There's nothing I want from HIM," Boris insisted.

Bela stared Mannix down. "Someone already tried to kill me once, so I fear nothing from you!"

Mannix was either good at playacting or he was genuinely remorseful. "Aw, now don't be that way. Look, Karloff, I'm sorry for all the rough stuff with your wife and all, but I wasn't myself. First that bastard Murphy tries to bump me off, then Jack Pierce wanted to sell me out to Siegel. That kind of stuff makes a guy angry."

Boris didn't look at all convinced.

"And I didn't really hurt her, did I?" said Mannix. "All the time it was that faggot in the dress, and he clocked me a good one. So, where's the harm?"

"You killed Billie Bennett," Rathbone pointed out calmly.

"Hey, she was supposed to be working for ME and she sided with Siegel. And don't think she didn't try to get me mixed up in her screwy ideas about blackmail. So when I wouldn't play along, that bitch tried to get me bumped off! She's the one who convinced Siegel that the only way he could be the new Big Boss of the West Coast syndicate was by getting me outta the way and frame Johnny for it."

Bela blinked in amazement. "You mean it was Mae behind this?"

"Right from the get-go. So I had to bump her off or she'd only try it again with some other poor bastard."

"I'm rather curious," said Basil. "When did you first suspect the whole thing was a set up?"

Mannix smirked. "They made two big mistakes, not counting playing me for a patsy. For one thing, there was that phony note incriminating Karloff. The ambulance boys told me they found it clutched in Murphy's hand, and the note wasn't even crumpled up! Not only that, there wasn't no burnt flesh on the paper, no blood, no nothin'!'"

"An excellent observation," said Basil, beaming appreciatively.

"Oh, my word!" Boris gave himself an admonishing slap to his rubber forehead. "I had completely overlooked that!"

"Don't be too hard on yourself, my dear fellow," Basil said with a bolstering wink. "Considering the stress you were under at the time, I'd say you made some very useful observations." To Mannix, he asked, "What was the other glaring mistake that tipped you off?"

"Trying to palm off fake blood for real blood," Mannix snarled disdainfully. "Like I can't tell the difference!"

"So from the condition of the note and the stage blood in Murphy's office, you deduced that you were being set up to be murdered?"

"Nah," said Mannix. "It wasn't that like that. Sure, I knew something was screwy, but I didn't know exactly what was gonna happen. But I got a instinct for this kind of thing. So I played along until somebody made a move."

"When exactly *did* Murphy make his move?"

"On the way to the crematorium. Pierce drove the hearse while I rode in the passenger seat. Murphy was stretched out in his coffin, see? Well, the dope used one of them prop coffins from *Dracula*!"

"Ah!" said Bela. "The one missing from the warehouse!"

"Right. Murphy was supposed to sneak up on me and knock me out with ether. But that coffin's got hinges designed to creak. So, I hear the coffin creak open and I look in the rear view mirror. Well, sir, nothin' fazes me, so when I see Murphy creeping up on me I wait for my chance. I reached my foot over and slammed down on the brakes, which sure sent Murphy flying. He hit the dashboard and I got the drop on him."

Boris rubbed his cheekbone thoughtfully. "So that's how Jack got that bruise on his cheek."

"Yeah. Pierce hit the steering wheel pretty hard."

"So," said Basil, "you killed Murphy and put your ring on his finger. That way everyone would think that Murphy was really your corpse disguised as Murphy's dummy."

"Yeah, I even buffed up his fingernails to look more like mine. I got an eye for details."

"Which reminds me," said Basil, reaching into his pocket, "I have a present for you." He pulled out an envelope and handed it to Mannix. "Your stone and the melted gold from your ring."

**"I guess you're all wondering why I'm walking around free and still have my job at M-G-M."**

Mannix's eyes brightened as he tore open the envelope and poured the contents into his hand. He looked up and smiled. "Gee, this is swell! You don't know the hell Toni's been givin' me for losin' it! Now I can get it reset!"

"I'm curious about why you stole Murphy's pants."

Mannix shrugged. "I figured leaving Murphy's pants at Mae's crime scene would keep the cops busy lookin' for Murphy."

"And your death mask?" asked Boris.

"I had Pierce make it up on the spot so he could say he had proof I was dead. I had to stall long enough to get even with Mae, Siegel, and Cohen, didn't I?"

"Speaking of which," Basil said, "I guess we can safely assume Mr. Siegel and Mr. Cohen are wearing appropriate cement attire a few miles off of, and a few fathoms down in, the ocean somewhere?"

"Nah. Why kill 'em when I can let 'em live and make 'em sweat? Especially Siegel. Then, maybe someday when Siegel least expects it—."

"If you don't mind my asking," said Boris, "when did you become Jack Pierce's house guest?"

"I had to lie low somewhere and Pierce knew too much. I kept him in line by threatening to hurt Blanche if he squawked to Siegel or the police."

"But Pierce DID call Siegel," said Basil.

"His telephone has a long cord. He took the phone out to the garage and tried to put Siegel wise. I caught him and lost my head." Mannix looked like a remorseful little boy. "I grabbed Blanche and took her for a ride in Pierce's heap, first to the garage where I keep my car, and then to Mae's, and finally to the hospital." With a heavy sigh, he added, "I didn't mean to really hurt Blanche. She was all right. In fact, I'm gonna try and make it up to her."

"I see," said Boris. "And I suppose you want to do the same for us?"

"That was the idea. I mean, it's Christmas."

Boris folded his arms and gave Mannix a reproving look. "Which is all well and good, but I'd like to know how you managed to avoid criminal charges for Miss Bennett and Mr. Murphy's deaths."

Mannix smiled and shrugged. "Hey, I'm a fixer! If I can cover other people's asses, I can sure cover my own!"

Bela said, "But what about working again with Mayer and Strickling?"

"True," said Basil. "To say the least, the working relationship must be, shall we say, awkward?"

"Well," Mannix said, hands in his pockets, making circles in the ground with his big toe, "let's just say those rumors Mae was havin' her girls spread around about me were kinda sorta true."

Boris glared at him in disbelief. "You mean you actually DO keep incriminating evidence for the purpose of blackmail?"

Mannix shrugged. "Hey, a guy needs insurance. So, a couple of free samples of what I got, and with a little muscle from my good pal Jack Dragna, suddenly Hollywood and me are all square. Same thing with the Law. We got an understanding, you might say."

Casting a scornful look at Mannix, Boris said, "So, obviously if you wanted to, you could kill US, get away with it, and not think twice about it."

Mannix appeared genuinely hurt. "Aw, come on. If it wasn't for you guys, Siegel and Mae might have just gotten away with murder, MY murder! Anyway, forget about those goons. I'm here because I figure I owe you."

Bela frowned. "What do you mean, you owe us?"

"Anything you guys want," said Mannix with a magnanimous wave of his arms. "Name it, sky's the limit! You wanna drop motion pictures for a sweet part on Broadway, just as a for instance, I got connections that can arrange it. Better contract with a bigger studio? No problem! I'll give you one at M-G-M for life. Or any studio you want."

Boris looked to his companions. He jerked his head to a far corner of the lot. "May I see you gentlemen in private?"

Bela and Basil joined Boris in a huddle. Mannix tried to listen, but couldn't make out what they were saying. At least not until Bela disagreed strongly with whatever Boris was proposing and shouted vehemently, "But I want a contract!"

Dwight Kemper

Apparently, after some arguing, Boris and Basil managed to convince the proud Hungarian to play along, albeit reluctantly. They broke from the huddle and approached Mannix. Boris said, "We know what we want."

"Okay," said Mannix, bracing himself. "Name it."

"Three things," said Basil. "First, regarding James Whale. You're to make every effort to find Colin Clive's ashes."

"If that's not possible," said Boris, "at least give James cremains without the ironic telltale evidence that they aren't Colin's ashes."

"Okay," said Mannix. "Ashes, got it. What else?"

"Jack Pierce is to have a pension and you'll pay all his hospital bills."

"Don't waste a favor. I already said I'd take care of his wife."

"Yes," said Basil, "but we want to make sure you look after *Jack* and not just his *widow*, if you catch our meaning."

"In other words," Boris insisted, "no assassination attempts on Jack!"

Mannix grumbled a little but finally sighed and said, "Okay, no revenge and a pension. That one, I gotta say, really hurts. Okay, two favors down, one to go."

"This last favor is a BIG one."

"Go ahead, Karloff, I can take it."

"Lay off the Unions."

Mannix did a double take. "Do WHAT?"

"You heard me," Boris insisted. "No more strike breaking. No more harassment when new Unions try to form in Hollywood. In fact, I INSIST you PROTECT the Unions from underworld involvement. Is it a deal?"

Mannix snorted like an angry bull. He took out a cigar, bit off the end and lit it. He took a couple of thoughtful puffs and said, begrudgingly, "Okay. You got it. From now on, I leave the Unions alone."

"AND?" said Boris.

Rolling his eyes, Mannix added, "And I get Roselli to lay off. I assume I'm to keep a special watch over the Screen Actors Guild, in particular?"

"Exactly," Karloff smiled.

"Now we're even, right?"

The three actors nodded. "Right." Well, two of them did. Bela sort of sulked as he weakly grumbled, "Right."

Mannix gave the three actors a jaunty wave and said, "Well, boys, nice doin' business with ya. Merry Christmas."

"And happy New Year," added Basil.

"Now that I got the ring back," Mannix said, "that's a big possibility."

After Mannix left them alone, Basil put out his hand and said, "Well, gentlemen, as I said before, I say again, 'All for one!'"

"And one for all!" said Boris, putting his hand on Rathbone's.

Bela hesitated, but after Basil and Boris cast the Hungarian their expectant looks, Bela relented with a shrug and a grin and joined in the gesture of

camaraderie. "Yes, and one for all," Bela said. "But a contract would have been nice."

"Come on," said Boris. "We'd better finish the day's filming before our beloved director has a coronary."

Soon Basil Rathbone, with Josie Hutchinson and Donnie Dunagan, along with the extras who had been strategically situated in the shot to suggest a multitude of grateful townsfolk, were back before George Robinson's rolling camera.

"Herewith I deed to you the castle and the estates of Frankenstein," Basil proclaimed. "Do with them what you will. And may happiness and peace of mind be restored to you all. Good-bye!"

"BYE!" Donnie waved.

Boris Karloff and Bela Lugosi stood behind the camera and watched the scene unfold. Boris smiled at Lugosi and whispered, "And God bless us, everyone!"

"Amen to that," said Bela.

"CUT!" called Rowland V. Lee. "Print it! That's a wrap!"

THE END
A Universal Picture

Coming soon

Bela Lugosi
and the House of Doom

# A Good Cast is Worth
# Repeating
# or
# Separating
# Fact from Fiction
# (WARNING! Contains Spoilers)

SON OF FRANKENSTEIN—The making of *Son of Frankenstein* was indeed fraught with production delays due to Rowland V. Lee's unorthodox approach to filmmaking, and Martin F. Murphy wrote many memos regarding those delays. In fact, the memo presented in this book comes from an actual memo from the same Martin F. Murphy. However, no murder ever took place on the set. But Boris Karloff did indeed have a birthday party as described. Production began on 9 November, 1938 and was completed 5 January, 1939. It premiered at the Pantages Theatre, Hollywood, California on 13 January, 1939. As for exactly *where* the movie was filmed, well, I based my descriptions on a picture of Basil Rathbone and Donnie Dunagan taken in front of a clearly marked Stage 7. As for the Phantom Stage, I'm not sure if the Castle Frankenstein set was erected there or not. I made several attempts to get copies of production notes from Universals Studios. Apparently they had donated all their early production documents to the USC Performing Arts Archives, but did not include material regarding their classic monster films. So I had to deduce from watching *Son of Frankenstein* numerous times that such a large interior set could only have been erected on Stage 28. Besides, the Phantom Stage is a very fitting location for Castle Frankenstein. I'm sure Lon Chaney's ghost felt right at home.

BORIS KARLOFF—Mr. Karloff never investigated a murder case, but he did play one in the movies—Mr. Wong. Karloff appeared in over 160 films and on television. Best known as Frankenstein's Monster, Boris was respected by colleagues and is loved by legions of fans to this day, including yours truly. Known to many as "Dear Boris," Mr. Karloff is survived by his daughter, Sara Jane Karloff Pratt, who runs Karloff Enterprises. It was Sara's insights about her father and mother, and her suggestions and encouragement, that made this book possible.

BELA LUGOSI—Although the Hungarian character actor did indeed have an affair with Clara Bow, and had a nude painting of Miss Bow that was presented to him by the "It" girl herself, Mr. Lugosi never visited Mae's Brothel (at least not to my knowledge). Facts about Mr. Lugosi and his lovely wife Lillian came from sourcebooks such as *Karloff and Lugosi: The Story of a Haunting Collaboration* by Gregory William Mank and *The Immortal Count* by Arthur Lennig. As for the whole "Gypsy Curse" thing, well, pure fiction, although his widow Hope Lininger Lugosi reported that Bela believed in such superstitions and kept a glass of water by his bedside to ward off evil spirits as he slept. Mr. Lugosi is survived by his son, Bela Lugosi, Jr., who, according to one of my publishers, is as handsome as his father. Lugosi, Jr. is a prominent California attorney.

BASIL RATHBONE—A fine actor and an expert swordsman, Mr. Rathbone became rather disenchanted with playing Sherlock Holmes and never actually investigated a real murder. Most of the information pertaining to Mr. Rathbone comes from his autobiography, *In and Out of Character*. Oddly, never once in that book did he mention *Son of Frankenstein* or any of his other work with Boris Karloff or director Rowland V. Lee, despite re-teaming with them to make *Tower of London*, a gripping historical drama. Regarding the adoption of his daughter, there is a bit of a discrepancy between his autobiography that claimed she was his biological daughter and later biographical accounts that say she was adopted. So, I split the difference. She's adopted but Basil and Ouida know the birthmother and have arranged to adopt. If that's not correct, chalk it up to poetic license.

MAE'S BROTHEL and MAE alias BILLIE BENNETT—Both a real place and a real person. Although the exact address is never given, my description of the brothel is based on two sourcebooks: *The Fixers* by E.J. Fleming and *Hollywood* by Garson Kanin. It was Mr. Kanin's very detailed description of his many visits to Mae's Brothel that became my main source of inside information. As for Billie Bennett's ultimate fate? I don't know, but her murder in this novel is purely fictional.

LIONEL "PINKY" ATWILL—Mr. Atwill never committed the attempted murder of Bela Lugosi, since said murder attempt was purely fictional, but he was indeed obsessed with murder trials, had a bullet-riddled Rolls Royce, and *did* host weekend sex parties. These parties became popular with many A-list stars and executives at M-G-M including Clark Gable, Barbara Stanwyck, Marlene Dietrich and Eddie Mannix. His 1940 Christmas party included underage girls, one of whom, a 16 year old, took Atwill to court alleging she became pregnant at the party. Atwill was acquitted at the trial, but he was later convicted for perjury. The subsequent scandal ruined his career. But this fact hasn't lessened my enjoyment of his work in films like *Mystery in the Wax Museum* and especially his Inspector Krogh in *Son of Frankenstein*.

EDDIE "THE BULLDOG" MANNIX — Although Eddie never left threatening letters on Boris Karloff's windshield, Mr. Mannix was indeed a "fixer" of Hollywood scandals and was Vice President at M-G-M, but he never killed Billie Bennett or became a target of Bugsy Siegel: this was pure fiction. But all the juicy gossip, including his ex-wife's suspicious death, comes from true sources. He did help establish Mae's Brothel along with Howard Strickling, but his "secret apartment" is pure fiction (as far as I know). He later married Toni Lanier, who eventually became smitten with a young actor named George Reeves, best known to fans in the 1950's as Superman. Eddie, Toni, and George became involved in a strange sort of triangle where Eddie, who had heart problems later in life, wanted George to take care of Toni after Eddie's death. George eventually fell in love with New York socialite Lenore (aka Leonore) Lemmon, which devastated Toni Mannix. It has been alleged that Eddie had something to do with "fixing" the facts surrounding the "suicide" of George Reeves on 16 June, 1959. Sourcebooks about Mannix include *The Fixers* by E.J. Fleming, *Hollywood* by Garson Kanin and *Hollywood Kryptonite* by Sam Kasner and Nancy Schoenberger.

TONI "LEGS" LANIER — For the most part, everything mentioned about Toni, except for visiting Mae's Brothel, and giving Eddie the tiger-eye ring, is true. Actually, the ring described in this book once belonged to my father whom I haven't seen since I was 12. The ring is my only keepsake of him.

JAMES WHALE — Mr. Whale never visited the set of *Son of Frankenstein*. His whole involvement in this mystery is pure fiction. However, it was reported that he did attend a screening of *Son of Frankenstein*. He also really *did* have a morbid fear of funerals and for that reason couldn't attend Colin Clive's funeral service. As for his relationship with Mr. Clive, I'm not sure if they were lovers or not. That's pure speculation on my part, which was based on popular rumor.

COLIN CLIVE — All the facts mentioned in this book are true with the possible exception of his relationship with James Whale, which is purely speculative and based on innuendo. Clive did die alone at Cedars of Lebanon Hospital, his wife Jeanne had indeed refused to come to his funeral and, sadly, Rosedale Crematory did indeed lose Colin's ashes. His ashes may have later been buried in a common grave along with a lot of other unclaimed ashes found in the crematorium's basement, at least according to Gregory William Mank in *Karloff And Lugosi: The Story of a Haunting Collaboration*. Wherever you are, Colin, rest in peace.

ROWLAND V. LEE — much of Lee's portrayal and his unorthodox directing methods is based on the making of *Son of Frankenstein* as described by Gregory William Mank in the *Universal Filmscripts Series Classic Horror Films — Volume 3, Son of Frankenstein*. This sourcebook also has a very good diagram of the sulfur pit effects and insightful production photos, including a photo of Rathbone and Donnie Dunagan in front of Stage 7.

JULIAN WALKER—A purely fictional character, Julian is actually an amalgam of two real people: B-movie film director and transvestite Edward D. Wood, Jr. and Eddie Izzard, a stand up comedian and transvestite with a marvelous grasp of and funny insights about world history. If possible, check out his DVDs *Dress To Kill* and *Circle*.

DELLA THE MAID—She may be a real person. Garson Kanin described Della in his book *Hollywood*. As far as I know, she never witnessed a murder at Mae's Brothel.

ALBERT KIRKWOOD—Purely fictional. I never could find out who really worked the sulfur pit effects. Production credits for movies back then weren't as extensive as they are today, unfortunately.

PETER MITCHELL—Purely fictional. The actually identity of the photographer who took those birthday pictures at Boris Karloff's on-set surprise party remains a mystery, which is a pity since those candid photos were what originally inspired this book project. Several photographs were taken and one of them hangs framed on my office wall. This picture, along with candid photos of Boris having coffee in Jack Pierce's makeup studio, were my touchstones to *Son of Frankenstein* throughout my writing of this book.

MARTIN F. MURPHY—A real person. However, apart from what I could tell about his personality from his many, many memos complaining about *Son of Frankenstein*'s production delays and his reported admiration for James Whale's money-saving direction of *Wives Under Suspicion*, I know absolutely *no* personal information about him whatsoever, including what he actually looked like. All his motives and background are purely fictional. When, where and if he died, I haven't a clue.

CLIFF WORK—For the most part, information about Cliff is based on true sources, although I have no idea if he was married and if he was, to whom. As for his pill-popping habit, that was based on descriptions of movie executives in general.

OTHER CAST AND CREW OF *Son of Frankenstein*—all real people as described in production credits for *Son of Frankenstein*.

KENNETH STRICKFADEN—A real person with real gosh wow Monster-making machine effects that he apparently kept stored in his garage in later years. All information I used regarding the operation of his equipment and "Megavolt Senior" was taken from *Kenneth Strickfaden: Dr. Frankenstein's Electrician* by Harry Goldman. Strickfaden has been credited in films under different spellings of his name including "Strickfadden."

JACK P. PIERCE—The much-praised Universal Studios makeup genius was never beaten up by gangsters or involved in a murder plot. My primary source about Jack comes from material on the DVD, *Jack Pierce: The Man Behind the Monsters* by Scott Essman. Scott was also nice enough to answer my telephone inquires regarding the makeup man's private life.

THE MOGULS OF HOLLYWOOD—What scandal could Walt Disney have been involved with, you may ask? Well, I had nothing specific in mind when I mentioned him. However there *was* a scandal when the entire animation crew, including some rather pretty ink and paint girls, threw a wild wrap party after finishing production on *Snow White* that caused some embarrassment to the creator of Mickey Mouse. As for everyone else, it is my understanding they all had things to hide and that fact was later exploited by William Randolph Hurst when the newspaper mogul insisted that every print of *Citizen Kane* be destroyed. So, use your imagination. I sure did.

M-G-M STAR SCANDALS—The scandals I allude to are all based on alleged fact described in *The Fixers* by E.J. Fleming.

THE GAMBLING SHIP "REX"—a real ship, although it actually sank in the summer of 1938. But I really liked the idea of the ship, so I raised it from the deep and made it a location in this novel.

BENJAMIN "BUGSY" SIEGEL—A real hit man that really did charm Hollywood, was actually seen with Wendy Barrie, and was ultimately executed by being shot in both eyes on 20 June 1947 after the infamous Flamingo casino fiasco.

MICKEY COHEN—A real hit man and an associate of Bugsy Siegel and a friend of Eddie Mannix. His involvement in the murder plot mentioned here, pure fiction.

JACK DRAGNA—A real crime boss described by Mob scholar Carl Sifakis as "a man who thought small." It was for this reason that the East Coast syndicate sent Siegel out to L.A.

HOLLYWOOD PRESBYTERIAN HOSPITAL—A real place where Sara Karloff was really born and where Dorothy Karloff remained hospitalized for two weeks after a C-section because of an infection according to Sara Karloff. These days the old wing is used to store hospital records. Occasionally the homeless reportedly sneak in to take refuge in its boarded-up wards, and perhaps the ghosts of past patients reside there as well. Many thanks to Paul and Denise Ruben for driving around Los Angeles and getting photos and maps to locations in this book including the old wing at Hollywood Presbyterian and consulting with some Red Cross workers about what floors contained what units at the time.

ANGELUS-ROSEDALE CEMETERY—A real cemetery, and again, my descriptions of the cemetery, the wall and the mausoleum are based on photos and maps provided by Paul and Denise Ruben. Thanks, guys!

TRAINS FROM LOS ANGELES TO CHICAGO AND NEW YORK—Information about 1938 train timetables and stops and what trains would go where were provided by members of the Southern Pacific Railroad Yahoo Group (or Espee), specifically Louis Adler, Ken Harrison, Spen Kellogg, Larry Mullaly, and Tim Zukas. Thanks, guys! Trying to figure out those timetables was making me feel like I was doing third grade word problems again. (If the *City of Los Angeles* leaves Central Station at 6:30 p.m. and travels at a speed of—EEK!)

CHRISTOPHER DEAN—Fictional boy toy, representing, I'm sure, many a young lover of James Whale.

FRANKENSTEIN'S MONSTER—Mary Shelley was indeed inspired to write *Frankenstein* after witnessing experiments in galvanic response on a human cadaver, at least according to several documentaries I've seen on The History Channel. Definitely my favorite of the Universal Monsters, I always wanted to write a *Frankenstein* story, and I guess this book is as close as I'm likely to get. Although many actors have portrayed the Monster since Mary Shelley conceived him, no one would ever personify the Monster with greater depth of character than Boris Karloff—at least in this author's opinion.

# ABOUT THE AUTHOR

Photo by Ann Ozark, Photoimagesbyannozark.com

Dwight Kemper is an accomplished character actor with over 13-years stage experience including an engagement at Carnegie Hall in New York City as Sergei Diaghilev in *Anna Pavlova*, a biographical ballet he co-authored. He appeared six years on stage as Herr Drosselmeyer in *The Nutcracker*, as well as Doctor Copellius in *Copellia*, and Catallebutte in *Sleeping Beauty*. He is also a stage illusionist and member of the International Brotherhood of Magicians. As *Murder for Hire*'s Producer and host sleuth Detective Chief Inspector Kemper of Scotland Yard, Mr. Kemper presents original mystery plays for hotels and bed and breakfasts throughout the United States. His mystery shows frequently haunt The Sherwood Inn in Historic Greene, NY. Dwight Kemper is also a film critic for Phantom of the Movies *VideoScope Magazine* where he applies his "critical chain saw" to really bad movies. Visit Mr. Kemper at Murder for Hire's web site: www.murdermysterytheater.com.

If you enjoyed this book
check out our other
film-related titles at
www.midmar.com
or call or write for a free
catalog

Midnight Marquee Press, Inc.
9721 Britinay Lane
Baltimore, MD 21234
410-665-1198
(8 a.m. until 6 p.m. EST)
or MMarquee@aol.com

Dwight Kemper